Praise for
Song in the Silence

"Every time it looks as if dragons had been done to death, along comes a yarn like this to revive them. . . With excellent narrative techique, wit, and intelligence, Kerner weaves these strands into a brisk story capped by a plausible happy ending. A superior debut."　　　　　*—Booklist*

"This adventure fantasy by a gifted storyteller belongs on most fantasy collection shelves."　　　　　*—Library Journal*

"A solidly detailed and impressively developed debut. Expect sequels."　　　　　*—Kirkus Reviews*

"Elizabeth Kerner weaves her tale with a lovely blend of lyricism and invention. If you are one of those aspiring souls who fly with dragons in their dreams, this is the book for you!"　　　　　—Deborah Turner Harris

"*Song in the Silence* is an intelligently written romantic fantasy with a strong female protagonist. It will certainly appeal to fans of Anne McCaffrey and Mercedes Lackey."
　　　　　—Josepha Sherman

TOR BOOKS BY ELIZABETH KERNER

Song in the Silence
The Lesser Kindred
Redeeming the Lost

THE
❧ *LESSER* ❧
KINDRED

ELIZABETH KERNER

TOR®
fantasy

A TOM DOHERTY ASSOCIATES BOOK
NEW YORK

This is a work of fiction. All the characters and events portrayed in this book are either products of the author's imagination or are used fictitiously.

THE LESSER KINDRED

Copyright © 2001 by Elizabeth Kerner

All rights reserved.

Edited by Claire Eddy

A Tor Book
Published by Tom Doherty Associates, LLC
175 Fifth Avenue
New York, NY 10010

www.tor-forge.com

Tor® is a registered trademark of Tom Doherty Associates, LLC.

ISBN-13: 978-0-8125-6875-2
ISBN-10: 0-8125-6875-3
Library of Congress Catalog Card Number: 96-19126

First Edition: January 2001
First Mass Market Edition: October 2001

Printed in the United States of America

0 9 8 7 6 5

To the glory of God
and to
the men in my life:

My partner Steven Beard
strong and loving, valiant and true,
who holds my heart in his
and is a wildly brave man
to love and live with a writer;

my father Chan Ewing,
scientist, loved and honoured Papa-san,
who for so many years has tried to fight the good fight;

my brother Lester Ewing,
rally driver, husband, father and occasional dentist,
whose love and friendship
and memories of home
are so precious to me;

my brother in all but blood James Quick,
composer, singer, hearth-companion,
soulfriend of many years,
who always makes me laugh;

and

Christopher
clear reason to my emotion,
friendship deep beyond all reason,

I dedicate this work.

The First Morning of the World

I woke with the late winter sun in my eyes
and smiled because Jamie had let me sleep.
Ah.
Let us sleep.

It was the first morning of my wedded life, and my impossible beloved lay beside me. His long silver locks fell like water over the creased linen pillowcase. *Typical*, I thought, smiling. *He has been human for less than three moons and already he looks better asleep than ever I could waking. Look, not a tangle in all that mane of his.* I pulled my long frowsy braid around to glance at it. I'd seen better-groomed tails on horses. Ah, well. At least Varien—my husband—didn't seem to mind.

Dear Lady. My husband.

I gazed down at him, drinking in the physical warmth of his nearness, breathing in the smell of him. There had been only one or two nights, in our mad rush to get here from Corlí, that I had caught him sleeping when I finished my turn at watch; he tended to hear me coming and was almost always sitting up when I came to wake him. Those few times he had genuinely been asleep we were both so exhausted I'd barely had time to wake him before I fell into the warm patch he left and into dreamless sleep myself. We had only just arrived from the Dragon Isle when we had to leave the port of Corlí at a run, doing our best to escape my wretched father Marik's hirelings. We had assumed they sought our lives, for they had nearly killed our companion Rella; we managed to get her to a house of healing but we didn't dare wait to learn how she fared. As best we could tell, we had eluded them.

The sun, gathering confidence as it rose, streamed through the gap in the shutters and shone in his hair, silver taking fire from gold. It was like nothing I had ever seen—ah, save once! With a shiver the memory rose before my mind's eye. Before he was changed, while still my dear one had the shape he was born with, I had seen full daylight glinting off his silver scales.

I lay back slowly, gently, so as not to wake Varien, while the vision of him on that day rose bright before me. He stood then on the Dragon Isle, the home of his people, and his name was Akor, the proud Lord of the Kantri, those creatures whom men call the True Dragons. He was the size of a house and purest silver from the hammered metal of his horned face to the delicate scales of his tail, save only for the deep green of his eyes, and his soulgem like living emerald gleaming in the centre of the great mask of his forehead. I gazed at him now, fully human, changed beyond believing, gone through death and fire—but there was still a faint mark, barely visible, in the centre of his forehead where his soulgem would have been. Blessed Lady, what we had been through!

Varien sighed in his sleep and turned his head. He was so very beautiful. His skin was as soft and smooth as a child's. . . .

Suddenly I had to try very hard not to laugh and shake the bed. Sweet Lady, that I should ever be so besotted with anyone! Me, with my man's height and strength, my plain face and my foul temper. I almost pitied Varien. The only decent traits I have ever possessed have been strength and what Jamie would call determination, but everyone else would call bloody-mindedness. I had never thought so soft a heart dwelt hidden in me; it had most certainly been hidden deep beyond finding until now.

In my own defence I can only claim to have been brought up motherless by a father—well, I had always thought Hadron was my father—who grudged every breath I took and kept me a virtual prisoner at Hadronsstead, the horse farm where I grew up. When he died, no longer ago than the summer just gone, I learned to my great relief that Hadron was no part of me, and I had left Hadronsstead in the hands of my cousin Walther to find if I could truly live the life I had always dreamt of. From my earliest memories I have longed in the deep heart of me to travel the length and breadth of Kolmar, and to seek out the Great Dragons living on the mysterious Dragon Isle far away, west across the sea. I found them, true enough, but the tale that unfolded then changed me forever, and all the Kantri along with me.

Varien stirred and moved. I held my breath to let him settle again into sleep. So dear to my heart, so valiant, so kind. His bravery I had seen while still he kept his dragon form, for he had defied the laws of his people to meet with me, to talk, to learn, and although we did not mean it, to love. A kind of madness had come over us both, for within the space of a few days we who had never met knew in our deepest hearts that we each had found our match. It was wonderful and terrible both together, to know that you have found the one soul in the world that is the completion of your own, and to know that you must remain forever separate in body. This we had known without question, but we also knew that for us there was no other choice. We plighted our troth one to another, Kantri and Gedri, dragon and human, doomed to be forever separate but matched in our hearts and minds.

I reached out to touch Varien, stopping myself just short. In that golden moment I did not wish to wake him. It was a still and breathless time, watching him sleep, seeing the gentle rays of the winter sun strike gleams from his eyelashes, glorying in the simple smell of him. Hardly breathing, I followed the contours of his face with my hand an inch away from his skin. Here and now, after all these years have passed, I remember that moment as if it had been this very morning. My body has changed as time has taken its toll, and both joy and sorrow greater have followed, but that first morning of my new world shines in my heart yet new-made, as though the sun that blessed Varien's face had never shone before on living man.

I sat back, hugging myself, longing to be in his arms again, knowing I would be there as soon as he woke, enjoying the longing for itself. I had never dared to let myself imagine that such a love would come to me. In the years before Hadron died I had tried not to think of love at all. In the Kingdom of Ilsa, where I was born and raised and had spent every moment of my life until the autumn just gone, if you were not married by your twentieth year you were like to live alone forever. I had turned twenty-four on the Balance-day last autumn and I had expected to sleep alone all my life—but behold, here he was, the Lord of the Kantri lying beside me.

The Lord of the Kantri. The King of the Dragons. He told me that among his people kings are chosen, not born. They had hailed him as their king in his youth and he had come to the flower of his age with the good of his people foremost in his mind. His concerns for them had not ceased with his transformation: he feared still for their future. While I was on the Dragon Isle I had assisted the Lady Mirazhe with the birth of the first youngling for five hundred years; had I not helped her, at the expense of horrible burns to my arms, both mother and child would have died. Still, five hundred years is far too long a gap even for that long-lived race. Unless that changed, and swiftly, the Kantri were doomed, and Varien never forgot it. When he became human he surrendered his kingship to his dear friend Shikrar, the Eldest of the Kantri, but his people in Council had acclaimed him their king even in his new form. Shikrar had said that the Kantri would have to work out the details later, but we had heard nothing so far. I was lost in thought, lying there, but then Varien moved slightly and I gazed down at him again.

His eyes opened slowly, deep startling green beneath the

silver of his lashes. When he saw me, a smile that glowed as bright as the morning lit his eyes and transformed what had been merely handsome into love itself made human.

The people of his birth have a gift known as truespeech, the speaking of mind to mind. I had been astounded to learn that I too possessed it, for it is known among humans as Farspeech and is matter for fireside tales, not for broad daylight. He had truespeech still, but now it was nearly as hard for him as for me, and much use of it brought on blinding headaches. One blessing we had been granted, in that he and I could still hear one another without effort and without pain.

In that sunlit morning, lying beside me all gold and silver, he opened his mind to me. There were no words, but there was his soul, full of love—and there was music. Sweet Shia, Mother of us all, there was music! When we had joined our hearts and minds in the Flight of the Devoted, there in his dark chambers on the Dragon Isle, we had made a new song between us, and that simple melody spoke the truth of his love to my heart more surely than any words ever could. I could hardly bear the beauty of it.

"Good morrow, my dearling," he said then aloud, grinning as he drew me to him and kissing me soundly. His body felt strong and warm and welcoming against mine, and my longing melted into simple joy. "So glorious a morning for the first of our wedded life! Though I fear me it is long past time for us to rise."

"I expect Jamie is being generous, love," I murmured, smiling as we held each other close. His heart beat against mine, and in his arms was home and safety and love and all. I kept my voice light, for I could hardly bear the weight of that bone-deep joy. "If he has not sent for us yet, the morning is ours."

"Your heart's father is generous indeed," said he playfully, his hands beginning to rove. "And what shall we do with so great a gift?"

Varien

She wrapped her long arms around me and held me with all her strength, and to my astonishment I found that she wept.

"And still your eyes leak seawater, littling," I murmured, which made her laugh as I had hoped it would. Before I had learned the Gedri word for tears she had wept for joy to behold me in my true shape after all her years of dreaming, and those were the words I had used.

"Oh, Akor," she breathed, somewhere between tears and laughter, "Akor, I cannot believe you are here, here, human, and my wedded lord!"

"Yours as long as life endures, my Lanen," I replied, stroking her hair, revelling in the feel of it on my skin. "May the Winds and the Lady grant us many years together, that I might show you the long truth of a dragon's love."

She laughed at that, hard enough that I had to release her from my embrace, but once she had explained the joke to me I laughed as well. "Well, my heart," I said, stroking her shoulder gently, "I say again, what shall we do with so glorious a morning?"

She thought for a moment and laughed. "You're not going to believe me."

"Very well, I will not believe you," I said, mock-solemn, and gathering her close to me. "What do you wish to do that I will not believe?"

"I want to go riding in the Méar Hills, up in the forest."

I thought she spoke in jest until I saw the joy in her eyes at the very thought. "The sun doesn't shine much in winter here, and I—oh, Akor, I never had the chance to go riding in winter while Hadron was alive," she said. "I've always wanted to. The Méar Hills are so close by, and the Lady knows we have enough horses."

"Surely one each will be sufficient," I said, laughing and not releasing her.

"Ah, but when your new wife is the mistress of her own breeding stables, and they the best in all of Kolmar, the choice isn't as simple as it might be." She grinned. "So. Are you going to let me go, or am I going to have to force you?"

I was intrigued. "And how would you do that? Your abilities are admirable, my heart, and you have not yet ceased to surprise me, but I have still some measure of my old strength. I do not believe that you can break free."

"Power isn't always the answer," she replied, as I yelped. She had barely touched me, just under the ribs, but the sensation was remarkable and it certainly broke my hold on her.

"What did you do?" I demanded. "What was that?"

She laughed, long and loud. I could not help but join her, though I knew not what amused her. Her laugh was joy made sound and completely irresistible. "I never thought," she managed to gasp out. "Dragons aren't so easy to tickle, are they?"

"Tickle." I tried the sound of the word on my lips.

"Yes, tickle. Like this—" She reached for me again and produced that extraordinary twitch. I decided that acquiring this skill would be a useful accomplishment and tried the same on her. It seemed to work and made her laugh again. After a very pleasant diversion she stopped me with a kiss, told me we could indulge our other inclinations after the sun was down, and hurried to dress.

I was proud of my simple accomplishments. Clothing no longer held terrors for me. It was familiar now and my skin had become accustomed to the cloth, so that I no longer raised a weal from simply being dressed. I had managed to find boots to fit me when we passed through one of the larger towns on the way north from Corlí, and to my astonishment my blistered, aching feet had recovered swiftly without the need for a healer. I was delighted. I had not known that the Gedri, my new kindred, healed so quickly and without assistance. The Kantri require months or years to heal, depending on the severity of the wound, and we must enter the Weh sleep to allow our bodies to repair themselves. It might seem a terrible weakness—indeed, the Weh sleep is the single greatest weakness of the Kantri—but the time it takes does not concern us, for we are a long-lived race, and we are naturally so well armoured that we are not often injured.

I sighed and Lanen turned to me instantly. "What draws a sigh from you this bright day, my love?" she asked as she sat on the edge of the bed and laced up boots lined with soft fur.

"Ah, dearling. I am still of two worlds," I said. "A moment's thought of my Kindred, and 'they' becomes 'we' between one breath and the next. I am glad enough to be human, believe me, but my heart is taking its time to learn."

She came over to where I stood dressing and kissed me soundly. "Your heart can have all the time you like, my love, as long as you're here with me while it's learning." She whirled away to open a chest that stood against the wall and drew out a long, heavy woolen tunic dyed a rich blue: "It's cold out there, you'll need this. Do you want another shirt?"

"I thank you, no." I said. "I shall wear the tunic, but I have no need of another garment. I am overwarm as it is."

"I swear, Varien, are you certain you're really human?" asked Lanen, grinning. "I think you're still one of the Kantri inside and have just taken human shape. Have you tried breathing fire lately?"

I laughed. "Yes I have, and could barely speak for an hour after!" I caught her as she passed and held her to me. "I am fully human, my heart. Shall I prove it to you?"

She kissed me again lightly and drew away, pulling me after her. "Not now, man! Restrain yourself. I told you, the sun doesn't shine very often or very long in the winter. Come out with me, it's a glorious day. You can prove whatever you like later but if I don't get out soon I shall burst!"

It seemed so simple a thing, but I was reminded yet again of the brief lives of my new people. This swift heartbeat, so short a time in the world—so short a time would I have my Lanen beside me, so short a time might I live myself, who should otherwise have known a thousand years yet under the sun.

"Then let us go forth and glory in the day!" I cried, my heart racing with hers, but I pulled her to the side as she made for the outer door. I dragged her laughing into the kitchen, loosed her hand for an instant as I disappeared into the larder and emerged bearing some aging apples and half of yesterday's loaf. "Now for it!" I cried, taking her hand again and running out the door.

I had never known so extraordinary a joy in such ordinary actions. We laughed as we saddled the horses, who seemed to catch our mood. We were barely on their backs when they broke into a canter along the track leading to the northern hills. Lanen had told me of the Méar Hills, of her dreams of walking in them when she lay lonely in her room. So much of her life had been lived through dreams in the dark, but to the honour of her soul it had not soured her spirit or brought untimely bitterness to her heart.

We gave our horses their heads as they hurried along the road. Either they needed the exercise or they were simply trying to keep warm, for they kept up a canter of their own accord for some time. The hills rose before us, the skeletons of the trees drawn stark and sharp on the high ridges and merging into brown on the flanks. The horses dropped into a walk and we rode side by side. The air, touched now and again with wood smoke from the scattered farmsteads we passed, was a little warmer than it had been and the wind had dropped to almost nothing.

As we came closer to the edge of the winter wood we dismounted, tethered our horses loosely, covered them with blankets and left food with them while we walked deeper into the wood. I noticed, scattered among the bare branches, that there were trees that kept their leaves, deep green and glossy among their sleeping cousins. I asked Lanen about them.

"Those are my favorites," she replied, grinning. "Come, smell," she said, crushing some of the greenery. A delicious scent came wafting up from the broken pointed leaves.

"What is that?" I asked, delighted.

"Ilsan pentram," she said. "It's one of the few trees I know; I almost never got out in the woods with anyone who could teach me about trees. One year at midwinter, though, Alisonde brought in boughs of this stuff and put it all round the house, stuffed in odd corners. It smelled wonderful for weeks and I've never forgotten it. It's better outside, though, in the cold." She laughed and hugged me, and I heard in her mind a deep delight that warmed the very air. "Oh, Varien, it's all too wonderful!" she cried, breaking away from me. "I can't bear it. Come, I'll race you to the top of that rise!" She ran off at a good speed. I started to follow, but my legs were still learning their new gaits and I soon realised I would never catch her that way. So I tried the other.

What a fool I was. I should have known.

Lanen

I heard Varien cry out behind me. I ran back faster than I had come, to find him kneeling on the cold ground staring in horror at his hands. They were slightly scraped—he'd obviously fallen on them—but nothing to be distressed about. I looked at him, appalled as he stared at his own body, and knew that for the moment he was beyond words. The Language of Truth can be incredibly useful.

"Varien, love, what is it? Whence this deep distress?"

At least, I tried to use the Language of Truth. This had never happened before. He was closed, I could not bespeak him. My words returned to me like an echo from a cliff face.

"Varien, talk to me. What happened?" I said aloud, really worried. For answer he stumbled to his feet and put his back against the nearest tree. He was shaking all over, pale now. I think he would have fallen save for the tree holding him up. He still hadn't looked at me. As usual, my worry and my love for him roiled about in me and turned into anger. I went close up to him and whispered his full name furiously. "Varien Kantriakor rash-Gedri, Kadreshi naLanen!" He looked up at that, caught my eye at last. In a more normal tone I continued, "If you don't speak to me this instant I swear by all that's holy I will shake you until your teeth rattle. Talk to me, man. What happened?"

He was breathing hard, like a man who had run a desperate race. With a terrible effort of will I kept my mouth shut and waited. Finally he managed to force a few words past his lips.

"Running—after you—too slow." His face contorted again, pain and shame mingled; his hands clenched and un-clenched as if he were trying to master them and failing. I did not reach out to hold him, much as I longed to. I knew as if the Lady had spoken to me that he needed to go through this himself. I waited.

"Then—I knew how to catch you, be there first, waiting for you—ahhh!" He tossed his head as though he were being struck by invisible fists, and his throat tightened so terribly that he had almost to yell to get the words out. In a dreadful voice he croaked out, "Lanen, I tried to fly!" He gave a great cry and fell to his knees again, or they gave out from under him. That had been the worst of it, and now that it was out he wept, great sobs racking his body. I could do no more than hold him close.

If Varien had not been in so terrifying a state I would have laughed, for it seemed ridiculous, but I didn't dare. Bless the Lady for the right instincts just that once. I didn't know ex-actly what he was grieving for but grief it was without doubt. I said nothing. I simply held him.

Finally words came, all rough from their passage through that poor throat. "I fell to all fours and tried to fly, and they were gone. They are gone, Lanen! Ah, my heart, it is hard, hard to bear," he groaned. "They are gone forever. I am a creature of earth from this moment unto my death, the life of air is closed to me." He seemed to collapse into himself, sinking away from me back on to his heels and turning his head away from me; but he held on to my forearms in a grip so strong I feared for my bones. "I am nor Gedri nor Kantri but some lost soul caught between—oh my Lanen, what have we done?"

For an instant I thought of the words of Rishkaan, one of the Kantri who had bitterly opposed the union that Varien and I had forged. The Lady knows I had tried to forget his words but they weighed always on my heart. Where Varien and I had seen in our joining a healing for Kantri and Gedri, Rishkaan had the opposite vision. His words were clear in my mind, as though he had only just spoken them to the

Kantri assembled to determine my fate and Akor's. "I too have had Weh dreams, Lord Akor, but mine have been of death and ending. My people, she would mingle the blood of Kantri and Gedri! Her children will be monsters, the world will fill with Raksha-fire and none to stand between because of *her*!" Dreams that come during the Weh sleep, when the Kantri are healing or shedding their skins, are taken very seriously by that people. Rishkaan had died fighting a demon master, a noble death, and the shadow of his dream was not easily dispelled.

Varien had me terribly worried now. Had he had some vision the equal of Rishkaan's?

Even as I thought that, bless the Lady, he rallied. He loosed his tight grip on my arms and knelt more upright. "Forgive me, my heart," he said quietly, and let a little of his thought through the strong shields he had put up.

I wish he hadn't. I had never thought before how devastating it could be to hear another's true thoughts without the softening that words can provide. His outer thoughts were not so painful, but the underthought explained much, and for the first time I even caught, at the end, a soft whisper of the deep sensation that is less than thought and more like feeling.

"*My wings, my wings, alas for what is gone* **they are gone I am broken I am bound to the earth,** *bound to you* I have paid a terrible price for love\ *but I do love you in the deep heart of me at least that has not changed nor ever will* **forgive me this weakness** *I cannot fly my back is bare alas for what is gone* I am crippled for life\ [It is because of her]."*

The Language of Truth is just that, more's the pity. Truth is not always easy to bear, and after all we had been wed less than a day. Dear Lady Shia, was our joy so easily broken?

"It is not my fault, Varien," I said, suddenly angry. My new-wedded husband had killed the delight that had filled my heart moments earlier with his strange turn, and now it seemed that in the depths of his soul he blamed me for all his misfortunes. "Did I force you to become human?"

I shook him off and stood up. He rose immediately and put his hand out to me. I turned away.

"What is it? What did I—oh!" He sounded so surprised that I looked at him once more. "Ah, my dearling, I understand," he said, his voice a little less crippled now. "You grow stronger in truespeech very swiftly, Lanen. I am astounded! Only Shikrar has ever read me so deeply before. It is the *terishnakh,* the hidden words, that you have heard. Forgive me, dearling."

"Hidden words?" I cried. "Then I'm glad I heard them! I'm not a mind reader, Varien, even if I do have truespeech. If that's what you really think—"

"Please, Lanen, hear me," Varien interrupted. "You are new to this level of truespeech, and you do not yet understand. Those thoughts, they are—unbidden, to say the least. Have you never had unworthy thoughts occur to you, only for them to be rejected by your waking mind? I can no more control the murmurings of the *terishnakh* than I can stop a sneeze, but they mean little more than that. Unworthy musings that are dismissed even as they arise."

I whirled on him, furious. "You said I crippled you for life! That is not a sneeze!"

I could not help myself. I laughed.

Lanen

My soul to the Lady, I would have struck him then and there, but then I heard the words I had just spoken repeated to me in truespeech, lighthearted and loving.

Dratted dragon. He always could make me laugh, especially at myself.

Then he drew me to him and kissed me, long and deep, his strong arms holding me close, and I melted a little. I was still angry at him, but—well, a passionate kiss from the one you love most does much to disperse anger. When we stopped for breath I put my hand to his cheek. "So, Varien. Do you forgive me for costing you your wings?"

"No, *kadreshi,* I do not forgive you." I started to pull back, but he continued, "I cannot forgive you what was never your deed to begin with." He took my hand and kissed my palm, sending a shiver down my spine. "You did not change me, my heart. If you recall, all our meeting and our joining seems to have been arranged by those greater than we, the Winds that my people worship and Lady Shia of the Gedri. How should two such mortal souls as we stand against the gods?"

I kissed him lightly and drew away, smiling again at last. "By going somewhere a lot warmer," I replied. "I don't know about you, Deshkantriakor, but I am freezing solid while we stand here and there's not a dragon in sight to start a fire. Let's go back."

That made him laugh. Deshkantriakor was the name that his oldest friend, Shikrar, had given him in jest when first he became human. The name means "strange king of the Kantri" and certainly suited him, though in the end he chose another to protect himself.

We walked swiftly back to where we had tethered the horses, folded the blankets and made our way back to Hadronsstead. The winter sun shone yet, glorious in its setting as in its rising, and the tingle of the clear cold air mingled with the scent of warm horse and the occasional waft of winter rot that their hooves stirred up as they walked through autumn's fallen leaves.

I was content for the moment to let things rest even though I knew that this was not resolved; it stood now as a shadow over us, small as yet, and as Varien did not speak much of it for some time I let it lie. I think partly I did not pursue it because I had never truly known that depth of sorrow and loss and the anger that goes with it, and I was shaken in the face of such violent and unknown emotions.

Ah now, truth, Lanen. I did not know what to do, so I did nothing. If he felt in the depths of his heart that his transformation was my fault, there was nothing I could say in my own defence. Had I not gone to the Dragon Isle he would certainly have been there yet as its king, and in his own form. It was foolish and cowardly of me to leave things thus, I know, but what would you? I was very young in many ways; I had hardly left my home before I went out adventuring in the autumn, and even though I woke each morning to this changed world, it was still difficult to believe. Perhaps the ballad makers would have me ever wise, but I am not nor ever pretended to be. After all, the makers of stories are the worst liars I know of.

The sun was down and the twilight fading by the time we returned. Jamie welcomed us at the door with a grin, sat us down by the kitchen fire and set bowls of good thick lentil and barley soup before us, with great slabs of bread and butter. We set to with a will. Jamie was in a strange mood, but he seemed to be enjoying himself. He kept bursting out laughing at nothing, and when I asked him to take food with us he laughed the harder.

"What's so funny?" I asked, my mouth full.

"My girl, I thank you, but I am not presently insane with love. I made a good noon meal, and it's hours yet before I'll need my dinner. I'll wager you've not et a thing, either of you, all day."

Varien and I looked at each other. In the rush of the day, in the midst of storms of emotion, we'd missed breakfast and completely forgotten the food Varien had brought along with us—it was still in the saddlebags. We grinned at each other, and when I glanced back at Jamie, his eyes twinkling in the firelight, I knew that I would live this down in, oh, a mere ten years or so. Still, I suspected that all fathers—or in his case, nearly fathers—must have some such stories to tell about their daughters when they wed.

I have said I thought Hadron was my father—so I did, until Jamie told me the tale of my mother, Maran Vena. He said I looked like her, tall and strong and grey-eyed. I would not know, as she had left me with Hadron when I was but a babe. Jamie, it seems, had been devoted to her and had been her lover for three years as they travelled the length and breadth of Kolmar. Then she had met Marik of Gundar, a Merchant, and for some reason I could not understand (for Jamie didn't know it) she left Jamie and took up with Marik for three months. She was never entirely comfortable with him, and it was just as well: her curiosity had saved her life, for she had overheard Marik plotting with a demon master. Marik promised the life of his firstborn child to the Rakshasa, the Demon-kind, as the price for a Farseer, a glass globe in which he could see anything he chose anywhere in the world, and thus gain power over his enemies. My mother Maran and Jamie stole the Farseer just moments after it was made. They only just escaped with their lives, and by pure chance—I almost said "evil chance"—they found them-selves, six weeks later, in the village where I grew up, and Maran met Hadron the horse-breeder. He adored her from the moment they met, or so Jamie says; but she was already pregnant with me when she wed Hadron. She left when I was less than a year old, and for love of her and because I might just be his daughter—for even Maran was not certain who my father was—Jamie had stayed on at Hadronsstead, never speaking of the past out of respect for Hadron, always there for me to turn to when Hadron turned me away. Too tall, too man-like, too plain, too strong, too wild: nothing I was or had ever done had pleased Hadron and I had lived a desperately confined life, abandoned by my mother, rejected by the man I thought was my father. Little wonder that Jamie's gentle love and kindness had been all the world to me from my earliest memories. I had not learned the truth until my adventures began, not six months past—I only knew that I had always loved and trusted Jamie, always re-lied on him, and bestowed on him all the love that Hadron rejected.

I had learned since, to my deep sorrow, that my father was indeed Marik of Gundar, and that he still sought me as pay-ment for the Farseer. I had met him on my travels. It was his ship that took me to the Dragon Isle, it was his demon-mas-ter who summoned the Raksha to take me, it was he himself who tried to make me betray the Kantri and who gave me of his own free will to the demons. It was Akor, Varien in his dragon form, who had saved me from that, but Marik was too great a fool to let it rest. He tried then to steal a great treasure—the soulgems of the Lost, not gems alone but the very souls of some of Akor's people—and to protect himself he had all but killed Akor. I closed my eyes briefly and shivered at the memory. The battle had been dreadful, and I still woke terrified from time to time with the vision of Akor's silver scales drenched with bright blood. In the end Akor and his soulfriend Shikrar had found a way to defeat Marik. I don't know how or why it worked, but they broke his mind. He was mad and helpless, and like to remain so as long as he lived.

I never lost any sleep over that.

Perhaps it seems unnatural, to feel so little for him, but I had never known him until that journey, and he had tried to kill me and those I loved more than once. What would you? To my sorrow, he was, with my mother, the creature who made me—but in every sense that mattered, my true father sat now across from me, an eyebrow lifted, amusement dancing still behind his eyes.

"And where have you been wandering, my Lanen?" he asked, smiling. "I know that look. You're a hundred leagues away from here."

"You know me far too well," I said, grinning. "But I'm back now, so no matter. Is there any more of that soup?"

Varien and I helped Jamie with some of the chores—feeding and brushing the horses, cleaning tack, spreading straw—until Varien walked up to me and gently but firmly took the pitchfork out of my hands, took me by the arm and led me into the house. I was confused, for I tried to ask him what he was thinking and he would not answer aloud, and hushed me when I tried to speak. He seemed both intense and amused, a most curious combination. When I finally thought to bespeak him I was astounded by the depth of the feelings that I sensed—his mind roiled with his longing combined with the greatest good humour as we moved into the bedroom and he shut the door behind us.

I could hardly believe the passion in his kisses, in his body as we moved apart only enough to undress. It felt—I shivered—somehow, for the first time it felt like the depth of passion that had joined us in the first place, love and honour and desire strong as the bones of the earth. I was moved almost beyond words—how can I describe it to you? It was the first time I realised that the impossible was true: I was wed to *Akor,* a thousand years old, wise and strong—and celibate until very, very recently.

I laughed in the midst of our passion. "You do learn quickly, for such an old man!"

He smiled, a fierce joyful smile, and replied—well, you may imagine as you will what he replied, for the sweet things said in a marriage bed are not to be repeated.

ii

The Place of Exile

*Hear now the words of the Eldest, the Keeper
of Souls of the Greater Kindred. Here I commit
my soul to the Winds and give you my name for
truth-fasting: I am Hadretikantishikrar of the line
of Issdra. Hear now the truth of those times
that changed the world.*

I woke in darkness with a start and knew that something
was wrong. I had been drowned deep in the hcaling Weh
sleep, so that struggling back to awareness was not unusual
in itself—but the air tingled and the ground felt strange beneath me. The Weh always leaves a feeling of new health
and strength, especially in one as old as I, but this was different. My heart was pounding and fire grew within me, a re-
flection of what I could only think was fear. Why?

Then the noise that had wakened me struck my ears again,
moments after I felt it—a low rumble that started below
hearing, a vibration through the deep earth. Without thinking I was out of my chamber and had launched myself into
the night before I realised what was happening. I called out
in truespeech to the one living soul dearest to me.

"Kédra, my son, where are you?"

*"Father? Blessed be the Winds! I called and you did not
answer, I feared you still kept the Weh sleep. Are you
healed?"*

"Nearly, my son. Strong and well enough to fly, at any

rate. Where are you, and did you feel the shaking of the ground?"

"I am aloft, my father, with Mirazhe." He sounded almost as if he laughed, and was a little out of breath. *"Fear not, your grandson Sherók is in my arms. He is much grown since last you saw him, and this excitement is thrilling him. He has never flown before. Listen."*

Sherók, Kédra's littling, was far too young yet to use full truespeech, but through Kédra I listened to his son. What I heard was closer to emotion than to speech or thought, but the littling was no more than a few months old—and he was full of pure delight. *"How long have I kept the Weh?"* I asked, calmed and pleased by this link with young Sherók. I could just imagine him in my mind's eye—his tiny scales yet soft, his back ridge still forming and hardening, his stubby tail thrashing in delight. In colour he was a blend of Kédra's and my dark bronze and his mother Mirazhe's bright brassy hide. His soulgem was covered as yet, as was true of all younglings. Sometime in the next nine months the scale that protected it would fall away—but his eyes were golden, a rare colour among our people and most wonderfully beautiful. Not that I am biased, you understand; but grandsires know these things.

"Less than three moons, Father," he replied. *"Are you but now roused?"*

I tried to gather my scattered thoughts as I sought out the scant winds of the winter's night to help keep me aloft. My flight muscles were stiff, surely, and my shoulder ached from the wound the *rakshadakh* Marik had given me—ah, that was an evil memory!—but both were recovered enough to heal without further time spent in the Weh sleep.

"The ground has shaken twice?"

"Yes."

"Then the first woke me from deep sleep. It was the second that set me flying." I had been listening but had not heard that threatening rumble again.

A soft voice touched my mind. *"Think you it safe to return to the ground yet, Eldest?"* It was Erianss, a lady some centuries older than Kédra but still far younger than I, and she sounded annoyed. I stifled the laughter that came to my mind. *"I know exactly as much as you do, Erianss. It has not been so many years since the last earthshake, surely you remember."* Still, perhaps she had a point. I spoke in the broadest truespeech, that all might hear. *"Let those who wish to speak of this meet at noon on the morrow at the Summer Field, away in the south. This is not a Council meeting. I make no demand of any."*

"Then I will see you there, Father," said Kédra. *"Where are you bound for the rest of this night?"*

I had already begun climbing, pushing myself to rise in the cold night air. I would pay for this overexertion tomorrow, but now was the best time to investigate. The fires of the earth are more clearly seen in darkness. *"I go north, Kédra, to see what Terash Vor is doing. I will let you know what I have seen."*

"Good hunting, then. Mirazhe and the kitling and I will meet you at the Summer Field tomorrow. Mind you keep high and safe in the firewinds, my father."

I hissed my amusement, loud enough for Kédra to hear it in my truespeech. *"So I shall, my son, and I thank you for your concern."* I did not remind him who had taught him about downdrafts near the firefields, or how long ago. The experience of age can be so burdensome to the young. *"Bear my love to Mirazhe."*

"I will. Fare you well, Father," said Kédra, and his voice was gone from my mind as it was never absent from my heart. As I worked my way high and north, I thought for a passing moment of those other two whose lives were so closely intertwined with Kédra's and mine—Varien Kantriakhor, my soulfriend Akhor in his new self, and his lady Lanen Kaelar. I had meant to bespeak them the moment I woke from the Weh sleep, but for now this was the more important task. Still, I wondered how they fared, even as I flew through the cold winter's night towards Terash Vor, the Breathing Mountain, to see what the future held for us all.

Terash Vor is in the centre of the western half of the range of mountains that divide the north of the Dragon Isle from the south. The divide is abrupt where the gentle hills rise sharp and sudden into high peaks five times their height. From the shapes of the mountains it is clear that in the distant past they must all have been of the same kind. I remember hearing my father, Garesh, speak of other mountains in the range burning as well, from time to time.

My people, the Kantri, the Greater Kindred, whom the Gedri children call True Dragons, had lived on this island for nearly five generations—that is to say, as many thousand years—ever since our self-imposed exile from the four Kingdoms of Kolmar on the Day Without End, burned in the memory of our race forever. On that day one single child of the Gedri, the human known only as the Demonlord, arose in a great darkness, and in the space of only a few hours the world was changed.

In those times the Kantri and the Gedri lived together, short lives and long intertwined to the great benefit of each: the long lives of the Kantri gave a sense of time outside their own brief lives to the Gedri, the humans; the swift-living Gedri kept the Kantri from forgetting to live each passing moment for all the joy it held and would never hold again. However, on that dark day a young man, a healer, reached the final abyss of his discontent with the small gifts granted him by the Lady, the great mother-goddess Shia worshipped by the Gedri. He longed to be among the great of his people, but he was not granted that excellence by the Winds—or, the Gedri would say, by the hand of the Goddess that shaped him. In his fury and frustration he made a dreadful pact with the Rakshasa, the Demon-kind, third of the four original peoples (the fourth were the Trelli, all dead long ages since). In exchange for his soul, his very name was taken from him and from all the world for all time, and the Demonlord was granted a hideous power over the Kantri. He began by killing many of his own people, moving with a speed beyond flight from one kingdom to the next, until he murdered Aidrishaan, one of the Kantri, and for some unknown reason stayed beside the body. Aidrishaan's death scream had reached his mate, Tréshak, who told the rest of us instantly through truespeech—for the Kantri are blessed with the ability to speak mind to mind—and we rose, four hundred strong, to destroy this murderer or die in the process. It was not courage, for we have wings and claws, our armour and the fire that is in us and sacred to us: the Gedri are tiny, naked and defenseless before us. No, it was in no sense courage. It was anger. That one of the Gedri should dare to destroy one of the Kantri!

Tréshak arrived first, on the wings of fury, and she dove at the Demonlord, claws outstretched, fiery breath scorching the ground whereon he stood—but he was unharmed by her flames, and with a gesture and a single word, Tréshak was *changed*. Even as she flew she dwindled to the size of a youngling, her blue soulgem blazing as she cried out in torment. She fell from the sky, for her wings would no longer bear her up, and as she fell her soulgem was ripped from her by a horde of the Rikti, the minor demons.

It would have been better had the rest of the Kantri stopped to consider what had happened, for clearly no Gedri had ever withstood our fire before, far less done so evil a thing.

We did not.

The fire that is life to us blazed out of control in our madness, and four hundred of the Kantri flew straight at the Demonlord, setting fire to the very air as they flew. The Demonlord spoke rapidly, the same word over and over, and full half of the Kantri fell from the sky and had their soulgems torn from them.

He could not kill us all, even so. It is said he laughed as he died, as the Rikti around him disappeared in flame—they are the weaker of our life-enemies the Rakshasa and cannot withstand simple dragonfire—but whether he laughed from the heart of his madness at death and pain, or because some darkness in his soul believed even then that he would triumph in the end, we do not know. His body was trampled and torn until the youngest of us, Keakhor by name, called out, "He is dead, we cannot kill him more. For pity's sake look to the wounded."

The Kantri turned then to those who had been crippled by the Demonlord and his servants. We tried to speak to them, but in vain. The truespeech that allows us to speak with one another as we fly, where the rushing winds could not carry speech, also allows us to sense emotion as well as thought, but there was no reason, no trapped mind to touch—simple fear was the only response to our desperate attempts to speak with them. Among the ashes of the Demonlord were found the soulgems that had been ripped from our mates, our children, our parents—and even then the gems bore the taint of their demonic origin. In the course of nature, the soulgems of the dead resemble faceted jewels, and when the Kin-Summoning is performed by the Keeper of Souls they glow from within with a steady light. The summoner may then speak briefly with the dead. These soulgems gleamed— to this day they gleam—at all times from within with a flick- ering light.

We believe that the souls of our lost Kindred are trapped within, neither alive nor resting in death, and despite endless years of toil and trying they are yet bound.

The bodies of our brothers and sisters had become the bodies of beasts. We could not kill them, for old love, but we could not bear to see them either. They were first called on that day the Lesser Kindred, and it has become our only name for them. They breed now like beasts and live brief, solitary lives. Several among us try to contact the newly born every year but none have had any response. Never in all the long weary years since that time has there been even a shred of hope that one among them might have heard or tried to respond in any way.

We left Kolmar that very day, for already several innocent Gedri healers had been killed by Kantri wild with grief. Those who kept their heads in the midst of evil knew that the two peoples must be sundered until the Kantri who were left could see a human without needing to take swift and fatal revenge for the deeds of the Demonlord.

It has been almost five thousand years since that day, and there are among the Kantri still those who cannot bear even the thought of the Gedri without a fury rising in them. It does not matter that there are now none left alive who were even the grandchildren of those who were witness to the deed: the cry that Tréshak gave when her soul was ripped from her echoes down the aeons, its fury and despair as wrenching and poignant as if it had happened not a day since. The Kantri live for two thousand years, if disease or injury or accident do not intervene, and the great-grandsons and great-great-grandsons of those who were there know the story in the marrow of their bones. Forgiveness is difficult, especially now that—alas!—especially now that our race is failing.

My son Kédra's youngling Sherók was born in the autumn—ah, he is a perfect littling, you should see his eyes!— but until his birth, the Kantri had gone five hundred years without issue. Our King and my soulfriend, Akhor, has long pondered our decline, but even he with wisdom beyond his years could not tell whence arose this barrenness, or why. We were grown desperate now, lest our race should die out entirely. I prayed to the Winds that Akhor's miraculous transformation might have some great purpose beyond that of uniting him with the soul he loved, that perhaps he might learn from the Gedri something that would succor his own people. If he did not, the black truth was that we were doomed, and Sherók would be the last of us.

I shook my head, breathing deeply of the night air, taking myself through the Discipline of Calm even as I flew, dispersing such darkness of heart. Such thoughts would catch no fish nor lift me a talon's breadth higher as I flew. I tried to concentrate on the problem at hand. I nearly succeeded.

Some have occasionally wondered if the murmuring ground might have anything to do with our present plight. The ground beneath our feet on the island was seldom quiet for long and we were accustomed to its shaking, but it had been growing more disturbed over the last several hundred years, and such violent movement as wakened me from my Weh sleep was rarer yet and demanded investigation. Never mind the fact that my own curiosity would have sent me to the same place, and as quickly—now that I stood in the stead of Akhor, our King who was among the Gedri, I had to think of all of my people. It was a curious feeling. I wondered as I flew whether Akhor had ever grown accustomed to this sense of bearing the Kantri on his wings and in his talons wherever he went, whatever he did.

The sky above the mountain was red and grew redder still as I approached. I had expected something of the sort. When I was still far distant, however, I found that I was not prepared for all. Terash Vor was sending its fiery breath high into the air, one vast stream of fire flowing upwards only to fall again to the ground, like a single burning feather from a bird the size of the sky. I kept my distance as I flew round about it, to learn if there was aught else to see. To my surprise, there were several smaller flows on the north side of the mountain, and a few distant red glows on others in the range showed that this was but the surface of a deep disturbance. I called upon Idai, an elder of the Kantri and an old and trusted friend.

"Idai, may I bespeak you?"

"Of course, Shikrar," came the familiar voice of her thoughts. *"What troubles you?"*

"I am at Terash Vor and I would that you might see what I have seen. Will you come to me here? I shall await you at the Grandfather."

She replied simply, *"I come. I shall be with you in the hour."*

The Grandfather was the name of the mountain nearest the south, the first that rose dark above the quiet hills below. It was so called for that it had, in some lights, the seeming of a vast black dragon. There was a large ledge on the south side—what would have been part of a back, or a folded wing—where two could stand and speak together. It was often used as a meeting place. I used it on occasion but I never was comfortable there.

We of the Kantri are long-lived, as I have said, seeing as many as two thousand winters in the natural course of things. We are thus not inclined by our natures to take note of anything so short as an hour. However, time passes for us as it does for all creatures, and while I waited for Idai I decided to dare my wings again and take another quick look around the fire plain. By the time I returned to the Grandfather to await her I was deeply troubled.

I had often been to Terash Vor. It usually happened that some time in every kell—every hundred winters—the mountains took a deep shuddering breath and exhaled fire. Some of these episodes were more active and some less, but I had seen this level of fire only once before, when I was little more than a youngling myself. Thus this was the equal of the worst outbreak in living memory, for I am the Eldest of the Kantri. Not for sixteen kells had there been such unrest in the ground. I wondered what it might portend.

Idai bespoke me from a distance as she approached. *"Shikrar, how fare you? I had thought you still kept the Weh sleep until I heard your call to the Summer Field on the morrow."*

"The ground shook me awake, indeed, but I am healed enough that the waking has been no hardship."

I heard her gasp of a sudden and felt the fear in her mind, and I knew she had seen the great plume of fire. *"Name of the Winds, Shikrar! What has so blasted the very rock that it thus burns in anger?"* She spoke aloud then as she landed beside me, her great wings almost fluttered as she came to earth. I had seldom seen her so agitated. "I have never seen such a thing."

"I have, but I was barely fledged the last time. Come aloft again with me, let us take as close a look as we may."

We leapt from the ledge, spreading wings wide, and took advantage of the fire-made updrafts to keep us high aloft. We investigated the patches of brightness on the other mountains and found little to comfort us. It was a great outbreak, and like drenching rain on hard-baked ground it had spread far and wide. The flows on the north of Terash Vor were a little unusual; the fact that three other peaks in the range were also gushing fire was cause for deep concern.

It seemed every bit as bad as the memory from my youth, and I well remembered that at the time there had been much debate about our future on the island. The necessity of having to leave had been seriously discussed. Only the dying of the mountains' fire had ended the debate. I could not, however, trust simply to memory for something so important.

As Idai and I turned away south again, towards our chambers and the Great Hall, I bespoke my son. *"Kédra, are ye landed safe and well?"*

His voice sounded strong and confident in my mind and below all ran a current of quiet delight like a strong river. *"We are, Father, and Sherók is already pleading to go aloft again! He seems to have quite a taste for it. What have you found?"*

"Much, and none of it of comfort. I fear I must ask for your assistance. Is Mirazhe well enough to care for Sherók without you? I will require you for the Kin-Summoning at the next dark of the moon."

"She is, my father," he replied, instantly somber. *"I will begin my preparations."*

"You need not act quite so swiftly as that!" I replied, hissing my amusement even as I flew. *"I must speak with as many as come to the Summer Field at noon, and we shall have more than a full moon before I am prepared for the Summoning. However, if you will meet with me in the Chamber of Souls at dusk of the coming day we can begin our preparations."*

He agreed and bade me farewell. Idai and I flew in silence back to our several chambers, for we both had much to consider.

Berys

It is done! I have begun this record of my acts, on the eve of my flowering. For the price I have paid to the Rakshasa, the greater of the two races of the demons, my thoughts and actions will appear on these pages, for I wish to remember all but cannot spare the time to write at day's end when what I require is sleep. A minor making this, compared to others I have done and shall do, but well worth the time it will save. This book will be my secret and my truth, that when I am finally raised to my deserved eminence and all of Kolmar is at my feet for as long as I wish it, those I hold in thrall may read how they were defeated. Their despair will add greatly to my rejoicing.

Once the journal was accomplished, the time was come to summon back the demon I had sent to find Marik's daughter. A minor summoning with a binding woven in and it arrived, cords and all ready to my hand. I tightened my grip on the binding and the thing writhed.

"Speak and be freed," I said. "Where is she?"

"Followed the trace I have, foolish one, but find her I cannot," it hissed. "Release me and you sshall live."

"I have paid well for your services, little Rikti. Your threats are empty and your life or your service forfeit. Speak!"

"Shee isss hidden!" it cried.

I tugged hard on the binding and it screeched its pain, high and agonized. Good. "Do you tell me that you cannot find her?" I spat. "Do you speak to me of your own death, worm?"

The Rikti hissed as I released the pressure to let it speak. "I bear no fault for that the one you sseek iss invisible. She hass been ssought throughout both worldss, but a veil iss about her and a fear liess on her name."

"A fear? What kind of fear can affect the Rikti?"

I knew the only possible answer even before it spoke, but I wanted to hear its version.

"Kantrissshakrim," it hissed. "She iss protected—there musst be one that iss ever at her sside. It would cosst my life to go nigh her," it said with a sneer, "and for that you have not paid."

"Your life is mine if you do not complete the pact," I

snarled. Its petty self-importance annoyed me and I tugged again at the binding charm. It screamed nicely until I released it again. "Now, filth, tell me where she is to be found. If there is a True Dragon in Kolmar it must burn in your sight like iron in the fire's heart. Where?"

"There are two, Masster, and I do not know which guardss the prey. Which would you hear of for your price?"

"Both, creature, or you shall serve me a year for each drop of blood I have paid you."

It hissed and struggled to free itself, but it knew that I had the right to make the demand and the power to enforce it. Finally it stood on all of its legs and peered past my shoulder, several of its eyes staring intently at nothing. "The firsst liess in the high hills north of here, a sstrangeness in the high passess that reeks of drragon, that iss and isss not Kantrisshakrim. The ssecond is in the far north and west, between the great River and the Sea but ssouth of the wood and the hillss. Sssmaller than the firssst but sstronger, and iss and iss not Kantrisshakrim. More I cannot tell you, for more I do not know." A shiver passed along its body and I knew I would learn no more. "The pact iss concluded, all iss done, live in pain and die alone," it hissed as it disappeared, leaving only a stench of rotten eggs.

Not the information I wanted, but news indeed. I divested myself of my Summoning robes as I pondered it. Two Great Dragons in Kolmar! I had never imagined there could even be one without news of it spreading far and wide. And one protecting Marik's daughter, whom I desperately require.

It will not be a simple task to destroy one of the Great Dragons, though my apprentice Caderan managed it on the Dragon Isle itself before he was killed, and Marik may well have done as much using the Ring of Seven Circles, a powerful device I had prepared for him. I would have to make certain that this time I did not fail. If one was watching so closely over the girl—but it was nonsense! They are huge creatures, hardly to be kept hidden even in the depths of the great forest of the Trollingwood or amid the high stone teeth of the East Mountains! Still, the Rikti was bound and spoke truth as far as its limited understanding went. There was something that kept the Rikti from finding her.

I must learn what it was.

Lanen

The next morning Varien and I wandered to the kitchen to break our fast, delightful as it had been to linger in bed. We found Jamie warming himself before the cooking fire. "Good morning, you two," he said with a grin. "Or is it afternoon?"

"Nay, not yet, Master Jameth," said Varien, holding me close to his side. "Not while my dearling shines so bright in my eyes. Surely it is always morning where she is?"

Jamie snorted. "New-wedded idiot! Lady give me patience." He turned to me. "Or is he always like this?"

"I'll let you know," I replied, turning in Varien's arm until we faced one another. I could not get enough of the sight of him, or of the feel of him against me. "Are you always like this?"

He stroked my cheek with his palm, infinitely soft, and despite his human form I felt still the effect of immense strength under control. *"As long as we live, my dearest Lanen Kaelar, I am thine and thou art the light of my days. But perhaps it is not fitting so to display our love before Jameth? For all his love of thee, he hath no mate to share his life."*

My love for him burned fiercely then, growing even when I had thought it full-blown, and I kissed him lightly as I stepped away from him. *"Quite right, my heart. Bless you for thinking of it. I am far too selfish."* Aloud I said, "Hmm. Yes, Jamie, I suspect he is. We'll try to keep ourselves under control when we're in public."

"Just as well. There should be laws about such things," he said, shaking his head. Under his words his voice was rich with laughter. "I guessed you'd both be hungry, so I've had Lise come in from the village this morning to bring bread. She's been very kind about it since you left," he said, shooting me a wicked grin, "though her bread's nothing like yours."

I laughed. "Just as well! Honestly, Jamie, don't get Varien's hopes up, you know the bread I make can drive nails."

"True enough—though I tell you, Varien, I'd give a week's wages in silver for a goose roasted by the girl. It's the best thing she does. She's a good enough cook, even if she can't do something as simple as bake bread."

I looked around me, contented. Desperate as I had been to leave Hadronsstead the autumn before, it was home, and had been for all of my twenty-four years. In the winter morning a hundred memories came back to me, centred on the kitchen and on Jamie. "Are there any of the geese left that were destined for the pot this winter?"

Jamie smiled in earnest then. "A brace, on my word, none too young but not ancient either. Ah, Lanen, your kind heart has not deserted you! You'll make this old man happy yet."

I laughed at him, as he had intended. "You may hand over that week's wages in silver this evening when they're done," I declared, looking about me for an apron. "If I thought there were a chance of it, I'd get you to pluck them for me too."

A strong pair of arms took me prisoner from behind and turned me around. Varien looked deep into my eyes. "Dearling, before you begin this work that will occupy you until the evening, you must eat and so must I. Swiftly. Before I get a craving for man-flesh." His eyes flashed at me as he lifted my hand to his lips and kissed it, then kissed my wrist, then drew back my sleeve and made as if to gnaw on my arm.

I batted him away. "Jamie, would you show this poor starveling creature where the bread and cheese are kept, or the oats if he wants porridge—oh, and is there anything left of that last batch of preserves I made?" I ducked into the little cold pantry off the kitchen. Plenty of onions, bunches of rosemary hanging from the rafters and sage still bravely silver-green in the garden, a little of the chopped pork from the pig butchered for the wedding feast—and for the moment I was content.

Make no mistake: had I thought that such a life was all that lay before me, I'd have left before dawn with Varien and been as many leagues hence as the fastest horse could carry me. I knew well, though, that this could be only a brief respite, and I even enjoyed washing the vegetables in the freezing well water. It was a familiar feeling, safe and cozy, and I knew it would not last long.

I had not forgotten the attempt on Rella's life, indeed I still didn't know if she was alive or dead, but from what Rella had told me while we were on the Dragon Isle together and what I had overheard of a conversation between Marik and his demon caller Caderan, I knew Marik had allied himself with a true demon master. I had heard the name, heard Caderan say it a few times, but I was thinking then of other things and couldn't remember it now. Caderan was dead, thank the Lady, but his unknown master lived and I did not wish to bring the wrath of demons down on Hadronsstead and those I loved. The last words Rella spoke before she collapsed in my arms charged me to find my mother, Maran Vena. I knew of only one place to look: the little town where she grew up, away north and east, a place near the Trollingwood called Beskin. On our way here, Varien and I had decided that as soon as we were rested we would go and seek her out.

Meanwhile, there was stuffing to be made and a brace of geese to be cooked. Looking back, I am delighted that I enjoyed it as I did at the time. Life runs by so quickly and it is so easy to be always looking to the morrow. The best times I have ever had in my life were when I was neither fearing the future nor fretting over the past, but simply enjoying where I was and what I was doing, be it as lowly a task as cooking food for those I loved. Life itself is change, and you never know when such pleasures will be taken from you without warning and without hope of recovery.

The three of us sat round the fire in the kitchen that night for a quiet cup of spiced wine after supper. I was proud of my cooking for once, for if I say it myself the geese had been roasted to perfection. Varien had enjoyed it nearly as much as Jamie.

The two youngest stableboys, Rab and Jon, had just finished washing the crockery through in the scullery while all the rest went about feeding and closing in the beasts for the night. There was a frost in the clear night air, bitter cold in the nose and threatening.

Jamie had spent the short daylight hours showing Varien around the stead. "Varien tells me he has never seen a stead before," said Jamie, bemused. "Though if all you say is true," he added wryly, "he'd have had little enough reason to do so."

"And still you doubt, Master Jameth," said Varien quietly. He seemed a little amused. "How shall I convince you, beyond my word and that of your own heart's daughter Lanen?"

Jamie held Varien's glance as long as he could, but had to look away. "You'll never convince me with words," he answered, somewhat subdued. Varien's eyes were the strongest argument he had. "It'll just take time. But I'll know truth when I see it." One corner of his mouth lifted in a half-smile as he looked at Varien again. "You can't say you expected me to believe you right off? You have to admit, it's a little unlikely. You're a good man, Varien, on that I'd stake my life, even if your eyes are peculiar. You could be anything, I suppose—but come, tell me, have you anything left of your old people in you to prove it?"

"Beyond the memory of my life with my Kindred, I do not yet know," Varien replied. He seemed to be taking this all very calmly. "I have been in this body so short a time, only three moons, I believe." He grinned then, all sadness forgotten as he reached over to take my hand in his. "I have not been paying overmuch attention to the passage of time, or to what this new body can yet do that I could do before. So different, so wondrous—in truth I have been far more intrigued by the differences." He let go of my hand then and held up his own two hands, palms towards him, staring at them, then passed the fingers of one hand over the other. "These Gedri hands are so soft, so delicate, they can feel the passage even of air. Yet withal they are so deft, so capable and strong, you can thread a needle one moment and haul on a rope the next." He was lost in thought, gazing at his hands. "These were the things I truly envied you, those long years when the *ferrinshadik* held me and I dreamed of such a moment."

"What does that mean—ferrin—whatever you said?" said Jamie.

"*Ferrinshadik*—it is a word in our tongue for the longing that touches many of us, to speak with another race, to hear the thoughts of another people who can speak and reason," said Varien, thoughtfully. "Some are spared, but many of us feel it as a longing to speak with the Gedrishakrim—with humans, whom we call in our language the Silent People. To some poor souls it is a deep and lasting sorrow for the passing of the Trelli, who in refusing the Powers of order and chaos sowed the seeds of their own ending."

Jamie looked at him, shaking his head. "Varien, your pardon, but what are you talking about? What powers?" he asked.

"Jamie!" I exclaimed. "Don't you know the Tale of Beginnings? Sweet Lady, even I know that!"

Jamie shrugged. "Never spent much time listening to bards."

Varien smiled at me and shifted slightly in his seat, sitting up straighter and facing both Jamie and me equally as best he could. I grinned back. "So—this is the human version of the Kantri Attitude of Teaching, is it?"

"It is indeed," he replied. "If you do not know the Tale of Beginnings, Jameth, it is time you learned. It speaks very well of your own people." He moved his neck slightly, brought his chin a little down—and I knew that he was instinctively moving Kantri muscles to arch his neck and face his students more directly. He spoke surely but slowly. I later learned that he was having to translate an old tale of the Kantri into human language even as he spoke.

"When Kolmar was young, there were four *shakrim*, four peoples, who lived here: the Trelli, the Rakshi, the Kantri and the Gedri. All possessed speech and reason when the Powers of order and chaos were revealed to them, and all four learned at the same time that in the life of all races there is a time when a choice must be made. Each chose differently.

The Kantri, the eldest of the four peoples, believed that although chaos is the beginning and the end of all things, it is order that decrees this, and thus they chose to serve order. For this they were granted long lives and a way to remember all that had gone before.

The Trelli, the troll-people, chose not to choose. They did not wish to accept either and denied both. In that decision was the seed of their own ending, for to deny the Powers is to deny life itself.

The Rakshi were already of two kinds, the Rakshasa and the smaller Rikti. Both chose chaos and thus balanced the Kantri—but pure chaos cannot exist in a world of order without the two destroying that world between them. The Rakshi for their choice received length of days to rival the Kantri, and a world within the world for their own, with which they were never content.

The Gedri discovered after much debate that they could not agree among themselves, but unlike the Trelli they did make a choice. Indeed, they chose Choice itself, that each soul might have the power to decide which to serve in its own time. Thus they acquired the ability to reach out to either Power and bend it to their own wishes, and although both the Kantri and the Rakshi were creatures of greater strength, it is the Gedri who have the world as their own."

Varien smiled, his recitation over. "Come, Jameth, do you tell me you have never heard this tale? Surely your bards remember it?"

I looked to Jamie, who said, "If they do, I have never heard them sing it." His voice sounded strange, and I looked more closely at him. His expression was very peculiar. "Though I think, now, that I heard something of the kind from my grandfather when I was very, very young." He looked up, and his voice took on a tinge of wonder. "How old *are* you, Varien?"

Varien ignored him for the moment, which I suspect was just as well. He had raised his hands as if to massage a stiff neck, but he looked terribly awkward; he had turned his palms out and was trying to use the backs of his hands when he stopped, looked up at me, and slowly turned his hands over. I gasped as I realised—no claws. He had been accustomed his life long to turn his great foot-long talons away from his own scales lest he injure himself. The smile that had lit his face turned to a grin as he used his fingertips to release the tight muscles in his neck, that had tried to hold up a man's head as a dragon would have. He laughed then and I with him. "Name of the Winds!" he cried, leaping to his feet, delight in his eyes and his voice deep with his joy.

He turned to Jamie, his eyes bright, his whole soul in his gaze. "This second life is a wonder beyond words, Master Jameth. Would that I could tell you how it feels! I stop a hundred times in a day simply to breathe, to feel the swift beat of my heart and the passage of air through my chest. I tell you, it is a dream I never dared admit even to myself, this deep longing for human form, for the hands of the Gedri children. This and walking on two legs!" And suddenly he laughed. "You have no idea how convenient it is, Jameth, not to have to carry wood in your mouth. It tastes terrible, believe me."

I was grinning, for I had seen him do just that, and spit fire afterwards to char away the splinters. This was all purest Akor, if Jamie could but know it.

"I tried for years to walk upright," said Varien, "but our legs simply are not shaped for it. My joints ached for days every time I tried, and I finally gave it up." He had calmed down a little and stood now before the fire, warming his hands.

"How old were you then?" I asked, teasing him. "You told me you had practiced landing on two feet, but you never said a word about this."

He paused a moment, smiling at old folly. "I was past my majority, but not long past, when I first tried. I was in my sixth kell that first time, and just over a hundred years from my ceat when I admitted defeat." He turned and smiled at me. "It was hard to surrender such a desire, my heart, but I was nearly my full size by then and hard-pressed to explain to Shikrar why I found it so difficult to walk for a month. It hurt terribly, I was an idiot to try."

"What's a ceat?" I asked.

"For that matter, what's a kell?" asked Jamie.

"A kell is a hundred winters," said Varien, gazing now at the flames, his voice calm and peaceful in the firelit darkness, "and a ceat is the halfway point in the lives of the Kantri, when we have lived twice the time of our majority and half the full span of our lives. It is a time for celebration, for noting the prime of one's life and rejoicing in it. A ceat is ten kells, a thousand winters. My own ceat passed just twelve—no, thirteen winters gone now."

Jamie swore vigorously, and though the firelight obscured his face I heard the strange note in his voice as he spoke. "Are you seriously trying to tell me you're more than a thousand years old?" I couldn't tell if it was fear or disbelief or anger, or some mixture of the three.

Varien, unmoved, said, "I speak only the truth in this, Jameth of Arinoc. I have seen a thousand and thirteen winters, and were I still of the Kantri I should hope to see yet a thousand more. We are a very long-lived people; if nothing hurries it, many of us can hope to see the turn of our second ceat ere death comes to claim us."

"Damnation!" cried Jamie. He could sit no longer; he sprang from his chair and began to pace the room—away from the fire and Varien—then all in a moment turned and came straight to me, ignoring Varien altogether. He stood before me, his face to my amazement a mask of hurt. "Lanen, damn it, what has come over you? Why are you two doing this? You know there is nothing I would condemn, nothing I could ever deny you. Why invent so mad a tale? Do you not trust me to love you after all these years?" His voice thickened. "Have you gone so far from me, lass, in so short a time?"

I stood to face him, put my hands on his shoulders and looked him straight in the eye. Well, looked down. I have been taller than Jamie since I was twelve, but suddenly he seemed small and fragile. That came as a shock.

"Jamie, my hand on my heart and my soul to the Lady, I swear, I give you my solemn oath this is not a tale. It is the exact truth," I said. The look of doubt and betrayal in his eyes was terrible to bear. "Do you think I don't know it sounds insane?" I said angrily. "I haven't gone mad, and you know me too well for me to ever try to lie to you. It's all true, Jamie. All of it. If I hadn't been there I wouldn't believe it either, but I swear on my soul it's true. I first met Varien when he was Akor, the Lord of the Kantri, the True Dragons. I loved him even then, knowing that nothing could ever come of such a love. I saw him fight a demon master and I saw the terrible wounds that tore him apart. Sweet Lady, I saw bone through one of them." I shuddered and passed my hand over my face, trying to dismiss the vision of Akor so horribly wounded by my own father, Marik. "Shikrar, Kédra and Idai carried him to his chambers, and there he—well, we thought he died, and with his friends I mourned him. I myself found Varien, as he is now, mere hours after the death of my beloved Akor, naked as a newborn and lying on the ashes of the dragon he had been. His soul is the same, his heart, his mind, his memories—it is only his body that has changed." Jamie stared at me, still hurt, still unbelieving. I turned away and sighed, then realised I couldn't help the half-grin that crossed my face as I sat down again with a thump. "Hell's teeth, Jamie. I can't blame you. If I'd only heard the story, I'd think I was mad as well, or lying."

Jamie turned then to Varien, who stood silent, gazing still into the flames. "Well, Varien?" said Jamie, his hurt turned now to cold anger. "I will have it now, whatever it may be. Murderer, thief, demon master, penniless singer, mercenary, whatever you are—I charge you by your soul, by your hope of heaven, by your love of my daughter and as you hope to see the Lady's face on the day of your death, once and for all, tell me who and what you are."

"And why should you believe me this time?" asked Varien, beginning to grow angry in his turn.

"Because I will not ask again," said Jamie, staring straight into Varien's eyes.

To my surprise and Jamie's, Varien bowed low. "Very well, Jameth of Arinoc. My soul to the Winds, by all I hold sacred, by my love for Lanen and my hope of heaven, however different a heaven it may be from yours, I will tell you first and last who and what I am, so far as a little time will allow.

"My soul to the Winds, Jameth—and among my people that is a binding vow—I was born a thousand and thirteen winters past, the son of Ayarelinnerit the Wise and my father Karishtar, of the line of Loriakeris. I had a silver hide, like nothing that had ever been seen before among my people, and it was seen as an omen, though an omen of what none ever knew. My eyes and my soulgem were green, as they are yet, but that is not unusual among my people. I flew at the age of thirty winters, full twenty-five years before most others. I reached my majority at the turn of my fifth kell, as do all of the Kantri, and less than a kell later I was chosen as the new King when old Garesh, Shikrar's father, died. I first knew the *ferrinshadik* as a youngling, at the age of two hundred and forty, when I first saw the Gedri come onto our island. They had been lost at sea and some of our people took pity on them. We helped them repair their ship, though it was difficult, for our two peoples spoke very different languages. Still, we helped as we might. When they found lansip and discovered it helped to heal them, we allowed them to take away as many of the leaves as they liked, along with a dozen saplings. They left after a very short time, but I had watched them every waking moment and longed with a deep longing to speak with them. That had been forbidden. There was a Council called when they first arrived and it was decided that only the King would have direct contact with them, as many of the Kantri were still roused to fury by the very sight of the Gedri. When they left I had learned the meaning of a few—a very few—words of their tongue, and over the centuries I learned everything I could about them."

He looked to me. "When Lanen arrived I had almost given up hope that ever another ship would come for lansip, for it had been a long kell since any of the Gedri had stepped on our shores." He smiled, coming forward and taking my hand. "Ah, Lanen! Never as long as I breathe will I forget the sight and the sound of your first step on the island of my people! I saw you laugh with delight as you walked on the grass." His eyes locked with mine and the passion behind them lanced through me. "I watched you kneel down and smell the very earth on which you walked."

I shivered. My most powerful memory of my first moment on the Dragon Isle was the smell of crushed grass. I had not known until this moment that Akor was watching me then.

"The first night we met in secret." In my mind I heard him add, *"And you called me brother, my Lanen, across so wide and deep a chasm of hurt and hatred. I loved you even then."* "The next night we met under the eye of the eldest of us, my soulfriend Shikrar, who feared I was touched by demons or under the spell of a Gedri witch." He laughed. "He learned better in time! But he forbade our meeting again. And for the first time I, the King of my people and the most bound by our laws, I broke that forbidding, for I could not bear to say farewell so soon. I bore Lanen to my chambers, far beyond the boundary established to separate our two kindreds, and our fate was sealed that very night. For she loved me and I her, despite the barren future that must lie before us, despite the madness of Gedri and Kantri joining one to another. We flew in spirit the Flight of the Devoted, a sacred ritual of my people, as real and as binding as the marriage vows we took not four days past. From that moment we were joined to one another."

Varien kissed my hand and released it, and stood once more before Jamie, pride and compassion warring in his glance. "That is the truth, Jameth. That is who I was, and who I am. You may believe it or not, as you choose, but all thereafter happened as Lanen has said. Her father Marik drew down demons, which we destroyed; he tried to sacrifice her and I rescued her; he tried to steal the soulgems of my people and Shikrar and I stopped him with Lanen's assistance; my old self died of the wounds, and beyond hope or understanding, beyond possibility, I woke as you see me now in the very ashes of my own body, with my soulgem clasped tightly in my hand." He smiled, more gently now, as he saw that Jamie was beginning to be persuaded. "What she did not tell you, however, is the part she had to play in changing my people. Kédra, the son of Shikrar, and his mate, Mirazhe, were expecting the first youngling to be born in five hundred years to my people—it was seen as a wondrous sign—but the birth was going badly, and we all feared that both Mirazhe and her youngling would die. Lanen it was who helped birth the son of Kédra, who saved mother and child, and who by that one action has changed the hearts of my people forever."

Varien bowed once more and took his seat by the fire.

Jamie was long silent. I could see him weighing it all in his mind, and a lifetime's study let me relax when I saw him accept—something. The spark came back to his eyes and he nodded to Varien. "Every bone in my body says this must be a lie, but I have known many men in my time and I know truth when I hear it. You may be mad, of course, but that you have told me the truth as far as you know it, that I most certainly believe. I suppose that great green gem set in gold that you wore for the wedding—is that your soulgem?"

"It is," said Varien. "Shikrar set it in *khaadish* for me before I faced my people as a man."

"*Khaadish* is what we call gold, yes?"

"It is. We—in time, the Kantri turn the ground they sleep upon to gold. We do not speak of it. *Khaadish* is a base metal, useful on occasion and reflective when polished, but of little or no value to us."

Jamie snorted. "Ha! That circlet of yours would buy this farm, the village and several more nearby, and that's just the gold. If you are ever short of cash, the gem alone would—"

I saw Varien bristle and interrupted. "Jamie, please, it's not like that. Would you sell your leg for what it would fetch?"

"It is so much a part of you?" Jamie asked, taken aback.

"More," snapped Varien. Jamie watched him but Varien stopped there. "Indeed," said Jamie finally. "Didn't mean to offend, lad. And as for you truly being a dragon—well, what's dark now's clear later, as they say, and I'll try not to close my mind to anything."

Varien nodded. "That is a rare gift in any kindred. I thank you."

One corner of Jamie's mouth lifted in a half-grin. "You're welcome. You've certainly the manner of a king, wherever you come from."

"My people would not say so," replied Varien, with just a hint of humour in his eyes. "They always claimed that I was too frivolous, too lighthearted, too quick to accept change for the sake of the novelty. And speaking of change—I understand that, among the many skills that I lack, there is one that you have that I would welcome."

"What's that, then?" asked Jamie. He beat me to it by a short breath. Varien hadn't mentioned anything to me.

"As we are to be travelling in the wide world I shall have to learn to defend myself. I have never held a blade in my life. Lanen has told me that you are a master of that art. Might I prevail upon you to teach me as much as time allows?"

"As much as time allows?" asked Jamie. He sounded resigned, though, and I knew this was no surprise to him. Still, he deserved an explanation.

"Jamie, it's not just that I need to see the world," I said, and he raised an eyebrow. "Well," I said, laughing, "not *only* that I need to see the world. We're in trouble. I don't know if Marik is sane again, or if he ever can be, but if he recovers I don't suppose he's going to give up his sacrifice. I think he'll come after me, sooner or later, himself or some hired muscle."

"Nothing more likely," said Jamie, a gleam coming into his eye. "I thought the tale of your adventures ended too suddenly. There is no way to escape demon callers except by killing them. Trust me, I know."

"But Caderan's dead," I replied.

"From what you've said he was an underling. I know enough of the breed to know a real demon master wouldn't risk his precious neck on such a dangerous voyage. Did this Caderan never speak of a master?"

Suddenly I was on a path by the sea, hiding in a stand of fir trees, listening to Caderan and Marik talking about—"He said something about a Magister of the Sixth Circle. Does that help?"

"Hell's teeth, Lanen!" cried Jamie. "They don't come worse! A master of the sixth circle can summon and bind all but the greatest of demons." He paced the room swiftly, his agitation plain now. "Lady Shia's backside, Lanen, how in the name of all that's holy did you—tell me, did you hear a name? Did they mention a name?"

"I've been trying to remember," I said. "I'm afraid my mind was on other things. If they did speak a name I don't recall it."

"All the more reason, Master Jameth, for me to learn to handle a sword," said Varien.

Jamie winced. "Do you know, I wish I'd never told you that was my name. Call me Jamie, like everyone else. Of course I'll show you how to use a blade—but we will speak again about this demon master and what is to do about him."

He took an appraising look at Varien. "You look like you've some strength in those arms, but in a fight a blade grows heavy fast. Have you ever lifted a full-sized sword?"

Varien looked perplexed. "Is there more than one kind?"

Jamie laughed. "A hundred kinds, man! But I have one in mind for you to practice with." He rose and went to a long low box beneath the stair, drawing from its depths a great lump of a sword that I recognised as Hadron's. I had seen my stepfather take the blade from its hiding place once every year, when he set out on the road to Illara for the Great Fair at the start of autumn. He carried it with him for protection on the road, and as far as I knew had never drawn it in anger. It was the right length for Varien, but looked far too heavy for his slim frame. I sighed as I realised that Jamie was taking Varien's measure. Again.

"Here, see how it fits your hand," he called, and, lifting the point straight up, threw the sword across to Varien—

—who plucked it without thinking out of the air with his

right hand, then stared astonished at his arm holding the sword. "How in the name of the Winds did I do that?" he asked, looking to me.

"Very quickly," I said. I was as surprised as he, and quite pleased. He was *fast*. "You certainly didn't have time to think about it."

"That's often the key," said Jamie. "If all your instincts are that good you might be halfway decent after a few years. How's the weight of it?"

Varien, still holding the heavy sword rock-steady at arm's length, replied, "I do not understand your question. What should it weigh? I do not find it a burden, if that is what you ask." He casually swung it about him, and that great chunky blade danced in the air like a butterfly at midsummer.

Jamie would never have let it show, but I had grown up with him and didn't need truespeech to know he was swearing inside. I knew that look. "Yes, that's what I was wondering. I think it'll do fine as a practice blade." He was watching Varien even more closely now.

Varien lowered the blade. "I thank you, Master Jameth. Now that you are assured that I can lift this weapon, when shall we begin my training? And what have I to offer you in return?"

Jamie bowed ever so slightly. "Only your diligence. Catch." He threw the scabbard to Varien, who again caught it easily. "We begin tomorrow. I'll need a little time to set up the pell—I'll come fetch you at midmorning, after the beasts are cared for, and we'll make a start."

"I thank you." Varien sheathed the sword and laid it carefully by the hearth.

"Mind if I join you?" I asked, teasing. "Maybe it'll take better this time—at least I'll be awake, for a change. You must admit, Jamie, I did the best I could at midnight and after."

I got the grin I had hoped for. "Aye, so you did, and worked hard too—but as dearly as I love you, my lass, you've just not got the speed. That's not something that can be taught, I'm afraid. Oh, you're good enough to save your skin, granted, but whatever you are to do in this life it'll not be as a swordswoman."

I know he didn't mean it as a slap in the face but that's what it felt like. I was surprised at how painful those words were. I'd always known I wasn't very good with a blade, but I had held on to the hope that it was just a matter of practice, that someday I would be a fearsome warrior. I used to love the tales of the Warrior Women of Arlis and I think I had always hoped that my height and my strength would somehow be enough. I knew I had the soul of a warrior and I believed I could kill if I had to. I had so often been forced to restrain my strength when I was furious: surely that kind of rage would be useful if it were directed along a sword's edge!

The worst of it was that I knew the truth when I heard it, and it struck deep. Damn. Not a hearth-tender, not a warrior—what was to become of me? What in all the wide world would I ever be fit for?

My grief must have shown in my face, for Jamie leaned over to kiss my brow. "I'm sorry to be so blunt, and I know you're not happy to hear it, my girl, but I'm glad it's so." He gazed deep into my eyes and a strange passion took his voice. "Lanen, I've known women who were as good as I with a sword, and some who were better. They were strong and fast and hard of body and of mind, and they were suited to their lives and well content with them. And many of them died young, and some of them died badly, and I mourned more for each of them than I did for all the men who died beside them. Daft, perhaps, but true." He gently stroked my cheek in his callused hand and smiled. "I'd rather see you live to a good old age, my girl, and talk with every dragon who ever drew breath. It's a better life, believe me." He grinned then, and winked at me as he stood straight. "And for you, certainly a longer one. Nothing worse than trying to be something you're not. It's a good way to get yourself killed. Use the gifts you have and you'll change the world."

I yawned then, suddenly tired. "Right. I'll do that. But do you mind if I start tomorrow morning? It's been a long day."

I stood and stretched as Jamie and Varien both laughed, and Varien came to me and with one swift movement picked me up in his arms.

I don't expect that sounds too strange; the idea of a man sweeping a girl up into his arms is nothing new. However, most girls that happens to aren't near six feet tall and broad of shoulder. At first I was astounded, and he took advantage of the fact to lean over and kiss me.

Then I got mad. Really mad, really fast. I struggled to get loose but his hold was solid as iron and just as likely to give out. "Put me down," I said, between my teeth.

He stopped smiling and let me down. I heard the door close and realised Jamie was leaving us to it. Wise man.

"What in the hells made you do that?" I asked him, walking away from him towards the door, shaking with anger. "I *hate* that feeling." I clenched my fist, turned my back to the door and hit it as hard as I could, putting my body into the blow. I just about noticed something splinter but I didn't care. "I hated it when I was a child and I hate it even more now. How would you like to be caught and held helpless by one stronger than you?"

"Forgive me, dearling," he said quietly. "I see now that it was ill-judged. I thought—" He stopped.

"You thought what?" I asked sourly, rubbing my hand. "Stupid bloody thing to do."

One corner of his mouth lifted. "As I was walking with Jamie around the stead today, one of the—hands, you call them? The men who work with the horses—I saw one of the workers do so with his lady when she brought him his midday meal. She laughed and seemed to enjoy it." I never thought I'd see such a thing, but it looked to me like Varien was blushing. "Jamie told me then that they were new-wed, just this month past. I thought perhaps this was a Gedri custom—"

I laughed then, my anger gone as fast as it had come, and held him tight. "You idiot," I murmured to his hair. His body was warm and strong against mine, and his arms encompassed me like every promise of home I had ever longed for.

"Please don't try to be like a human, my heart. Just be what you are. You are the one soul I love most in all the world. We'll find our own way." I drew back just long enough to look in his eyes. "I appreciate you trying, my dear one, but Jamie's right. There is nothing worse than trying to be something you aren't."

"Very well, then, I shall be what I am," he said with a smile, his hands moving sensuously across my back. "I am your beloved and your new-made husband. You are weary and I must think ever of your welfare. Come to bed with me, my dear one, my heart's own, and I shall see if I can banish your weariness for a while." He kissed me then, hard, his passion swift as fire awakening mine.

We only just made it to the bedroom.

So Much to Know

Berys

I must be cautious a little time longer. As I was leaving the Great Hall of the College of Mages this morning, Magister Rikard looked long at me. "I still say you are ill-advised to leave the College just now, Magister Berys, but at least you are fit for the journey," he said sourly. He is always sour. He has been sour every moment of every day of all the years I have known him. "Indeed, I have never seen you look so well. It must be the morning light, I'd swear you look ten years younger."

I laughed and said it was the effect of the heavy mist. "If the ladies knew it smoothed out so many wrinkles, we could turn to weather-mastery to earn our keep," I said to him.

"It is no light matter," he replied nastily. He is very full of himself, Rikard, though he is but a kestrel in human form— small and skinny with a nose like a hawk. Suspicious bastard. "I am not the only one who knows what the essence of lansip can do, and it is known that you have lansip and to spare since you financed that poor mad Merchant to the

Dragon Isle. You meddle with forbidden knowledge, Berys, though I am certain you would deny it."

"Deny it! There is nothing to deny. Rikard, I know your motives are of the best, but you make much of nothing. You know I have not been well lately. If the lansip I have had the luxury of taking for healing has restored a brief semblance of youth so much the better, but I am no fool. Youth once gone has gone forever."

He just looked at me. " 'Ware pride, Berys," he said at last. "It has brought down greater men than you."

I smiled at him, secure in the knowledge that sometime in the near future I would be able at last to plunge a dagger in his heart. I have known Rikard for the last twenty years, during which we have cordially hated each other. However, he comes perilously near the truth and I am not quite prepared to let all my secrets go. None have connected Malior the demon master of the Sixth Circle with Berys the Archimage of the College of Mages in Verfaren, and I do not wish that to be known just yet. Not long now and I will not care, but for the moment my respectable life as Berys is worth protecting. Rikard may have to be—well, accidents happen, and I begin to tire of Rikard. He is the only one of the Magistri who knows anything of demon lore, apart from me, and his knowledge is not convenient.

We have made good time on our journey so far. The weather has favoured us, cold but clear and sunny. If it holds thus, Elimar is only six days' travel from where I stand. Had I prepared a demonline I had been there and returned in moments, but I carry one with me on this journey—one end anchored in my hidden chambers in Verfaren, the other to be set in Elimar when I arrive, to allow a future visit to be swift and untraceable. It will be good to have an escape route to Elimar. I will also establish the return journey, in case I require it, and will fix the "destination" at Verfaren when I return. Demonlines must be established physically at either end and they are not easily erected. Still, though they last for only one use they are worth the price—instant transportation between two places, no matter how distant. Even dragons cannot move so swiftly; and once used the lines disappear and none but the maker knows where the traveller has gone. Well worth the price. One never knows when such a thing might be useful. I believe in being prepared for all eventualities.

I am no closer, as yet, to learning how the dragons might be defeated, but I have collected every reference book from the library at Verfaren and I am reading them through. Surely someone, somewhere, has learned a better way of defeating dragons than risking themselves in combat! The Ring of Seven Circles works, but the worker must be within range of the beast, and when Marik used the one I prepared for him the creatures broke into his mind. I do not wish to take that chance.

I had not known they could do that. I must be more wary in my dealings with them.

First, though, I must heal Marik and learn all that he knows. I cast this very recording spell upon him when he went on his journey to the Dragon Isle, so that every thought, every word, was written as he thought it in a book in my own chambers. That was well, as far as it went, but when his mind broke so did the link. The book finished long before I had intended it to.

Poor fool. He thought, to the very end, that I aided him in his search for his daughter that he might be rid of his pain. He promised her to demons before she was born, in exchange for the making of a Farseer. Marik's incompetence allowed that particular object to be stolen as soon as it was made by Lanen's mother, one Maran Vena, but since the price was never paid the demons put pain into Marik's leg to remind him. The pain would never cease until his firstborn child should be given to the Lords of Hell. Search though he might in the years between, he could never find Maran again, or her child. However, the Powers Below look after their own; he met the daughter by chance last autumn. He intends to give her to the Lords of Hell to pay his debt and so be freed of the pain that has haunted him since that day.

I let him believe that I would assist him in return for the

body of his daughter after her soul was taken by the Lords Below. Marik has always been a credulous fool. Let him suffer agonies from now until the end of the world. I need his daughter, whole and unharmed, to fulfill the prophecy spoken by one of our number many long years ago.

> When the breach is healed at last,
> when the two are joined in one,
> when the lost ones from the past live
> and move in light of sun,
> Marik of Gundar's blood and bone
> shall rule all four in one alone.

The first two lines are yet unclear to me, though I have considered them. I have long wondered if the "breach" refers to the time the dragons left Kolmar, the day the Demonlord defeated so many of them. It has occurred to me that the breach—if it is the one between the Kantri and the Gedri—might already be healed, for I heard from those who accompanied Marik on his journey that his daughter Lanen and her companions were carried to the ship by the dragons themselves. I have no idea what the "two joined in one" might be. However, in the absence of other interpretations, I assume that the lost ones from the past are either the Trelli or the Rakshi, the demons who were banished from this world at the time of the Choice. The Trelli dwindled and died out many long ages since, and there is not one left that could ever live or move again. I therefore assume that the lost ones referred to are the Rakshi, who have no bodies as such and cannot live on their own in this world. It is therefore my task to find a way to provide a body or bodies for at least one of the Rakshasa, that the prophecy may be fulfilled.

However, I have learned much from my research. He who trusts in the power of prophecy without making adequate preparations is at best a fool and at worst a dead fool. I have therefore been quietly ensuring that the children of the Kings of Kolmar have been meeting with dreadful accidents. Many years apart, mind you, and with no trace of any evil-doing, and certainly with no way to trace the deaths of the poor creatures to me. It has been most useful to have Marik's Merchant House at my disposal. Each branch in each town has its own healer and many of them are my own carefully chosen men and women. After all, Healers are accustomed to working with power. It is only a small step from there to working with demons, and if the step is paved thickly enough with silver there are many willing to take it.

As for the healed breach, it is very much in my mind that the greatest threat to my ambition is the Great Dragons, now that they are again aware of us and have made a bond with the one person in the world I require for my purposes. I had thought them all safely out of the way on that island in the west and had left them out of my plans altogether, until Marik's ill-fated quest for the precious lansip leaves that grow there roused them like a stick in an anthill. By all accounts, three people had been carried to the ship by the dragons themselves; carried and protected, by those who before only killed! Until that journey, the beasts had done no more than allow the gathering of lansip—which will grow nowhere else—and kill any who crossed their boundary. Then of a sudden they were become the champions of a hunchbacked old woman, a silver-haired man who came from nowhere, and Marik's long-lost daughter, Lanen. So much the accounts of those who were there had taught me.

I lit my dark lantern and blew out the candles in my summoning chamber. With a swift gesture and a whispered word I locked the door and sealed it against prying eyes. Any could find the door or knock, but should he touch the handle he would forget why he was there and wander away. It was unlikely that anyone would do such a thing, but safe is best. All perfectly harmless, all done with pure Power untainted by the Rakshasa.

The lantern lit my steps back up the narrow stair to my very sedate College chambers. Once through the hidden door beside the fireplace, I stirred up the fire and sat at my desk. There was much to consider.

The hunchback the dragons favoured was one Rella, a highly placed member of the Silent Service and long an enemy of mine. When I learned she was on the ship I had arranged to have her killed if she should manage to return from the voyage. A swift knife in the ribs appeared to have done the deed, but I have had a report in the last few days from the Corlí branch of Marik's Merchant House—Rella lived. It appears that Marik's daughter Lanen and the silver-haired stranger had taken the woman to a Hospice and left her there. The Healers were well-paid enough not to be willing to release her until she was fully fit, they would not allow any of the "visitors" I sent in to see her, and by the time she was healed she was on her guard and gave my men the slip. They had been able to find no trace of her. Pity, really. They had never failed me before. Still, there are always others willing to take on such tasks.

I opened my ink-pot and drew the candle closer to the paper.

"Devlin, I require your services. You and each of your men will earn four silver pieces for every fortnight you serve me, as well as expenses for your journey, and a bonus of ten silver each will go to the men who find what I seek, upon delivery. You must divide your forces into two groups. One is to search the country just north of here, in the Súlkith Hills between Verfaren and Elimar. The other will go to the north of Ilsa, west of the River Arlen and south of the Méar Hills. Find for me a tall, plain, grey-eyed woman with light brown hair, of about five-and-twenty winters; one who has been away through the autumn, or one who has recently arrived in a new place and acts in a strange manner or has peculiar companions, notably a man with long silver hair. If she is using her right name, it is Lanen Hadronsdatter. Bring her to me unharmed."

It would do for now. When my preparations are further advanced I may seek her more urgently. I could use demons, but the price they demand for such things is far higher than silver, and I must conserve my resources. There is much to do, and most of it men cannot accomplish. Let Devlin and his men do what they can, it is a simple enough task. I shall need all I have to bend the demons to my will when the time comes.

On a slightly different note, I should mention that I have been engaged in a little experiment since Marik returned. My share of the lansip harvest was considerable, and I had found in the archives of the College of Mages a method for extracting the essence of lansip that legend said could restore youth. It had cost a third of a ship's crew, Caderan's life and Marik's mind to get the lansip back to Kolmar from the Dragon Isle, and to me it was cheap at that. The wretched plant grows only on that one island: every sapling, every seedling, every half-grown tree that has been taken away in the past and planted in the earth of Kolmar has died.

Lansip is a heal-all, strong to cure all the ills that beset men. A weak infusion of even a single dried leaf in water is said to be a sovereign remedy for everything "from headache to heart's sorrow." The rare lan fruit, of which an astonishing three dozen were found on Marik's ill-fated journey, can heal all wounds save death alone. I sold the dozen that were my right for enough silver to purchase anything I might need for the rest of my life. Their worth was roughly that of Verfaren, this town that supports the College of Mages where I reside as the beneficent Archimage. Is it not a supreme jest?

Better than that, though, better than all, is what I have learned about lansip and its properties. Legend, that true servant of those who would learn from the past, records the old belief that essence of lansip can restore lost years. I have long known the tale of the rich merchant who was found dead and forty years younger than he should have been, for though that tale has been much corrupted in the telling I found the original report here in the great library at Verfaren. I have not repeated his mistake. He took a great draught all at once and died of it. I have been taking infusions regularly but in small quantities.

Legend was right.

I am growing younger by the day.

Lanen

"Good morning," I murmured happily, turning to face Varien. He stretched and casually put a long arm around my waist. "Good morning to thee, my dearling," he replied, kissing me lightly. The sun was only just up; it was pale and grey behind the shutters and I was glad to be still warm and in bed. Even in that light Varien all but shone. I braced my head on my hand and leaned back a little, just looking at him. Sweet Lady, but he was beautiful.

"Surely, I have not changed so much in the night?" he said, smiling at me. "Or is there something amiss that I should know?"

I reached over to stroke his hair. "Every now and then I still have to convince myself that you're real," I said, smiling back. "Sometimes I wonder."

"I am here and I am real, my heart. Why should you doubt?"

I ran my hand across his chest, revelling in the feel of him, of his skin beneath my fingers. "Until I went to the Dragon Isle I had spent the whole of my life alone, and I expected to spend the rest of it so. And now here you are, my own husband, so much more than I . . ." My voice faltered for an instant before I spoke my worst fear aloud. "I swear to you, Varien, sometimes I dread that I shall wake one day from this dream and curse the waking forever."

He drew me to him and held me tight, his arms strong around me. The scent of him was making me giddy, like too much strong wine. "I am here," he murmured in my ear. "I am no dream to fade with waking." He drew back just enough to kiss me, a blessing, a promise. "You had best believe that and grow accustomed to my presence, for you are mine, proud Lanen Kaelar, and I will not leave you as long as life remains."

"You'd better not, or I'll bloody well come after you and find out why," I growled.

I'm afraid my anger wasn't very convincing.

After Varien had shown me how un-dreamlike he really was, and we were resting again in each other's arms, I said quietly, "You know, Varien, I was wondering—have you ever yet wakened in the morning and wondered what happened to your tail?" I grinned. "Or why you were lying on your back? I'd wager the Kantri don't do that."

He smiled back at me. "Ah, but we do—at least, younglings do so sometimes, while their wings are still quite small, but it quickly becomes uncomfortable." He grinned. "As an adult I have only rolled on my back a few times, when I had a terrible itch and there was no one around to help scratch it. I did so envy human their long arms! Why do you ask, darling?"

I took a deep breath. "I was wondering if you were regretting the change."

He was silent for a moment, thinking. I have always loved that in him—that he never replied with some easy answer but thought about everything that he said. "I will not lie to you, my heart. There are times when I miss my life as it was," he replied honestly. "We are creatures of fire and our feelings are deep and strong, and we are not used to sudden change. But even if I have mourned the loss of my wings and the joys of the air, if I have missed the strength that could protect us both, I have not yet wished to undo this change that the Winds have sent. I know not the purpose of it, beyond loving you and seeking to aid the Lost, but I have so far delighted in being human." He gently swept an errant lock of my wild hair away from my face. "Lanen, *kadreshi*, the love of the Kantrishakrim is not given lightly. I would have loved you my life long no matter what shape my body held. Why should I regret that we now may join in body as well as in spirit? No, dearling, I do not regret being human." He leaned across to kiss me again and smiled. "What wind blows that shakes you so this bright morning?"

I loved the way his voice echoed in his chest. Deep, clear, resonant.

I drew back a little so I could look at his eyes. "I don't know. Sometimes it just comes over me. I never really planned—I had only just started living when I went to the Dragon Isle. I had no larger idea of what to do with my life beyond wandering through the world, learning new places and new people, finding new ways of seeing the world." I laughed. "It seemed enough—and to be fair, you and your Kindred have taught me a great deal. But for all my life until then I had dreamt only of travelling through Kolmar. And now—"

"Now?"

I sighed. "Now Shikrar has put a duty on us. I know that we are bound to do what we can to help restore the Lost. That duty is an honour, but I fear—" I sat up and looked away. "And Rella told me to go to my mother. I know I will have to do that sooner or later. And now I don't know which is more important, which I should do first—and of course it's not just me anymore, we are both going to have to decide what to do, and in what order. Sometimes I swear this is all beyond me. For pity's sake, Varien, I grew up on this little stead a hundred leagues from anywhere!" My voice rose with my frustration even as I wondered where this flood of self-doubt was coming from. "I'm not some clever, brave warrior in a bard's tale, I'm flesh and blood and more likely to be wrong than right about most things. I know a bit about horses and gardens and enough about crops to keep from starving, but that's about it. I'm not some great and glorious hero in a ballad, I'm—I'm the bastard child of a madman and a mother who left me as a babe!"

"Is this what troubles you, my heart?" asked Varien gently, as he sat up and took me in his arms. I held tight to him, for I was filled with a terrible sense of being overwhelmed, of frustration and anger at the expectations that had been put upon me, and suddenly I was weeping.

Bless him, he didn't try to comfort me or talk me out of crying, he just held me close until the storm passed. When my tears were spent I lay still in his arms, heart to heart, and I could feel his beating against mine strong and steady.

Only then did he speak, and his heart and his voice were light.

"Lanen, my true Lady, I shall never cease to be astounded by the depths of you. So young as you are, not even old enough yet to fly, and each day I learn more of your great soul." He moved a little away from me so that he could see my eyes, which was very brave of him. I once caught sight of myself in a mirror after I had been crying—I have seen some women who only look more beautiful when they cry, but my eyes go bright red and puffy and my nose runs. Bless him, he kissed me anyway.

"Dear heart, if you believed that we would soon accomplish all that Shikrar hopes we might one day achieve, I might be pleased at your enthusiasm but I would be seeking some way of telling you that it was unlikely. At the very best, I would assume that we have long years of work ahead of us, my dearling, of searching and learning in the knowledge that all may come to nothing in the end despite our best efforts. Sometimes so great a thing can only be faced if it is known before we start that it is impossible. Only then are we free to know that we cannot do worse than fail."

"I wish I knew why I feel so awful about it," I murmured.

He stroked my hair. "I cannot know, dearling, but I begin to have a sense of you. I know how deeply the tale of the Lost affects you. Have Shikrar's words made you feel responsible for them?"

A few last tears leaked out and I nodded. "Yes, they have. I do feel responsible for them," I muttered. "And what if I can't do anything? What if we make no difference to them at all, after all that has happened, all we have been through?"

"Kadreshi," he said gently, "we of the Kantri have believed it to be impossible for years thick as autumn leaves, but every year we try again to speak with our distant kin. If it is impossible we have nothing to lose." His voice grew soft and low, the words barely loud enough to reach my ears, and beyond us not even a whisper escaped. "The weight of the world is not on your shoulders, my Lanen, nor is the fate of the Lost in your hands. If we are to attempt to help them, we must do so out of concern for our fellow creatures in this world, not for glory or because you think Shikrar believes you to be some heroine in a bard's tale." Varien smiled at me, melting my heart. "He does not, and he would be distressed to think you took his words so. I know him well, and like me I am certain he hopes that a fresh mind might bring a new insight—that in looking at the problem from so different an angle, from the point of view of the Gedri rather than of the Kantri, perhaps something will arise in your mind that would never have occurred to us. That is all, my dear one. He does not expect the two of us to work miracles for him. But he always hopes for one."

He gazed long at me and I was drawn in and comforted by the ageless depths of the emerald eyes that filled my vision. "Once you know that a thing is impossible, my heart, and that in all likelihood you cannot do anything about it at all, you are suddenly free to think of it differently than you would if you had any hope in the matter. If a thing obviously cannot be done, it becomes a game, a mystery, a challenge, to think of a way around the impossible part." He grinned at me. "You have, this moment, already mourned your failure—our failure—to help the Lost. The Kantri have tried for five thousand years and accomplished nothing at all. Therefore we have nothing to lose, for we cannot make matters worse or do less than has been done before." I could almost see the flame behind his eyes as he added, "The only truly unforgivable thing is not to try."

"Then in the name of the Winds and the Lady, let us begin!" I cried, all ablaze to be up and doing.

He grinned at me. "Even as we are? I admire your spirit, my heart, but I fear that even you might find the winter air frosty on bare skin." He ran his hand over the nearest bit of bare skin he could reach and I began to regret that I had taught him what "tickle" meant. For all my enthusiasm I couldn't help but laugh.

Joy lit his face like the morning sun as he drew me close

in his arms. "We will leave soon enough, but for now, *kadreshi*, let us see what love can make possible at this very moment."

I laughed again, from pure delight. It was still so strange and new to be desired.

"Varien Kantriakor, I swear you are getting addicted to this. I thought the Kantri only mated a few times in their lives!"

He stopped kissing various bits of me just long enough to say, "Behold, another of the joys of being human!"

And yet we managed to be dressed and ready by the time Jamie sent for us. It's amazing what you can do when you put your mind to it.

It was a heavy, cold, grey morning, cloudy with the kind of damp cold that gets in your bones. I knew I would only be watching as Jamie instructed Varien, and I had hunted out every warm garment I possessed, leggings under my skirts and a tight woolen shirt under my heavy linen shirt under a long-sleeved wool tunic under a hooded sheepskin cloak. I looked half again my normal size but I was warm. Varien was also dressed in woolen tunic and leggings, but he refused to wear a coat. "I shall be warm enough, I trow, an Master Jameth hath his way," he said.

"He will," I replied. "But for pity's sake don't call him Master Jameth this morning. Jamie hates that name and you really don't want your swordmaster mad at you."

I saw Varien take a breath and I knew he was going to ask why. "Trust me," I said. "Come, Jamie's waiting in the courtyard."

Jamie was trying out the pell he'd set up, a tall thick log braced upright in the middle of the courtyard. It was a lovely sight and one that brought back a hundred memories, though the light here was considerably better.

Jamie had taught me what little I knew of fighting over a number of years and, as my stepfather Hadron opposed such knowledge for his daughter, we had been forced to practice in the feed storeroom in the dead of night. I remembered every move of Jamie's, though, and the patterns made my own muscles twitch in response. Jamie made it look like a dance. Forehand low, backhand high, forehand high, backhand low, head strike, then again, and again, until the muscles knew where to go without having to be told—then vary the pattern, practicing, building strength and endurance—then learning to parry, which took me forever—then the first tentative matches against Jamie, against a thinking target, when patterns disappeared and you had to rely on reflexes, and parrying badly got me a thump with the flat of his sword and a cry of "This isn't an exercise, girl, you're fighting for your life!"

I sighed, watching him finish the pattern and straighten up. He was right, I just didn't have the speed. If I paid attention I should survive a brief skirmish, but in a pitched battle with a half-decent swordsman I'd lose every time. The worst of it was that when my opponent got the upper hand I kept wanting to drop the sword and start swinging my fists, which is deeply stupid and a good way to get yourself killed. I used to think he was terribly disappointed in me, but his heartfelt words the night before had gone deep to heal, and my lack of ability didn't hurt nearly so much as it used to.

To my surprise I heard Jamie calling my name. I walked slowly over to him, picking my way carefully over the cold stone cobbles, and gazed at Jamie out of my woolly nest. "What did you want?" I asked contentedly.

"To find out if you can still fight," he said briskly, moving swiftly behind me and twitching my hood off. "Just because you'll never make a living at it doesn't mean you don't have to defend yourself. Come out of there and take up a sword." I don't know if it was the cold or the practice, but Jamie looked ten years younger and his eyes were sparkling.

Muttering to myself, I shrugged off my cloak, shivered, and picked up the practice sword Jamie had brought along. By the Lady, it was heavier than I remembered! I hauled it upright and Jamie pointed gaily at the pell. "Five minutes there first, while I talk to your other half," he said, swatting me. I raised my sword and growled and he danced lightly away. "Do you remember your drill?"

Without a word I stood before the pell and readied my sword, thanking the Lady in my heart that Jamie had thought to scatter earth on the cobbles around the pell to keep us all from slipping.

Right. Deep breath, concentrate—*go*.

It helped that I'd just watched Jamie go through the pattern, but after a few passes my arm seemed to remember anyway. Truth to tell the practice felt good. On my trip to the Dragon Isle there had been several times I'd wished I was better with a blade. Strange to be doing this in full daylight, though—and with room to swing the sword at full stretch at last! I settled into the familiar movements—one, two, harder, harder, *overhand*, use the weight, two, three, harder, *overhand*, one, two . . .

Varien

I watched Lanen, fascinated. When she first started hitting the log—the "pell" was a tree trunk a handspan in width—she stood stiffly, aware of other eyes watching, but after a very few strokes she relaxed into it as a familiar action, using only the muscles that she needed. I didn't know why she kept her right arm crooked high in front of her chest, but I expected I would learn soon enough.

Jamie walked over to me as Lanen was practicing. He stood before me and said, "Draw your sword."

I laid the sheath gently on the cobbles.

"Now, feel the edge."

"There is none to speak of," I replied immediately, for I had examined the blade the night before. "Is it meant to be this dull?"

Jamie just looked at me, but even with three moons' practice I could not read that expression. "Forgive me, Master Jam—Jamie—but I cannot tell what you would have me understand."

"Unless you want to lose an arm by accident, yes, it's meant to be dull," he replied dryly. "The sharp one comes later. Have you got the pattern that Lanen is practicing?"

"I have watched the sequence. Is there a particular meaning associated with it?"

One corner of his mouth lifted in a half-smile. "No. Just practice." He walked with me to the pell. "That's enough, my girl," he called out, and Lanen straightened, lowering her sword and allowing her right arm to drop. She shook it for a moment. "Damn. Stiff already," she said, ruefully. "Sweet Shia, but I'm out of practice."

"No, are you? I'd never have dreamt it," he said. "You can have another session later, and you will practice every day until you've got some strength back into those arms. Now, young Varien, step up and show me what you saw Lanen doing. Start slow."

I lifted the sword and swung it. It felt awkward and alien. I attempted to follow the pattern as Lanen had, but I overbalanced on the third stroke and nearly fell.

Jamie stopped me. "Are you sure you're left-handed?" he asked. "You looked damned awkward."

"I know not. I am doing as Lanen did. What is 'left-handed'?"

Jamie sighed, taking the sword out of my left hand and put it into my right. "Try it that way," he said, and it felt better immediately. He stood beside me at the pell, guiding my arm. "Forehand low, backhand high, forehand high, that's right, let the weight of your sword do half of the work for you, now backhand low, yes, now head strike—straight over the top, and every now and then vary that with a side strike to the head." He showed me, moving my arm with his, and soon I could feel the rhythm of the swings on my own. Then he had me crook my left arm up and forward, as Lanen had her right. "That's where your shield will go one of these days," he said. "Might as well get used to having it there. Remember to keep this arm angled to the side, where an opponent's sword would land."

"Surely this overhead strike is slow and clumsy," I said, keeping up the pattern. "Does not the foe see the sword coming and have time to get away from it?"

"Aye," said Jamie, "you're right, as a killing stroke it's

practically useless. However, believe me when I tell you there's nothing like seeing a sword coming towards your eyes to make you step back and reconsider. Besides, once his shield's up you've a better chance at hitting something vital next stroke, if you're quick and he isn't. Just you keep at it, I'll come stop you in a moment." He took hold of my left arm, which had wandered down to my side, and lifted it again. "Remember, keep your shield arm up." He left me working at the pell.

Lanen

Jamie wandered carelessly over to me, but his glance was sharp and he spoke urgently. "Now, my girl. If you want to convince me once and for all that your tale is true, use that Farspeech of yours to tell him you're in trouble and he should drop his sword and come help you."

Ah, well.

I answered quietly. "If you want proof I'll ask him to come over here, but I can't lie to him. It doesn't work that way."

"Why not? Just say those very words. Surely that's not so hard."

"Jamie, it's called the Language of Truth for a reason. It's not like writing a message, it's like—like overhearing a conversation. Some of the older dragons can hide a little of what they are thinking, but I've only managed it once and that was with a lot of help. Flat lies are impossible; your thoughts would show the lie even if you don't mean to. At the very least it'll make him angry."

He raised an eyebrow. "Interesting. Very well." He looked around at Varien. "Ask him to try practicing with his left hand again."

I did not bother to answer but bespoke Varien. *"Dearling forgive me but Jamie is putting us to the test again Jamie has asked me to request that you try the pattern with the left hand again, I wish to goodness he'd just know the truth when he hears it."* I tried to keep silent about what Jamie had actually asked me to do, but I was still fairly new to true-speech and I never was much good as a liar in any case.

Varien

Lanen's underthought was obvious, as was the fact that she was trying not to show it. *"You'd have thought he'd re-alise by now, he wanted me to lie to you, I told him I couldn't/wouldn't he still doesn't trust you or me for that matter, I wouldn't lie to you aloud much less in truespeech."*

I instantly switched to my left hand and became instantly awkward again. I went through the full pattern three times to emphasize the point, but I could feel my anger building with each stroke and on the last I let loose my full strength and drove the sword deep into the wood. I left it there and strode over to Jamie and Lanen.

Jamie impressed me, for by the time I arrived he was al-ready moving and wary. So he should be. If I had still had my old shape I might well have killed him out of hand.

"How darest thou ask Lanen to lie to me?" I cried. Even as I spoke, a detached part of me noted both that I was using a form of speech that was far too old, and that my body was physically shaking with the effort of holding back from striking him. "The Language of Truth is so named for a rea-son! How should we deceive each other when our very thoughts are made clear? Truespeech is not some idle amusement, it is deep communion with another. You cannot open your thoughts, your very self, to another soul without revealing the truth of your mind and heart. Never think it again, Jameth of Arinoc, nor ask Lanen to do so."

Jamie nodded. "It's true, then," he said. "You really can hear her." He looked at me. "You'd like to hit me, wouldn't you?"

"Desperately," I said, still shaking.

"Go ahead and try," he said. "Even if you manage it, I'll live."

"I dare not," I replied, turning away from him, breathing

far too fast and too deep, "lest I have still some of my old strength and I injure you."

"Ah. Come over here," he said, catching my arm and leading me back to the pell, but never turning his back on me. Wise man. "Now. Pull your sword out with your right hand and use your full strength when you're drilling. Take out your anger on it—and don't worry, if you damage the pell I can make another one."

It was a relief to let out my anger in striking something, to feel the steel bite deep into the wood and to pull it out again by main strength. I thought it was dissipating until Jamie cried out, "Now! Kill it!"

His timing was superb. I had just begun a high forehand swing, and I put all my anger and my whole body into the stroke, shouting as I hit.

There was a noise of tearing wood, a loud crack, and a dull thump and clatter as the top third of the pell landed on the cobbled yard.

There was deep silence for a moment.

"Hellsfire, Varien," said Jamie then, very quietly. "Let me thank you now for not taking me up on my offer to let you strike me. Lanen's lost one father this year, that's enough for anyone." He kept staring at the lump of wood on the ground.

I grinned. "You are welcome."

I was calm again, all my anger gone in that last stroke. I had seldom had the satisfaction of using my full strength as one of the Kantri. It was good to know that I could do so in my new form. "In any case," I said to Jamie, "at least you believe in truespeech now."

"Varien, lad, I believe absolutely everything you two have told me," said Jamie, still gazing at the severed lump of wood. I could not entirely recognise the tone of his voice, but it sounded a little like awe. "Absolutely everything."

"Shall I continue my practice?" I asked.

He looked up at that, clapped me on the shoulder and smiled. "No, lad, I think this will do for a first session. Besides," he said as he took me by the arm and led me into the house, "I need to make a new pell."

Lanen

I was still a bit dazed as I watched the pair of them disappearing into the mud room off the kitchen. I leaned down and picked up the sheath of Varien's sword, forgotten for the moment, and like Jamie stared at the result of Varien's anger.

He had cut through a block of wood a hand-span thick with a blunt sword.

Jamie was right, Varien didn't really need too much practice. All he needed to learn about swordplay was how to avoid his opponent's strokes—and how to aim.

Roughly.

Shikrar

On my return from Terash Vor I landed in a clearing some distance from my chambers, in cold darkness. Judging from what Kédra had said, I guessed it must be no more than the first full moon of the new year—there were then several hours of darkness yet to come before dawn brought better hope and clearer thought. I remembered from my early youth having seen what looked like the end of the world in the darkness over Terash Vor. My father had taken me back the next day to show me that daylight would restore my perspective wonderfully. I had seen in the sunlight that day that there was not nearly so much fire as there had seemed. I had little hope on this occasion that daylight would bring any more illumination than the sun itself provided, but I would have to go back and make certain.

For the moment, however, I decided to walk the rest of the way back to my home, for my wings were stiff and sore and my new-healed shoulder ached with the chill of the high air. Winter lingered still, but the calm cold of the ground felt positively warm compared with the moving chill of the high winter wind.

Seeing the red glow of the earth's wounds is very like watching the ground bleed, and it is profoundly disturbing. Seen in darkness it inspires fear even beyond its merits. I kept repeating this to myself as I walked, for the little comfort it brought, for I knew in my bones that when I returned to the firefields this noontide I would find no comfort in that sight.

As I drew near my own chambers I was delighted to see that Kédra was there before me and had lit a fire in the pit to welcome me. Of course he had warded the Chamber of Souls while I kept the Weh sleep, it was his duty, but I was deeply cheered nonetheless to see the light. Warmth engulfed me as I entered my chamber again and I sighed deeply with relief.

"Ah, Kédra, I rejoice to see you, and the blessing of the Winds upon you for lighting a fire. This night has got into my bones." I stood in the flames, revelling as the fire licked around me and the piercing cold of the high air left me. Fire is life to us, and though it warms, no flame born of wood could possibly harm us. I closed my eyes and arched my long neck, putting my nose almost to the base of the fire to let the friendly flames warm my faceplate, sighing delightedly with the warmth. The fire licked gently at the soulgem in the centre of my forehead, sending a shiver of heat through me. I pulled my tail into the circle and folded my wings tight against my sides, letting every surface be caressed by the fire. Kédra hissed his amusement at my self-indulgence as I bathed in the generous warmth.

He had a large bowl of water warmed for me as well, flavoured with *itakhri* leaves. This brew is not for us the sovereign remedy that *hlansif* is for the Gedri, but it has a pleasant taste and warms from within, and it is cheering on a winter's night. As soon as I could tear myself away from my fire-bath I drank deeply.

Kédra had waited a long while but he was far too curious for much patience.

"Well, my father?"

I did not answer immediately. The vision of the firefield

was before me still, and the words to encompass it did not come easily.

"My father, what did you find?" he asked again. His voice was grown a little solemn, for he knew me well.

My own voice would have turned traitor had I allowed it. Instead I said calmly, "Kédra, my son, you have kept well since the birth of your littling? You do not neglect your exercises in the air for the joy of beholding your son?"

"Mirazhe and I both fly every day," he said, smiling. "A good two hours each, as you taught me long ago."

"And Sherók enjoyed being held as you flew last night. That is well." I closed my eyes. "He will not be wing-light for many years yet, poor littling, and I fear there may be a great deal of flying to be done long ere that time comes."

I do not know if Kédra was being stubborn, or if it was only that he had not seen what I had. "To what end? Why all this talk of flying, Father? The firefields bear watching, surely, but what need has my Sherók of flight at his age?"

I bespoke him, showing him in the privacy of our minds that which I could not yet put into words.

Kédra swore. "Name of the Winds, Father. Are you certain?" he asked quietly. His voice held little hope—as I say, he knew me too well.

"Ask Idai if you will, for she flew with me," I replied. "I have seen—once, when I was barely past my second kell, I saw the firefields roiling in the starlight. What she and I overflew last night makes that seem as perilous as cloud across the moon."

"I see." Kédra heaved a sigh and was silent for a moment, then looked at me and said wryly, "You know that there will be some who will blame even this on the Lady Lanen and Lord Akhor. So soon after that great upheaval, our very home destroying itself—I do not envy you, Father. How will you convince them otherwise?"

"I shall knock their heads together until I rattle some sense into them," I replied shortly, for Kédra had said aloud what I had been thinking. I had known since Akhor left with his lady that every ill for many years to come would be laid at their feet, but I had never imagined that anything so drastic would happen so soon. Ah, well. Life delights in catching us napping. I yawned.

"My son, would you watch here with me yet a few hours? I feel the need of rest. The earthshake woke me from the Weh, and I am weary yet."

Kédra was instantly solicitous. "Your pardon, my father. In the turbulence I forgot you had been wakened untimely. Feel you the need to return to your Weh chamber?"

"No, I thank you," I replied, settling on my bed of *khaadish*. "For the most part I am healed. My shoulder is stiff and a little sore, but no more than I can bear. No, I need only rest, and meat when I wake." I had shaken my wings just so and was tucking my tail under my head when Kédra said, "Father, truly, are you well enough to deal with the Council and what may come after?"

I glanced up at Kédra, who was gazing down at me and standing in the Attitude of Concern. I looked away and sighed. "Perhaps you are right, my son, and I am simply growing too old," I said, attempting to sound piteous.

It had the desired effect, though I could not sleep until he stopped laughing.

The Summer Field is so called for its loveliness in high summer, when the flame's heart, with their bright crimson flowers, bloom in their vast numbers alongside the deep purple and vivid green of summer midnight and the spiky yellow blossoms of the sunstars. I have not made a study of such things and know no more than their names, but their beauty always cheers me in the warmer months. The field itself is no more than a broad expanse of grassland, with enough room for all of us who remain to gather comfortably.

In the winter it tends to be a hard, frosty plain full of old stubble, neither comfortable nor lovely even in a stark winter fashion. However, it is outside and a wingbeat away from open air and safety, rather than being warm, underground and a constant danger, as is our Great Hall when the earth is unsettled. I knew not how many would come, as I had not called a formal Council.

The day was grey and cheerless when Kédra roused me from sleep, wing-stiff, sore and muzzy-headed and not at all inclined to tell the gathered Kantri that it was possible that we would all have to leave our home. Kédra had let me sleep as long as he could, leaving me only time enough to eat the haunch he had brought me before I had to leave for the gathering. I had hoped to have time to consider further what I might say, to soften the blow perhaps, to have alternatives to put to them. Still, sometimes it is best simply to lay the truth in all its starkness before those who must hear it and be done with it. No matter how much blame was laid at Akhor's feet—or more likely thrown at his absent face—we still had to consider what to do, and that quickly.

I drank deeply of the cold spring near my chamber and that roused me enough to think straight. I started walking to warm my muscles, but eventually I had to stretch my stiff wings and fly the rest of the way to the Summer Plain, not knowing who or what I would find there.

As it happened, there were fewer there than I had anticipated. Earthshakes even as violent as the ones in the night were common enough not to inspire much fear in us, and the others had not seen what Idai and I had seen. Still, a score of the Kantri had gathered in that cold, windy place, one in ten of our number, to speak of what was to do.

I thought I had landed reasonably well for one both stiff and sore, but Idai bespoke me with her concern. *"All is as well as may be, my friend. Help me now."* I replied, and bowed to the assembly. "I give you good morrow, my friends, and I thank you for attending," I called out loudly. "There is much to be done."

Kretissh spoke first, a soul nearer my age than Kédra's. His voice was a strong comfort in the feeble daylight. "Shikrar, Keeper of Souls, what have you to tell us beyond what we know? The earthshakes were strong last night, truly, but no stronger than others have been and others will be. I know you of old, Teacher-Shikrar. What has moved you to call your students together?"

That raised a little laughter. I have an old habit of teaching. I taught flight to the younglings when there were enough to teach and I cannot seem to get out of the way of it. Akhor used to tease me about it as well, calling me Hadreshikrar, that is Teacher-Shikrar. How I missed him.

"Kretissh, would that there was aught I might teach any of you now. I am rather in need of knowledge myself, and hope that one among you might enlighten me." I had no need even to raise my voice, so few of us were gathered. "My kindred, I went to Terash Vor after the earthshakes last night, and it was . . ." I closed my eyes for a moment. "It was worse even than fear could imagine. Never in all my years have I seen the firefields so active, so much of the ground flowing like water. It has shaken me to my bones. As witness I call the Lady Idai, who met me there."

Idai addressed us all in truespeech, valiant, angry, bitter with the telling, for she was farsighted and knew what lay before us even as I attempted to deny it.

"Shikrar, the Keeper of Souls, speaks truth. Terash Vor is alight, and Ail-neth, and both Lashti and Kil-lashti burn. The other mountains do not sleep, but they are not yet as awake as are those four. My people, I have seen the Wind of Change sweeping over the very earth we stand upon. We must consider this deeply."

From among the mutters a voice called out. "Eldest, you have seen such things many times. If this is worse than you have seen before, what of it? All things pass in time."

"I hear you, Trizhe," I replied. "And I too have had that thought, which is why Kédra and I are preparing for the Kin-Summoning. Perhaps one of the Ancestors might know more than we, might have seen such an upheaval before."

I looked out over them. Most were not seriously concerned and seemed to think as Trizhenkh did, that this was merely the worst that had been for a while and, like all the others before it, would go away in its time. Maybe he was right.

Then in that cold and barren place I saw again in my mind's eye the firefields alight, the ground all but boiling, and knew that he was not.

"I will speak of the outcome of the Kin-Summoning on the morning after the second full moon from this day. Let us gather here, for I shall here summon you all to Full Council for that time. Until then, I would ask three things of you gathered here. First, that others fly to Terash Vor to see for themselves why I am so filled with foreboding. Second, that at least one in each household might begin to keep watch. If the earth sleeps but lightly, so must we." I hesitated, but knew I had to speak of this. "It may be, my friends, that our time on this island is at an end. I would therefore ask a third boon—that the younger of us should fly far, east, south, north and west, as far as wings will bear you, to learn if there is another place where we may make our home. We will ask the Ancestors, but sometimes newer knowledge is useful as well."

That brought a surprised silence from most, but I was not the only one who had had that thought, for a voice rang out, saying "And what if there is no such place, Eldest? You know that we have long sought such a place and have never found it. What then, Teacher-Shikrar?"

I turned to Kretissh, for it was he who had spoken. "Then, my old friend, we are going to have to think very seriously about returning to Kolmar."

"And the Gedri?" he asked angrily, amid loud murmurs.

"Let us not borrow trouble from the morrow, Kretissh, for surely we have troubles enough this day. If we must deal with the Gedri, we shall, but that day may be far, far distant, and in any case such a decision would have to be made by us all. Let us speak with the Ancestors first and learn what we may."

Kretissh was not satisfied but in truth there was no more to say. When all who had come were scattered again, I bespoke all of the Kindred, letting my concern colour my thoughts as I called out the words of summoning that were used when a special Council was called. Never used for nearly six hundred years, then twice in six moons. Truly, the Winds must laugh at us sometimes.

"*Hearken, O my people. Let all who are wing-light come*

to the Summer Plain at midday on the first day of the second full moon hence, and let those who cannot attend be certain to share truespeech with one who is present. I, Shikrar, Eldest and Keeper of Souls, in the name of Varien the Lord of the Kantri, call a Council of the Kindred, for there are deep matters to consider and much to be done to guard our future. I summon ye, my people all. Come to the Council."

I sighed and set out for my chambers. If I was to perform the Kin-Summoning there was much now to do.

The Mercenary's Tale

Callum

Don't know why you're asking me, I was only there the once.

Well, twice.

Yes, that's why we'd come so far from Sorún. Devlin, the master of our troop, told us we'd been hired to seek out a woman, up north Ilsa way. Why the man would need a whole gang of mercenaries to find and take a woman had us all thinking maybe she was a witch, but Devlin said she wasn't. And she was not to be harmed, just found and brought away.

It was my first job with them. I'd just come into Sorún from—well, never you mind—and I thought I'd try this mercenary lark. I'd been a soldier for a little while, and since I'd managed to live through that I decided it was an easy way to make a living. I was a titch then as now, you know, small built, and I'd found that if you make a living with your sword men are less inclined to make fun of you.

Aye, aye, I know. I was nineteen at the time. I'll wager you were wise as Shia at nineteen. Everybody is.

'T any rate, we'd been travelling for nearly two moons when we first started to realise we were in the right part of the world. Our instructions hadn't been the best but Devlin was used to that, and the buyer wasn't stingy with our pay so time wasn't a problem. Or it wouldna been if it had been summer instead of bloody winter. There were eight of us and we had to camp a lot more often than we'd have liked. The cold got into my bones, lying on the hard ground, but I never let on. Too busy telling myself and all the others that I was fine, I could take the cold, I was man enough. Never mind that the others were all old in the trade, to a man scarred inside and out, minds of stone and skin of leather. Never occurred to me that their faces would be mine, did it? Old is something that happens to other people when you're nineteen.

Well, we finally found the right village, or Devlin did. He and Ross, his second, left us all in a quiet little tag end of a wood while they went along to the nearest inn for a bite and a sup. Came back that night half-cut with the drink and laughing, they'd found word of her right enough. She was some local farmer's daughter, her da had died summer last and she'd gone away soon after, come back just before Midwinter Fest with some man she'd married on the longest night. That got some laughs, me the loudest. I said she must be ugly to need all that dark and the others laughed some more.

The stead was a scant hour's easy ride west from where we stood. Devlin told us we'd ride at first light, to somewhere close but sheltered, and he'd go in on his own to spy out the place, learn how we could capture the lady quick and quiet. I wondered why he was worried, for I liked the fighting and I was good at it, but he seemed to want as little fight as he could manage. I remember thinking he must be a bit of a coward.

The next day was cold, bone-chill cold, and as grey and cheerless a winter's day as you'd grumble to find. I remember thinking the horses were sluggish first thing, but then so was I. It got better as we rode, but we came up on the stead faster than we'd thought, and without warning. Worse, there was no convenient clump of trees nor houses or anything. We just had to stop at the edge of the marked fields, tramp out a place in the frosty scrub ground to set up a fire, and tend the horses until Devlin got back. I was well content to think of getting as warm as I could and was about to take the saddle off my horse when suddenly Devlin calls me out and says I'm to go with him. Ross wasn't best pleased, but Devlin laughed and said nobody'd believe he had a son so old as Ross. We left our horses with the others. The stead buildings were just a few fields away.

I was happy as a pup in a mud puddle to be in the thick of it at last. Devlin explained as we walked. I was to be Devlin's son, weak with cold, "So lean over and look weary, idiot, not like you're aching for a fight," and we both were to be strangers from the south looking for my "aunt" who had moved away north and might live thereabouts. They wouldn't know her, as she didn't exist, but we'd learn soon enough who lived in the place and what protection they had.

I was mighty impressed by Devlin, coming up with that so quick. It seemed so clever.

Well, we came up to the stead to find hardly anybody about. Dev was well pleased about that and he started walking around the buildings, having a good look at the double doors on two corners of the main square. It was a hell of a big place and the doors were good and strong, made from thick wood and hung from the stone walls on forged hinges made so you couldn't take out the pins. The main stables—for we heard the horses—ran along three sides of the square, as best we could tell, with what looked like a granary at one corner and what Dev guessed was a tack store in the other. The fourth side was the house, only a little ways from the stables. We could see from the roofline that the stone wall was double thick between the stables and the house. There were other barns dotted around the place, but this had to be where the really valuable horses were kept.

Devlin was talking to me, quiet-like. "Somebody here

knows a little something. This place is made to defend. They don't have to step outside these walls unless they damn sure want to."

We'd been getting the lay of the place for near half an hour when we got back round to the doors we'd first come to, which were open. Devlin raised up his voice and called out "Hallo the house!", loud, and just a minute later out comes a man. He was no more than middlin' high, grey at the temples but strong-built and walked like a man much younger. He came up close to us right quick, like he didn't want us to come no closer to the house.

"I see you, lads. What is it brings you here on such a cold day?" says he, looking at me and Devlin in turn.

"We'd be mighty glad of a place by your fire for a minute or two," says Devlin, tryin' to sound old and weak. "My boy here is weary and my bones are chilled through. We slept on the cold ground last night, and truth told I'm gettin' too old for that sort of lark."

The man just stood there, never offered us water or chélan or even room by the fire, so Devlin started tellin' him the story he'd thought up, about how I was his sister's new-or-phaned boy and she'd just died and we was looking for my ma's sister. I tried to feel and act wretched, but I couldn't help watchin' the old man's face. He stared at us for a minute, like he was lookin' through us, then he started in to laugh. "You damn fools, is that the best you can do?" He laughed harder, and I could see Dev workin' to keep quiet. The old man just kept on laughin'.

"Stranger, my captain gave us that same story to use thirty years ago. Either it's come back into use or it's never gone away, but in any case I know it too well to believe it for a single breath."

Devlin never said a word, just looked at him.

The man straightened up and stopped laughing. "I don't know your names, lads, and I don't want to. Only thing I need to know is—

Then he started talking nonsense, least it sounded like that to me. None of the words made sense. I near fell over when Devlin answered him in the same language.

Jamie

I hadn't used merc—mercenary cant—for many years, but these things never really leave you.

"Right, you. Are you what you seem or just an upstart wanting to make a dirty living? Can you understand me?"

"Of course I can, granddad," the leader answered. His accent was strange, and he was surprised to say the least. "Never thought to find a brother here."

"I'm not your grandsire nor no more your brother than that youngster is your son, and don't you think otherwise. I left your life a long time since and I've no mind to rejoin it. What are you doing here, and what do you want?"

"A mark."

I instantly slipped into the darker tongue of the assassins. "You don't have the look of this about you, but if you know what I am saying you are bound by blood to answer. Are you here for death or for taking?"

"What in the hells did you just say? That wasn't cant," the man responded in merc, angry. Well, that was a blessing in any case. He didn't look bright enough to lie that well.

"Very well," I said, speaking in common again for the younger lad's benefit. "This is fair warning. I know who you are. I don't know why you're here but I can guess. Know that I have lived your life, and a darker one yet than that, and you do not frighten me. Go now, tell your buyer you couldn't find what he sought. Come back here, by sun or moon, and I will not waste time in speech. If I see either of you again I will assume that you mean death or harm to me and mine and I will kill you the first chance I get. Be warned. Next time I will not stop to speak."

The older one nodded ever so slightly and I knew he believed me. "I give you leave to go, right now," I said. "Once you are out of my sight don't come back."

Callum

I couldn't believe Devlin was just taking this. Here was this skinny old man, no sword on him, not even a knife, and he was threatening Devlin and me both. I'd seen Devlin kill a man, right in front of my eyes, for a lot less, and here he was backing down.

"You don't scare me, old man," I cried, standing up to him. Small as I was, he was only a little taller. "Talk never won a fight! You're old and slow, you'd best watch your back or some dark ni—"

I had to stop speaking. I didn't want to, I had a few good insults I'd thought up, but when a man has a knife to your throat and your arms pinned to your sides, there's not a lot to say. Damn, I'd have *sworn* he was unarmed.

"He's not worth it," says Devlin, calm as can be. "Hells, he's green and stupid, but don't take it out on him."

"I'm not in the habit of slaughtering idiots," says the old man. He put away his knife and turned me around to look at him, still holding my arms pinned. He was lot stronger than he looked.

He looks deep into my eyes and shakes his head, real slow. "You're brave enough, lad, but you're cocky and you're slow. Get out of this business now, while you can. There are other ways to get through life and almost all of them will see you living a lot longer than this one. You're not made for it."

He threw me towards Devlin, who caught me before I fell on the cold ground. "Warning taken, master," said Devlin. "But I'm nor green nor foolish. And I've been paid."

"Hells help you then," says the man. "You've been told." He turned on his heel at that and went back through the big double doors and closed them behind him.

Devlin pulled me away with him, swearing. When we were out of earshot, I had to ask. Just casual, as we were walking back to the others.

"What was that you two were saying?"

"It's merc's cant," says Devlin. "Shows we're both merce-naries with some years of fighting and a measure of blood behind us. I'm not sure what that other noise he was making was, but I've a feeling it was rather worse than better."

We walked in silence a few moments more. "You're not afraid of him, are you?" I said.

Devlin just kept walking. "Yes, I damn well am. He's faster than I am, and I'd wager he knows everything I know and more as well. Even without the cant I was worried. He's sharp. Like a knife he's sharp."

"So what are we going to do?"

Devlin sighed. "*We* are not going to do anything. I'm going back to the others, and you're going to get on your horse and go home."

"What!" I cried. "You can't believe that old man, he was just lucky, I wouldn't—"

And for the second time in half an hour I was held helpless. Devlin wasn't as strong or as quick, but he managed all the same. "If I can do you, lad, that other one would have your heart on a stick before you knew you were dead. I've thought it before. He's right, you're just too slow. Go home. Find a girl, work on a farm, join the King's Men somewhere, find any sort of life you want but get out of this one. You're not right for it."

And what really scared me was that Devlin wasn't angry. He talked like he was talking about the weather. "I'll do what I please, it's my life!" I cried, struggling.

He let me go and kept walking. "So it is. Please yourself, Callum. But when you're dying in some ditch before the year's out—or maybe the week—remember I warned you. So now your dying curse can't touch me." He brushed his hands one against the other. "I'll not say word more, I've done what I could. The rest be on your own back."

I shook myself and walked alongside him. I was mad: at myself, at Devlin, at that scary old man. I wasn't about to give up. But even then I wasn't completely stupid, and in the hidden part of me that admitted to fear I started to wonder if maybe there was something in what they said.

When we joined the others we drew back to that little bit of woodland we'd left the night before—it gave at least some shelter and there was enough wood to burn without spending every second looking for more. Our cook started up a good fire and put some potatoes by to bake in the foot of it, then made up a broth from the last of the meat we'd bought at the market some days since and a handful or so of barley. It wasn't much, but it was food and it was hot and that's all that mattered.

Ross and Devlin called us all together in the twilight of that early winter's night. We all sat as near the fire as we could. I was shivering something awful despite the food and regretting the mild southern winter we'd left behind when Devlin started talking.

"Right, lads. We're up against worse than we thought. I never saw the woman, but I'd swear my life she's there. Problem is, she's got a lot of help. The man we met, who-ever he is, has been a merc, and he's told us straight he'll kill us if he sees us again. You all need to know that." He de-scribed the man so we'd all know him on sight.

"If you think I've come this far and been this cold just to walk away now, you're daft," says Ross.

Devlin smiled. "Aye, so I thought, but you had to know. And make no mistake, he surely will kill us quick enough if he sees us. So we can't let him see us. We move tonight. And he's been a merc, knew our story off pat, so he'll also know all the standard distractions and ignore them. So no cries for help in the middle of the night, no stray saddled horse come rattling into their courtyard, no howling wolves too close to the house. I need some fresh ideas and I need 'em fast."

"Our luck, the bloody wolves'll howl fine on their own," said Jaker sourly.

Ross spoke up. "That courtyard's mostly stables, isn't it? The lad in the village said they breed horses."

"Aye," says Devlin. "And so?"

"Horses hate fire, don't they?"

"You don't say," put in Jaker. He was in charge of the horses—guess that's why he said that about wolves. "They hate it, and it makes 'em stupid. I've seen 'em run back into a burning barn just to get killed—and a hell of a noise they make."

Then Ross says, "So why don't we set fire to the barn?"

Even in that company there was a hiss of quick-drawn breath. Fire happens when it happens and every man alive works to put it out. We were mercs, not outlaws. My da had once told me about a fire he'd seen, a house caught somehow and they couldn't get the people out. He'd said he'd heard the screams for what seemed like hours. I still sometimes had nightmares about that.

Dev just waited, but nobody else said a thing.

"Not as easy as it sounds," he says after a few minutes, thoughtful. "They build with stone around here. Those barns are stone to the rooftree and slate tiled above. Not much to burn there." He stared into the fire for a moment, then he smiled real slow and looked around at us. "But the stalls have windows on the outer wall, and they're closed with wooden shutters," he says, right pleased with himself.

"But fire . . ." says Hask. I was surprised. I'd always thought him a hard man.

"It's not as bad as that," says Devlin. "We won't burn the people, we'll just scare the horses. Jaker, we'll all ride halfway there and walk the rest—you keep the horses where we stop, safe for our retreat. The rest of you—if Old Man Merc comes out to fight, you kill him before he can do you. Anybody else, just take them out the fight fast as you can, no need for killing unless you've got to. The girl's tall as a man, she should be easy to spot. Soon as one of you has her, let out a long whistle and all scatter. We'll meet back at the village—not here, it's too close."

"I don't like it, Dev," says Hask. He stood up. "Fire ain't right. I near got kilt in a fire when I were young. Fire ain't right."

Dev just looked up at him, for Hask was a big man. "You got a better idea?"

Hask shook his head.

"Then it's set," says Dev. "Jaker, you reckon Hask could take care of the horses for the time?"

"Sure," says Jaker. He and Hask had been working for Dev a long time, and they were as close to being friends as men got in such places. He took Hask aside and started talking horses at him.

I got out my knives and started in to sharpen all three of 'em. I planned to take Old Man Merc myself, pay him out for making me look a fool in front of Dev. My speciality was throwing knives and I was damn good at it.

Well, I thought I was damn good at it.

Lanen

Jamie told us about the mercenaries at the noon meal. Varien was appalled by the idea of men that were paid to fight but he wasn't stupid, and even he could tell that the expression on Jamie's face wasn't one that invited questions.

"I'd guess that someone from your trip isn't happy about the way it worked out, my girl. Maybe Marik got better," he said. "I certainly haven't done anything to rattle anyone lately. Can you think of anyone else who'd come this far and pay mercs to look for you?"

"Only Marik, or the demon master he works with," I said. "He's the only one I know of with a reason, but I'd be amazed if Marik could even speak yet, let alone plan such a thing."

Jamie thought for a moment. "Must be the demon master, then. Why in all the Hells has he sent men instead of demons?"

Varien spoke, but his calm voice was belied by the anger in his eyes. "Demons demand quite a price for their services. Perhaps he is not wealthy, or has run out of blood he is willing to part with."

"Where is Marik, anyway?" asked Jamie, looking relieved that we weren't going to have to fight demons just yet. "Someone must be looking after him, surely. Who would it be? You said he was the head of a Merchant House."

"His men carried him from the ship," said Varien quietly. "I know not where they took him."

Jamie sighed. "Truth to tell, I've almost been waiting for this. Stories are all well and good, my Lanen, and they sound fine coming from a bard, but real people who are after you don't just let you get away. You've come away the winners of this last bout, but it sounds like there is too much at stake for it to stop just because you give up. There are always loose ends from any weave. You seem to have left a right trail of them behind you."

I laughed, imagining a ravelling bit of rough-woven cloth trailing behind my horse, but I was the only one. Varien looked thoughtful.

"What are they most likely to do, Mas—Jamie?" he asked. "Would they attack such a stronghold as this?"

"Depends on their numbers," Jamie said. "If there's a score of them they might try it, but if they're less than ten they'll think of some distraction to make their way easier. We need to know what they're after first."

"Could it be the gold?" I asked quietly. "I don't think anyone saw it, but we brought back—quite a lot from the Dragon Isle."

"What!" cried Jamie. "Lanen, you never said word!"

I grinned. "You never asked. I was going to leave it as a surprise. The dragons—well, they—they have plenty, and we decided it might come in useful here."

"How much do you have with you? I've seen the circlet you wear," he said to Varien. "That's bad enough. Most men don't ever see that much gold in their lives. Many don't see gold at all. Did you bring—is there much more?"

I went to fetch my pack and brought it to Jamie. "Inside," I said.

Jamie felt around inside the nearly-empty pack. When he found it his eyes grew wide. He lifted out a lump of gold, that the dragons call *khaadish*, about the size of his fist. He stared at it, his jaw slack in wonder.

"Lanen tells me that *khaadish* is rare among your people, Master," said Varien calmly, "yet I have no sense of its worth. I saw no scrap of it on our journey here. What could you do with that much—"

"Gold. It's called gold, Varien." Jamie blinked. "Hellsfire. What could you do with it? Varien, a silver piece is worth twelve coppers. You can pay a man two coppers for a day's work and know he has the full value of it, for coppers are cut into halves and quarters—they're called haves and farthings, and most men deal in coppers for daily business. We sell horses, the best in Kolmar, and we occasionally see a gold piece for our best stud stallions. There are a hundred silver pieces to a single gold coin. A man's work for two years, that's what gold is worth. And that's a single thin coin. There must be—gods, there must be the best part of two hundred gold coins here. Enough to buy this whole farm and every stud and mare on it, and the work of the men for years to come."

Varien bowed his head briefly and closed his eyes. "I thank you," he said, sighing. Glancing up again he looked to me. "I think I begin to understand why so many of the harvesters over the long years dared to breach the Boundary and face our wrath. Your legends tell of—of dragons stealing and hoarding this metal, do they not?"

"Yes, they do." Jamie watched Varien carefully. "Is it true?"

"No. We do not seek it out. We do not regard it at all. The Gedri obsession with it passes our understanding."

"And yet here it is, a fortune—"

"Jameth, it is in our nature," said Varien, beginning to grow angry. "A man once betrayed his friendship with the Kantri for the sake of this yellow metal, a betrayal that cost the life of the one who had trusted him. The metal is of no worth save as ornament, and yet you tell me it is so highly valued among you—by the bright sky above, I do not understand!"

"If you do not seek it out, how then have you so much of it?" persisted Jamie.

"I have told you, it is in our nature," replied Varien, his anger plain now. "Where we sleep we turn the ground to this stuff. It is simply the way things are."

Jamie let out a low whistle. "By the Lady," he muttered.

He replaced the gold in my pack and handed it back to me, shaking his head. "Well, you learn something with each new day, true enough. But this doesn't answer the question. If you've kept that close hidden, it's not the gold they'd be after. Besides, it was the wrong story," he said. "They'd need to have come in to look over the place for that—they'd have cut the young lad and brought him here for healing, so we'd be too concerned about him and not notice his companion looking in every room. No, the story he used was only for finding a way in, or for finding a particular person." He looked up at me. "Hell's teeth, Lanen. Silver to horseshit it's you." He sprang up from his chair and started pacing the room. "Hells take it . . ." I let him get it out of his system. He swore pretty well when he worked up to it, he even used one or two I'd never heard from the sailors on the Harvest ship, when I went to the Dragon Isle.

"You said that bastard Marik wanted you for a sacrifice while you were on that island," Jamie said finally. "Well, I'd wager my year's earnings these men are here to finish what he started."

I shuddered. It made a lot of sense. Marik had been desperate to give me to that demon—it had been stopped only because Akor had rescued me. I looked to Varien and saw sadness in his eyes.

"Were the same to happen I could not save you now, dearling," he said in truespeech. *"I am a man, more so each day, and only a Lord of the Kantri can battle one of the Lords of Hell and hope to prevail."*

"I expect you're right. What are we to do now, Jamie? Do you think they would attack the house?"

"They will if they've been paid enough. We'll set a watch tonight, and you come sleep in the common room—it's the easiest to defend and it has a fireplace."

I felt terribly confused and vulnerable. "But Jamie, the stablehands, they're not fighters. What if . . ."

"I'll warn them, my girl, don't worry about that. You get working on the evening meal, that needs done and it'll keep you inside. I'll post a guard and set a watch." He seemed almost pleased; certainly his eyes were bright and sharp. "They'll not catch us sleeping, not if I can help it. Brew us up some chélan, there's a good lass. We'll need it." He turned to Varien. "And you bring that sword to the tack room just now, Varien, and we'll put an edge on it."

Jamie

Lanen was right, though. The lads weren't fighters. I warned them, but though they nodded and agreed to do as I asked, they all were convinced I was making a lot of noise over nothing. They knew better than to disobey me, but for all that I walked up and startled them several times after darkness fell. And I wasn't even trying.

I kept walking around the buildings, checking the doors, trying to quiet the horses. They seemed bothered by something but I couldn't tell what.

I'd been inside the common room warming up, and I must have stayed longer than I realised. It felt like the middle of the night when I went out again. I could feel the frost crunch under my boots. The quarter-moon was bright, the sky was clear, and it was bloody cold.

All of a sudden the horses in the west stable started complaining, loud and urgent. I turned and was making for the door when suddenly, between one step and another, the noise from the horses changed from restless to flat-out panic. That cry for help is unmistakable and reaches through your gut to get your feet moving without bothering your brain. I was already running.

When I reached the main stable door I threw it open. The smell hit me instantly, stronger even than the noise of terrified horses.

Smoke.

Hellsfire and bloody damnation.

"FIRE!" I yelled, loud as I could. "FIRE, FIRE, FIRE!" Over and over. I had no idea what had happened to the lad who normally slept in this barn but there was no time to wonder. The smoke was coming from the farthest stall on the left. I pulled off my coat as I ran, lifted the latch on the stall, threw the door wide and tossed my coat over the head of Row, our best stallion and one of the founders of Hadron's stock. He was scared stiff and drew back, tossing his head in panic, fighting me. I spoke to him, calm as I could manage, knowing I couldn't spend much time even on him with so many others to get out. I managed to get my coat over his eyes, and thank the Lady, he changed his mind all of a sudden and came out with me.

I was almost surprised to find the courtyard full of folk, busily getting out every horse they could. I caught one of our young stable lads in passing. "Rab, quick, take Row out to the paddock and take any of the others that'll follow. And make sure someone's fetching water to douse the fire!"

I didn't stop to hear his reply. I was already running back into the barn, through the smoke, to the other stall nearest the fire.

Lanen

When I heard Jamie yelling "fire" at the top of his lungs I was up and moving before I realised I was awake. I'd slept in my clothes, for we had expected something, and somehow I managed to slip on my boots. I snatched up a coat as I hurried outside. Varien moved more slowly behind me, but then he didn't understand about fires and horses.

When I emerged after even those short moments, the courtyard was full of our folk. Some were fetching water and dunking rags in it for the others to use to cover the horses' eyes and noses with. The horses were screaming with terror, and I could hardly breathe myself as I grabbed a damp rag and ran into the stable.

The smoke was up to the roof in great grey clouds, lit from below by the flames. The fire seemed to be running along the hayloft as fast as a man can walk.

One of the lads cried out to me as I passed. "She won't come, Lanen! Shadow won't come!"

"Then leave her and save another!" I yelled. I opened a

stall at random and found myself facing Jamie's own gelding, Blaze. I didn't stop to think—I hadn't had a conscious thought yet—just threw the damp rag over his eyes, called him by name and spoke to him in as normal a voice as I could, and tried not to panic myself as I led him out. To my immense relief he came with me. As we emerged into the sweet cold air outside the barn I heard Jamie yelling that the horses we'd got out should be taken to the paddock, so I grabbed a passing maidservant who was being no use and told her where to take Blaze. She said nothing but seemed glad to have something to do.

By now there were a fair few horses being led out of the courtyard, but not enough. Not nearly enough. I remembered to grab the rag off Blaze's face and went in again.

The air was torn by the sudden screams of a horse. I tried to get to the sound, but the fire was too hot and burning fragments were starting to drop down from the burning hayloft above. It was sickening and the smell of burning horsehair and flesh made me gag, but I didn't have time to cry. I found myself in another stall fighting with Daft Sally, one of our brood mares, who didn't want to come, when I heard the most astounding thing. It took me a moment to realise that the voice was not coming from behind me.

It was Varien. His mindvoice was calm and he was speaking to the horses in broad truespeech. He was not using words, just feelings, of calm, of sense, of safety outside the barn, of trusting and following the people who were trying to help.

I couldn't be certain, but it seemed to help. Daft Sally calmed down enough to let me throw a halter over her neck and she followed me out, terrified but willing to go. I walked her as fast as I could to the door and gave the lead rope to young Tam. Every soul on the stead was working hard to get out as many as we could, but in the pit of my stomach I knew that the fire was well caught and if we could get any more of them out it would be by the grace of the Lady.

I was heading back to the stable door when on the edges of my mind it occurred to me even in the midst of that mad chaos that there seemed to be an awful lot of folk about, even with every soul we had—maybe some of the villagers had come—I was all but through the door when something fell over my own face, filled my mouth and blinded me, and I felt myself grabbed from behind with my arms pinioned to my sides. The man was big enough to drag me with one arm and keep the other tight around my throat. I tried to scream and got a mouthful of cloth, which set me coughing. I cried out in truespeech to Varien, as loud as I could, and tried desperately to stop coughing and breathe.

I had just managed to take one breath—I know this sounds slow, but it happened all in a moment—when in the midst of trying to kick backwards with my heeled boots, aiming vaguely for a shin, I was pulled off my feet. Only after being dragged backwards for a while did I remember what Jamie had taught me and tried to twist out of my captor's hold. He seemed to have been expecting it, though, and tightened his stranglehold around my neck. It was clearly either breathe or fight, and even at that my breathing was terribly limited.

"Varien, quickly, help me!" I cried, with all the strength of mind I had.

"Lanen, you must focus your thought. Where are you? Are you in the barn?"

"No, no, some bastard has me by the throat so I can't scream. He's dragging me across the yard!"

"Dearling, be calm if you can. You are casting your speech too wide and I cannot find you," came Varien's voice, strong and calm and reassuring. *"Send your thoughts to me through the smallest opening you can imagine. I shall follow you."*

It wasn't easy to think straight—I was furious that I was so easily held helpless, my mind was filled with getting the rest of the horses out of that inferno, and just on the edges of thought came the worry about what whoever it was that had me would do when he got tired of dragging me across the cobbles. However, desperation concentrates the mind wonderfully. I tried to think of a pinhole, just big enough for my mindvoice to get through, as Varien had taught me. *"I'm here love I'm here, the bastard's dragging me backwards, even in all this madness I should be easy enough to find— Goddess, that was another of the horses in the barn, I'm going to be sick—damn, we're off the cobbles and outside on the grass damn it I need to breathe—"*

The noises were receding, or at least changing. I could still hear horses yelling, it twisted in my gut, but now it was an outdoor sound, not the echoing noise they'd made in the courtyard, and around and about me were the sounds of quite a few horses and people. *"We're passing the paddock, damn this bastard I can't get a foothold to stop him he's moving me too fast, can't anyone see me he's too damn strong **watch out there are more of them!"***

We had stopped. The other voices were low and terrifyingly calm as they tied my hands together. I struggled and tried to scream again, but I couldn't get enough breath to make any difference, and I was kept off balance quite successfully. The word "overpowered" occurred to me, and now I truly knew what it meant. It struck me then that I might just die there, alone and trussed up in the middle of my own field.

Fear always makes me furious. I twisted and fought harder, kicking when I could, but my captor tightened whatever he had around my throat and I had to give over. *"Varien, quick, they're tying me up and I still can't breathe,"* I sent in truespeech. I was terrified and it was harder than ever to draw a simple breath. *"Help, help, I'm here, I'm here, please, help me find me get me out of here they're tying my feet I can't stop them help help **help."***

I could do no more, I was exhausted and now my head was pounding from using truespeech. I felt I was only a few breaths away from fainting for lack of air, so I concentrated on just breathing.

Varien

I summoned my strength and went swiftly over the Kantri Discipline of Calm as I sought her. I knew I could be of no further use to the horses, for Jameth had stopped us all from entering the barn. The fire was raging now and it was plain that nothing else could be done. For a fleeting moment I longed for my old form. I could have simply lifted the horses out, for the fire would not have harmed me.

I noted as I sought the direction of Lanen's voice that Jameth had begun clearing the horses from the other two stables. Ah, *there*.

Old habits die so slowly. I had spent my entire life being certain of my power over the Gedri, knowing that they could pose no real threat to me. Had I thought about it for even the half of a moment I would have called for assistance, but I did not. I suspect I was not as calm as I believed, for I followed Lanen's thought and hurried after her, my sword in my hand. I was too far away when I finally realised that I had been foolish, but by then I could do nothing but finish what I had begun. I sent a prayer winging to the Winds as I came up to the dark knot of men who were busy tying Lanen hand and foot. We were too far from the walls of the stead for any to hear a cry for help, amidst all the mayhem.

I did not stop to announce my presence, I simply raised my sword and rushed at them. I must have made some sound—I think I may have growled in my anger—but in any case they heard me and easily avoided my ill-aimed blow.

"Kill him," said one quietly, pointing to me. A large man left the others and came to meet me. What little training I had had that morning deserted me as old instincts took over. I nearly dropped my sword to swipe at him with my claws, but I managed to remember at the last moment that I had none, and by pure chance managed to avoid his sword. I was off balance and tried to back away, but he kept coming towards me, menacing in the darkness.

"Akor!" came Lanen's mindvoice, weak now. Just that one word, but the fear in it rang like metal in my soul and focussed my thoughts into cold, calm fury. I leapt back and found my feet, then began to advance, growling, towards the one who stood before me. He struck and his blade glanced off mine and hit my arm, but I ignored the flash of pain.

Time seemed to change around me, for I moved as fast as I could and suddenly the other was slow and clumsy. I was able to strike at his unprotected body before he struck again. He faltered and dropped his sword and I struck once more, putting my body into the blow.

He dropped to the ground and I turned around to face the others, only to find a second body on the ground before me and the others in flight. I turned and slipped on the wet grass, and sat suddenly upon something soft. Another body. This one had a drawn knife in one hand and had been just behind me—but I certainly hadn't killed it.

"Lanen!" I called, shaking my head as I stood and slowly returned to the normal passage of time.

"Here, love, and safe now. I'm here with the horses they left."

I strode over to her. "Dearling, how did you . . . ?"

"She didn't. That was me. Good even, Master Varien."

Callum

Well, there's not much left to tell. When Ross has room to swing, it doesn't matter if they parry, he's just too strong and his blow works anyway. It didn't then. That skinny git with the silver hair should have gone down with half his arm lopped off, or broken at the very least, but he stopped Ross's blow with his bare forearm. He didn't even yell, he hissed, and then he moved up and struck out fast as a snake. I've never seen anything like it, you couldn't even see his sword move. Ross was hit, bad. Dev kept trying to tie up the woman, but she was fighting like fury and Dev had to keep tight hold of her. I tried throwing a knife or two, but I was scared witless and my aim went all over the place. This wasn't Old Man Merc, this was something worse: something that couldn't be hurt with steel and moved like the wind. He swung that damned huge sword round again and near cut Ross in two, killed him sure, but while Jaker had come up behind him and was about to knife him, I heard a quiet sound like a butcher cutting meat, and saw Jaker drop to the ground without a sound. Then Porlan, who had come up in front to take him out while he was busy with Ross, dropped as well.

Dev swore and yelled "Run!" He tried to bring the woman along, but she kicked and fought and got out of his grip and by then he just let her, grabbing my arm and hauling me away over the dark ground. I didn't resist. Who had sent those knives through the air from nowhere, in the dark, and killed Jaker and Porlan in the instant?

Well, none of us wanted to wait and find out. We ran like fury. They didn't follow us.

We got back to where Hask was waiting with the horses and stirred up the fire. Dev told Hask what had happened. I hadn't been sick, though it had been a close thing. I'd never forget the sound of that knife hitting Jaker. I wasn't shamed of running, for we'd all run, but the more I thought about it the more I thought that maybe both Dev and Old Man Merc had been right. And Ross and Jaker and Porlan hadn't even been threatened. They were just dead, just like that, with no warning.

I really didn't want my last thought to be *where did that knife come from?*, and to judge from what had happened that seemed like to be my future, and there didn't look to be much of that future to think about. And you know, just there and then, 'twixt one breath and the next, I decided I didn't give a damn what anybody thought, and there wasn't enough money in the world to lose my whole life over.

I went up to Dev when he had stopped talking. He looked grim. He and Ross'd been working together for years. They were nearly friends.

He'd just told the others that we would wait for them to come out, for he knew Old Man Merc would send a party at some point. I knew I'd sound like a coward, but like I said, all of a sudden I didn't give a fart for what anyone thought.

"Dev," I says, walkin' straight up to him, "you're right."

"About what, Cal?" he said. He sounded awful tired.

"About me bein' slow. I fired two knives at that feller and

neither one came close. And I was scared out my mind, and I ain't going back."

Dev just looked at me, then he did the damnedest thing—he smiled at me. He stood up and put his hands on my shoulders and smiled. "Well, bless the Crooked One who looks on all thieves, there's somethin' good come out o' this. Callum's off to find a girl, lads, and live a real life."

And as I looked around the fire they all looked as pleased as they were able that I was leaving. Not much good for my pride, that, but in the time since I've come to think maybe they felt like my living would mean something to their dying, and they feared that would come all too soon. Hask even said, "Kiss her for me, lad, whoever you find." I got up on my horse, and Dev give me a little money to get me to somewhere I could find work. I bade 'em all farewell that very moment, but never a soul among 'em said a single word to wish me on my way.

I've never killed a man, before that night or since, and I've never passed a butcher's stall in a market without hearing that knife cut Jaker's life from him. Old Man Merc was right. I wasn't never meant for that life.

v

Endings and Beginnings

Varien

"Lady Rella!" I said, astounded as I recognised her voice. "What wind bloweth thee to this place, in this very moment of our need?"

"Later, Varien. You couldn't take one of their daggers and help me, could you? I'm trying to get the rest of these ropes off young Lanen and my fingers are damn near frozen."

By the time I had found a dagger, Rella had freed Lanen. My dearling was desperate to get back to the stead, for the sounds and the smells that came to us across the fields were terrible. We would have run at that moment, but Rella caught me by the shoulder. "A moment, master Varien," she said. "How's your arm? I thought I saw that big bastard hit you."

Her words recalled me to my hurt. "So he did," I replied. Now that my life was not threatened and I could think of it, the wound was indeed painful. "What must I do, Lady?"

"Wait here," said Rella. She ran off but was back in a moment with a dark lantern. She opened the panel and shone the light on my left sleeve, stained dark and damp. "In the heat of anger I paid it no heed," I said. "What is to be done? I cannot flame it clean."

"Just hold still," said Rella. I was beginning to understand that tone of voice. It indicated forbearance under great strain.

She drew a long strip of cloth from her scrip, and a small pot. Lanen gently pulled back the sleeve of my tunic to reveal a deep cut that still bled. She held my arm still while Rella put a strange paste from the small pot onto the wound, which made it hurt worse than it had before; then she wrapped the strip of cloth around my arm to cover the cut. "Leave that there for at least two days," she said. "It looks clean enough, it should heal well."

"I thank you, Lady," I said, bowing to her in the strange human fashion. It still felt stilted and somehow wrong, but with practice I was becoming better at it.

"Thank me later. Lanen is going to kill us if we don't get back to the stables," said Rella.

"This instant," said Lanen.

Lanen

We stumbled into a jog-trot as we hurried back. It took us only a few moments to come level with the paddock. As we drew closer I could hear the horses running out their fear, and there was a steady stream now of people—some leading out terrified horses from the other barns, some carrying blankets, some bringing warm water and hot mash, come to bring what comfort they could to the creatures out in the cold. I stopped someone—for the life of me I can't remember who—and told them to start moving the yearlings and the pregnant mares into the summer barn up the hill, it was drafty but it was shelter. They told me Jamie had already told them to do so and when I looked closer I saw a slow line of half-panicked horses being led farther away from the fire, the noise and the smell of the burning.

As we drew nearer to the stead the noise grew louder and the smoke grew thicker, and the smell—dear Goddess, the smell of burnt hair and flesh and hide, it was everywhere, thick and sickening, catching in the throat. My stomach roiled with it but I did not stop, in case there was anything I could yet do. Then above other sounds came what I thought for a moment were the shrill screams of a last dying horse trapped inside the stable. I started shaking, but Varien held me up and told me, "It is the wood, dearling. Believe me, it is the wood." He was right, the sound changed a little and I recognised it as the gigantic version of those strange high-pitched sounds that you sometimes get from a log on a fire. The thick beam of the rooftree cracked as we arrived and I could feel the sound in the soles of my feet. The timber made a terrible racket as it burned, sometimes high-pitched, sometimes low as a rumble of thunder, as if the wood itself were in agony.

I was in the lead when we entered the ordered confusion of the courtyard. It turned out later that my cousin Walther had run a ladder up to the roof of the tack room—the room nearest the fire—and had thrown off the roof tiles, cut a gap in the beams with an axe and thrown water on whatever he could see. He got himself pretty badly burned and the roof had collapsed at that end of the stable, but it was he who had stopped the fire from spreading to the other buildings round about. His lady Alisonde was tending his arms now as he stood in the courtyard shouting orders. The rest of the horses had been taken out and away, and the few of us who were left did what we could, but there was only so much to do. The surviving horses were as well taken care of as we could manage until morning, and the house was safe. We threw buckets and buckets of water on the nearby buildings and doused the sparks that flew in the blessedly light wind, but in the end we could only let the fire burn itself out. Mercifully the trapped horses had died long since, but no one even tried to sleep. Every soul from the stead stood there in the cold, watching until the last of the flames faded just before morning light. The blackened beams glowed demon red from within, and the hot stones cracked loudly as they cooled.

When the walls had grown cool enough and the last of the embers was put out, and we could bear to go inside the ruin of the stable, we found that we had lost eleven of the twenty-four horses. Yet again I felt bile flood the back of my throat at the sight and the smell, that acrid, hideous smell: it hung in the air and clung to my clothes and my boots and the back of my throat, so that I feared I would never be rid of it. By that time, though, we were all so exhausted by sorrow and anger that it felt somehow as if it was happening to someone else, and even the sickness that threatened could not overwhelm.

Jamie was only a little better than me. I had seldom seen him so grim, but when he spoke he surprised me. "It could have been much worse, my girl," he said, standing in the ruin of the ashes, staring at nothing. "I've been through a stable fire before, many years ago, when I lived in the East," he said, and I knew the rough edge to his voice had nothing to do with weariness. "We lost a lot more than half of them that time. Damned if I know what it was, but just before the fire took over at the last, I'd swear that something drew a lot of them out of that barn last night."

Varien said quietly, "Let us be grateful for that mercy, at the least." I wanted to tell Jamie what Varien had done, but I knew my dear one was right to keep silent. How should he claim to have helped with truespeech when there was no proof to any but the two of us?

Meanwhile the morning was wearing on. I went to help Alisonde set about making food and hot drink for everyone, while Jamie and the others saw to the surviving horses, made sure they were fed and warmed and made as comfortable as they could be. The stablehands began the long and grisly job of clearing the burned stable down to the stone. The Healer from the nearest town, who had been sent for at dawn and had finally arrived, began to treat those who were in most need, starting with Walther.

Varien was next. We took the bandage off and the Healer put forth his power willingly, saying as he did so that simple cuts responded far better than burns did, but after just a moment he stared at Varien's arm.

Nothing was happening.

He drew a deep breath and tried again. I had watched Healers working several times and was used to the way the blue glow around them seemed to go into the wound. But it didn't now, not on Varien.

"Have you ever been to a Healer before?" he asked Varien, who of course said he hadn't. The Healer frowned. "I have heard of such things, but I have never come across one such as you. I fear, good sir, that you are a rare case. I have heard of those who cannot be touched by the healing power, and it seems that you are one of them. Thank the Lady you are not too desperately wounded." He leaned over and smelled the salve that Rella had provided. "You are using the right simples, and with time you will heal as well as any—pray forgive me, good sir, but I can do nothing for you, and others require my care." He bowed and moved on to the next who needed his help.

🐾 The poor horses that had burned to death were to be buried in one deep grave not far from the north side of the main stead buildings. It was a huge pit, wide and deep, and it took every kind soul who had come from the village to help dig it. With all of us working like madmen it was finished that very afternoon, and the dreadful burned bodies, mercifully covered with rough burlap, were lowered into it as carefully as possible. I had learned that my Shadow, my little mare, had been trapped in the fire. When I thought back I remembered someone shouting something about her, but I had been too distracted to pay much attention at the time. Coward that I am, I was desperately grateful that I could not see through the burlap and did not know which of the shapeless bundles covered her.

It wasn't until we were filling the earth back in that I realised I had been crying gently most of the time. Shadow had been with me for so many years, a friend in a world where friends were scarce. So many of the horses had been under my care, so many I had known and ridden, taught and learned from—so many lost.

Oh, Shadow, ever my willing companion. Sleep soft, dear friend. I will miss you.

When the last of the earth was laid on the mound, Jamie came and put his arm around my waist and looked up at me, his red-rimmed eyes locked on mine. I slipped my arm about his shoulders and we turned and walked back to the house together without a word.

🖋I introduced Jamie to Rella in a brief stolen moment, but he didn't hear our full story until that night, when Rella had gone to sleep and the three of us sat exhausted around the kitchen fire. After we had told him what had happened the night before, he demanded to hear everything I knew about her, which I soon realised wasn't much. "We met on the Harvest ship, on the journey out," I told him. "I looked after her when she was poorly and we started talking. We shared a tent at the Harvest camp, when the whole ship's complement was out gathering lansip every waking moment, but I still didn't know much about her until I was in Marik's power. She told me then that she is a Master in the Silent Service, and that Marik was far too bound up with demons for anyone's good. She helped me get away, and when the demon caller caught me again she went to Akor and told him." I put my hand on Jamie's shoulder. "The demons would have had me if it hadn't been for her, Jamie."

"The Silent Service. I see," said Jamie, distantly.

He saw a lot more than I did. I had heard of the Silent Service only once or twice in my life. They are based in Sorún, the great city on the bend of the River Kai. They are the reason for the other half of the saying about the famous port city of Corlí: "If you want to know anything, go to Corlí; if you want to know everything, go to Sorún." It was said they would find out anything or anyone for a price.

Jamie just stood there, thinking. I couldn't stand it. "For goodness' sake, Jamie, she saved my life again last night!" I said.

He turned to me. "Yes, I know, but I don't know why."

My turn to be surprised. "What?"

"Members of the Silent Service don't give away the time of day if they're standing beside a sundial. Why is she here?"

I frowned at him. "In case you had forgotten, Varien and I saved her life in Corlí."

"Yes, and she had saved yours already, helping you escape Marik, calling in the dragons—why, Lanen? Always find the source. Who is paying her fee?"

I realised in the midst of being surprised at his attitude that I was up against my ignorance again. "She couldn't just be a kind soul who's worried about—hmm. I see what you mean." I thought for a moment. "In any case, she certainly saved my life last night. Our lives. Whoever it is wants me living."

"So did Marik," said Jamie tightly. I shivered.

"She can't be working for Marik, she helped me get away from him—"

"No, I never thought that. It's not Marik she's working for. But until we know who it is," he said, taking me by the shoulders, "please, Lanen, a little caution."

I nodded, chastened by my blind acceptance of Rella's goodwill. She was no part of me, true enough, why should she risk her life? Find the source . . .

I was torn. I generally trusted Jamie's instincts, but he had not been with us on the Dragon Isle. I was convinced deep down that Rella's heart was true. The Kantri would not have trusted her as they had, Kédra would not have admired her, had she wished me ill.

Varien and I both slept like rocks that night, the night after the fire, and did not wake until midmorning. We rose groggily and met with Jamie and Rella at breakfast. Jamie had posted triple guards round the stead during the night just in case, but they saw and heard nothing.

"I hear that I must thank you for saving Lanen's life, mistress," said Jamie to Rella. "I did not know it in all the confusion yesterday. I owe you a great debt."

"Nothing so great that another cup of chélan and more

porridge won't go a long way to pay it," said Rella easily. "I'm starving. That was rough work last night."

"And how long will we have the pleasure of your company?" asked Jamie politely. Well, he tried to sound polite. It has never been one of his strong points. On Jamie it just sounded suspicious.

"I hadn't thought that far, I fear," she replied cheerfully. She looked to me and nodded. "I came here wanting to repay these two for saving my life. I seem to be halfway there at least."

"Well past, Rella," I said, "for we would have both been lost without your help."

"You may consider the debt paid, my girl, but I don't. Not yet. And as I appear to be a free agent at the moment, I will be glad to assist you whatever you decide to do." She looked to Jamie. "If that is acceptable to you, Master. I can see you don't trust me, I'm used to it—a crooked back tends to worry people, after all—"

"Nothing to do with that," said Jamie roughly. "Lanen tells me you're with the Silent Service. I never heard that such people were ever free agents."

Rella laughed at that, loud and long. "Ah, I see! And here I was blaming my poor back for making me look suspicious. No, Master, I won't ask you to trust me, but we are allowed time off from our duties, and I truly owe this pair for my life several times over. Did Lanen never mention her ability to use Farspeech?"

Jamie looked wary. "She has said something of it."

"Or that she used that ability to save the whole ship from a demon-spawned disease as we returned from the Dragon Isle? No, until I have repaid my debt I shall keep these two company, either with them or following them. For unless I miss my guess, they are not long for this place."

"You're right," I said before Jamie could speak. "We have talked about it and we both think its time to get moving."

Jamie opened his mouth to object but he soon shut it again. I could only guess why, but it seemed clear to me that Rella would be either with us or behind us no matter what we did. When I put it to him later he said he'd rather have her under his eye than wandering about on her own. However, for now he seemed willing enough to accept Rella's presence and did not insist that she leave before we discussed matters. I was relieved at that, for she had proven her worth and her intentions to me both on the Dragon Isle and in that fight in the dark, when she had only to leave us to our fate if she intended us ill. I still could not believe ill of her, and if she still felt that she owed us a debt I was very glad of her assistance.

We had quite a council of war. Jamie wanted Varien and me to stay put in a defensible place, but I did not want to risk the lives of our people and the rest of our horses if I was the one the mercs were after. The argument got quite heated about then. It didn't help that despite a night's sleep we were all still exhausted.

"What do you hope to gain by our staying here, Jamie?" I demanded, finally. The four of us, Varien, Jamie, Rella and I, were sat around the kitchen fire drinking chélan and trying desperately to stay awake and make some kind of sense of things. "If whoever it is really wants me, Jamie, they know now where I am and they can send more and more men until either we're all burned alive or they get what they want. I'd rather lead them a chase and make sure Walther and Alisonde have a chance to rebuild than just sit here and let them find new recruits." I turned to Rella. "Do you have any idea whose men they are, or how many of them there are?"

"Only an inkling," she said. She seemed the least affected by the lack of sleep, and was calmly sharpening her knives, some of which she had reclaimed from the site of our battle in the dark. There were quite a few of them. "I followed them for a few days, since we were both coming this way. There were eight of them until yesterday. We buried three this afternoon. That leaves five, not really enough even for desperate and angry men to want to attack a stronghold. But the longer we leave it, Master, the sooner they'll find reinforcements and be back."

"And what if they find those reinforcements and come

upon us on the road?" asked Jamie angrily. "A man who would use fire would do anything. It's forbidden, even to assassins. It's too wild, it can do too much damage. Only rank outlaws would even think of using it."

"I think Rella's right, Jamie," I said quietly. Something about her words had struck a chord. "I think they may be that desperate. You know, for the most part Marik didn't use force on me, he used amulets and demons. If whoever hired these men is a demon master, maybe those bastards aren't just working for money. I would guess that demon masters can take quite a price for failure."

"That's what I was thinking, lass," said Rella, impressed. "But such men almost always have protective spells for themselves. These ones died fast. A simple knife wouldn't touch the demon-protected."

"Such men never protect their tools," spat Jamie. "I still say they could find us and kill us all and still get Lanen."

"Us?" I asked, surprised. "I thought we were talking about Varien and me."

Jamie snorted. "And how long do you think you two would last on the road with this kind of idiot after you, eh?" he asked angrily. "I let you go once, to my sorrow. I'm not letting you out of my sight again until all this is done."

"Jamie, you—"

"I'll brook no argument, my girl." He put his hand on mine and challenged me with his gaze: his resolve showed in his eyes, strong and sharp as steel. "You are the only daughter I have, Lanen. You're a good man, Varien, but you are new to the sword and I cannot let my girl go forth again with none to guard her back."

"I would not gainsay you, Jameth," said Varien quietly. "In truth I welcome your offer, for if you had not made it I would have asked it of you."

"Good," said Jamie shortly. "Then perhaps you will listen when I say we should stay here."

Rella narrowed her eyes. "You know, Master, if I didn't know better I'd say you were frightened."

"Know better, then, woman," growled Jamie, rising from

the bench and starting to pace. "I hate those bastards more with every breath I take, but I was not there to protect Lanen last night. They got past me, the seven-times-damned sons of bitches got past me." He began to pace, his feet pounding into the floor, shaking the boards. I had seldom seen him so angry; you could feel it coming off him like steam. "They took her from under my nose, Mistress Rella. I'm getting old and slow and stupid. It never occurred to me they'd use *fire* just for a diversion. The bastards got past me and I never noticed until you brought her back to me. She might have been gone forever and I'd never have lifted a finger to stop them. May all the demons of all the Hells find them some dark night"—he whirled on me—"and *you* want to go out into the depths of winter, just the three—"

"Four," said Rella quietly.

"Just the—four of us to face the rest of them and whoever is behind them! I never thought I'd raised an idiot, my lass, but I'm beginning to wonder."

I was growing angry myself—I can barely hold back my temper at the best of times—but it was Varien who spoke. "For a people who do not truly breathe fire, you manage to come very close."

"Hah," muttered Jamie.

"Do not let your guilt overcome your good sense, Jameth. You are mistaken in this and you know it. We must leave, publicly and very soon. You must not let your fear blind you to truth."

"I'm not afraid of them!" he growled.

"I did not say that you were," replied Varien gently.

Jamie stopped then and stared at Varien. "Failure once is seldom true defeat, Jamie," said Varien. "It is there merely to let the wise soul take note that something is not as it seems to be. I thought I could fly when I had seen but twenty winters; my wings were large and I was strong. When I jumped from the low cliff where those twice my age were taking off, I flapped long and hard and still fell straight into the sea thirty feet below. It was not that flying was impossible, only that there was more to it than I had thought."

I couldn't stifle the laugh. "Did it hurt?" I asked, grinning.

"Enough to stop me trying it again that day," he replied lightly. "Yet I worked on in secret, and in the end flew not five years later, a quarter of a kell before the rest."

"Spare me your sympathy, dragon," growled Jamie. He glanced at Rella and frowned. "And why aren't you asking whether he's mad or not, talking about flying?"

"Because I saw him just a few hours after he changed and I know all about it," she said, grinning. "Any more questions?"

"Only to wonder why all of you are so intent on getting killed. You're good with a blade, mistress, but even I wouldn't trust myself against as many as may come," he muttered. "I know my own limitations."

"Jameth of Arinoc, you are spouting childish nonsense and I'm getting tired of it," said Rella suddenly. "Don't be a fool. They are right, and you're feeling guilty and sorry for yourself. Poor old man," she taunted, "you're just not up to it anymore, are you?"

He drew his dagger even as she finished speaking, and even though she knew it was coming Rella was still within his reach. His blade stopped just short of her heart.

She was grinning. "If you're so slow, idiot, how did you manage to do that? I'm very, very good at what I do, and *I* am certainly not out of practice." The rage on Jamie's face turned slowly to wonder, and she pushed his hand away gently. "Now put that thing down before you hurt someone with it. We need to take Lanen away from here. I'd suggest Sorún, but then I would."

"Why?" I asked, while Jamie sputtered.

"It's home. Well, home for the Service," she said.

I spoke up then, quickly, before Jamie recovered. "There is another possibility. I know it's a longer trip, but I—we— perhaps we could aim for Verfaren."

"Hells' teeth, why Verfaren?" asked Jamie. His voice was rather more normal, which was a relief. He seemed to have a lot on his mind.

"Lanen has told me of the collection of wisdom there,

which she called a library," said Varien. "It is a journey she and I must take at some time or another, and since we must go somewhere it seems as sensible as any other destination."

We kept arguing.

Four days later we were sitting round a far-too-small fire in a little clearing just inside the Trollingwood. We'd gone straight east from Hadronsstead, telling my cousin Walther we were bound for Sorún and would catch a riverboat all the way down the Arlen. It seemed as good a story as any, and to be honest Walther didn't care in the slightest. He was still mourning the horses and seemed to think that I had got myself attacked just to make his life more difficult. He wished us well and turned at once back to the business of getting the stables cleared of debris so the horses could go back in. I did not think it would be so easy as that, for the dreadful smell of death and burning lingered in the air, lingered in the very ground. If I were a horse I would never go near the place— but that was now Walther's problem. True, I was Hadron's heir and the stead was mine by right, but I had arranged it with my cousin half a year before that he and Jamie and I would have equal shares in it all if he would take care of the horses, which was all he cared about in any case. So far it had worked well for all of us.

When we were a day and a bit out from Hadronsstead, Jamie led us slightly north to get into the edge of the great Trollingwood. It wasn't much shelter but it was a great deal better than nothing. We were still debating where to go.

"We need to learn as much as we can about the Lesser Kindred, Jamie," I said. "Surely in all this time someone has learned something about them. Wasn't it you who told me that the great library in the College of Mages in Verfaren is the best place to look for anything?"

"Yes, girl, and he's right," said Rella, "but must you go there first? It's a lot easier to catch a riverboat from Sorún, or even somewhere along the Arlen, than to tramp overland all the way south—and where were you planning to cross the river? Besides," she said dryly, "I have an errand in Sorún. I have an idea who hired those lads, but I want to find out for certain. The ones who are left will almost certainly be looking for reinforcements."

Jamie took another small sip of his beer, for we hadn't brought much. "I wouldn't worry overmuch about that. He'll not find anyone hereabouts in any case."

"There are always idiots for hire," said Rella sourly.

"Aye, but the idiots are the only ones left," said Jamie, grinning unexpectedly. "I've already found every likely lad for thirty miles around and got them working for me."

Rella grinned back. "I should have realised. Very well, Master, so they are stuck with the five of them. That's good. But it's still more fighters than the four of us."

"I can take us by roads they will not know," said Jamie quietly.

"So can I, Master, and the roads have changed since last you travelled them. I know you know the way, but if you follow me we'll get there faster."

"And that's another thing—why do you call me that?"

Rella raised her eyebrows and looked at Jamie. Then she said something in a language I couldn't understand, but whatever it was it shocked him. I nearly cheered. Jamie was all the better for a shock every now and then.

Jamie

She spoke the tongue of the assassins far too well. "Don't try to tell me you don't remember. The Master of Arinoc was a legend when I joined up, and you'd been out of the game for ten years by then. Never missed a kill, never injured, never caught—you were our hero."

I spat at the ground and answered her in plain speech. I knew the Blood Cant, but I hated it and the memories that came with it. Bad enough I'd had to use it with that merc some days before. "Damn fools. And if anyone ever called me that, it was far enough behind my back that I couldn't hear them. I never realised you were one of them."

"So were you and don't forget it," she snapped back. "And just because I speak Blood Cant doesn't mean I go around slaughtering people. Yes, I've killed in my time, in fair fight and foul, but seldom for pay and never for pleasure. Don't you dare to judge me, Jameth of Arinoc."

I glanced quickly at Lanen. She was staring thoughtfully at the fire, but when she looked up at me the condemnation I dreaded was not in her eyes. She had truly accepted me, then, for what I was and had been. Blessed be the Lady for that at least.

I turned back to Rella. "I would not presume, Mistress Rella. Those in the Silent Service have their own motives and their own sources. And how should I dare to judge you, with my own past laid here before me? No, lady. Rather I pity you from my heart, and for the good you have done my Lanen I can only hope you escape the Service before you die in it."

She was about to reply when Varien spoke up. I hadn't been paying attention to him, but he sounded sick to his stomach. "Lady Rella, do you tell me that you have killed others of your kind for *khaadish*?" It made me believe his story just that bit more. He was too old to be that innocent.

"What?" she said.

"For gold, for money," said Lanen quietly.

Give her credit, Rella looked him in the eye. "Yes, Varien. I have."

He stood up quickly, his arms wrapped around him and pacing a little in front of the fire. He favoured the injured arm a little. "And you, Master Jameth. You have done this as well?"

I looked up at him. "The last man I killed died this autumn past, for he would have killed both Lanen and me. Before that I had not put blade to flesh for thirty years, but in those days, yes, to my soul's darkening I killed for money. It was Lanen's mother Maran who—" I shook myself. No need to go into that now. "Never mind. Yes, I have done so."

He turned and walked without another word into the dark wood. Lanen stood, not knowing whether to stay or go.

"Go after him, girl," said Rella quietly. "If he doesn't need you now, he will soon. And don't let him get far. This isn't a pleasure trip."

Lanen rose and followed Varien into the darkness.

"And so, Mistress Rella," I said, sitting again and warming my hands.

"And so, Master Jameth—though I'll call you Jamie, if I may."

"Jamie is just a horseman, Mistress. He's only ever killed to keep himself alive."

"That suits me. And I'm just Rella." She looked over at me. "I've only ever had the paid duty once, you know. We are all taught any kind of cant we can learn—I thought that one might stand me in good stead."

"It's foul on the tongue and worse on the soul," I answered. The old familiar darkness was coming over me and I did not welcome it. "I left that life hating myself. If it hadn't been for Maran I don't know what I would have done."

"I know. She told me."

I didn't realise my jaw had dropped until Rella told me to close it. She had the grace not to laugh, at least. I finally managed to speak.

"You knew Maran Vena?"

"I still do," she said, smiling briefly. Against all likelihood she had a good smile. "Why do you think I turned up just in time to save young Varien? I might have done so for friendship's sake, true enough, or to pay back the debt I owed the two of them, but I wouldn't have tracked them across the breadth of Kolmar just for the privilege. I'm on duty."

"Sweet Lady. Maran!" I rose and paced much as Varien had done. "Name of—what's she doing in all this?"

Rella raised one corner of her mouth. "She *is* the girl's mother, after all. Just because she's not here doesn't mean she's not paying attention."

I stared at Rella and realisation struck me like a blow. "Hells' teeth. The Farseer," I breathed. "She's using it to watch over Lanen, and when she saw her leave Hadron-sstead—"

"She hired me. Damn fast, too, and at that I only just made it to the Harvest ship in time." She winked at me. "You're sharp. I can see how you earned your reputation. It wasn't your killing we admired, you know."

I stood silent, my thoughts racing, my heart full of hope one instant and fury the next. When I finally thought I could speak I was about to ask a question that would tell this woman far too much about me, but I was interrupted by a loud yell from the darkness. We were both moving before the echo stopped; I was the faster, but Rella had had the good sense to grab a burning branch from the fire to bring with us.

Thank the Goddess, Lanen has a good pair of lungs on her.

Lanen

I had followed Varien at a little distance, leaving him to his thoughts. I know how I had felt when I first learned of the darkness that shadowed Jamie, less than a year past, but if Rella was right, I should be near Varien if he needed me. I was about to call out to him not to go further into the wood when I heard his voice in my mind, very quiet, very sad. *"Kadreshi? Are you there?"*

"I am here close by, dearling. Say something aloud so I know where you are, it's dark as all the hells out here." I heard his voice away to my left and I hurried to join him, though it wasn't easy or fast. There were tree roots everywhere, hidden under a blanket of dead leaves, just waiting to catch an ankle. I all but fell into him in the darkness. He caught me up in his arms and held me close. I didn't speak, just held him tight to me and kept quiet. This had to come from him.

"By all that's sacred, Lanen," he said, his voice deep and rough with the hurt. "Your heart's father is one who kills for his livelihood. This is a deep evil. I tell you truly, dear one, it weighs on my soul and my sight is darker even than this night. How can you bear it? How can *he*?"

I was trying to be understanding but it was hard. I knew the Kantri killed my people without a thought. "Varien, you must remember that this all happened long ago. He told you, he gave up that life long since. Surely that tells in his favour? He told me that he was paid very well indeed, he could have lived like a nobleman if he chose, but he did not choose. When he met my mother he had already decided to leave that life."

Varien stood away from me. "Forgive me, dearling. I knew the Gedri killed one another, those who chose to follow the path of the Rakshasa—but to kill for no reason! To be the claw of another, without even the poor excuse of fury or the saving of one's own life . . . name of all the Winds, I cannot bear it."

"Do the Kantri never kill one another?" I asked, trying to control myself. I could feel my temper rising. I loved him dearly, but who was he to judge Jamie?

"No. Never since time began has one of the Kindred killed another," he said passionately. "It is a deed worthy of the Rakshasa." I could barely see him, but it looked as if he had wrapped his arms around himself.

That did it.

"It might well be," I said sharply. "Remember, we Gedri are the ones with a choice. Very well, it's true, Jamie chose wrongly all those years ago, but he has done better since. We have all our short lives to get it right, and Jamie did so before I was born. I'd be dead if it weren't for him. And you'd be dead if it weren't for Rella taking out that merc behind your back."

"She killed to save my life, not for pay!" he answered, stung.

"Probably," I said. "But he's just as dead. Have you thanked her for saving your life?"

"Too late," said a deep voice I'd never heard before. I screamed as a dark shadow lunged towards Varien.

I drew my boot knife and stabbed as hard as I could, but I could feel the blade being turned off the stroke. Whoever it was wore a thick leather jerkin for the purpose. "Varien!" I yelled, trying to pull the dark shape off of him.

I might as well have saved my breath.

I'd forgotten just how strong he was.

I heard a grunt and saw the shape being tossed back into shadow and crashing into the undergrowth. "Are you hurt?" I asked, helping Varien up with my free hand while staring wildly into the darkness round about us.

"There are others. Watch and ward, Lanen."

"Jamie! To me!" I cried, loud as I could.

"Lanen!" cried Jamie, already close, and there was light from somewhere, I could see a little. A shadow on the far side of the light drew back. Rella threw down the burning branch she carried and drew us all back from the light towards our own fire, just visible in the distance. "Jamie, you're point, you two in the middle, back to the camp, *go*!"

We moved as fast as we could, but the tree roots made the going hard. Not just for us, thank the Lady, but it was terrifying trying to move at speed over treacherous ground in the dark. I clutched my knife for comfort, but I had already learned it was no use.

We were just at the edge of the clearing when I heard a sound behind me. I turned around, trying to see through the border of shadow. "Rella?"

"I'm here, girl, save your breath. That wasn't me. Go on into the firelight." And we were in the clearing. Jamie threw more branches on the fire and it blazed enough for us to have a look around. Nothing to be seen. I stopped Varien and made him look at me. "Are you hurt?"

"No more than I was before, dearling," he said. He turned away and found his sword lying by his pack. He drew it, saying ruefully, "Wisdom learned late is better than none, is it not, Jamie?"

"Keep your eyes on the trees, man," said Jamie, scanning the undergrowth for movement. "And remember what I told you, keep your sword raised, if it's halfway through the stroke by the time you start you're ahead of your enemy."

Rella stood, as did Jamie, with her back to the fire, "You take north, I'll take south, eh Master?" she said. Jamie just grunted assent.

I wish I could say I was thrilled at the prospect of battle—certainly the ballad singers would have it that way. Idiots. They've never been able to understand one simple thing. I'm terrible with a blade, and even then I knew it. I'm *not* one of the Warrior Women of Arlis, much though I might have wanted to be, and I was afraid. In the dark, the four of us against who knew how many—in fact I feared it was more like two against the enemy, for I thought Varien not much more use than me.

We are all mistaken from time to time.

Certainly when the four of them burst through the trees, every man of them armed with swords and shields and coming straight at me, it took all my courage to hold my dagger ready and not run. "Hells' teeth," I muttered; then my blessed temper rose past my fear and I yelled something at them. I've no idea what I said, to be honest, but it did seem to stop some of them, or at least slow them down.

Jamie

Just before they came through into the clearing, I saw out of the corner of my eye that Varien was holding his sword exactly as I'd taught him, very correct, looking like the greenest of recruits.

They came in from the side nearest Lanen, across the fire from me. The second they showed themselves Rella was moving, looking for the best way in, as I was. And Lanen?

When I saw they were all headed for her I despaired. If they were really determined to kill her they'd probably succeed before we could do anything. Then she yelled, my own Lanen, in pure fury, "Stop where you are, you bloody bastards! Any closer and you're all dead men!"

I nearly laughed. Some of them stopped, and Rella had
long enough to throw a knife—flat, deadly. He dropped and
barely even gurgled as he died. I thought that might slow
them down, but no. Fools.

The big one came straight on to seize Lanen, but suddenly
Varien was in his way. Varien tried to strike with his sword,
of course, but I'd not had time to teach him about targes, and
all of them had those little shields that are so useful in hand-
to-hand battle. I couldn't watch, for I was faced with one of
my own to worry about, but Lanen told me later how it had
gone.

Lanen

Varien was hard put to it in his first swordfight. I tried to
distract the bastard but he kept fighting Varien. When he realised how badly Varien handled a sword he laughed.
"Fool!" he cried, dodging even a fairly well-aimed blow
easily. "Give it up. She'll feed the demons no matter what
you do."

I thought I was the only idiot stupid enough to throw away
my sword, but when Varien heard those words he did just
that. I heard what could only be called a hiss as his sword
clattered on the ground, and he was inside the other's guard
in the very instant, his hand drawn back to strike. I saw him
put his whole body into the blow, direct to the face. There
was a sickening crack as the man's neck snapped backwards
and he dropped.

Varien roared, turning to the nearest foe, the one fighting
Jamie. He struck him from behind, sending the man reeling
forward full onto Jamie's sword. Then suddenly I wasn't
watching anymore, because the last of them had turned from
fighting Rella to seize me from behind. I felt a knife at my
throat and heard him yell, "Move and she's dead!"

Everything stopped.

"Drop your swords!" ordered the voice. He stood directly
behind me. Jamie and Rella threw their swords on the ground.
Varien just watched, his eyes never moving from his prey.

"She's no good to your master dead, you know," said Jamie quietly.

"She's no good to you dead either. Keep back and she'll live," he growled, backing up and pulling me along.

And there I was, helpless again until he stumbled on a tree root and lost his balance. I pushed back and fell on top of him as hard as I could. I heard the breath go out of him all at once. He lost interest in holding the knife at my throat and I scrambled up, getting out of the way so that Jamie could grab him.

Except that Jamie was too slow.

In one movement Varien, growling, hauled the leader of the mercenaries upright by the front of his tunic and hit him full in the face with the heel of his hand. The man went limp instantly. Varien dropped him as if he hadn't existed and came to me. "Lanen," he said, taking my hand gently.

"Shia save us. How in the Hells did you know to do that?" breathed Jamie.

"I have no claws, but my arms have much of their old strength," said Varien. "It seemed to work, in any case."

Jamie

Rella and I moved the bodies deep into the woods. Even as I dragged away the poor dead mercs, even as my soul burned within me in the private darkness at having killed again, though it were only to save my own life, I clung to one solid rock in all the shifting sand of this cursed night. Lanen had not killed anyone. The worst she'd done was fall on to a man who held a knife at her throat.

Thank the Goddess for that.

Lanen hadn't killed.

Lanen

That was when it started, right after that terrible fight in the dark. I'd never been so near to death before, feeling it all around, knowing that only by harming others could you survive. It was awful.

Ah, now, speak truth, Lanen: it was awful after I realised Varien had killed the one who held a knife at my throat, and that he was the last. I had felt a fierce rush of joy when I saw him drop. You can't help but delight in a victory that means you're going to live, but death is death and when I saw four bodies that had but moments before been living men—well, my supper hadn't been much to keep down anyway.

It was late when we were all gathered again round the fire. Jamie insisted on setting a watch, just in case there were others we didn't know about. All of us who weren't on watch slept like stones, but with our weapons in our hands.

Exhaustion caught up with me as I lay thinking about the dead men away there in the woods. My last thought was that, dreadful as their deaths were, they had attacked us and would have killed us if they could. I slept better than I thought I would, but all night I kept thinking I heard voices.

I roused early, as you do sleeping rough, and if it was possible I think I was wearier on waking than I'd been on going to sleep. The voices murmuring in the back of my mind were a little easier to ignore now I was awake, but they hadn't stopped. I wasn't about to mention this to anyone. I thought at the time I was imagining the ghosts of the dead men cursing at us, so I resolved to ignore it.

I was also hungry enough to know that food was going to be the most difficult thing about this part of our journey, now that we did not need to fear immediate attack. We had brought some food with us but there was very little to spare, and we were a long way from the nearest market. Breakfast was oats cooked in water with a little salt. I had been chilled through from sleeping on the ground, and I felt gnawed with hunger, but still the heat I got from it was a damn sight better than the taste.

We left immediately after we ate, carefully avoiding the place where Rella and Jamie had taken the bodies. I was nearly sick again when I thought of them, but distance helped. We went vaguely south, for though we had still not decided where we should go, all of our destinations lay to the south of where we were.

We rode through the day, stopping only briefly for food at noon, but we made camp early in the afternoon for we were all weary, and I the worst. I was still shaking slightly, and though I kept it to myself I still thought I heard voices at the edge of hearing. Varien and I were told off to see what we could find in the way of small game. How we were meant to catch anything I can't imagine. I had a bow and I was usually decent with it, but I couldn't hit a thing that day. We spent much of our time searching in the slanting light for arrows that I'd sent into the undergrowth. At least the walking warmed us a little. Jamie had his bow and was out looking for something more substantial. He said he'd seen deer scat, and he was a much better shot than I.

Varien and I were coming back empty-handed to the camp when I heard the scream. It was like nothing I'd ever heard before—not human, but a living creature seeing its death and crying out in fear and pain as its life was torn from it. It brought me to my knees, retching, poor Varien beside me holding my head and wondering what was wrong. "What in the Hells was that?" I asked feebly, when I could speak.

"What ails thee?" asked Varien, deeply concerned. He could not keep his thoughts from reaching me. *"What didst thou see/hear/what hath touched thee?"*

I couldn't explain aloud, so I tried responding in true-speech. *"It was a cry of pain, a creature meeting its end, I heard no words just pain and fear and the falling away of life. I am frightened it was so real so near, death so near, Goddess keep it from us all."* Even truespeech was difficult. *"Can you see it, hear the memory of it in my mind if I think of it?"* I asked, and when he nodded I thought again of what I had felt and heard and tried to let him see it. It seemed to work, for he immediately stood upright, his hands on my shoulders.

"Lanen, *kadreshi*." His voice was deep with astonishment. "Truly the Wind of Change is blowing wild upon us, for surely you are being shaped even now." He raised me to my feet. The memory was fading a little, it was easier to stand, to think. Varien took my chin in his hand and turned me towards him. In the cold afternoon light his silver hair gleamed like frost, and his deep green eyes were solemn with realisation. "Lanen, what you heard was the death cry of a deer. Jamie must have found what he sought."

"That's ridiculous! Why on earth would I hear such a thing?" I cried, really frightened now. "Don't tell me deer have truespeech!"

"No, my heart, of course not. But it happens sometimes, when one of the Kantri grows old or infirm, that they begin to hear such things—the day-song of birds, the rush of sap through the heart of a tree, the death screech of small creatures in the long grass when owls are hunting. Dearling," he said gently, "do you hear anything else?"

"Oh Hells," I said, my eyes wide and filling with tears against my will. This was vastly worse than the attack in the night. I was filled with dread, fear like a pit opened bottomless before me. You can run from or fight with other living souls but your mind is with you always. "Varien—oh Hells. I've been hearing voices, just out of range—I mean, I know they are voices but I don't know what they are saying."

He closed his eyes, just for a second. "Lanen." Then, looking up, "I do not know how this can be. You have an affliction that falls only upon the Kantri. When did this start?"

"Last night." I swore. "Hells blast and damn it!"

There, that felt better. "Why do you ask?"

His eyes looked less haunted immediately. "Then it cannot be the same. Are you well otherwise?"

At least that made me smile. In fact it made me laugh. "What, you mean apart from being exhausted and having been captured twice in five days and fighting for my life and watching my farm burn down around me and my husband kill men with his bare hands? Apart from that?"

"I do not jest, *kadreshi*."

"I'm sorry," I answered, recovering myself. "We do that sometimes, it's the only way to deal with things that are too hard to bear, we just have to laugh about it."

"I know. We do the same. Are you well otherwise?"

"As far as I can tell, yes. I'm weary to my bones and ravenously hungry, but aside from that I think I'm well enough. *Why*, Varien?"

"It usually affects us at the end of a long life, and only after a prolonged time without food." He was shaking his head. "Forgive me, dearling, I do not mean to worry you. I am wrong, I must be. Know you of any such illness among your own people?"

I managed to smile. "Only madness, my dear. And last I checked I was as sane as I ever have been."

He caught me to him, his arms strong about me as if he were holding me against one who sought to take me from him. "Come, my heart. Let us go back to the fire, this setting winter sun warms nothing. Perhaps I make more of this than is in it. You are cold and weary, it could be mere chance or imagination. Come."

But when we got there, Rella and Jamie had taken the deer's carcase a little way into the woods to clean.

It got worse from there.

To use words is misleading, for there were no words then. Only feelings, sharp as the light after a thunderstorm, and the unformed shapes of thoughts like shadows in a deep pool.

There was longing, for I had not seen him or heard his voice in many years. There was loneliness, for though I did not know where to go I knew that I needed to be with him, needed to know that he lived. I flew high many nights, searching, wondering, yet too full of fear to leave the home I had made for myself.

The thought of him was remembered joy, family, home—his absence a bitter wound that bled sorrow. I needed him, needed his presence. The world was changing, moving towards a place where no light shone. I could not be sure any longer even of my own kind. I had seen fighting among us and death that shocked me to my bones, made even heart's-fire cold.

Where there should have been calm waters there were thorns, and a feeling in the blood of darkness like deep winter spreading over life and light. I needed him—teacher—friend—Father. I needed to hear the sounds he made, on the edge of understanding, so near, so near . . .

vi

Recovery

Maikel

The poor madman, my master, sat up in bed. He was still fast asleep but he was laughing this time, which was better than before. The last two mornings he had wakened screaming bloody murder, rousing not only his watchers but full half the household. When I went to release him from this dream he did not fight me as he had, but relaxed into my arms and slept again without waking. I almost had some hope that his cure had begun.

I had been a Healer in the House of Gundar since first I came into my power. He had been thirty-five then, and I in my early twenties. Over the last fourteen years I had watched the changes that had overtaken him and seen his association with Magister Berys of the College of Mages draw him into the worst of himself. I had willfully blinded myself for many years, but on that voyage to the Dragon Isle, Marik had revealed himself as a soul lost to the Rakshasa. I had planned to leave him when we returned, but then he had pitted the strength of his demon-centred power against the

Lord of the Dragons. I did not know precisely what had happened; but when his guards carried him to the ship, mindless, helpless as a newborn, I knew I could not leave.

Without the lan fruit we would have lost him. I had heard of such things, of course, and knew the theory, but I had thought it merely legend until I saw the miracle that one of those fruits had wrought on the Lady Lanen. Horrible burns, to the bone, burns that would have taken months to heal—if she had even lived—with the most skilled and constant care in all of Kolmar, had disappeared overnight. Arms that should have been hideously scarred for life had no more than a few traces of those ravages wrought by I knew not what fire. True, I saved her from the fever that raged within her, but for all my strength she would have died that night without the fruit from a lansip tree.

The first that I fed him, on the ship, saved Marik's life; the second that I fed him, after we reached Corlí, had a more subtle effect. I had summoned the Healer's deep vision that I might watch as he ate; it was astounding to see his ravaged mind begin to knit before my eyes, see even the disturbance of minor ailments pass from him, and to observe the war between the virtue of the lansip and the years-long pain that he bore. When he had finished, that old wound was nearer healed than ever it had been before, and it did not grow worse again after the healing as had been the pattern for so many years. I did not imagine this could be a direct effect of the lan fruit, however virtuous. Myself, I think that with his mind gone the evil creatures couldn't find him, though I presumed his old punishment could not be entirely revoked while he lived.

I half expected him to rise up from his bed as his old best self, fully recovered, but that fool's dream soon deserted me. After more than four long moons of work and healing, he no longer required the care of a babe in arms, but his mind was not restored. It was more as though a deep wound had finally stopped bleeding. It was not healed, but at least it was not getting any worse and healing might take place in time, though my hopes on that score were dwindling. He could understand simple words but he had not yet regained his speech.

I had managed as well to keep Magister Berys from him ever since we had returned from the Dragon Isle. Perhaps if I had kept him away longer my master might have recovered fully in time—but speculation is idle. Word had arrived some days since from Berys to let us know that he was coming. Despite my status as the Healer in charge of Marik, Berys was the head of the College of Mages in Verfaren, where Healers are trained.

When the Archimage is chosen, the choice is meant to be based on a combination of qualities, such as strength, integrity, honesty and compassion. In Berys's case it had been pure power. He had more of it than any other Mage alive at that time, more than most of the others combined. The faction supporting his election had put about a rumor that the presence of so powerful a Healer must be a sign that his power would be required for some great work in his lifetime. It had swayed many—though I was not among them, I am pleased to say—and he had risen to the highest position afforded any Healer in all the lands of Kolmar.

He made my flesh crawl.

And he was on his way, indeed, would most likely arrive in Elimar before nightfall. Why he had journeyed so far I could not imagine; at this time of year it was a good ten days' ride from Verfaren to Elimar, for the road was treacherous in this second moon of winter. In the meantime, I washed Marik and shaved him, and spoke to him as best I could. It was not rewarding. His stare was nearly as blank as it had been this month past. Even though I had been resting for some days and was able to put forth my full strength that morning, I got no further in healing his poor broken mind.

There are some who would say that his piteous condition was judgment for his wicked ways. However, until they can explain why those who live spotless lives are as likely to die young as those who scurry to destroy themselves and others, I will not believe such words. Am I to think that the Lady would so callously discard her son? True, he had gone down a dark road, but the only certainly irredeemable creature in this world is a dead one. I must confess that in my heart of hearts I had occasionally hoped that his body would grow weary of keeping the shell alive. Some nights I even begged the Lady, prayed, to the peril of my soul, that if he could not be restored to himself he might be allowed to die while at least he was doing no evil.

She did not have so gentle a fate in store for her errant son.

When Berys arrived at nightfall he demanded my report. He made a token effort at courtesy, but it was clear that he had no time for the niceties. He listened carefully to my assessment of my patient and then informed me, not unkindly, that I had done well in difficult circumstances and that he was taking over.

I had expected as much. Indeed, had it been anyone apart from Berys I would have been delighted at his arrival, for surely no living Healer could be as great a help to my master as could the Archimage of Verfaren. As it was, my stomach churned at the thought of those hands touching my master.

In the end I surprised Magister Berys and astounded myself. As he moved to Marik's bedside I stood in his way, moving between him and my master. I had not taken a decision to do so. It was as if my body had moved of itself in response to my deepest instincts.

"Yes, Healer Maikel? What is it?" he asked briskly.

To my astonishment, I heard the words escaping my lips. "Your pardon, Magister, but I do not release him into your care. The patient must be consulted if the attending Healer does not accept the offer of assistance, and my patient is in no condition to consent."

Berys hardly glanced at me. "And why, Healer Maikel, do you choose not to accept my aid in this matter?" he asked as he continued his preparations.

"Magister, I have been the Healer of this House for fourteen years. Marik knows me and trusts me. In his current condition, trust is a very valuable and very fragile thing. I have sealed the breach in his mind, with the help of the lan fruit, but that is only a first step. Fear is behind his every breath. He screams if any touches him beside myself. For the time being, I must insist that he remain in my care."

For the first time I had his attention. He looked full at me, his eyes narrowed. After what seemed forever, he shrugged. "Very well. I challenge thee, Maikel, in the name of the Powers, show that thou art more fitted to heal this man than I."

What? A formal challenge? Here?

In those few seconds of surprise he had summoned his power. He glowed bright blue with it, painful to look at. While I was still struggling to call in what strength I had left, he struck. No warning, no mercy, and precious little of Healing about it. It seemed to me, in the instant before I lost consciousness, that the Healer's blue aura that struck me was shot with black.

When I woke the next morning it was to a changed world, and I the most violently changed of all.

🜚 The first thing I saw when I opened my eyes was the face of Berys close to mine. He smiled. I realised then what a good smile he had, open and honest, and wondered at myself for having harboured such dark thoughts about him.

"So, Maikel, you are with us again. How are you feeling?" he asked. His voice was soothing, and I saw now why he had been so successful at Verfaren. His very presence made people feel better.

"I am well enough, Magister," I replied. My voice was weaker than I would have expected and I was more than a little hazy as to why I should be in bed and under Berys's care. Why was he here?

He sat back. "I fear that I owe you an apology, my young friend. I was so weary and so concerned about my old friend Marik that I was far too abrupt with you when I arrived last night. I only asked you to let me see him, and when you refused I fear I lost my temper and challenged you. I do beg your pardon. If you would like me to leave him in your care, I will gladly do so."

"Why should I deny your right to serve him, Magister?" I

asked, even more confused. "I confess I do not remember aught of last night. You say I would not let you see him? What reason did I give?"

"Nothing very coherent, I fear." He took my wrist to check the progress of my heart and smiled. "Strong again. Good." He looked at me. "I must say, though, it's just as well I have come. As it is I had to work long on you to draw you back from the fever that beset you."

"Fever?" I asked, putting my hand to my forehead. It felt normal.

"No longer, I am glad to say," he said, smiling. "I can only assume that it already had you in its grip when I arrived, else why should you deny me the right to see an old friend who needed my help?"

"Why indeed? I must beg your pardon, Magister." I smiled ruefully. "You say you challenged me? And I accepted? I must have been feverish, I'd never do such a thing in my right mind. I have the greatest respect for your abilities." I tried to reach back for the memory, but there was nothing there. I shook my head, smiling. "I must have fallen like an autumn leaf, I remember nothing about it."

"You were swaying when I had done no more than summon my power to me," he replied. "I barely touched you and suddenly there you were in a heap on the floor." He laughed softly. "You had your revenge in that moment, though. I feared I'd killed you. Never mind, all's well now and the harvest in, as they say. Do you feel well enough to rise?"

I essayed it and found I could stand, though I felt a bit dizzy. I saw that I was in my own chambers—presumably the servants had brought me here when I fell. Berys led me to the table he had placed in my anteroom and he joined me in a light breakfast, as recommended for those who are convalescing from a fever. Now that I was more myself—like most Healers, I make a terrible patient—I could see that he looked better than ever he had before. He glowed with health and looked years younger than he had when last I had seen him.

When I mentioned it, he smiled. "Ah, it is obvious now! Yes, I thank you, I am very well indeed. I have been experimenting with the lansip I acquired from my late venture with the House of Gundar." He leaned closer and whispered conspiratorially, "Do you know, I had heard that old tale about an elixir made from the leaves that would bestow youth to the aged, and I thought that since I now had both the need and the wherewithal I would attempt it." He sat back and shook his head slightly. "Alas," he resumed in his normal voice, "the claims were exaggerated, but I certainly feel vastly better than I have in many a year. If it is making a difference to the eye of the beholder, so much the better! I have not been aging gracefully, I fear, and any delay in the process must therefore be a good thing."

He looked at me with his Healer's sight then and seemed content. "You looked recovered. Will you come with me to see our patient?" His eyes twinkled. "Or must I challenge you again?"

We both laughed. "Not until I'm feverish again, if you please," I replied. "I'd prefer to keep as many of my few wits about me as I may, I thank you. Let us see what we may do together for my poor master."

Marik slept lightly in the morning, but he did not wake until I spoke his name. When he was himself he had risen every day before the sun. Even now he seemed to wish to do so but could not. Whether some obscure fear kept him asleep or whether his body was simply trying to heal his mind as it rested, I did not know.

Magister Berys asked me to recount all that had happened to bring Marik to this state. He said he had heard rumors but wanted to hear directly from me all that was known, as I had accompanied Marik. I told him all that I could—all that I had gathered from the mysterious Varien on the journey home—but he seemed none the wiser. I had not been present when Marik was stricken. I was only summoned after the fact to find his mind wandering in some far field where I could not follow.

"Was he injured physically?" asked Berys, gazing at my

master. "Had he any wounds, large or small, when you saw him?"

I sighed. "There was a small puncture wound on the middle finger of his left hand, and a number of ragged scratches on his chest. They were all infected, whatever caused them, and grew worse almost as I watched. I managed to make a poultice of lansip leaves to stop the infection spreading. After that I used my own strength, day after day, and fed him on the lan-fruit he had found. At first it did no more than keep him alive, but even that was more than I could have done on my own. I did as much as I might on the journey, but it was not until I returned with him here to Elimar that I could put forth all my strength. And as you see, that has only healed his body. I fear his mind is still adrift."

Berys summoned his power about him and used his Healer's sight to look at Marik. I knew what he was seeing. I had not spoken of it, lest I cloud the Magister's sight with my own interpretation, but the vision haunted my sleep and my waking.

Where a normal mind was full of colour and movement to the healer's sight—bright with pain, or dancing with golden joy, or even shimmering grey with fear—Marik's was a field of dry earth: barren, cracked with heat, hard as bone, brittle, and scorched by a blazing, merciless sun.

We are taught to attempt the healing of the mind (it is far harder than healing the body) by countering the vision with its natural opposite as we open a way for the healing power. A mind full of darkness is to be gently, gently introduced to the dawn—nothing sudden, no flaming sunrise that would overwhelm, just a first slight suggestion of growing light that heralds the morning. Often the suggestion is not even noticed by the patient, but with time and talk and much hard work, this kind of healing can take place. While we are working, it is as if we are "there," inside the metaphor, and can feel the results of our own work.

I had tried to heal Marik with visions of morning mist, of low soaking cloud, even (in desperation) with a gentle rain—in each case the "water" of my healing disappeared instantly when I ceased putting forth my power, as if something was drinking it, and the broken brown dust of the vision remained untouched. It was as if he were drinking in all that I could offer but was still dying of thirst, even though I could feel myself getting soaked through as I was working.

This time I drew my power about me—and feeble it looked indeed beside the pulsing blue of Berys's healing mantle—and watched, for we can "see" what is happening even when another Healer is working. The two Healers might not see the same metaphor of the patient's mind, but the effects are mirrored in both.

I was there again, standing on the hard cracked ground of Marik's mind, barren of all life and of all promise of life. I felt Berys stretch forth his strength—and there, a cloud was coming over the sun, and a breeze sprang up. I drew in a deep breath and I swear it smelled of rain.

If you have ever been proud of a small skill, one you have worked long and hard for, and then seen a master of the craft surpass your very best work without the slightest effort, you will know how I felt. Over three full moons of work I had managed several times to put an image of gentle dampness in Marik's mind that stayed with him for an hour or so. Berys had called up a thunderstorm upon the instant.

Deep inside myself, I was uneasy—surely this was too sudden, too rough. A broken mind needs to be brought back gently if it is to regain its wholeness, or so I was taught. However, I could hardly argue with the Archimage of Verfaren. I stood and watched, felt a cold wet wind blow lazily through my cloak, chilling me, and heard thunder far off. The first large drops fell, raising dust as they hit. I could feel them on my skin, cold, heavy, even painful when they struck. They did not immediately change the dryness below my feet, though I could see a few patches of dampness that lasted for an instant before they too fell away.

However, I knew from the feel of the air that this could not last. The drops came faster, heavier—and I was standing in the midst of a downpour, like a bucket being emptied from the clouds. It felt dangerous. I found that I was terrified even as I was fascinated. I suspect I was drenched in the first instant, but I never noticed—all my attention was riveted on the ground.

For ground it was becoming. Nothing could stand against that much water, and even as I watched the cracks filled with dark liquid, the edges softened, and that barren land crumbled into mud. Soon it was a pool filled with more rain than it could hold. I began to fear for Marik and called out, "Lord Berys, enough, surely that is sufficient for now!"

There was no reply, but the rain did not stop and the air grew even heavier. Something began to emerge from the pool.

It was a creature of nightmare, a dragon the size of a mountain. The falling water fizzed and disappeared as it touched the gleaming black skin, but still the rain fell in sheets. The creature stood on its back legs and roared, terrifying—and there was an answering roar of thunder from the heavens, and a spear of lightning split the sky, stabbed down at the dragon and struck it between the eyes.

I was blinded, there in the realm of the mind. I shook myself, drew deep breaths, returned to the waking world, and saw a miracle.

Marik was sitting up, his eyes focused on Berys, and though he was trembling his voice was surprisingly sure.

"What took you so damned long?"

I had grown since I left him, both in body and in spirit. I had walked in the deep woods by moonlight, drinking its rays like water, feeling the currents in the ground beneath my feet like living things. I had flown, one hot summer night, high and far, rising and circling on air strong as stone beneath my wings. I had seen many like him, two-legged, walking like him but fearful in the shadows under the trees, and some like me, four-legged, winged and tailed and scaled and taloned.

There were more of his kind than of mine.

Even when I was very young I knew we were different. As I grew I wondered when I would lose my wings and stand upright and whether it would hurt. I knew he was older than I and wiser and looked and smelled so strange, but I also felt love sure and strong. I never questioned, until one bright morning I leaned over to drink and saw my face in a pool, the colour of an autumn sunset, and knew in my blood that my great shield of a face would never go soft or be covered with fur like his. It did not make me love him less, but I knew then that I must go from him and seek my own.

I sought, I found, I made my life with my own kind, but I did not and could not forget that loved face and form. And now that there was a great change coming over us all, a deep desire arose in me to be with him again. Long I wavered between stay and go, long my fears kept me from doing either, but in the end I chose to leave my safety and seek him. I will never know why I so chose, or how I found the courage; but I did, and the world changed.

Lanen

I had never objected to deer meat before, but I couldn't eat it even when Jamie had managed to cut some small and cook it quickly on a skewer in the fire Rella had set going. It smelled good, but at least for the moment I couldn't get rid of the echoes of that cry in my mind. I found myself hoping that vegetables didn't scream as I bit into a carrot, one of the winter store we'd brought from Hadronsstead. My gut was in a terrible state and the very idea of meat turned my stomach. Even the carrot tasted terrible.

"What's up with you, my girl?" asked Jamie, when I refused the deer. "It's well cooked and we all need hot food."

"I'm sorry, Jamie," I said. I couldn't face explaining what was only a guess. He'd had enough trouble believing in true-speech between people. I wasn't sure I could ever tell him. Maybe it would just go away. "I'm not hungry. I can't face food just now."

He looked closely at me for a moment, then shrugged. "Suit yourself. We should cook as much as we can, though the cold will keep it fresh enough for a few days." He smiled at me. "If you're not hungry you're the very one I'm looking for. Keep an eye on the rest of this lot while I set up camp."

He left me to tend skewers of small chunks of deer cooking over the fire while he untied his bedroll and mine from our saddles. "Thank the Lady those poor bastards were in such a hurry to get you they left our horses alone," he said after a time. "I'd rather ride than walk."

"Ride where?" asked Rella, kneeling on the cold ground as she cleared a space for her bedroll near the fire. "We never did decide exactly where we're going." Her voice hardened. "I still vote for Sorún. I have my suspicions but I want to know for certain who hired those poor buggers."

"Are you suspecting anybody I know?" I asked, half a smile tugging at my lips despite myself.

"Not unless you've heard the name Berys, no."

I frowned. It seem familiar, somehow, though I couldn't be sure—and then I heard Jamie hiss, "Berys." His voice was so deep and intense I turned to stare at him. He had stopped what he was doing and knew nothing beyond Rella's words.

I had to concentrate hard to hear anything. My mind was suddenly filled with voices again, louder than before. I tried desperately to ignore them. Something Jamie said had raised a memory, something I'd heard him say once and couldn't quite remember. It was hard to think with all the noise.

"I know him," he said. "Do you?"

"Yes, and I wish I didn't," she answered. "He's been watched for years now and none of the news is good."

"It never has been," said Jamie, almost in a trance. "I've known him for the last twenty-five years and I've hated him ever since I first heard his voice."

"Ah, you're a man after my own heart, Jamie." Rella took in Jamie's stance and voice and came to a decision. "I suspect I could be dismissed from the Service for telling you this but I think you need to know. He's now the Archimage of the College of Mages in Verfaren, where the best of the young Healers go to learn their art and better their skills. It's still a good place, by all accounts, but he's rotten to the core and as far as we can tell always has been. Rumour has it the place has started to stink of demons."

"At least for the last twenty-five years," said Jamie. His voice shook me and made Rella turn to look at him even more closely. He stood there in the winter wood, his pack dangling unheeded from one hand, his other on his sword hilt, and he was hot with fury decades old. The voices in my head were a little quieter now.

"Lady guard us, what did he do to you?" asked Rella, her eyes wide with surprise.

"Tried to kill Maran and me with demons," Jamie said, the words rough in his throat, "but that's by the by." And I remembered with a shock, as if it were the day before, Jamie telling me of a demon master linked with Marik. But that was before I was born, a quarter of a century since, and Berys had not been young even then by Jamie's account. Jamie had told me that this Berys had killed an innocent to create the Farseer, a globe that allowed the owner to see whatever they desired, no matter the distance. The Farseer for which Marik's first child had been the promised price— me, yet unsuspected in my mother's womb, the unborn child of Marik of Gundar.

"I made a vow to kill him with my own hands and now I have the chance to do it," said Jamie. "He's at Verfaren, you say?"

"I know what you're thinking and it can't be done, Master. He's the head of the College of Mages! Untouchable. Nearly everyone believes he is what he claims, a kindly servant of the Lady who oversees the training of the young Healers with a very powerful benevolence. The Silent Service knows better and obviously so do you." She flashed a quick grin at me. "Ah, well. Guess we're not going to Sorún. We can make straight for Kaibar and cross the river there, that's the fastest way to Verfaren from here."

Jamie dropped his pack and knelt beside her. "Mistress," he said fervently, laying his hand lightly on her arm, "this is not your fight. I go into danger to fulfill an old vow. Lanen and Varien go where the Lady and their destiny lead them. You do not need to come."

"Is that so, Jamie Horsemaster?" said Rella, gently removing his hand and drawing out an extra blanket from the depths of her own pack. "You don't listen very well, do you? I'm on duty, remember."

I was going to ask her what kind of duty she was talking about when I heard Shikrar's voice clearly saying my name.

"Wake up, girl!" Rella's voice interrupted my thoughts. "If you burn that deer meat you'll eat it yourself."

I managed to save most of it and was laying it by on a stone to cool when Jamie said, "Where's that man of yours?"

"He's not far," I said. "I heard him just now." Silently thanking the Lady for truespeech, I bespoke him. *"Varien? Where are you/are you well?"*

Varien

I was not so squeamish as Lanen and ate well of the deer that Jamie had killed. I had occasionally heard the death cry of creatures I killed for food—certainly I saw their faces.

It is a hard truth of life that we live, all, on death. We of the Kantri give thanks to the Winds for the lives that sustain our own and ask forgiveness of the creatures we must kill, but we cannot live only on the fruits of the earth. Indeed, one of the Kantri tried it when I was young—Kretissh, it was. He ate only roots and the fruit of the trees, and though lan fruit is sustaining for a time, eventually he grew weak and then ill. It was Shikrar, my old friend, who came roaring into his chambers with a great fish he had caught. Crafty soul, he knew Kretissh was partial to fish. Shikrar was not Eldest then but he had taught Kretissh along with most of the rest of us, and when he ordered Kretissh to eat, he ate. He could only take a little flesh at first, but as he grew stronger he returned to himself. As Idai once said, how do we know that the fruits do not feel pain and cry out in their own silent tongue when we eat them?

I found my thoughts turning more and more to my old

friends and my heart grew heavy. So far away, my people. I had almost forgotten that I had the means to bespeak them. I drew out from my pack the rough gold circlet Shikrar had made to hold my soulgem. I did not put it on immediately but held it in my hands and gazed at it.

How shall I explain it to you? A soulgem is not an ornament dug from the ground, it is a part of us, part of our bodies, as much as wing and talon, blood and bone. I still missed my wings, though the wonder of being human delighted me, but the absence of my soulgem was a constant sorrow. It was as though a human had lost all but the least of hearing and sight, and yet could hold the loss in their hands. The Kantri can sense emotions and hear truespeech. It is the way we are made—without truespeech, how should we speak one to another, up in the high air riding upon the winds, and with at least two wings' distance between us? Lanen was the only child of the Gedri who had ever been known to have truespeech.

I raised the circlet and put it on. My head began to ache immediately but I did not care, I so desperately longed to hear the voices of my kindred. *"Shikrar, soulfriend, canst hear me?"*

"Akhorishaan!" came the response, immediate, delighted. *"Ah, blessed be the Winds, I hear you! And I must call you Varien, of course. Your voice is welcome as summer in winter, my friend. How fare you?"*

I wrapped my arms around me, hugging his voice to myself. It was Shikrar, speaking to me mind to mind as of old, the lifelong friendship between us deep and strong as the sea. *"All the better to hear your voice, my friend. The winter is long, and life among the Gedri is not always simple."*

"Life is never simple, Kantri or Gedri," he replied. Now that I was past the first joy of hearing his voice again, I caught undertones of concern in his voice. *"Much has happened of late, Varien. Have you time for speech?"*

"As well now as later," I replied. *"Come, Shikrar, how fare you? Since you reply so swiftly, I must assume the Weh has released you."*

"I am recovered, I thank you. How keep you and your lady?"

"We are as well as may be, though trouble has sought us out of late. I am learning hard truths about my new people, Shikrar."

"Truth hath ever sharp edges, as you know of old. Keep you in good heart despite what you learn?"

"Good heart enough. Lanen is ever the delight of my eyes and the wings of my soul—ah, forgive me, Shikrar! We are but new mated and I am wont to speak of my delight."

I could feel his joy, tinged as it was with regret. *"Akhorishaan, long years have I waited to hear you speak thus. I rejoice for you, my friend, though in all truth my heart would be lighter had thy brave-souled dearling become one of the Kantri instead. Still, the Winds blow over all, and we must trust they will blow us to safety in the end."*

"Great heart, I so believe as well, though now I pray to the Lady of the Gedrishakrim as well as to the Winds. Surely the Winds and the Lady between them can well look after us all! But enough of that. Shikrar, speak to me. How fare the Kantrishakrim? What of my people?"

"All is well with us, Varien. It is not thy people that should concern thee, but the land upon which we live. Terash Vor swells with fire again and the earthshakes wakened me from my Weh sleep."

"Shikrar!"

"I am healed enough. It is our home I fear for, Akhorishaan. It is not Terash Vor alone that breathes fire. There are others—even Lashti and Kil-lashti are alight."

"Name of the Winds," I swore softly. *"Shikrar, have you called a Council?"*

"It will take place less than two moons hence—if we are given so long. I fear we will not be. There is something in the air, Akhor, a high sound on the edge of hearing that grows louder and softer but does not stop. I do not know what it means, but it is—unsettling, to say the least."

"Would that I were with you!" I cried in frustration.

"You are better where you are, my friend," said Shikrar

dryly. *"If we must leave here, we have only one place to go. We will need all the friends we can find to speak for us."*

A thought occurred to me, belatedly. *"Have you spoken with the Ancestors? Surely the Kin-Summoning—"*

"Kédra helps me prepare. It must take place at the dark of the moon, as you know, but that is upon us now and I require time to prepare. I will have to wait until the moon is dark again, but I do not hold out much hope. If ever this island had been so violent before, we surely would have heard of it."

My head was beginning to pound with pain. *"My friend, forgive me, but I must go. Truespeech is painful for me now, alas! Know that I am with you in spirit, and I pray you, bespeak me again when the Council begins. I will listen as long as I can."*

"I shall do so. Be well, Akhor, and send my true regard to thy lady Lanen," said Shikrar, sending me as he left a benison that washed over my weary mind. I returned the same and removed the circlet. Almost at the same moment I heard Lanen bespeak me, asking where I was. I turned and walked slowly back to the camp, reassuring her as best I could while I told her Shikrar's news, and deeply relieved that truespeech with her did not require me to wear my soulgem crown.

We were to make for Verfaren.

vii

Salera

Salera saw I   first in fire—
Sorrow sealed her,   lone child and lost.
Friendship's flame   burned fierce between us—
Dear as daughter,   she fixed my fate.

Will

I've always thought there should be more to that—a whole song maybe—but I'm no bard. Still, that much appeared without being called and no more came to mend it, so perhaps that's all it is meant to be.

I came across her nine years ago. I was on my way home from gathering the tiny blue salerian blossoms. Salerian grows only in the hills, I've tried cuttings and seeds and all sorts but it just won't take and grow in a garden. Still, as it's the best remedy known for maladies that make the head ache, it's worth the trip. The plant is a large one, more a bush than anything else, but the flowers are small and at their best and strongest in the early spring. It was no more than three weeks after the Spring Balance-day, all those years ago. I'd gone gathering early in the day, before the rain came. I was on my way back home with my bag full, racing a big black cloud, when I smelled smoke.

It was cold enough for a fire, true, but I lived deeper in the wooded hills above Verfaren than any other and my cottage was a good two miles away. I knew of no charcoal burners thereabouts and, well, yes, I was curious and followed my nose.

I hadn't far to go, but even in that little time I knew fine I would find no ordinary fire. The smell was not of wood smoke. There was a wildness to it, a tinge of something I didn't know at all, but under and over all as I drew nearer was the scent of burning flesh. I slowed as I drew near, for it was well off the path and I did not care to lose myself in the trackless wood. Even so, I gasped when I peered round a great oak and saw her.

She was walking in the midst of a raging fire, nosing about in the very flames like a dog seeking a scent, making the most pitiful noises. As I watched, spellbound, she threw back her head and screamed.

The sound hit me like a blow. This was not the voice of a beast, a lost dog abandoned by an owner, nor was it her death-agony. It was not physical pain at all. There was not the slightest doubt in my mind that this was grief, and that the creature before me suffered terribly in the full knowledge of what it had lost.

I had never seen a dragon so close, and never imagined that they were more than beasts. I had also thought they were larger. This was no more than the size of a big dog.

Oh, Lady keep the poor soul, I thought, as I realised I could see now the vague outline of where the fire was—or had been, for it was dying rapidly. A much larger shape, indeed, lay traced on the rough ground in ashes. I had heard any number of reasons why no dragon carcases were ever found, and before me was the explanation that made the most sense. Seems that when they died they burned, fire to fire, leaving nor tails nor scales nor wing-tips, only ash and a few small hunks of charred bone.

The little dragon cried out again, its eyes tight closed, all its teeth bared and its nose pointing to heaven, for all the world like any human soul in pain. The world's fool I was and am, for I couldn't help myself, I moved to comfort it as I would do for any man or beast. I'm no Healer, but even a herbalist has a need to lessen pain if it can be done, and my sister Lyra always said my heart was as soft as my head. Still, it was not as foolish as it might seem, for I'm a good size and strong enough in myself to deal with most things.

The creature was suddenly aware of me and hissed a warning, like a great snake. It bared its teeth, watched me through eyes now become mere slits, head low to the ground.

For some reason best known to the Lady, I spoke to it.

"Now then, now then, no need to worry, I'll not harm you," I said calmly and quietly, as I'd speak to a child or a hurt dog. *And let us keep it that way on both sides, shall we? I thought to myself.* "What's brought you to this pass, eh, little one? For you are that, aren't you? Just a kitling who's lost yer mam and got nowhere to run and hide. Don't you worry, Willem's here, I'll help you if I can."

My voice seemed to be soothing it—at least it relaxed enough to open its eyes some bit wider, and I got another surprise. Its eyes were brilliant blue, the very blue of the salerian flowers I'd been gathering. "Salera," I said aloud. "That'll do you for a name, unless you've one already. Salera. Don't know if you're lad or lass, but it don't matter much." I had been very slowly drawing nigh it, moving smoothly as one does with unknown animals. I stopped just before it shied away and kept talking as I knelt down with one hand outstretched. "Nah, then, Salera, what are we to do, eh? I'll wager your mam's been ill some while, hasn't she? I can count your ribs, ye poor thing. And now she's left you without wanting to or meaning to, but you're left all the same."

It was warily coming a tiny bit closer, stretching out its neck, sniffing at my hand. *At any rate it's got something else to think about now*, I thought, *and that's all to the good.* I didn't know if I could bear to hear that scream again.

It moved its attention in a moment from my hand to my pouch and started sniffing at my salerian flowers, and before I could move or think, I give you my word, that creature tore open my bag and ate up in a few quick mouthfuls what I'd spent hours collecting. I just sat back and watched. Maybe it knew the flowers by the scent for their healing powers, maybe it was just attracted by them, maybe it was just so weary with grief and pain it didn't care—but it had been in need and had taken food with my scent on it. It grew braver then, or had lost any fear of what could be worse than had already happened to it. I kept still on my knees while it came and carefully sniffed me all over. It smelled warm and somehow spicy, like cinnamon, but with a sharp tang under all of fire and danger.

Then, it looked me in the eye and tried to say something.

I know, I know, it sounds mad, but I'd swear it was trying to talk. It moved its mouth and made sounds, its eyes were bright and full of intelligence, I just couldn't understand it.

Like an idiot I said, "What? What was that?"

I would swear it said the same thing again. Near enough, anyhow. But I was no nearer to understanding. And I had forgotten my hurry, but the reason for it arrived and reminded me. A few big drops splashed on my arms and face, and the kitling looked up just like I did to see the clouds upon us and the rain smelled only moments away. I looked around, but the kitling was already moving. The big rocks away on the far side of the clearing weren't solid like I had thought; one moment the dragon was there and the next it wasn't. Well, I'd about made up my mind to go home and come back later, despite the rain, when I heard the creature cry out. It was nearly a mew, nearly a bleat, but more than either. If it wasn't calling for its mother then it was the next best thing.

Well, it was join the beast in the rocks and stay dry or keep out in that rain and get drenched, so I went to join it.

I'd never heard tell of anyone going in the lair of a dragon of their own free will—I reckoned I was the first in many long years at least, if not the first ever. Sure enough, folk saw the little dragons from time to time, though there didn't seem to be many of them—but they were shy, skittish creatures for the most part and stayed away from people. I didn't have time to think about that or about what to expect, I just ran in to keep dry.

There was some light from an opening overhead, in fact, the whole wall at the back was lit from above, though just at the moment it was right dim and there was more rain coming in than light. There was a smell in there of decay and illness, but it wasn't overpowering. Just one small heap of half-digested something in a corner that had come back up, and one or two piles of not-quite-covered droppings away to one side. Otherwise it was dry and bare, almost you'd call it clean. No skulls, no bones, but no gold either. I was almost disappointed, when I had the time to think about it. I'd heard dragons slept on a pile of treasure and human bones.

Well, I walked in and stood with my back against the wall near the entrance, and the kitling came up to me. I don't know if it didn't like rain or was just so desperate with need it would take any kind of comfort, but it came right up against me and stared into my eyes. I kneeled down again to get closer and it reached up its long neck so we were nose to nose. I couldn't resist, I reached out and let it smell my hand. It sniffed once, briefly, then slid its head under my hand.

That did it. I sat down with my back to the wall and patted it, my hand light on its scales. They were smooth, like nothing I'd ever felt before, and the colour of bright copper. If it were now, I'd say they felt like finest silk, but I'd never seen silk then. Its hide was warm to the touch. It worked its way closer, carefully at first, slowly, as if still not sure whether I'd up of a sudden and treat it ill—then all in a moment it gave in and just crawled into my lap.

I'd had enough dogs in my day to know that they mourn every bit as much as people do, but this was worse. It knew more, somehow, and its misery was the deeper for knowing what it had lost. I could do no more than hold it, speak to it, let it feel a fellow creature's touch and know it wasn't all alone in the world. That's about all anyone can do around death in any case.

Eventually it slept, right there in my lap. I hadn't the heart to move it even after the rain stopped. I was amazed as I sat there, my back against the wall, the weary little dragon curled warm in my lap like a great cat, its half-formed wings tucked neatly along its sides, the tip of the tail resting under its cheek. I felt light-headed, trying to understand the strangeness of it one moment, the next knowing full well that the creature would have gone to a cow for comfort as readily as it came to me, I just happened to be passing.

I thought hard as it slept, for I knew fine that kitling needed food, but I had no notion what the creatures ate aside from salerian flowers. What did I have in my house, what could I catch—come to that, how old was it, and was it going to die because I didn't know how to make up for its mother's milk?

That at least I dismissed, first because I didn't know if dragons made milk in any case, and second because I took a good look at the fangs sticking out from its lower jaw. Those were made to tear meat, sure as life. I wondered if it would be happy enough with rabbit, which was all I had in my larder, or if I would have to fight to keep it off my chickens.

Just then it woke and stretched, and it near broke my heart. I knew that moment, I'd done the same when I woke the morning after we laid our mother in the earth—the first time you wake after such a shock and it all seems no more than a bad dream just for that very first instant. That stretch was utterly natural for one heartbeat—then it stopped and contracted, just like a person thinking, *My world has changed I'm alone I can't stretch or breathe or move as I did before, ever again.* It was startled and scrambled away from me quick, sharp, scratching me with its claws as it went. That hurt, I can tell you for nothing. I yelled and it stopped running and looked back. I was angry and I scolded it. Damn stupid thing to do, but it's hard to fear a creature that has slept on you, and those claws had been sharp.

"Look now what you've done, Salera. What was that for? Here I sit with you for comfort, wasting away my morning, and I get ripped trews and a handful of scratches for my pains. What would yer mam have said, eh? Is that the way to treat a friend?"

Well, it was full awake now, and damned if it didn't come

back to my hand, even tried to lick the scratches on my leg as if it was sorry.

Believe me or not, when I left that cave, the little creature came along behind. I had a brew heating at home, I had to get back before the fire died out entirely, and bless me if Salera didn't follow me all the way to my house. I stoked the fire, stirred the brew, then went to my little larder and brought out the rabbit I'd caught. I sighed just a little as I realised I'd have only roots for my own supper.

I took the carcass out to Salera. She had stopped to drink at the stream that runs by the edge of the clearing to the north, whence we'd come. I'd cleared only enough land for my house and a little vegetable patch. I've always thought that trees deserve life as much as we do.

She—well, yes, I was only guessing she was female, but I couldn't think of her as "it," and somehow she struck me more as a she than a he—anyroad, she came in a hurry when she smelled the meat. That was the real shock, though: she sat back on her haunches, took the carcass gently from my hand with her front claws—her hands—and ate that rabbit like any lady, save that she took only three bites to do it and crunched the bones as she went.

Poor thing. Game isn't very plentiful, that time of the year. She licked her claws, then licked my hand clean even of the scent, then walked very calmly to the stream and washed.

I couldn't think what to do with her, but in the end it wasn't really up to me. She stayed with me all that year, through summer and harvest and all through the winter, until spring was come again. She had grown quite a bit in that year, must have been nearly her full height, for towards the third moon of the year it was like living with a horse in the house. I was grateful for my own height and strength then, for I could just about make her shift herself when I needed her to move. Still, she had learned for the most part not to knock things over. She slept in front of the fire and I moved my chair well to one side, and we managed well enough.

By the end of that year I couldn't imagine life without her.

We had been constant companions. I had hunted for her, fed her up—and that took some doing, I'll tell you for nothing—but when she was old enough and strong enough, just after the Autumn Balance-day, she got the idea, and after that she provided for me. I ate better that winter than ever I had, enough that I could share with others in the nearby village who were in need of a bit of help and grateful indeed for meat in winter.

And she was someone to talk to. I spoke to her as to another soul, and though I don't think she understood my words, she seemed to try to reply. As time went on, I almost thought I heard a word every now and then. I must have been a little daft.

In spring, though, when the first warm wind blew through my little clearing, when I'd just put the early vegetables in the ground, she came out and felt the breeze. She lifted her head, sniffed for all she was worth, and spread her wings. She'd had trouble with them as they were growing, when the skin and the tendons stretched it bothered her, and I'd tried all my simples until I found a few that helped her. A soft ointment made with oil, mint, pepper and a scented resin, much as I'd use to salve an old man's bones in winter, seemed to work best, and she chose the resin herself. Nosed it off the shelf, she did, while I was wondering what would be best. It would be one of the ones I have to trade for, and to be honest it convinced me I'd been right about her being female. I usually saved it for perfumes to sell at market, but—well, I couldn't deny her, now could I? So she not only had her pains soothed, she smelled of the most amazing combination of exotic perfume and dragon.

However, when I saw her ruffling her wings like that, I got a feeling I didn't like. I knew the time was coming. It wasn't natural for either of us, living together, and though she had taken well enough to my ways they were not hers. I hoped she'd be able to learn to fly on her own, though. Not as if I could teach her!

Didn't need to. She tried a few times, flapping and looking terribly awkward, then somehow she managed to stay aloft for a moment or two. That did it. She just kept at it after that, and by the next moon she was flying better than I thought was possible for the creatures. I had always heard they could barely fly, but she seemed to manage it without any trouble.

Then one morning, as spring was drawing towards summer, I rose after her and found her in the most open bit of the clearing. She was waiting for me. I don't know how I knew, but I did. She was leaving and this was farewell. I walked straight up to her and she watched my every step. I put my arms around her neck and hugged her, and she wrapped her wings about me just for a moment.

It felt like saying farewell to a daughter, and I couldn't just let her go like that, could I? So I held her big face in my hands and gazed into her eyes. "Fare thee well, then, my Salera," I said, stroking her cheek ridge. "Kitling. Lady keep you wherever you fare, little one. I'll miss you. Fly well and strong."

She closed her eyes and touched my forehead to hers, that bump on her forehead warm against my own brow—she was always so warm to the touch—then she straightened up and looked at me. She said something then, I'd swear, but even after all that time I couldn't understand it. I think I tried in my mind to make it sound like my name, but in truth it was a long way off from that.

"Lady keep you," I murmured, and stood back. She crouched, then leapt, her great haunches launching her into the air, her wings sweeping down, beating fast. I watched her flapping madly until she found warm air. Then she stretched out her wings and rose smoothly in a gliding spiral upwards. I give you my word, she was the most beautiful thing I'd ever seen. She turned her face south—deeper into the forest, towards the Súlkith Hills—and was gone.

"Blast the child, she's trodden all over my new lavender," I muttered. "Wretched dragon. She never did look where she was going in the garden." Then I realised I'd walked on fully half of the new plants myself and broken most of them, and I started to swear at her, at myself, at the seedlings for being in the wrong place. I was so angry I could hardly see straight.

Well, it might have been anger.

I never saw her again, though I surely did look. I stayed there another two years, tending my garden, helping those I could, selling my potions and oils and perfumes at the market, waiting for Salera. She never came back. In the end I decided I had to find out what I could about her kind, for I'd never known a thing save what I learned from her, and she was raised by me, poor soul.

The only place I knew to go was Verfaren, where the Healers are trained. I'd heard they had a library, writings from as far back as writing went. Surely someone must have studied the creatures in all those years. So I packed up my bits, left the door open and the fire laid just in case she returned, and went to learn what I could at the College of Mages.

That was seven, nearly eight years ago now. I learned what there was to learn but I had to search the library through to find it. I helped in the garden to earn my keep. In time I came to know the library so well that when the master of the books was taken ill, he asked me to stay and help. I stayed, and helped, and when he passed on I was asked by Magister Berys himself if I would take the books for my work. I told him true that I hadn't come planning to stay, but that if he was willing I'd stay awhile, until my way was clear to me and it was time to leave.

"And when will that be?" he asks me.

"When the wind's right and the sky calls," I answered. It wasn't respectful, but then I never liked him. To be honest I was only staying to honour old Paulin. "And I'll not give up the garden."

He just laughed, and said that if I knew the books and didn't mind the students, it was good enough for him, and he'd get a gardener into the bargain. So I've stayed on here, learning what I could, getting to know a few of the students passing through, enjoying their different views on life and learning. The only difficulty I have is putting up every year with the new young girls, who find a tall, fair-haired man not so much older than themselves a great temptation, or perhaps a challenge. I'm not boasting, you understand, it's all a bit wearisome as far as I'm concerned. I can't help my looks, and I don't encourage or take advantage of the girls.

However, it has changed me, being around so much learning. I've read everything I could find, and I speak differently now than I used to. You can't read so many words without starting to use some of them. My sister laughs at me but I think she is secretly impressed. She was the only other person who ever knew Salera and she misses her. I go back home occasionally, to visit with Lyra and to make sure my cottage in the wood has not fallen down. In fact I was there before midwinter just past, making all snug before the frost set in. I still returned to Verfaren though, to see in the new year, despite the fact that I have never felt that I belonged here. I have never felt the need to go back home, either.

Until a few years ago, when I met Vilkas and Aral. Interesting that almost the only lass who has been able to see me as no more than a friend from the beginning has been Aral, and that she has captured my heart so completely.

Life does that to you sometimes, when you're not looking.

Maikel

I was speechless with wonder. "Marik? My lord?" I whispered, not daring to believe what I saw.

"Who did you think it was, Maikel? And what's wrong with your eyes?" he asked, frowning at me. Berys laughed.

"He has not been well, Marik. Worn out with fussing over you. Still, you are both under my protection now, so there is no need for concern."

Marik seemed to get angry at that but he was not really strong enough for anger yet. "For now," he murmured. Why he should be angry at Berys's words I could not understand. I worried for a moment that he was not as fully recovered as he seemed.

"How is your leg, master?" I asked.

He seemed surprised. He glanced down and flexed the muscles. "It hardly hurts at all."

"Wait until you stand up," chuckled Berys. "Maikel tells me you have been unable to get out of that bed for more than five minutes together ever since you returned, and that has been full four moons by my reckoning. It is time you took some exercise." He grabbed the blankets and tugged them off the bed. "Come, man, it's midmorning, time you were up and doing."

The Magister dragged my Lord Marik out of bed and got him to stand, which is more than I had managed to do for many months, but I barely noticed it. He was weak, he was disoriented, but he was himself again. His mind was healed. I could scarcely believe it. I had not yet dispersed my Healer's sight and without thinking I used it to look into his mind.

No longer did I see that desert that had haunted me for so long. His mind appeared at first glance to be much like any other, bright with flashing thought and swirling with colour, but there was an obvious difference just below the surface.

I know not how I may explain this to you. Imagine a hut made of twigs and branches of all different shapes and sizes. At first glance it appears solid, but when you look closely you see that it has been made hurriedly from shoddy materials, and the nails that hold it together are poorly forged and too short. It looks whole but one good wind would blow it to pieces. Or a bridge—yes, that's it, imagine a single slim bridge spanning an abyss, barely long enough to reach across. There are no handrails and it shakes at every step. It is possible to cross, but the link is dangerously weak and could shatter at any time.

For a moment I stared at Berys, horrified. He had not healed Marik, he had patched him together with thin cord and weak glue. It was a dreadful, irresponsible thing to do, for if that patch came undone my lord would be worse off than before. The undermind trusts only once. If Marik's mind shattered this fragile link, it would never accept Berys's healing again. It would probably never accept any healing again.

I looked up to protest, then thought better of it. Best not to mention such a thing in Marik's presence. I must speak to Magister Berys later, alone.

In the meantime, Marik practiced walking. He was dreadfully weak, as might be expected, but he managed a few steps several times that day. And he finally ate real food, not just the infants' mush we had managed to get down him before.

Perhaps the mend would hold. Certainly the habit of sanity was the best cure. The longer he remained well, the stronger his mind would become. But I didn't like the slapdash way he had been healed, and I resolved to say something about it when I could catch Berys on his own.

Salera

I sought him then, following instinct, even as I trembled at the thought of the journey before me and wondered if I could find the place where I was raised. I had travelled far and wide in the years between and was not certain where to look, but there lived in my mind a quiet woodland up in the hills, where there was a cave once and pain, and a house in a clearing with a stream at the side. I knew somehow in the confused heart of me that it was there I would find him.

As I followed the mind's trace that drew me to him, I saw many of my own kindred in passing. Some came to me with a glad sound and that was very good. I saw more than I had dreamt there might be and my heart knew joy at the seeing. But as night follows day so there is darkness in all things, and I also passed many of the Hollow Ones. They were shaped as we but there was nothing within them but pale fire and the need for food. They turned upon one another, rending in anger where kinship was lost, and my blood grew cold as the ice beneath my feet when I saw them.

I travelled long, by sun and moon, flying where I could, walking when I had to, seeking any sign of him or of my old home on the ground or in the air. I stopped to eat and sleep as need found me and hope carried me, until finally I began to recognise the land. The trees were naked so early in the year, though I remem-

bered them with white flowers and red berries, but it was the
same place. We had walked here together of a morning. I was
come home.

   Alas, his smell was cold, and my tail dragged in the dust that
lay soft and gentle upon the threshold. I did not smell death, but
neither did I smell present life. But there was food to be had in the
wood, and water and shelter, and I could keep myself strong as
I awaited his coming. For I knew in my soul that he would come,
as I knew that day followed darkness. I had only to wait and
watch.

viii

Journeys

Shikrar

The moon was dark. Full six se'ennights had passed since the night of the earthshakes that had wakened me from my Weh sleep.

My dear son Kédra and I waited in the entry to the Chamber of Souls, watching the sun set. The winter days were growing longer, noticeably so now, but the cold had returned with a vengeance. Frost was in the air, sharp and clear, and this night there would be no moonlight to soften the ice with beauty.

Kédra was fully trained in the Kin-Summoning but I had decided that this time I should undergo the fasting and meditation, for he still kept watch over his youngling. However, it was not necessary to spend every waking hour in preparation. Even though I had to keep to my chamber for the full fortnight before the Kin-Summoning, to fast and to quiet my soul, Kédra brought young Sherók to visit me every day to lighten the waiting.

The little one was astounding and filled me with delight. I

had forgotten how swiftly they change when they are so very small. Each day he was more steady on his feet, each day it seemed that his wings grew. It would not be many months now before they were in proportion to the rest of him. He was already making the sounds that would flower into speech, and soon thereafter he would begin to send his thought-pictures to more than his mother and father. True-speech was still a few years in the future, of course, but after a mere quarter of a year he was grown half again as large as he had been at birthing.

He was lighter in the scales than his father, for his mother, Mirazhe, was a burnished brass, and his colouring was somewhere between that and Kédra's dark bronze, but his eyes were golden as an autumn sky and beautiful beyond words. When his soulgem was revealed he would receive his true name, but that would not be for nearly a year. The gem is too soft at birth to be uncovered and has a natural scale of skin that protects it. Eventually, when the soulgem has hardened, sometime in the first year, the scale dries and falls off. It is the first coming of age, the first step towards life as one of the Kantri, and a time of great rejoicing.

His very life was rejoicing to me. Every time I saw him, every time I picked him up and held him close, wrapped him in my wings, laughed with him, played with him, I saw behind him the form of Lanen the Wanderer, who had saved his life and that of his mother on the very day of his birth. And sometimes I imagined, or felt in my heart as deep longing, my lost Yrais. She was my one true soulmate, mother to my own Kédra and more dear to me by far than my own flesh: but she had died young, when Kédra was yet a littling. I had never stopped missing her, and from time to time of late I found myself speaking to the air, telling her of her new grandson. How proud she would have been.

The last rim of the sun disappeared behind low cloud. "It is time, my father," said Kédra. He bowed to me, then stood in the formal Attitude of Respect. I was hard put to it not to laugh, he was being so serious, but I did manage to contain myself. I bowed in return and mirrored his stance. "Let us approach the Ancestors, in all humility, in this our time of need."

I took one last deep breath of the night air and turned back in to my chambers. Kédra remained until I should call him.

All was prepared within. With a brief invocation to the Winds, I drew breath and sent Fire into the heart of the wood piled high in the firepit, for Fire is sacred to us and the Kin-Summoning a solemn duty and honour. Light blossomed with the heart of flame, flickering and gleaming off the walls and the floor of *khaadish,* set thick with the soulgems of the Ancestors. I cast onto the blaze certain leaves and branches, representing each of the Winds. They made a sweet smoke, which I inhaled deeply.

I had fasted full a fortnight in preparation and so was light-headed to begin with. The smell of *kirik* and *tel-aster, merisakis* and *hlansif* (that the Gedri call lansip) rose and blended in the still air of the cavern. The fire shone bright on the gathered soulgems.

The back wall of the inner cavern was studded with them. They were ranged in order, eldest highest, set deep in *khaadish* to protect them. Now, you must not imagine that set in that wall was every soulgem of every one of the Kantri who had ever lived. Even apart from the soulgems of the Lost, with their never-ending flicker of light and darkness, it had been several lifetimes after the Choice before we had learned of the Kin-Summoning. Also, it had happened from time to time that some of us had died in far-off places with none to retrieve our soulgems and bring them home in honour. I bowed before them all, with a private thought of sorrow over the newest of them—the soulgem of Rishkaan, who had died in the autumn fighting a demon master. He had killed the *rakshadakh* who had threatened us though it had cost him his life. "Lie safe on the Winds, old friend," I muttered, then turned back to the fire and settled down, still breathing deeply of the smoke, and began the Invocation.

"In the Name of the Winds, humble I call upon thee, Ancients of our Kindred. O ye who sleep, graciously wake ye to listen. We who live call upon thee in our need. Lend us thy wisdom, speak again in accents of life, teach us who are thy children those things that are needful. Hear, speak, aid us. It is one of thine own who calls. I hight Hadretikantishikrar, of the line of Issdra. I beseech thee in the name of our people, speak."

Kédra heard me and entered the Chamber, sitting far from the fire. I nodded at him, knowing I was protected now, and let my mind follow the smoke out the airhole far above.

I felt myself rising as on wings of mist even as I knew that I sat solidly on the ground. It is almost impossible to describe the sensation. I am told that the Gedri when they are desperately ill can feel something akin to it. My eyes would not focus but my mind was sharp and aware. Kédra tried to bespeak me, and when he could not he knew the time was come.

"O my ancestors, I summon thee," he said. "It is Khétrikharissdra of the line of Issdra who calls. The Gift of the Choice of the Kantrishakrim, the way to remember what has gone before, is needed sore by thy children. My father Hadretikantishikrar, the Keeper of Souls, stands near to welcome thee."

I felt my throat change, and in the voice, much deeper and harsher than mine, that takes me at such times, I responded, "Speak, Khétrikharissdra. What so concerns the living that they take counsel with the dead?"

"Revered Ones, we have two questions for thee. First, we seek knowledge of the firefields of our homeland, the Place of Exile." That is how we name the Dragon Isle in our own language. "The earth shakes with greater violence than any now living have known. The mountains burn and run like water. Revered Ones, know ye aught of this?"

I felt myself falling again, down deep under earth and clear water, and rose with a different voice. It was lighter and more resonant than the Speaker. I had never heard it before.

"I bring thee greetings, Khétrikharissdra. I hight Khemirnakunakhor. In life I was called Keakhor, who led our people to the Place of Exile after the Day Without End. It was I who had found it long years before, for in those times I was a wide-traveller, flying to the limits of strength for the joy of it. I it was who saw the Isle much as thou hast described it, many years ere we arrived. But surely the earthshakes have never stopped, my child? What so stirs thee, thus to waken us?"

Kédra bowed again. "Of thy courtesy, Keakhor, see in the mind of thy vessel, my father Shikrar, that which we fear. He hath overflown the firefields. They burn in his mind and he hath known no rest from that sight."

I felt the touch, gentle, ancient, of that mind upon my own. I felt its surprise.

"Thou hast done well, Keeper of Souls, to summon us." I felt my head and neck bowing to Kédra. "Would that I had better tidings for thee. At the worst, when we feared for the life of the island itself, there was not half so much fire." I could feel the astonishment of Keakhor whistling through me. "Name of the Winds, youngling, if thy seeing be true the very mountains begin to melt like snow in summer." My head shook, sadly. "I fear me thou art in peril, my child, that all the Kantri are in peril, but I can be of no service to thee. The like hath never before been seen by any of us."

Kédra bowed. "I thank thee, Revered One, nonetheless. And from thine own words, it would seem that thou are the best source for my second question. Far-traveller, Keakhor, who didst lead the Kantri to the Place of Exile, knowest thou aught of other lands apart from Kolmar where we might live? For thou hast seen the doom that awaits us here. If we are to seek another home, where must we fly to find it?"

Keakhor within me sighed. "Alas, youngling, again the truth I have for thee is not what thou wouldst hear. In life I flew high and wide, sleeping on the winds, seeking new lands. Thrice I came near death for that I had nowhere to rest or to drink. Keeper of Souls, there is no land that we can reach save Kolmar. West, south, north, there is only the vast ocean. Do not forget that Kolmar is our home, littling. Perhaps it calls us back. If you must fly there, know that two days east and a little south there is a small island with sweet water, where younglings and the wing-weary may rest for a time. I know of no other lands."

Kédra responded swiftly, "Then I thank thee, Keakhor, for thy visitation, I honour thee for thy wisdom, and I release thee to sleep again on the Winds. Go in peace."

"I go, littling, but do not let thy good father waken yet. There is one here who would speak, if thou wilt hear her."

Even in the depths of my trance I was surprised. I had heard of this happening, when I was trained by Leealissenit, but it had never happened to me before. Kédra nodded. "If there is one who would speak, we honour and welcome her. Farewell, Khemirnakunakhor."

"The Winds bear thee up, youngling," said the ancient one, kindly, and was gone. Again the feeling of falling, dizziness, then caught up all in a moment by another.

Oh no. No, please, I cannot bear it.

"I give you greeting, my Khétri—what are you called, my littling?" said the one who spoke through me. It was the wonder of the Kin-Summoning that I could hear her voice and not mine. Oh, my heart.

I knew that voice as I knew the air that I breathed. It was Yrais, my beloved, my soul's other half. I had not heard it in eight hundred years.

Kédra was shaken, though he knew not why. "I am called Kédra. Who speaks?" he asked, his voice heavy with awe.

"I am your mother, Khétrikharissdra," she said. Kédra shivered to hear his true name spoken, but not with fear. The love in her voice could not be mistaken.

I knew that tone in her voice, she only ever used it when she spoke with me or with our son. *Oh, ye Winds, bear me up in this.* "Littling, I cannot stay, but when Keakhor looked in your father's mind he saw bright and shining your own son. Know that Shekrialanentierók is known to me now, for all time, and know that my love comes to him through your father."

Yrais!

"Fare you well in all your travails, my kit, you and Mirazhe your beloved and Sherók your son, and may the Winds carry you safe wherever you fare."

And she was gone, save for a sweet gentle touch on my mind as she left—a phrase, an echo, of the Song of the Devoted we had made together so very long ago.

I rose out of the trance of the Kin-Summoning racked with a pain I had thought long since healed. It was forbidden to call up the Ancestors for personal reasons. I had never dreamt to hear her voice again.

Kédra came near and held me, helpless, as I cried out my agony to the Winds. Sorrow endless as the long years, longing like torture pierced my breast, against which the pain of the end of the Kin-Summoning passed unnoticed.

Unless you have lost one you truly love you may not understand, but I would gladly have fought demons to have been spared that sweet, gentle touch, that voice so well beloved and so swiftly silenced forever, and the memory of a song I would never hear again this side of death.

Maikel

Soon after my lord Marik was restored to himself, Berys arranged for us all to leave my master's home in the Merchant quarter of Elimar. We were to take up residence in Verfaren so that Magister Berys might continue his work at the College while looking after Marik. We travelled slowly: what should have been little more than ten days' journey even in winter took nearly a fortnight, and it was hard on my master even so. I spent several days simply helping him recover from travelling.

Once he was feeling better both Berys and I took a great deal of time working with him, helping him to walk and, eventually, to ride again. His recovery was wonderfully swift, all things considered, but I was still concerned. The vision of his patched-together mind haunted me.

It was late one night towards the end of the second moon of the year, just as the worst of the winter was leaving and the days were getting longer, before I had the chance to speak to Berys alone. My master was asleep. He had ridden some few miles through the fields that day and eaten well afterwards, all good signs. I was delighted to see him doing so well, even as I feared it was but temporary.

I knew that Berys could not be working so late on anything of importance, but I was passing his chambers last thing at night on the way to my own and saw a light under the door. I knocked quietly and to my surprise was answered immediately by his servant Durstan. He welcomed me and took me in to Berys's study after only a very short wait. I found him seated behind his desk, plainly busy but pleasant enough.

"Master Maikel," he said, nodding to me. "You are welcome. I trust our patient is no worse?"

"He recovers still, Magister," I replied, somewhat absentmindedly. There was a peculiar smell in the room and I was trying to think what it was. I thought I remembered it from somewhere.

"Then what brings you here?" he asked, smiling.

It was difficult to say, he seemed so kind and so concerned, but I knew I had to say something. "Magister, I have sought the chance to confer with you about Marik. I fear for him."

"In what way?" he asked, genuinely surprised. "Has his condition deteriorated?"

"No, he is as he has been since you healed his mind," I said. "But—"

After a moment's silence, he said rather more pointedly, "But what, Healer Maikel?"

"It's not right." I managed to get the words out. "Magister, I have the greatest respect for what you have done, but I have seen his mind. It was lost and broken, and true enough you have healed it, but the healing is patchy and largely on the surface. The break is still there, the rift between sanity and madness, and the bridge is very insecure. It would take very little to drive him back across and very little more for him to fall off altogether. My fear is that he would then be worse off than before."

"Are you questioning my methods?" asked Berys, smiling. "He has done nothing but improve since I brought him back. He grows stronger every day, mind and body. What you are objecting to, Maikel?"

"I—well—forgive me, but yes, Magister, I question your method. I admire beyond words that you have brought my master back from that dry, dead place, but surely a slower approach would have had more lasting results. This patch, this overlay of healing—I fear it cannot last." There. I had said it.

Berys stood up from behind his desk. He came close to me and stared into my eyes. "Hmmm. Seems to be wearing off."

"What, already?" I asked, shocked. Did he know something of Marik that I did not? Surely that fragile sanity was not breaking already.

He laughed, a sharp, unpleasant sound. "I was not speaking of Marik. No, he will last some time yet. Perhaps in time my quick work will take root, though I do not know. However, he is well now. Is that not what you desired?"

"Not this way," I said. Suddenly I was reminded of my old reservations about Magister Berys. I had perhaps been too critical, but there was still something wrong about him. Something about his eyes—oh Goddess. What were Marik's first words to me? Not a simple greeting, not so much as "Hello Maikel," no, he'd said "What's wrong with your eyes?" I had wondered at the time. Now of a sudden I was frantic to be gone, to look in a mirror, to see if I had the same taint as Berys. In the same breath I remembered what the curious smell was.

Raksha-trace.

Dear Lady, see me safe out of here, I begged silently.

Her answer was swift in coming.

Lanen

It was raining. It had been raining for-bloody-ever. The weather had turned foul a week after that fight in the dark, with a cold rain driven by a colder wind, and I had caught a sniffle that would not go away. We had been rained on for what felt like a solid fortnight: as we crossed the Arlen to travel south through the western reaches of the North Kingdom, as we rode through fields and woods to keep off the main roads, as we seemed to crawl our way south: sometimes harder, sometimes no more than a gentle mist that got into our packs and soaked everything, sometimes just a dreary never-ending drip all day long.

The Spring Balance-day was still more than a fortnight away. We'd been travelling a full moon and a fortnight on every back road in Kolmar ever since the night the mercenaries had attacked, with never a sniff of an inn or a hostel, and it had been raining forever.

Well, it felt like forever. When your best fire is a few tiny flames dancing on a stick for a few hours, believe me, patience and understanding fly out the window in a hurry. Jamie was growling at Rella, Rella was growling at me, and I was growling at everybody. Varien, maddeningly, was calm and unruffled. He was making me furious, but then, so was everything. In my poor defence I should say that the voices in my head had not stopped. They seemed to come in waves, sometimes loud enough to stop me from being able to think, sometimes barely there at the edge of hearing. I couldn't decide which was worse, but I was heartily sick of them and of everything else, especially myself. At least there had been no more attacks, thank the Lady for small favours.

Jamie had spent a little time every day training both Varien and me in swordplay. I was very little better than when I had started, but Varien seemed to take to it like breathing, and after less than two moons he was better at it than I was. This, of course, made me terribly jealous.

I seemed to spend every waking moment in a foul mood. I did try to fight it, but for some reason every least little thing made me snarl.

"Lanen, how fare you?" asked Varien quietly when we stopped in the poor shelter of some ancient trees to take our midday meal. At least the rain wasn't quite so hard there.

"Just as I've fared every time you've asked," I growled. "I can't get any peace, inside my head or out." I stomped away, looking for any vestige of dry wood I could find. I didn't find any.

We ate cold bread and cheese and strips of salted meat that were drier than we were. "I swear to you," grumbled Jamie, who was not much better off than I was, "if this keeps up much longer there'll be murder done."

"Stop bragging," said Rella. She was for some reason in better heart than she had been for some days. "We're nearly there."

"Nearly where?" I asked.

"There's a way station half a day's ride from here."

"And what is that?" asked Varien. "Of your good heart, lady, tell us that it hath a fire and shelter from the rain."

"No and yes," she replied. "There is nowhere to light a fire, in case it should smoke, but way stations have roofs and four walls and a dry floor, and there is always a stock of dry wood for the taking. There are also things there more precious than lansip, if none have been there before me."

She refused to tell us what she was talking about, but the thought of a solid roof over my head sounded wonderful, even without a fire. We all cheered up a little, and the voices grew that bit quieter for a while. It just shows that anticipation is a strong influence. Just as well. When we finally came upon the way station, it had grown even darker than the grey murk we had travelled through all day, and it took Rella a few minutes to find it even though she knew what she was looking for. It was well hidden, certainly. It was also no more and no less than she had said. When Jamie finally managed to light a stub of candle, we saw that we were in a small room with four low walls, a roof that kept out the rain but was so low that Varien and I couldn't stand upright, a small chest against a corner, a tiny grille high up in a corner to let in air, no windows and no place for a fire. I started grumbling and threatened to light a fire on the floor as I piled the wet saddles and other tack in a corner. The horses were in a sheltered brake; we'd fed and watered them, but the poor things had naught but the wet ground to sleep on. They each had two blankets, and we had to hope that would do.

"And how will you start a fire in here without setting light to your own foot?" said Rella, offended. "Honestly, girl, you're foul-tempered these days. Have some consideration for those of us who have to live with you. This is a way station of the Silent Service, not the common room of an inn! If anyone found out I'd let you in at all, I'd lose a month's wages and have to stock way stations until the next quarter day. There's nowhere for the smoke to go in any case. It's well sealed, though, and with all four of us sleeping here we'll be warm enough and dry for a change, and there are candles enough to keep a light as long as we want. That reminds me." She took the candle and carried it to the chest. When she opened it she laughed with delight. "Oh, the Goddess bless the poor bastard who's in disgrace! Dry blankets, by Shia, and enough waterproofs for all!"

She started hauling out bundles of folded material and handing them round, a blanket each and another bundle. These last were surprisingly heavy, but when I took my sodden leather gloves off I felt the curious texture. It was like a medium-weight burlap, a finer weave than I had expected, but it smelled of something that wasn't cloth. I sniffed.

"Beeswax," said Jamie, grinning. "Waxed cloth, by the Lady! Mistress Rella, I beg your forgiveness, and grant you mine despite the fact that I'm frozen to the bone." He stripped off his sodden tunic, wrapped himself in a dry blanket, put the waxed cloth over all and settled down with his back to a wall. "Blessings upon the Silent Service, I'll never curse them again without good cause," he said, and Rella laughed.

"Why doesn't the wax break when the cloth bends?" I asked, copying Jamie. The dry blanket was the first real warmth I'd felt since we got soaked through two nights since, and though the waxed cloth wasn't warm in itself it kept the heat in and I began to thaw a little. Varien sat beside me and wrapped the two of us in his cloth. He was, as always, nearly hot to the touch, bless him.

"None of your business," said Rella smugly. "Why do you think we're called the Silent Service?"

"How far are we from the Kai, do you think?" I asked. I had tried not to ask that every night for the past week. I was losing the battle.

To my delight Jamie said, "I am not certain of these roads, but unless I am far out of my reckoning we should strike the river in the next day or so."

Rella raised an eyebrow in approval. "Not bad for one who's been on a farm for a quarter of a century. I expect to reach Kaibar tomorrow," she said.

"Where we will find an inn, with a large fireplace and a real bed and hot food and cold beer," said Jamie. "I don't care if every assassin ever spawned is after our blood, I am going to sleep in a bed tomorrow night."

"Hear, hear," I said. "If I could get warm enough and stay warm, maybe I could shake this blasted cold."

"You won't get any argument from me," said Rella. "My back is killing me. I've been ignoring it something shocking ever since we started out."

I tended to forget about Rella's crooked back. She had exaggerated it when I first met her, to appear helpless and crippled in the presence of my father Marik, but it was not a disguise she could do off. I hadn't known how it bothered her until we started travelling together. She was made of stern stuff, but the cold and the wet got into her bones and every now and then she'd swear at the ache. Varien had taken to sitting back-to-back with her when we had our meagre meals, for she said the heat was a great relief. Still, that very morning she had not been able to contain the groan when she mounted her horse.

She wasn't the only one. My long back was starting to bother me too, and to add insult to injury I had a growing sense of discomfort below the waist. I had taken to running alongside the horses as often as I could stand it. It wasn't that I was getting fat, really, but I felt the way I did each moon just before my blood time. I was concerned, because I was a week past that time, and still my fingers were swollen, and my belly, and I had to wear a breast band to keep the soreness at bay. My bloods had been much lighter and shorter of late as well. I felt decidedly peculiar below the waist, and I could seldom eat much. Half of what went down came back up again later, but I tried to keep that as secret as I could. I put all down to short rations, too much cold and too much riding. The idea of a night in an inn—or two if I could convince the others—sounded like heaven. A chance to clean my clothing, my hair, my grubby self—blessed Lady, what a delight! And perhaps, I said in my inner thoughts, a good long visit with a Healer.

As we began to relax and to warm ourselves, I asked sleepily, "So, we are near to the South Kingdom at last. I have never been there. What is it like, Jamie?"

"Much like anywhere else," he grumped, but his heart wasn't in it, for he let out a muffled laugh. "Now, there's a thing. I never thought."

"What?"

"That's where the little dragons live."

"What!" I asked again, more sharply now, and I could feel Varien beside me sit straight up.

"You're right, Jamie. I'd forgotten. Well, you almost never see them, do you?" said Rella. "Shy creatures they are. I have only seen a few in my travels, though that's not so surprising, they don't go where they know there are men." Her voice softened in the darkness. "They are quite beautiful, really."

"The Lesser Kindred, kadreshi," said Varien in true-speech, as excited as exhaustion would allow. *"It is well. Perhaps we shall find them a little more easily, you and I."*

We slept sitting up in that tiny way station, drier than we had been but still damp around the edges and not really warm enough, and dreamed of the simplest of pleasures. Being warm and dry may not sound like much, but it is the very stuff of heaven if you can't get it. As I drifted off to sleep, trying to ignore the voices that were now muttering constantly just below hearing, I almost smiled. For years I had wanted to see the wide world and move out of the four confining walls that I felt were drawing in around me. *I had heard that all things come full circle at the last, Lanen, but surely this is a bit quick even for you*, I thought sleepily to myself.

It was only just over the half of a year since I had first set out from my home.

That thought was nearly enough to keep me awake. Nearly.

Varien

I waited until they were all asleep. It did not take long. Indeed, the most difficult part was to remain wakeful myself, for I was weary and the dry blanket was a blessing. Still, it had been far too long. I missed my people.

I drew my soulgem in its circlet from my pack and put it on.

The moment my soulgem touched my skin I felt Shikrar's presence. I knew that feeling: it was as if he called me without words. We did so often, he and I, when troubled or lonely.

"Hadreshikrar, my brother, I hear you. What weighs so weary on your heart?"

"Akhor!" he cried, and I found myself in the centre of a wild storm of emotion that overpowered words. I feared at first that something had happened to Kédra, but I swiftly bespoke him and was answered.

"Lord Akhor! Blessed be the Winds! My father is in need of you."

"Kédra, what is it? You sound almost as bad! Shikrar, soulfriend, I beseech you tell me what wrings your heart so. I hear your pain, my heart aches with it, yet Kédra is well. This is—" I stopped, stunned. *"Shikrar, how—what hath befallen thee? I know this sadness of thine from of old, from my youth, yet it bleedeth like a new wound. It cannot be—"*

To my intense relief, I began to hear at least the slightest hint of recovery in his reply. *"Akhor, soulfriend, thy voice is balm to my shattered soul. Alas, Akhorishaan! It was the*

Kin-Summoning—it has only just come to an end. Akhor—I could not stop her. Yrais—Yrais—she spoke through me, she spoke to Kédra with her blessings for young Sherók. I heard her voice, her words, felt the touch of her soul—ah, my heart. Akhor, Akhor, it was **Yrais***.*"

I bowed, so far away as I was and despite the pain in my head that was growing steadily worse. Shikrar had been mated for so short a time before Yrais was taken from us. Their love had been remarkable among a passionate people, and Shikrar's grief had been deep as the sea and nearly as boundless. *"I have no words, heart's friend, soulfriend. Is there aught to be done?"*

"No, Akhor, do not fear for me. I begin to recover. But oh, alas for that wound that will never heal!"

I would have been shocked at his anguish had I not known how deep was Shikrar's love and how long grief had claimed him after her death. I could only call his name, sending my friendship without words to comfort him. It was a blessing that he had the ordeal of the Kin-Summoning behind him, for as soon as the worst of his grieving was past, as soon as he felt my mind-touch and that of his son and felt our love and friendship surround him, he was taken gently and irresistibly by sleep.

"May sleep bring healing," I said softly to Kédra. *"Did you learn much from the Kin-Summoning before—"*

I could hear the sad smile in Kédra's voice. *"Fear it not, Lord Akhor—forgive me! I should say Lord Varien."*

I smiled myself. *"I answer to both Kédra. Lanen frequently calls me Akhor and does not even realise she is doing it. It was my name for a very long time, after all."*

"And my mother, may her soul rest on the Winds, has been dead for a very long time. Do not fear to speak to me of it. I was astounded to hear her voice—she called me by name. Akhor, she remembers!—and pleased beyond measure that she somehow knows delight in Sherók, but I am not devastated like my father. The Kin-Summoning was extraordinary, in fact. Keakhor himself wakened to speak with us. Alas, his words shed no light. This island has never been so violently

disturbed, and for all his travelling he never found another place that we might live. He even suggested that Kolmar was our rightful home and we were being called to return!"

"In the midst of all that has happened of late, Kédra, it would not astound me. The Kantri on Kolmar again! It would be a wonder."

"It might also be a disaster, Akhor. Not all of our Kindred are pleased at the thought.' "

"I never thought for a moment they would be." I replied. "Yet remind them for me, Kédra, this is a vast land. We forget, on our little island, how broad the back of Kolmar is. Few as we are, those who do not seek out the company of the Gedri need never endure it."

"Ah, my Lord King, your wisdom is sorely missed, and not only by my father! I will tell them, my Lord Varien. And a thought to pass along to your lady Lanen Maransdatter—did you know that Keakhor took the name Far-Traveller for his own? In the old speech, he was Keakhor Kaelar!"

"I will tell Lanen when she wakes," I said, smiling. "She will be pleased. Forgive me, Kédra, my head aches terribly, it saddens me but I must go. Give my regards to your father when he wakes."

"I will, Akhor. And do not be too sad. You may be seeing us all far sooner than any of us expected!"

I removed the circlet and held my cool hands against my aching head. It helped a little, and the ache passed swiftly enough, but exhausted as I was I remained wakeful long enough to send a prayer winging to the Winds, that Shikrar might wake and find the armour of time and distance that had been stripped from him intact once more.

Will

Just before it all came to a head I found myself outside Vil's chamber of a winter's day. I heard voices through the door as I approached.

"Vilkas ta-Geryn, put me down!"

"Be quiet, woman. You're in no danger." A pause. "There, back in one piece."

"Not if I get hold of you," came the sharp reply, then the voice softened a little. "You're getting better at that."

I decided that at the very least someone had to tell them they could be heard. I knocked twice, loudly.

The swearing was reasonably muffled and the delay before the door opened not too long.

Vilkas flung open the door. His face was a picture, though he tried hard to keep his thought from showing. If he were a normal lad, he'd have been scowling at the interruption and been halfway through telling whoever had disturbed him just what they could do to themselves before he recognised me. Thankfully his face changed when he saw me. He drew me into the room and shut the door quickly behind me.

"Keep it down, you two. I could hear you in the corridor," I said as I sauntered to the chair before the tiny fireplace.

"I thank you for the warning, Will," said the girl. "Was anyone else out there?"

"No. Everyone else is at their classes, Mistress Aral, as you well know. What excuse have you today?"

"No excuse and none needed. Did we not tell you? Vil asked Magistra Erthik if we could work together, try combining our powers as a special project. She seemed happy enough to let us."

"And yet you are here, and not a patient in sight," I said. "Not lying now, are we?"

"Not in the least and you know it," replied Aral stoutly. "I'm a servant of the Lady, you know, and She doesn't take well to liars. We've already been down to All Comers—you know, where anyone can come who needs healing and isn't afraid of students—and we worked together on two people."

"Any luck?"

"Yes, if I take your meaning aright," replied Vilkas with a brief smile. "One badly crushed leg, caught under a cart wheel, and one with a chest you could hear rattle from the next room. Not often we get such acute cases, but they served our purpose well."

"It was wonderful, Will," added Aral, her dark eyes shining. "Once we got them asleep, we combined our coronas and—it was—oh, sweet Shia, Will, it was amazing." Her voice grew thick with emotion. "That leg especially. I could—we could see the whole structure, and while Vil drew out all the bone fragments and put them back in place I knitted the muscles and the blood vessels back together. Together we cleansed the wound of dirt and infection, and I smoothed the skin. It was as if it had never happened." She laughed, delighted, and the joy in her smote me like a blow. My heart started pounding as she gazed up at me. "When we woke him he couldn't even speak at first. He just kept looking at his leg, and then he stood on it." She laughed. "I think if his clothes hadn't been bloodstained he would have thought it was a dream."

"I was prouder of the chest case," said Vilkas, his voice deep and slow and lazy. It pleased me to see him so relaxed. It didn't happen often. "We do work well together. Aral has a way of calming folk down and getting them to accept the healing that she ought to teach. The woman was nearly blue at the lips with it, and you know how those breathing cases panic."

"So would you if you were fighting for every breath," said Aral indignantly. "I had a bad chest infection once and it was terrifying. Don't dismiss people like that. As if you wouldn't panic if you couldn't breathe."

Vil bowed to her. "Quite right. Your pardon."

"Oh, get on with it," she said, flapping a hand at him.

"There's not much to tell, but it was harder work. The purely physical, the gross injuries are just a question of structure," said Vilkas, sounding briefly like Magister Rikard on a dull day. "It's the cause behind the infection that was such a challenge. She's one of those who gets a rattling chest every time she gets a cold. We didn't just clear up her lungs, we managed—"

"*You* managed," corrected Aral.

"*We* managed to find the underlying weakness in her lungs and repair it, though she's still got her cold." He grinned briefly. "She didn't seem to mind. And don't underestimate yourself, Aral. You were already there intuitively by the time I found it."

"So Magistra Erthik was pleased?"

"She will be when we tell her," said Aral, mischievously. "We finished ages ago and came up here to practice—other things."

"Magistra Erthik is always pleased when we find a reason to be elsewhere," said Vilkas. "She is a kind woman but there is nothing more she can teach us."

"That's enough, Vilkas. There is no need to speak so of Magistra Erthik," I said sternly.

It was hard to object, though. He was right. Magistra Erthik was wise in her way and had a deep understanding of human nature, but she had never had much to teach Vilkas that he could understand. Still, Vilkas was too inclined to judge everyone and everything by his own impossible standards.

It was part of his great gift and part of his difficulty with life. He was the strongest Healer to appear before the Magistri in many a long year. Some said he would one day be as strong as Magister Berys himself, but that was because Vilkas had held back when he was tested. There was untapped power the limits of which no one knew inside that long, lanky frame. Aral and I were the only ones who had any idea of it and Vilkas had sworn us to silence. He'd had no need to do so, really, for we knew little beyond the fact of its existence.

"Quite right. My apologies, Will. Can I offer you a cup of chélan? It's bloody cold out there."

I grinned. "Then close the window, idiot. And yes, please, chélan would be a pure gift, I'm frozen."

Because I was the only outsider there, Vilkas sat back in his chair and closed his eyes, frowning with concentration.

The window creaked in on its hinges. Despite myself, I let out a low whistle. "By the Lady, Vil! You're getting good at that."

Aral let out a sharp laugh. "Ha! Good? He's getting insufferable. Just before you came in he lifted me off the ground and held me there for a quarter of an hour." She glowered at him.

"It was nowhere near that long, and you came to no harm. I don't see why you're upset," said Vilkas calmly as he made a pot of chélan for us all in the conventional manner.

"I don't appreciate feeling helpless, idiot," she replied. "Just let me catch you off guard and I'll keep you still as a stone for an hour, then you might get the idea."

"You might be able to, at that. Interesting thought. We should try it."

"Oh be quiet and make the chélan, thou great and powerful wizard."

"Honey for you, Will?" he asked. Their sniping was a good sign, it meant that all was well with them.

Vilkas and Aral—how to begin their story, they who have shaped so many stories since? At that time I had known them both for a little less than two years, ever since they first arrived at the College of Mages in Verfaren, young and fiery and green as grass in spring.

For a start, to look at, they were wildly mismatched. They could not have been more opposite in their appearance or in their approaches to life. Where he was quiet, solitary and withdrawn, she was all light and laughter, sound and movement. She spoke and acted according to her heart, he according to his head.

It was rather the friendship between them that was astonishing.

Aral was an attractive lass. She was on the short side of medium build, with long brown hair that curled and flowed like water when she let it escape from the braids wrapped around her head. Her deep brown eyes sparkled with the life in her, but she kept her generous curves hidden beneath what she called "work clothes" and what the rest of us called men's clothes—trews and a tunic that came below her knees and was belted loosely around her waist. I could understand her reasons, though. On those rare occasions when she wore a fitted dress and let her hair loose, she drew every man in the place—including me—to her like moths round a candle. Every man except Vilkas.

He was on the tall side but young enough yet that he might stretch even more, and so thin that he always looked even taller than he was. His skin was very pale and his hair black like a raven's wing, with the same blue depths, and his eyes when he unveiled them were a shocking brilliant blue. He wasn't handsome, or that's what the girls tell me, but he was certainly striking enough to look at. Soon after he had arrived he grew a neat beard and the picture was complete. A great Mage in the making. Several of the lasses tried for him, as they were honour-bound to do, but he showed no interest beyond friendship. Most of them found him too uncomfortable for that. Certainly it was the sense of mystery about him that drew Aral.

Not many knew it, but I had heard that of all the students she was nearest to Vilkas in strength and intellect. The Magistri had admitted her into the college only months after Vilkas had arrived. She worried them. Magistra Erthik told me once that the Magistri thought the arrival of two such powers would mean either internal strife or some dire threat to the world, and were relieved after two years to see that neither seemed to be the case. Shows how much they knew.

It might be that that was what started their friendship. She never expected any more of him than friendship—well, not at first—and he found in her kindness and a mind equal to his. After a little time, though, they could not be separated. It was never love in the usual sense—not on his part, anyway—though they had a partnership that most would envy. I think it was simply that they found in each other the presence of something they lacked. For her, a sharp mind equal to her own that would challenge her, power even greater than hers that was willing to work with her, a friend to rely on who, despite all the boundaries he put up to keep the world out, was always willing to help, and even let her come close on occasion. For him, it was the contact with a loving heart, one that listened and gave a damn about what he thought and felt and did with his life, a friendly hearth-fire at which to warm himself when the roiling power within threatened to overcome him.

We worried about Vilkas, Aral and I. In a college full of intense young men, Vil was unique. He was fond of drink and could usually hold it well, but Aral told me that one time, in his cups, he had let slip his defences, just once, just for a moment. It had left her shaking. She had not needed her corona or even simple Healer's sight to see what it was Vil was defending against. It was not that he was keeping the rest of the world out. He was defending the world from that which lived inside him. It terrified him, exhausted him, spurred him to learn and to control and to live life as full as he could, for he was convinced that he would never see thirty winters.

I for one was determined that he should live to be ninety, if only to prove him wrong.

Aral felt the same way, but lately for very different reasons. I knew the signs. She was young and passionate and spent most of her time with Vilkas, taking risks, working with their shared power. No wonder she fell in love with him. His complex intensity, which he shared only with her, must have been completely intoxicating for her, and their shared work was all their lives. It was hopeless, worse than hopeless from the outset and even Aral knew it, but love, like weeds, grows where it will, and the mind has very little say in the matter.

I was their one friend, being just that bit older, and both together and on their own they came to me when they needed someone to talk to. I enjoyed their friendship, in fact I was honoured by it. When I realised the awful depth of the hole Aral was digging for herself I simply decided that come what may I would be there to help her out when she finally fell in, for so she would one day, and I would not leave her to be alone when that happened.

Of course, the fact that I was deeply in love with her myself might have had something to do with it.

"What in the world are you thinking of, Will?" said Aral, smiling and handing me a cup of chélan. "You're miles away."

"Quite right, lass. I beg your pardon." I shook myself. "So," I said, sipping the hot chélan and enjoying the simple feel of the warmth in my throat. "Magistra Erthik has approved your activities, has she?" I smiled. "Somehow I find that hard to believe."

Vilkas lifted a corner of his mouth and Aral laughed. "Right as ever, Will," she said. "Vil and I only told her that we were going to try working together on a healing or two. Turns out that's her dearest cause."

"Indeed. And how long ago did you two first manage to work together?" I asked. I knew them well, these two. They would not lie, not outright.

Vilkas turned to Aral. "End of last summer?"

"Aye. Before harvest, in any case. Perhaps two moons after the solstice?"

"Sounds right."

Aral turned to me. "In any case, I can't believe you've come here simply to pass the time of a winter's day."

"I might as well. There's precious little to do in the garden this time of year, and my few simples are well stocked." That made me smile. A college of mages, the best healers in the world, and there was still a demand for the teas that would ease a sore throat, or the warming grease that kept old bones from seizing up in the frosty weather. More serious things were treated every day, but the abiding curses of humanity still included growing old and catching colds in the winter, and there was nothing any Healer had ever found that could slow down the one or hasten the cure for the other.

"You know, if either of you were wealthy I'd be well off forever from the blackmail. If Magister Berys ever found out what you were doing you'd be tossed out of the nearest window so fast you'd hit the ground before the glass did."

Aral instantly looked sombre. Vilkas snorted. "I'm not so

sure. I swear, Will, I have caught traces of things in this college that should not be here, and the nearer you come to Magister Berys the thicker the smell. And have you noticed that he seems to have been reversing time lately?" Vil was now as serious as Aral. "It's true, Will, I swear it. I didn't know anyone could do that, demon master or not. He doesn't look much changed in passing, but the last time I saw him I swear he had tried to make himself look old. He stood straighter than I've ever seen him, there were traces of players' paint on his jaw and his hands no longer have wrinkled skin or age spots. There is something very, very wrong about Magister Berys."

Berys
It has been a day for news. I have just had word of Gorlak, followed not an hour later by news, at last, of the fate of the mercenaries I sent after Marik's daughter.

Ah, Gorlak. My apprentice, my assistant in conquest. The King of the East Mountains, with a large and powerful army, a brutish son, a thirst for ever greater power and a weakness for flattery. He had come to my hand willingly when I sought material assistance in my aim, for why use demons when there are men who will fight among themselves instead? Gorlak's was the only line of the Kings of Kolmar untouched by disaster, for only Gorlak had agreed to wage war on the other three as my proxy. I would leave him untouched, as I had not left the others; I would assist him as I could with information, silver and provisions, and he would conquer the other three Kingdoms for me.

Why should any man do so? For power, of course. I have no heir nor ever will, and Gorlak knows it. I have even sworn that should such a one be born he might kill it with impunity. No, I have promised Gorlak the thrones of the Four Kingdoms when I am done with them. And I am an old man, am I not? How long would he be forced to wait—ten years, perhaps fifteen?

I may have forgotten to tell him of my experiment with

lansip, that was restoring my youth. Ah, well. I am some-times forgetful. Doubtless he will learn of it in time.

For the moment, however, I knew that some weeks since he had set a muster for the northwest border of his Kingdom of the East, so very, very close to Eynhallow, the capital of the North Kingdom. It is well known that it would be insane to attack Eynhallow in winter, so of course the Northerners were completely unprepared.

I had already heard, through word passed by my sources in Marik's Merchant House of Gundar throughout Kolmar, that Gorlak had fallen with no preamble upon the fortified city of Eynhallow. King Karrick for all his age was no dotard, even taken unawares, and it took Gorlak nearly a full moon to take the city, but it is taken. It is mine now. Ancient Karrick, cut down in battle, was buried with honour in the chapel of his ancestors. It cost Gorlak nothing, and it kept the populace from rising against him.

One accomplished, two to follow.

Gorlak is no fool. He immediately fortified Eynhallow with his own men, and when the assembled army of the North, under Karrick's surviving generals, came upon him, he was ready for them. They were badly prepared and far fewer than they should have been. After only one more moon he has subdued the North and managed to keep word of it from reaching beyond the borders, for the most part.

However, a spy of the Silent Service has managed to find out this very day, as swiftly as the news has reached me, and it is known now to those who can pay for the information.

I am not overly concerned. It will be a good first test—what will happen to Gorlak, now that he has taken such a desperate and irreversible chance? If he survives until spring, the next step in the plan is Ilsa. It is a kingdom of farmers, sparsely populated, and unlike Karrick, King Ter-shet can barely remember his own name. The army of Ilsa, such as it is, has not been mustered for ten years. Those few with some claim to the throne have been hovering like car-rion birds for years now, doing nothing. If they are cut down at the same time as Tershet, who will mourn? Not the people. The people don't give a fart who the king is, as long as the taxes are low and life goes on much as normal.

So much for Gorlak. He has done well and I am pleased. Several large boxes of lansip leaves are on their way to him, guerdon for his good work. It may not seem much, but if you assume that the old man you are secretly fighting for is going to leave all to you, it would be enough.

Gorlak, as I have said, does not know that I am now physically no more than thirty years of age. I have stopped taking the lansip essence, for having lost more than half my years I am well enough content. No more stiff joints, no more failing eyesight and diminished hearing, no more aches and pains to plague me. No more, no more of those times when the glass showed Death looming over my shoulder, far too near.

As for the mercenaries, I had word early from those I sent north, to the Súlkith Hills between Verfaren and Elimar: they found something curious but it was not what I sought. The folk in the villages reported seeing far more of the little useless dragons about the place than ever before. Dragons are not all that unusual, though they tend to be shy of contact with men. Try as I might, however, I cannot see how they, the small, common dragons, might be connected with the Kantrishakrim. It is said in some of the oldest histories that far back in time they were one people—it is possible, I suppose, in the same way that the Rakshasa came originally from one kind. The Rikti said "Kantrishakrim and not"—I can only assume that the stupid thing mistook a large number of the little dragons for one of its larger cousins. Therefore Lanen must have been protected by the other "not Kantrishakrim" in northern Ilsa. In proof thereof I have had no word from those I sent to that place until this morning. It seems that only one of those who were in my pay survived. He left the others before they were killed. That must be only the second clever thing he has ever done, for the fool only bothered to send me word written by a public scribe and sent by the Long Riders, and even that was done many se'ennights after he must have known the fate of his comrades.

The Long Riders are swifter than normal travel, but I had paid the leader to send word far more swiftly by means of a device I had given him. It must have died with him.

The only other clever thing the survivor has ever done was not to sign a name to his missive, nor ever to touch it himself. I cannot trace him. Alas.

Life, Death and Fire

Maikel

A brief knock at the study door and Durstan came in without waiting. "Magister, your patient is awake and in distress."

Berys seemed unmoved. "Can you not assist him?"

"I will come, Durstan," I replied. "No need to bother the Magister. He has spent enough of his precious time with me already." I bowed to Berys and turned to leave, but he laughed and came around the desk to take me by the arm.

"Ah, Maikel, your dedication does you credit, but it is no trouble. I will come with you. Surely together we can put Marik at his ease."

"Quickly, please, gentlemen," said Durstan, leading the way at a trot.

When we arrived it was to an all-too-familiar scene and my heart grew leaden. Marik was sat up at the head of the bed, his back pressed against the carven headboard and his bony shoulders shaking despite the heaps of blankets and furs that covered him. The look of blank terror in his eyes was one I had hoped never to see again. My worst fears were dispelled in the instant, though, for however deep his fear he retained his fragile hold on sanity. "Maikel, help me!" he cried when he saw me. I was deeply grateful that he had called upon me and not Berys. "It's back, it's come back."

I strode to the bedside, summoning my corona, and put a hand on his shoulder. His hand reached out for me and gripped my arm like a talon.

"What is back, my lord? Are you in pain?" I asked, gently sending my healing power into him.

He shuddered and relaxed enough to breathe. I kept up the flow of healing, trying to soothe his panic, and in a moment he turned to me. *Ah, well,* I thought, *at least the terror in his eyes is focussed now.*

"No, no, not pain, it's the voices." He let go my arm and grasped his hair in both hands. "I'm hearing those damned voices again. Make them stop!"

Berys sat on the bed on the other side of my master and spoke quietly. "What are they saying, Marik? Can you make out speech?"

I started. Certainly this was a novel approach. It had never occurred to me that the voices might be saying something real.

"But there are so many!" he wailed.

"Try to choose one, any one, just a single voice, and listen to it alone. Can you do that?"

Marik concentrated. I admired him even then, able to think when he was so frightened. I am a creature of loyalty, you see. It can be a terrible handicap.

"There are two that are louder—the rest are only like whispers in another country."

"Choose one of those two, then," said Berys calmly. "Concentrate. What is it saying?"

He closed his eyes, frowning. "Something about . . . recovering . . . alas for the wound that will not heal—" He opened his eyes. "The two loud voices have gone. What in the Hells am I hearing, Berys?"

"I do not know. Listen longer and perhaps we will learn. Can you hear anything yet?"

"Wait!" interrupted my master. He was showing genuine interest for the first time in many months. I could not help but be pleased. "There's only one now, but it's stronger. 'Did you learn much from the—summoning,' I think—it's stopped, but I think it's waiting for an answer—yes! 'I answer to both, Kédra, Lanen frequently calls me Akor and does not even realise'—Hellsfire, Berys!" yelled Marik, and Berys and I jumped. My master's eyes were open and clear and his voice was strong, even though it was shaking with emotion. "Hellsfire, it said Akor! Lanen and Akor! Someone who knows Lanen is talking to that damned silver dragon that almost killed me! I'd have sworn it was dead!"

"Listen! Tell me!" commanded Berys.

Marik, still shaking with fury, closed his eyes again. "It's talking to someone called Kedra—'it would not astound me, the Kantri on Kolmar again, it would be a wonder.' Now it's stopped—wait—'I never thought they would be . . . this is a vast land. We forget how'—something—'Kolmar is . . . those who do not seek out the company of the Gedri need never endure it.' Now it's gone quiet—wait—'I will tell Lanen when she wakes—my head hurts'—no, it's over, it's gone."

Marik sat back, shattered, astounded, but no more astounded than I was. Berys, once the first shock was over, appeared calm, but I would swear he was as amazed as we were.

"Be at peace, my friend," he said to my master. "I fear you are overtired. I will prepare a sleeping draught for you." He turned then to me. "My thanks, Healer Maikel, but Marik and I will pursue this on our own. It is late, and I think we have all had enough excitement for this night. Go you to your rest, my friend. I will tell you of it in the morning."

I was about to object when I realised that there was a nimbus around Berys. The faintest of hints, but he was calling his power to him. I had no wish to be struck down again and to waken once more as his willing slave. I bowed. "I trust to your greater knowledge, Magister, and to the strength of your gift. I give ye good night, my lords."

I trotted off, the obedient servant, and as soon as I was certain I was not observed I rushed back to my own chambers. I am not a vain man and had not for several months gazed into a mirror longer than it took to shave, but now I stared intently at myself, at my eyes.

There was nothing to see. If I had had a glamour cast upon me my eyes would be dimmed, that I might see only what I should. A glamour cast by a lesser Mage would last a few days at most. Berys's had been in place for nearly two months.

That was not possible. He would have to have renewed it several times, no matter how strong he was.

And why not? I thought to myself bitterly. I had slept in the same shelter as he ever since the deep winter, he could have drugged me or—yes, if he had no principles he could have cast me into the sleep all Healers use for desperately wounded patients, and then sent the glamour upon me like any hedge wizard, any night he chose, as often as he chose. Demons made all such work much simpler.

Glamours are the work of the Rakshi, not of Healers.

Goddess. That smell.

My poor master. I could do nothing to save him from Berys. I was simply not strong enough. And his daughter, that valiant lady I had come to know on the return from the Dragon Isle—what had she to do with all of this?

I stopped in midstep. Sweet Lady. The voices Marik was hearing were real. Who was he listening to? I cursed to myself as I realised I was still too weak, too alone, and I returned to what I was doing. That poor girl, caught up again in Berys's machinations. My only ray of hope was that the dragon, Akor, had been mentioned. I had seen him bring the Lady Lanen, desperately wounded, back to the camp for healing, and he had threatened Marik with death or worse if he did not take good care of her. The dragon Akor must therefore be in some sense her protector. I could only hope that his protection would be enough to keep her safe.

My loyalty fought against me even as I drew out my small pack from the chest at the foot of the bed and filled it with my other tunic, my small clothes, the few possessions I had with me. *Stay, you must stay with him, you took an oath all those years ago and time does not diminish it,* my conscience argued as I prepared to flee.

My response to this thought was one that had occurred to me often enough. The man I had taken an oath to was dead indeed. His mind was held together with demon-forged nails and I could do nothing about it. Unless I wanted to become a Raksha-slave myself I had to leave now, before Magister Berys dragged me under his influence again.

All I owned made a small pack indeed. I had little money, but I could always live by my gift. Others did so all their lives. And perhaps I might one day find a way to fight the Archimage of Verfaren, though I held out little hope.

I did not allow myself to consider what else Berys might have done while I was helpless and under his influence.

I habitually left my chambers neat and I made certain there was nothing to show that I had left them not intending to return. I slipped out into the night-filled corridors of the College of Mages.

I made my way swiftly to the main hall, past the open doorway of All Comers, where any who were wounded were welcome, whether they could pay or not. There was no door into that chamber, only an archway, to show the goodwill of the College to all men and the willingness of Healers to serve.

To reach All Corners, you had to pass through the main doors.

What could let in could let out.

Marik

Berys left me to my thoughts for only a few moments before he was back, carrying two mugs of hot chélan. "So. The voices are real," I said, surprised at the smell of what he had brought. "Some sleeping draught."

"Ah, but I want you awake," said Berys, smiling. "Did you recognise the voices you heard?"

"Hells' sake, Berys," I snarled, "it's not like overhearing a conversation in the next room. These were voices in my *head.*"

"The phenomenon is called Farspeech. I thought it was mere legend, but here you are just recovered from madness with it in full bloom. I want to know how you have managed it."

I shuddered. "Tonight before you came, it was—I felt as though I had gone mad again. I heard voices all the time then. Talking, talking, they wouldn't leave me alone no matter how I screamed. You can't know how it was, Berys. I had no peace, they were always there—but it was worse when they left me alone. Then there was only—no, I can't."

"What precisely happened to you, Marik?" he asked, staring intently at me. "You have not been strong enough to tell me before, but somehow I think it will not be beyond your powers now." When I shook my head and gulped the chélan, he said "Come, Marik. All is past, the damage done is healed now. The best thing you can do to reestablish your strength is to tell someone all about it, with all the details. Leave nothing out. Come, my friend, speak to me."

I had indeed recovered enough now to be wary of his concern. Berys had never been concerned for another except as that other affected him and his plans, and he was no one's friend and never had been. Still, his offer was tempting. I could feel my mind returning, both it and I were stronger every day, and it would be a relief to speak of it once and have done. Besides, I had been out of my mind for a long time, and Berys has ways of learning things. For all I knew he was testing my trust.

"Caderan and I fought them, two of the dragons, a silver one and one of dark bronze. The silver one was Akor, the Guardian, the one that had brought Lanen for healing and had stolen her away when I tried to give her to one of the Lords of Hell." I shivered at the memory. "It came through the *wall*, Berys. The damn things are tremendously strong.

I'd wager its head was as long as I am tall, and the rest of it in proportion. It wouldn't fit in a house."

"That was some time before the final battle, Marik. Come, man, face it. Leave nothing out of your account. You and Caderan were fighting the two dragons."

"Yes. They spat fire at us but Caderan's spells kept us safe, and the beasts could not reach within the cast circle to touch us. I used the Ring of Seven Circles to fight them—the first five had nearly done for the silver one—when another one we never noticed roared down at us from the sky. Caderan killed it, but its body fell full on him and crushed him. I flung the sixth circle at the bronze one and wounded him, but before I could get the last one off Lanen knocked me down. She bore no weapon, so Caderan's spells of protection could not stop her. In my fury I tried to kill her with the last of the Seven Circles, but I had forgot it was proof only against the dragons. I then tried to send forth the last circle to kill the silver one when I heard—they—oh Hells, Berys." I was breathing as though I had run a race, the terror of that moment alive in my mind. "They—I heard screaming, as from a distance, and suddenly it was in my head. I can't recall if I sent off the last circle in the end or not. I think so, but I'm not sure. I couldn't get them out of my head, they cut me off from my body and cast me loose in the darkness. I wandered lost, dismal, only coming back every now and then to a voice or a time."

A few scattered images returned to me. "I—all I remember after is something about a charm Caderan had cast. He had warned me about it, said over and over how deadly it was, so I'd make sure he survived. I've no idea why we didn't all die—either Caderan was lying or they found the charm and destroyed it somehow."

I turned away from Berys's face. "I seemed to remember Lanen's voice speaking to me in that darkness, but that's not possible." I shivered. "I imagined all kinds of things in my dreams."

"After that I knew only Maikel, now and then, speaking words I did not understand, feeding me something that tasted like nothing I'd had ever known, the ripest pear, the sweetest apricot—oh Hells' teeth!" I swore then, for I had only that moment realised. "Damn it! He gave me lan fruit, didn't he?"

"If he hadn't you'd have died, you wouldn't eat anything else. Be at peace, Marik, there were still plenty for each of us, and your Steward has sold yours for an obscene amount of silver. I have eaten some and sold some of mine."

I stared at him. I had never dreamed he would be so wasteful: but then, he never did know the value of things. "If I didn't know better—I swear, Berys, you look younger." I peered at him in the dim light.

"That does not matter now." He frowned, rubbed his chin, and began to pace the room. "I believe your story, Marik, but on the face of it, it is impossible. What they did to you would only work if you had the gift of Farspeech in the first place"—he frowned at me—"which apparently you do, but how did they know that? Unless . . ." He started muttering. I heard only phrases—"but why should they—only if . . ." Suddenly he looked up and stared at me across the room, and his face blossomed into a smile that would terrify strong men.

"Lords of all the Hells," he said in an awed, delighted voice. "They have sown the seeds of their own destruction. The balance will call for it." He stared at me, his eyes boring into mine from ten feet away. "Marik, had you ever had any idea that you might have Farspeech?"

"Of course not. I have only ever heard of it in children's tales," I replied. "Would that it had stayed there."

"Oh, no, Marik my friend, no, no, we have been given a great gift. The power of Farspeech has never been truly understood." His face changed, slowly, and he came to look remarkably like one of the demons I had seen him conjure. "You were forced into this power, but at some level they must have known you possessed it. That means that at least one of them has it, and if you are hearing more than one voice—"

"It seems like hundreds of whispers, sometimes," I said.

"Then it is likely they all have it." He laughed suddenly, a plain laugh, full of delight. "Ah, Marik, we have them now!" He grinned and walked slowly towards me. "For if you can hear, if they have *forced* you to hear, even one of them, then we have them." He leaned over me, his too-brilliant eyes not a handspan from mine, his breathing short and quick. "Can you speak as well?"

"Back off, Berys," I snarled. "Why in all the Hells do you care?"

"Do this for me, Marik. For us. Try to speak to them."

"And how should I do that?"

"Can you hear any voices now?"

"Berys, I don't want to—"

"I don't care what you want! Listen! Can you hear any voices?"

His voice demanded obedience, though I swore I'd get him back for this. "There is one soft one, a long way away. I can't tell what it's saying at all."

"Listen closer. Can you make out the words?"

I closed my eyes. "No, nothing. I can tell someone is speaking, that's all."

"Try to say something."

"How?" I demanded.

"I have no idea. Just try it."

I tried thinking at the voice, but I felt and heard nothing. "It's useless, Berys. Nothing. Nothing at all."

"Perhaps you can only hear, then." He moved back with a sigh. "Still, it is a great deal better than nothing."

"Whatever you say. My head hurts like fury, you bastard. Fix it."

He laughed, loud and long, as the pain went away and I grew sleepy once again. "Are you content now?" I asked.

"Content, Marik? Yes, I am content. You are saner than you have been since you left Kolmar, and this gift that has been forced upon you will be the undoing of every dragon ever spawned. Think of it, Marik, dream of it. The hurt they have done you will prove their death. Sleep with that in mind, and dream of power untold."

I was too weary to care. I lay down and slept like the dead.

Lanen

We woke to a sunny morning. The rain had moved off at last, thank the Lady, and it was a little warmer than it had been. If I used my imagination I could almost smell a hint of spring in the air, but that didn't make me feel any better.

In truth I was really beginning to worry. There were far too many things happening to me that I could not explain. It was not simply the voices, though they were bad enough. For the last week I had had a constant headache, and for the last few days my lower back had been aching as well. I was just over my blood time for this moon, and that had been so light and short as almost not to have happened at all, but all the symptoms had stayed with me, the aches and the bloating. I rose that morning sick to my stomach and sore all over, with a burning desire to find a healer as quickly as possible.

However dreadful I was feeling, though, Rella was as bad. When we woke that morning in the cramped way station, she cried out and cursed when she tried to stand. I knew better by then than to offer to help, but I did it anyway and was snarled at for my pains. She hobbled out the door and we all sat talking quietly, pretending that we couldn't hear her gasp of pain as she pulled herself upright. When we heard her stomp off towards the horses we all went out to help, carrying the saddles and tack. We managed to give the poor creatures a bit of a brush before we saddled them, though they were all in a shocking state. Looking around, I realised that the four of us weren't a lot better.

Rella was first packed and mounted, despite her pain, and we all hurried to join her. To break our fast we ate as we rode, cheese with hard edges and a few last crumbs of travellers cakes—made with oats and wouldn't go stale, but sweet Lady they were dry—and followed Rella's promise of

Kaibar. I often had to ride with my eyes closed to keep out the light, for it made my head hurt worse.

We smelled sweet water long before we saw anything, and heard the rush and tumble of the river through the bare branches as we rounded a last stand of trees. The Kai was before us, and there to the west still some miles away across the plain we saw the tall white buildings and the red rooftops of Kaibar. We were at the gates just after noon. Jamie, Varien and I were all for stopping at the first inn we saw, but Rella dragged us deeper into the city and nearer the river, to an inn called the Three Kings.

Kaibar is a large city that sits on the banks of the great River Kai, just where the smaller River Arlen joins it from the north. The Arlen is the boundary between Ilsa, where I was born, and the North Kingdom that we had been travelling through for two moons. If you stand on the pier at Kaibar facing west, your feet are in the North Kingdom, before you across the Arlen lies the southern border of Ilsa and across the Kai to your left is the northern boundary of the South Kingdom—hence the three kingdoms and the name of the tavern. I didn't think of the kings very often, for though I knew old King Tershet of Ilsa sent his tax men to the farm and the village once a year, they never demanded anything that couldn't be paid easily by all, and we never heard tidings of the other three. There had been peace between the four Kingdoms for many years, and even though the barons, the great landholders, were always squabbling amongst themselves it didn't make much difference to the rest of us.

When we finally stopped at the inn, Rella went in and was out again in a very few minutes, looking happier than I had seen her in weeks. "We're to take our horses to the stables while he makes up the beds in our rooms, I've got us the use of the scullery all morning to wash our garb, and I've claimed the first bath, so there!"

The horses were drooping even as they stood—I knew how they felt—but we all four managed to brush them down decently for a change, feed them a good mash of oats and corn with plenty of warmed water to drink, put their blankets over them and let them lie on clean straw. I managed to hide the fact that I was feeling terrible, and in fact the stretching helped a bit. Jamie's Blaze let out a huge sigh of relief when he finally lay down, and we all laughed for we felt exactly the same way.

Despite being grubby we ate first, for the afternoon was passing and we'd had nothing since breakfast to sustain us. And such a feast! Or so it seemed to us—imagine the change, from what felt like weeks of little but tough strips of dried salt beef, oat-cakes, hard cheese, and salted porridge for breakfast every day of the world, to fresh brown bread and soft white cheese, hot soup with carrots and barley and a venison pie cooked with strong red wine. There were even spiced roast apples afterwards. We all fell on it like starveling souls, the innkeeper must have thought we hadn't eaten in weeks. It felt that way to me, too, and for once I was hungry enough to do the meal justice. I only hoped that enough of it would stay down to do me some good. The headache had eased a little as well.

While Rella had her bath I chose out my least filthy tunic to wear as I washed everything else I owned and paid one of the kitchen girls to put my clothes to dry before the kitchen fire and keep an eye on them.

The inn, miraculously, boasted a little room on the ground floor with a little fireplace, a high window to let in the light, and a real bath. When Rella finally came out and the maid-servant brought in clean water I leaned over and scrubbed my hair first, then knotted it on my head and lowered myself into the water. I nearly wept when the heat started soaking through and warming my cold bones. Never mind that I was far too long for the bath itself, that my head was pounding, that I was still swollen—warmth and the prospect of being clean did wonders for my spirits and I lay back as far as I could, revelling in the luxury. I had not realised how stiff my shoulders had been until I felt them relax. I was almost falling asleep when the first pains hit me.

It felt like little more than a muscle cramp, at first. A twinge below my waist, no more. I ignored it. Then as I sat

back in the water and started to relax it cramped again, a little harder and a little longer this time; but it gradually went
away and I gently began scrubbing off the grime. I made
fairly quick work of it and was leaning over in front of the
little fireplace drying myself off, but when I stood up
straight from having dried my foot I felt pain like a knife
blade in my gut. I cried out, as much in surprise as anything.

Then, I felt a strange dampness between my legs that was
not water and realised that I was bleeding. Not much, but
my blood time was past. It frightened me well and truly, and
fear I had to rush out of the bathing room to be sick in the
garden. So much for that lovely meal. I managed to get
back to my room and get a blood cloth in place before I
called for Rella.

Rella

I'm glad Lanen called me to help her. Varien was bathing,
for which I was grateful. This was not something that either
ex-dragons or husbands would be much good at.

I took one look at her and called to the landlord, who immediately sent one of his lads for the local Healer.

"Thanks," she said, when I came back in. "I thought I'd
need one soon. I don't know what's wrong with me, Rella,
but it's getting worse." She told me then, finally, all that had
been affecting her. I began counting the moments until the
Healer would arrive.

"You idiot child, why in the name of all that's sensible
didn't you say something before?" I asked her, keeping my
voice as calm and reasonable as I could. "How long has it
been since you kept down a proper meal?"

She couldn't answer me right away. I think that's when I
began to realise that she was very unwell indeed.

The Healer finally arrived in the late afternoon. It was a
woman, middle-aged and sharp-looking, very brisk and
blunt in her manner. I was not impressed, and that was before she set to work.

She called her power to her with the ease of long practice

as she took a deep look at Lanen. "Sweet Shia's tears, girl, how long have you been like this?" she asked, as she reached out to send her power into Lanen.

We should have known, I suppose.

"Like what?" asked Lanen. "The bleeding only just started, not the half of an hour gone."

"No, I mean how long have you been so ill with this pregnancy?"

"What!"

"My dear, I must warn you now that it is not going to last, but you are most certainly with child."

Lanen was pale before, but now she went white. "Shia— what do you mean, it won't last?"

"I'm sorry. This is your first, isn't it?"

"My first what?" demanded Lanen, her voice a little blurred. She was so terribly pale.

"The girl's in shock, woman. Help her," I snarled. The Healer nodded and sent a brighter blue pulse towards Lanen, who relaxed a little. "Your first pregnancy, my dear. I'm sorry, I'm not often called in as a midwife, but I have done enough work in the field to know when the body is intent on rejecting that which it carries. Believe me, it is for the best. If the unborn is too weak or too ill-formed to live, your body is the first to know. It is always best to simply assist the body to cleanse itself. Rest assured, I will make you comfortable while it happens."

She covered Lanen with a bright blue haze and started moving her hands.

"What are you doing?" I demanded. Lanen's eyes were watching but unfocussed. The woman was a horror.

"The body has rejected the unborn, but at this stage it is not difficult to remedy," she said, her voice calm and steady. "I have only to encourage the natural—oh."

She stared at her hands for a moment, then closed her eyes and began to glow much brighter. She opened her eyes again and sent a thin blue river of power through Lanen, who instantly started screaming.

I had the Healer flat against the wall and my hand about her throat almost without thinking. It worked, for the flow of her power stopped. "What in the Hells are you doing!?" I cried.

"It should have worked," the woman said, removing my hand but otherwise bizarrely unperturbed by my actions. "And it most certainly should not have hurt her. I don't understand."

"You'd damn well better try. What were you trying to do?" I demanded.

"What I said, attempting to assist the girl's body to rid itself of the pregnancy, which is obviously causing her great harm," she said. "It would cure the girl and ensure that the next pregnancy would be more likely to be successful." She frowned at Lanen, who was now holding her belly in pain. "Her body doesn't seem to know what it is doing, which is very odd indeed," she said. "It seems to be at war with itself, at the same time trying to protect and trying to be rid of the unborn." She held her hands out towards Lanen again and sent a far softer blue glow her way. The pain faded from Lanen's face but the anger did not.

"I can do no more, young woman," she said. "You should get yourself to a Mage as soon as possible. You need to rid your body of that child before it kills you."

That did it. Despite her pain, Lanen was on her feet in the instant and had struck the woman across the face, hard. "How dare you!" she cried, in a towering rage. "Touch me again and I swear, my soul to the Lady, I will knock you senseless. Get out!"

The woman was as sensitive as a stone but she did have at least some sense of self-preservation. She left, but she managed to say as she went, "You may not like me but I am not wrong. That child is feeding off of you, it can only be got rid of by a Mage. If you do not rid yourself of it you will surely die."

Lanen aimed a kick at her backside but the woman had scurried off.

"My girl, she's not worth kicking downstairs, just think of trying to get the bloodstains out of the wood," I said, desperately trying to defuse Lanen's fury.

"Bloodstains on wood! On my knife, more like. Rella, she

was horrible—Goddess, what a hideous, unfeeling cow! How could such as she ever—I mean—oh Hells," and Lanen deflated all at once. "Oh, Goddess help me," she said weakly. "Hells, Rella, she's a bitch but do you think she could be right?"

I sat Lanen down and held her by the shoulders. "My girl, I think she's right that you're pregnant, don't you?"

She just looked at me, desolate, then she burst into a strange mixture of laughter and tears. "Yes, now you mention it, I think I am. But I feel so ill with it."

"Well, I think she may be right about that too. Remember two things, though—first, she was not able to rid you of the pregnancy, which tends to mean that there is good healthy life in the child." Lanen nodded and looked a little brighter at that. "And second—well, I'd wager there is a qualified Mage somewhere in this town who will be able to do rather more than that idiot could." I snorted. "I've seen them before, barely qualified and they think they know everything. I wouldn't trust that—that unspeakable, inhuman piece of refuse to cure a wart!"

"You don't think she was right about me dying, though, do you?" asked Lanen solemnly. I knew I could not lie to her, she'd know it in a moment. Thankfully I didn't have to.

I gazed into her eyes. "We all die, my girl, but I would wager my next seven years' pay that you are not destined to die in childbirth. If nothing else, there are plenty of Mages in Verfaren and that's where we're headed. We'll get you there in one piece, never fear." I leaned over and kissed her cheek. Sweet Shia, that girl could touch my heart. "Now get yourself dressed and come down to dinner—I expect you're starving."

"I'll be down in a moment," said Lanen quietly.

I nodded and left her to her thoughts.

Shikrar

I flew over the firefields one last time, only seven days before the Council was to take place, and I waited until dark that I might see the true extent of the unrest.

I was still far too many leagues away when I saw the glow. It lit the low cloud from beneath, turning it bright red and giving the whole north end of the island a hellish look, as though legions of demons were breaking through a hole in the world. I had seen the effect before but never from so far away. My heart turned to stone in my breast as I flew, for as I drew nearer the light grew brighter, filling my eyes with fire. I had never in all my life seen anything like it. Surely those three active mountains could not throw so much light abroad, unless . . .

I topped the high crest of the Grandfather, which had hid some of the worst from my sight, and the full horror lay before me. I nearly fell from the sky as the heat tossed me back like a feather on the breeze. I barely recovered my balance in time. Taking heed, I turned away from the cliffs and spiralled much higher, having to work hard in the cold air. I kept away from the worst of the turbulence, though the air was still choppy, and the steam through which I flew was full of the stink of the yellow earth that appeared sometimes when stone melted.

Once I was over the firefields, much higher than I would normally fly at night, I used the strong thermal updrafts to soar higher still and to behold the full extent of the fire.

Every mountain for miles ahead of me, and to left and right, had its own part in the inferno. Nearly every peak in that great range of mountains was throwing rock and flames into the air or, worse yet, sitting brooding in a series of lakes of molten stone.

Worst of all, most frightening, was the way the land had changed near the Grandfather and the other heights of the southern cliffs. I was used to the great round pit on top of the high mountain that stood sentinel above the Grandfather, extending north from the harder rock of the southern cliffs. At some time, long before the Kantri had arrived, that mountain had run with fire, and when it cooled the deep round pit had formed.

When I looked for it now, it was gone, the pit was filled; and the black and fire-yellow and red surface boiled like water, throwing flame aloft here and there, almost like a living thing. From time to time a gout of flowing red stone would escape away towards the north and run swiftly down the mountain, but on the southern edge—I gasped—the Winds preserve us, there was very little darkness now between the fire and the Grandfather mountain. I could not believe that the slender barrier of stone would hold much longer against that great weight of fire and molten rock.

The peaks on the far northern edge of the firefield held their own silent menace in the great bulges that distorted them, and everywhere I flew that high scream, of rock or fire or the very earth itself, assaulted my ears and rattled my thoughts.

It is difficult to surprise one as old as I, for the years building each upon each tend to even out all things—but the devastation before me shocked me to the bone, and I saw no slightest sign that there was an end in sight. On the contrary, it was vastly, hideously worse than it had been mere days ago. The heat was immense, and the smell of burning rock was acrid in my nostrils and grew only stronger as I fought to hold a steady way through the violent updrafts. At least they helped me put more air between myself and the raging earth. There was also a great deal of steam, which made it harder to see, and the red light was sometimes more hindrance than help.

From what I could make out through the smoke and the stink and trying to see through that dreadful light, Terash Vor, at the centre of the widening ring of fire, was now much larger than it had been, and there was a darkness around and about it. No fire sprang from its top or its sides, but it showed an ominous bulge on its southern flank.

I realised that the terrible high screech was combining now with a rumble deep in the earth, and I banked in panic when I realised that the rumble was directly below me. Even as I flew off, fire spewed beneath me where moments ago there had been only a dark bulge on a mountainside, and I had to swerve again violently to avoid the fire-rock, spurting from the mountainside like blood from a death wound. Despite the height at which I flew I had been singed, tail-tip and wing-tip, albeit not badly. It must have been a quarter as high again as the mountain that had birthed it.

I gave up then, scorched, exhausted, my wings grown as weary as my heart. I turned away south towards the chambers of my people. I had still over an hour to fly, and my new-healed shoulder was aching.

I must tell my people what I had seen. I could not wait another sevenday.

This was the death of our home.

Wearily, wearily, sorrow bowing down my heart, I bespoke the Kantrishakrim.

"My people, my Kindred, hear me. It is Hadreshikrar who calls. We have no more time. Come to me at the Summer Plain at dawn."

A confusing babble greeted me, including many voices protesting that I had arranged the Council for half a fortnight hence. I heard their protests for only a moment. *"There can be no argument,"* I said coldly. *"Behold what I have seen."*

I concentrated on the manifestation of the hells that I had just flown through, on sending the image of that devastation to all of my people.

It was met with absolute silence. I was not surprised. We are not a stupid race and we all knew death when it threatened. *"My people, we must leave. I hope that we will have this night to prepare ourselves, but we must all be ready to take off instantly if need be. If there is aught of value you cannot bear to leave behind, bring it, remembering that the journey will take some days and there will be little chance to rest save on the Winds. If you know of any who keep the Weh, call to them and pray the Winds they hear you. If there are any who are not wing-light, tell me that we may find a way to bear them with us.*

"If we are to survive, we must leave this place in a very few hours. Kédra?"

"I am here, Father," came his voice. Strong and sure, my anchor.

"Come to me at the Chamber of Souls, my son, once you

and Mirazhe have Sherók safe. I will need your assistance to prepare the Ancestors and the soulgems of the Lost for the journey."

I would not listen to any who tried to bespeak me. I was weary beyond belief.

The Place of Exile had been our home for more than five thousand years—it was the only home, the only world, any of us had ever known.

And as I flew, I seemed to hear my own voice chanting to a succession of younglings over the long, long years.

First is the Wind of Change, Second is Shaping,
Third is the Unknown, and Last is the Word.

It is the first of the teaching verses, the basis of our understanding of the way the world works, the four Winds that blow through our lives. But she who taught me that verse when I was no more than a kitling never told me that the wind of change, on wings of flame, could blow so very, very cold.

Berys

The problem of Vilkas has come to a head at last. I have alerted the other Magistri. Finally, the chance to get him and that wretched girl out of my way! Now it has come to the point, it has been so very, very easy. And Erthik and Caillin at a stroke—ah, life is sweet.

Vilkas has been a student here at the College for two years. He tested nearly as high on his entrance as I did all those years ago, a once-in-a-generation power—but I would have wagered a day of my life that he was not working to his capacity for the test. I suspected at the time that he was a powerful wastrel who could not be bothered to exert himself and would come to nothing, for I have seen others of that kind, if never any so strong. Still, his capacity was high enough for me to keep a watch on him. I made certain that my occasional observations of him were well hidden from the other Magistri, and went out of my way to befriend him. He was not interested in my friendship. Given the power available to him, that made him my enemy.

Not long after he arrived, the girl Aral appeared. She also tested very high, not in the same class as Vilkas but with more real ability than even her test results would indicate. She is not a threat, however, and may even be an asset, for she is his weakness. They are both far too powerful for their good or mine, but they are young and ignorant enough to be outmatched without overmuch effort.

I timed it well. When Magister Rikard unlocked the door this morning and swiftly threw it open we caught them in the very act. Vilkas was surrounded by a brilliant corona, the Healers' Power without a doubt, and he was using it to hold an unconcerned Aral some three feet off the floor.

"Vilkas!" cried Rikard, appalled.

Every member of the Council, assembled for this very purpose, saw the tall young man turn his head, acknowledge us with a nod, and gently lower the girl to the ground. The moment her feet touched the floor she would have started forward, but Vilkas raised a hand and she stopped where she was, bristling with righteous indignation. I suppressed my laughter with difficulty.

Vilkas bowed to the Council, calm and faintly amused. Aral stood unmoving, with a defiant flush on her cheeks. "Very well, gentlemen, you have found us out," said Vilkas with a smile. "I hope you will allow us to explain our actions."

"Vilkas, how could you!" cried Rikard. "When Magister Berys told me I would not believe it. How can you act against all we have tried to teach you?"

Vilkas only lifted an eyebrow. "I have acted against nothing you have taught me, Magister Rikard. We have invoked the Lady with every breath. All is well. And Aral is unhurt, as you see."

"We've done nothing wrong," said Aral. She was bristling now, all five feet of her, in defence of her friend. So, he was her weakness too. I had not known that for certain. "What is it that you object to?"

I turned to Magistra Erthik. "Do I understand that you have not warned these two against using the Power for purposes other than healing?"

Erthik was the least concerned among us, with the possible exception of Vilkas, and spoke lightly. "Berys, really! You know perfectly well that if you desperately want an entire class of students to do a thing, all you need do is say, just once, 'Don't even think about doing this, it's dangerous and unpredictable.' We don't even mention such possibilities one way or the other until the third year, and it never occurs to one in a hundred that our power might have other applications before then. Only one in ten of those ever try it." She looked at the pair before us and smiled crookedly. "Well—two in ten. Though I must say that's the most impressive result I've ever seen." She had the insolence to sound impressed.

"Then there is a prohibition against the use of the Power for anything other than healing?" said Vilkas, unperturbed.

"Of course there is," said Rikard sternly. "And despite Magistra Erthik's indulgence you should know it is a most serious offence."

"So I gather. However, given that we were both ignorant of such a prohibition, you can hardly condemn us for attempting to discover the limits of our gifts."

"On the contrary, Master Vilkas," I said, "condemnation is precisely the word. There is a harsh penalty for what you have done."

"A penalty for ignorance? Then the whole world owes a debt," said Aral sharply. "We have acted in the name of the Lady at every turn."

"Why?" I asked her, and when Vilkas attempted to speak I silenced him. "No, I would hear Mistress Aral." I turned to her. "Why did you feel it necessary to be so assiduous in your devotions, Mistress? Surely a simple prayer of invocation to begin would be enough."

She spoke her defiance without hesitation. "It might have been, indeed, but I am a servant of the Lady. We were making sure there was no room for the Rakshasa, Magister."

"What made you think there might be?"

Vilkas laughed. "Magister, I know you have chosen to keep all of your students in the dark, but after a year and a half of working together we have learned that any extended use of the Power draws those of the Demon-kind like cats to a fishmonger. I do not know, but I would guess that Power is like food and drink to them, or like sunlight, and the more you use it the nigher they come unless you do something about it."

His gaze lingered on me just that fraction too long.

"Magistri, you may leave us," I said. "I will deal with this."

Erthik was loath to go and began to grow angry. "This is not a matter for you alone, Berys," she said. "This must be dealt with by all of us. You do not know these two, but I do. Let them be disciplined, certainly, but you cannot think either of them Raksha-touched."

I let slip some of my anger and directed it at her. "Erthik, you do not know what can happen to even the stoutest soul when it perverts the Power. I do. That is all my study, night and morning. You treat this far too lightly! I will bring them before the Assembly this afternoon, but I have a few words to say to them first."

For a moment I feared she would not go—she is stubborn—but after a last long look at the two of them she nodded and left. Fool. Rikard seemed more hurt than angry, for these two had been in some sense his apprentices. He left with the others, muttering sad phrases. I closed the door swiftly behind them.

"Magister Rikard informs me that you have been experimenting with the Power," I said coldly. "That you have attempted Farspeech, and moving objects with the Power, and that you have tried to read the future. Do you deny these charges?"

"No." Vilkas, straightforward as a knife and every bit as malleable.

"For Shia's sake, we've never tried to hide it." Aral, armoured in justice. Fool.

"Know you the penalty for such a misuse of power?"

"It was not misused. We simply applied it in a different way," said Vilkas. He was controlled as always: unconcerned, his eyes half-lidded, his voice steady and calm. "We have done all in the name of the Lady, invoked her with every breath. There is no Raksha-trace on either of us."

"Indeed," I said sternly. I assumed he had noticed. "Unfortunately I have been doing research on certain of the Demon-kind and am tainted myself at the moment, else I would investigate your claim. However, that is not the issue."

"Then what is?" demanded Aral. "We've done nothing wrong, Magister."

Vilkas simply stared at me, a challenge which I ignored. Instead I let my voice rise in anger. "On the contrary. By the laws of Verfaren, young woman, you have incurred the harshest possible penalty."

"Our work has been harmless. How could it possibly be a threat to the Magistri?" asked Vilkas. His stance and his gaze annoyed me, his lazy voice grated, and of a sudden I tired of the game.

"The threat is this," I replied. I called up my power and sent a bolt of pure force against Aral's midsection. She reacted swiftly enough to deflect the blow in part—I must admit, that surprised me—but the point was made. She fell to the floor.

I turned again to Vilkas, who without an obviously hasty movement stood now between me and his companion, incandescent with Healer blue. "You may dismiss your nimbus, young Vilkas. I have done with my demonstration," I said, letting contempt show in my voice. "That was but a gesture, a tiny fraction of my power. If I were to focus it at either of you in earnest you would die on the instant. That is what happens when the Lady's gift is perverted—inflicting pain and death rather than healing, rejoicing in our power for its own sake rather than for the good it can do others. If this were a mere hundred years ago, you would both be tried and executed for your crimes. Deviating from the Healing way leads inexorably to the misuse of Power, and almost always to the summoning of demons."

"Then what shall we say of your misuse, Magister?" purred Vilkas. His voice was still soft but now it held the edge of menace. Aral had recovered her feet and moved away from him, her corona in place now, her stance defensive. The corona about him, however, shone bright and clear, and I caught a glimpse of just how strong he was. I decided to make a trial of his strength and resolve. If I were fortunate and he failed, it would look like an accident.

"Ah, the last resort of the guilty," I said with a sigh. "Lay all the blame on another. Of what do you accuse me now, apprentice?" I asked, not releasing my own power but putting my hands behind my back. There I was free to move my fingers in a specific pattern to release a calling-on spell I had prepared for just such an emergency. "Do you say that I— Bright Shia, beware!"

The two Rikti appeared in midair and launched themselves, one at Vilkas and one at me. I cried out in some surprise—quite convincing, I suspect, as they might have gone for any of us—and made great show of attempting to fight off the one that was before me. It had orders not to harm me, of course, but the one on Vilkas was not so hampered.

However, the thing's talons were mere inches from his eyes when both it and the one facing me were stopped and held motionless. The source surprised me, however. It was the girl. She was chanting some kind of prayer aloud as she approached and held tight to something on a long chain about her neck. The Rikti fought to free themselves, but her cage of power was strong and her will implacable. Indeed, for that moment she shone brighter than Vilkas, until she touched whatever sacred symbol she wore with one hand and the creatures with the other. Each in turn cried out and vanished, leaving only their stench behind. That done, she loosed whatever assistance she had received from her prayers and her corona shrank to its normal dimensions.

"How dare you!" I cried, outraged. I did not have to practice my player's skills, for I had hoped that at least they would be injured. "Do you still tell me you have never encountered demons? How shall I believe that, with such evidence!"

"We never said we had not encountered them, Magister," said Vilkas, and his voice was calm and cold as dead midwinter. "As I believe I mentioned, we have found that they are drawn to any use of the Power, and we have had to dispel them on several occasions."

"Then how do you explain that one's appearance?" I cried.

"*We* did not call it," he said, his gaze locked on mine.

I knew in that moment that he was better than I had thought. Not only did he know who had summoned the Rikti, he had hung back and let his assistant do the work using some kind of amulet, so that I would not know his strength. He sealed his doom thereby. I will not suffer him to live. But slowly, slowly, perhaps he *could* be of value to me alive. For a short while.

"You will destroy all trace of your work in this room and come to the Great Hall before midday," I said coldly. "Do not fail to appear or attempt to leave, lest you force us to bring you back in irons."

"We will be there," said Vilkas smoothly, moving to open the door for me. I saw in his eyes that he would appear though all the Hells should bar his way, if only to spit in my face. Good. I wanted him angry.

In a way it is a pity—I would have preferred to have Vilkas's power on my side, but it was clear that neither he nor the girl would ever consent to it. It is just possible that Vilkas and the girl will attend the Assembly and suffer the fate in store for them, but I do not expect it. I will send Erthik and Caillin to guard their room. I will arrange for horses to be saddled and ready in the courtyard, complete with valuable articles from the library and a ring of Erthik's that I found some months ago.

If they are clever, they will run. If they take the horses they can be charged with theft if it comes to that—but I have a better fate in store for Vilkas, and for Erthik. Both at a stroke. Ah, this is the first, this small matter, but in later times it will be seen as the first moment in my rule. The first act of King Malior, truly, for I shall rule in the name I have taken for myself as a master of demons.

Erthik and Caillin will die soon after I send them to guard the room, for I need their deaths to be unmarked at first and I do not know how long it will take for the prisoners to decide to leave. However, when the bodies are discovered outside the empty room that held Vilkas and Aral—ah, life is sweet.

In the meantime I have sent word to every Mage in Verfaren to prepare to block a great power, in case Vilkas is a fool and decides to face the Assembly. I do not expect it, but one must be prepared. Should the two young idiots submit, I have a delightful fate in store for Master Vilkas. I can make far better use of his death than of his life. Once the block is in place, and they are banished and walking the world— well, it is not chance that Maikel has disappeared. I will not miss his meddling. To challenge me! For his presumption I have prepared him carefully over the last weeks, while we have been "working together." I have set a Sending in him, planted in his mind a deep need to find—well, whoever I wish him to find, I need only send a Rikti to touch him to engage the spell. He will find and follow whatever quarry I set him on, for weeks if I require it, though I do not intend to wait so long.

When I require my prey—Vilkas if he is a fool, some other if he is not—I need only summon forth the demon I have planted in Maikel. It is enspelled to establish, in only one hour, two ends of a demonline that starts here in my chambers. Such a task normally requires weeks of preparation.

I am very, very good.

When the demonlines are set I will be able to appear wherever Maikel has gone, capture my prey and return here in little more than the blink of an eye. Poor Maikel will not survive the experience, of course. He should never have challenged me. And should Vilkas prove a righteous fool he will be the subject of my slave Maikel's hunt; with his power blocked, he will make a fine sacrifice.

All is now set. If they run and do not take the horses, I shall send Rikti to deal with them, enough to ensure their death and defeat. If they submit, Vilkas will live—briefly—despised, disgraced and powerless. Let him face that for a day or so until I have him safe, when he will have just enough time to despair before he becomes demon fodder. It is too good a fate for him, to be the means of rebirthing the Demonlord, but better him than me.

Ah, the Demonlord, the Nameless One! The first to follow my calling, and the best of us. His natural gifts left him discontent, for he was a mere first-level Healer without the ability to go further. He had studied healing all his life. When the Magistri of his day tested his power and found it so paltry, he knew he must do something to change it. He knew the Tale of Beginnings, that the Gedri had the power of choice, but it is said that he was the first for many centuries to have the courage to call upon the Rakshasa for assistance.

His greatness lies in the fact that when he called upon them he knew that he had nothing to lose. He had thought long upon the pact and told them in detail what he required—more power than any alive possessed, the ability to destroy the Kantri, and a way to survive should they live long enough to try to kill him. When the Rakshasa demanded his true name for payment he agreed without hesitation. His name was stripped from the world, from the memories of all who had known him—so much is known to all men. What most do not know is that the spell of the Distant Heart was performed at the same time. Like the great wizards of legend, his heart was taken from his living body and laid in a distant place for safekeeping. It was a great work that he wrought. In essence he became a demon himself at that moment, with all he had demanded, beginning with more power than any human had ever before possessed.

When the Kantri attacked him, he managed to destroy fully half the great beasts before he was killed. He died valiantly, laughing at his murderers in the knowledge that he would live on as a Raksha and in the certain knowledge that it would be possible for him to live again under the sun when a demon master of sufficient strength and resolve should arise to summon him.

I am that man.

I must go and meet with Erthik and Caillin in a moment, but first I need to renew the players' paint and powder that conceal my youth. This will be the last time. Sometimes I can barely stand still for the power that is in me now, when I emerge from my hidden chambers trembling with excitement.

I can feel in my bones that all the world is rising to join in battle. I do not intend to be alone.

However, one thing eludes me still. It is simply not possible for two of the Kantri, or even the shadows of them, to remain hidden in Kolmar so long. Perhaps the large number of common dragons in the hills might smell like one of the Kantri to a Rikti, but what is this Akor that lurks in Ilsa? I sent word by demon messenger, at great expense to myself, to the Healer under my control in Marik's branch House in Illara, the capital city of Ilsa. She is skilled in the dark arts, but even though her powers extend a hundred miles in any direction she could find no trace of the Kantri, nor has she heard any rumour of a dragon. There is something very wrong, something I am missing.

I begin to feel a sense of urgency. All is carefully timed from this moment forward, that my coronation might take place on Midsummer's Day. I must have Marik's daughter by then—by preference, long before that day. I am concerned at the words Marik heard—"the Kantri on Kolmar," it said. All of them, perhaps?

Even in the fullness of my power I do not wish to battle all of that nation at once.

Though I could do it, for the Demonlord, brought back into life, will surely be the final death of that people. Indeed, as I think of it, my problems would thus be resolved at a single stroke. For behold, I know now how to summon him, how to raise up a body to enshroud him, and my power over Marik will provide the required sacrifice of a living soul when the body presents itself to me.

I have been searching much of my adult life, reading all, daring all to ask very particular questions of very particular demons, and now I have found it. He was clever, the Demonlord, but he could not have expected that one such as I would arise. He was the greatest power of his time, thanks to the Rakshasa, but even without their help I am a hundred times stronger than he.

He could not have known that Healers as a class would grow more powerful as time went on, and that the use of the Power would expand as it has. Where only the very best of his time could smooth a broken bone and hasten its healing, that is now routinely performed by Healers of the third rank and above. Now we can cure illnesses of the mind, which difficult and delicate accomplishment they never even dreamed of.

I know where he is and how to bring him back, and I have that which alone will summon him. My final accomplishment will come tonight, when I discover how to be rid of him when I am finished with him, for he who cannot banish the demon he summons is the greatest fool of all.

Oh, yes, he was clever and daring, the Demonlord, but I am more clever than he, for I can bring him here and make him do my will, and tonight I will learn how to kill or banish him when I require him no longer. That is true power.

Two days later I will be prepared to complete the summoning that was begun at the change of the year, on the darkest day of midwinter. Somewhere—I neither know nor care where—earth shakes and fire spews skyward as the demon creature grows to maturity. I would not care to be there when it is birthed.

However, enough of such pleasant speculation. I must go and have a last word with Erthik.

Will

Rumour flies as fast as thought in this college. I was passed in the corridor midmorning by four of the Magistri: Erthik was muttering something about Berys, and then I heard Vilkas's name.

I was approaching Vil's chamber when I heard someone leaving, and the voice made me shiver. I ducked around the nearest corner, heard footsteps going, thank Shia, in the opposite direction and fade to silence. I went up to his door and was dragged inside almost before I had finished knocking.

"The bloody bastard!" said Vilkas, with a heat I had never seen in him. "To threaten us so for experimenting! Every time I see him he reeks worse of the Rakshasa." Vil looked directly at Aral, which was unusual enough to catch my attention. He seldom looked directly at anyone. "Are you hurt?" he asked.

"No, I managed to turn most of it," she said, rubbing her arm and not seeing his glance. Just as well for her, for the care and concern he allowed himself to show might have undone her. "But I swear he meant to wound me badly. If I hadn't been on my guard, I'd have been thrown across the room at least. Lady curse him to death and darkness—"

"Stop right there, you," I said quietly. "No curses."

"Will, you weren't there. Damn it! If I'd had a knife I'd have gone for him."

I put a hand on her shoulder, briefly. I didn't dare leave it there very long. "I know, lass. But that would make it worse, not better. Knives are not the way for that one."

"Will, he's insane!" she cried, whirling away from me. "He tried to injure me, then stood there lecturing us about how misuse of the Power is forbidden, and then he called up a pair of demons! With no altar, no incantation that I could see, he called two demons into the room and pretended to be helpless. He made us get rid of them. As it was I could barely breathe for the stink of demons all around him. And we're called up before the Assembly in only two hours, and the Lady only knows what they're going to do."

"Hells' teeth, Vil. Was it really that bad?" I said to Vilkas as I steered Aral into a chair before the fire. She subsided into muttering to herself. I tried not to listen to the words.

"In fact it went a little better than I had hoped, though there are two very different aspects of this to consider," he replied coolly. He had regained his composure and was watching Aral with a cheerfully bemused expression. "To be honest, we have long suspected that what we were doing was not widely acceptable. Magistra Erthik doesn't seem all that worried, but then she knows both of us." He paused for a moment. "Interesting that Berys felt threatened enough to want to defend himself, even if it was quite amazingly feeble. Claiming research to explain the Raksha-stink, indeed! And he took the trouble to insult me, which I find unsettling."

I looked at him. "Insulted you? How? And why should that bother you?"

"By disparaging my Power. He called it a 'nimbus'." Vilkas stood behind Aral's chair and leaned over slightly, and I noticed he was surrounded even as we spoke with a subtle blue cloud. I guessed he was checking Aral to be certain she was uninjured. It took only a moment. "I don't give a damn what he says, Will, it only concerns me because I have been careful never to show him enough of my ability to draw attention to myself." He half grinned at me. "I believe he has noticed now."

"Noticed *you*? That's good. Who did all the work?" complained Aral, turning round in her chair to look up at him. "Nimbus, indeed! That's what they call the lowest level of Power, Will. Healers who haven't started their training or who don't have a gift beyond the first level have a 'nimbus' when they summon the Power." She snorted. "I expect Vil has one when he's fast asleep. His corona is every bit as bright as Berys's and a damn sight cleaner."

Vil nodded to me and walked over to the fire, warming his hands, leaning against the mantelpiece. Aral, on the other hand, leapt to her feet, her frustration not letting her sit still. "Have you any chélan, Vil? I'm dry as the great southern desert and I can't sit still when I want to kill someone."

"The leaves are in the cupboard and I suspect we need more water. Make enough for us all, would you?" said Vilkas. She got on with it, knowing her way around Vilkas's chambers as around her own. Vil went to stir the fire while I wandered over to the window and stared out at the bright morning, trying to take it all in. That Berys was on easy terms with demons I could well believe, but to summon one in broad daylight where both Vil and Aral could see him do it—it did not bode well at all. I had in my gut a cold certainty that great things were now moving and we had best deal with them by assuming the worst. I glanced over to where the two of them were making chélan, she growling at him, he speaking quietly to her.

Typical.

"What's caught your mind, Will?" asked Aral a moment later, still with a brow like thunder but a little calmer than she had been. "I asked you three times if you wanted honey in yours. You've got some now, want it or not."

"A cold day like this needs the sweetness, I thank you."

Vil had taken up his post, leaning that slim frame of his against the side of the fireplace while Aral and I sat before it. We had gathered thus many a time, ever since I had first come across them arguing in the gardens soon after Aral arrived. I had stood watching them full five minutes before either noticed me, and by then they had been standing on my seedlings for quite some while. They brought me others a few days later, by way of apology, and a friendship developed. I was just that bit older than either of them, perhaps a matter of eight years older than Vilkas, who was the younger by a year, and I had become a kind of mentor to them both. It pleased me greatly. They were good souls and I enjoyed their bickering. It was very much like my sister Lyra and me at their age—though what I felt about Aral was most certainly not the love of a brother.

I was about to ask them what they were going to do next when there was a knock at the door. Instinctively I hid myself as Vil opened it. Don't ask me why.

It was Magistra Erthik and Magister Caillin. "Hullo, you young idiot," said Erthik cheerfully. "Berys has decided you need guarding, which just goes to show how well he knows you. Caillin and I will be here until you two are due at Assembly. I thought you should know."

"Magistra, surely you do not believe—"

"Vilkas," she said, "the only thing I truly believe is that Berys is as twisted as a corkscrew. I'm not a fool, you know, I can smell the Raksha-stink as well as you can." I couldn't see, but her voice sounded as if she were smiling. "I've been waiting years for this particular Assembly, my lad. We may even manage to get Berys tossed out on his crooked ear. Just you tell the truth, all of it, and you'll be fine. Now go away, I'm not meant to be talking to you."

Vil shut the door, and he and Aral made enough noise to cover my retreat to the window, where we were far enough from the door to speak in whispers.

"So, Vil," said Aral quietly. "What next? Sounds like the Assembly is going to be nice and lively! I just wish I knew what they are planning to do to us."

"I have absolutely no idea," replied Vilkas, his voice barely loud enough to hear. "I can't believe it will be only a lecture, we've already had one of those." He grinned, looking for an instant like an overgrown imp. "Do they throw folk out of here, or are we more like to face a slit throat and a gutter for a graveyard?"

"Mages are not allowed to kill, idiot," said Aral. "Remember? Though I don't suppose they'd hesitate to toss us out."

"Mages aren't allowed to deal with the Rakshasa either, but Berys does so all the time," said Vilkas with some heat.

"That's quite an accusation, Vil," I said sternly but very

quietly, "and for Erthik's sake, you'd best be sure you have proof if you say it in the Assembly."

"The things don't just appear, Will. Someone has to call them. We didn't." He looked across at me slowly. "I think it has come to the point, you know. I think he was hoping we'd react too slowly. If we hadn't been ready that demon would have killed me and it would look like an accident. I'd be dead and it would be Aral's word against his."

"Goddess," breathed Aral. "You're right, Vil. Sweet heaven. Has it gone so far? Does he really want you dead now?"

"That is the only reasonable explanation I can think of for his summoning those Rikti," said Vilkas. He was very cool about it.

"You're certain he did it?" I asked.

Vil frowned at me. "I told you, they can't just show up. Besides, can't you smell it on him?"

"Smell what?"

"That acrid stink that clings to him and everything he touches. It's the Raksha-trace. He fairly reeks of it, I can smell it across the room."

I smiled a little sadly. "You know, I should be flattered that you keep forgetting, but I must remind you that I have no Healer's talent at all. None. Not the slightest hint. I'm every bit as able to smell demons as, oh, that brick in the hearth. I'd know a demon was behind me if it bit me in the ass, but that's about it."

Aral sniggered but Vilkas remained solemn. "Will, do you have any idea what they might be planning to do at this Assembly?" he said.

"No, lad, I'm sorry," I said. "I've never heard of students being called before the entire Assembly. One or two of the Magistri have joined Berys for a disciplinary hearing, yes, but never all of them." I grinned. "Sounds like Erthik has a few ideas of her own, in any case. You might find that you are able to fade into the background when the real show begins."

"Possibly, but I don't expect we'll get away untouched," he said.

"Well, they can't kill us, there isn't a prison here, and they can't take away our power," said Aral, then her eyes grew wide. "Sweet Shia, Vil," she said, struggling to keep her voice low, "they *can't* take away our power, can they?"

"No," he said decisively. I looked the question. "I've done quite a bit of research on that subject, Will," he replied. Unexpectedly, he smiled. "Just making sure. But no, Aral, there is no known way to decrease or disperse a Mage's inborn power, though it is possible to put—a—block . . ."

And Vil started swearing, loud and creatively, pacing up and down the room like a caged heron on his long legs, and throwing in a little blasphemy for good measure. He didn't often crack like that. I watched, interested. I wouldn't have tried to stop him or even slow him down for worlds. He soon got himself under control again, but he was physically quivering with rage. I'd heard of such a thing but never seen it. In someone as intense as Vilkas, believe me, it's frightening.

Just then there came a strange soft noise from outside the door. I looked for somewhere to hide and found only bare walls behind me, but the noise was not repeated and no one knocked. In a moment Vilkas spoke, still in an undertone but with absolute fury in his voice.

"That's it, Aral, that's what they're going to do," he managed to growl. "I've read about it. They won't kill us. They'll just put a block on us that we won't be able to lift for *three years*. That's what the records say. Then we get sent away and warned not even to try to use our power lest it destroy us in the backlash." He stopped pacing and looked solemnly at her. "The only question is, do we run for it now, or do we hope they don't have the measure of our ability and try to get rid of the block once it's in place?"

Aral stared at him. "Do you really think we could run for it? How would we get past the two on the door?"

Vil said nothing but bowed and gestured at the window.

"We're two floors up!" hissed Aral.

"I've been levitating you for weeks now," murmured Vilkas, one corner of his mouth tilting up. "What makes you think I've forgotten so quickly?"

To my delight, Aral grinned back at him. "Hmm. Good point. I like it."

"I don't," I said. "What if Berys is ready for you?"

"I'd be willing to wager that Berys has never even considered that we might run," replied Vil urgently. "I saw him. He assumes that we'll come along to the Assembly if only to spite him and make accusations we can't possibly prove." Vilkas pulled himself to his full height, looming over Aral. "The more fool he," he said in a whisper, but with immense dignity. "I will not put myself in his power. Are you coming, Aral?"

"I can't talk you out of this?" she said with a sigh, knowing the answer.

"Are you coming?"

"Hell, blast and bugger it. Yes, I'm coming. Let me get my cloak so I don't freeze."

"Where will you go?" I asked quietly.

"Away," said Vilkas shortly. "If you don't know you can't be forced to tell."

"True enough, though I don't think it has quite got to the stage yet where Berys can torture the staff without someone noticing," I replied calmly. And suddenly it all seemed so unreal, so stupid, that I refused to play the silly game anymore. Honestly, grown men huddled whispering in a corner! "In fact," I said, standing up and speaking normally, "this whole thing is ridiculous." I felt like I was shouting, but suddenly I refused to allow this nonsense to continue. "Come on, you two. I need to speak to Magistra Erthik." I strode to the door and opened it.

Well, I wasn't to know.

Magistra Erthik was there but I wasn't able to speak to her. No one would ever speak to her again. Both she and Magister Caillin lay in crumpled heaps, like puppets with cut strings. His face showed only surprise. Hers was set in a mask of rage.

I leaned back into the room. "We're leaving. Now," I commanded. Don't ask me why they didn't argue or wonder—

Aral told me later I was snow-white and just for that moment had a voice like her father. They came without question.

Vilkas took one look, grabbed Aral by the arm and started dragging her away towards the front gate. I followed.

Ah well, I thought as I hurried behind them. *That's me in it up to the eyeballs, at any rate.*

As soon as we hit the deserted corridors outside the first years' chambers, we started to run.

The Price of Belts and Bright Days

Varien

I learned that evening why Lanen had been so ill. Rella met me on the stair as I was returning from my bath.

"Varien, there's been a Healer in to see Lanen," she said, stopping one step above me. We each carried candles and the flickering shadows were disconcerting. I could hardly see her face, but her voice was grave. "She's a little better but she's not well."

Rella's concern seemed greater now than before we had entered the city. "Was the Healer not able to aid her?" I asked. "I have seen Gedri healers bring Lanen back from the brink of death. What did the Healer say? What afflicts her so?"

Rella held the candle away from her face. "Go to her, Varien. She needs you."

I stood back to allow her to pass on her way down the stair. I climbed slowly, breathing in long deep breaths, taking myself through the first stages of the Discipline of Calm that was so helpful in controlling the fierce passions of the Kantri. I did manage to slow the rapid beating of my heart.

I opened the door to our room slowly, lest she should be sleeping.

I have tried to forget that moment, but I cannot. It is an odd trait—both Kantri and Gedri remember events in much the same way, but I find there is a curious effect when the heart is most deeply involved. The strangest visions choose to stamp themselves on the memory.

The long side of the bed faced the door with its head against the right-hand wall, and the single candle by the bedside shone on Lanen's gleaming hair, for her face was turned away from me, her knees drawn up to her chest and her arms around them. I thought she was gazing out the small window directly opposite the door.

"Lanen," I said softly, as I put the candleholder on the shelf by the door. She did not move.

"Lanen?" I called again. She did not respond as I closed the door, and I knew could not approach her. I was beginning to learn the Attitudes of the Gedri, and Lanen's especially. There is a set in the shoulders, a something in the tension of the back even under her shift, that speaks as loudly as words and warns off even a husband from a too-swift approach. I "listened" for her mindvoice and heard nothing.

I addressed her in truespeech, for my heart's fears threatened to break through the fragile calm I had imposed on them. *"Dearling, forgive me, but I fear for you. Rella told me a Healer had been to see you but that you are not yet well."*

I listened in the dark and the quiet and heard only the faintest response. As though from a great distance I heard her calling in truespeech, longing, desperate, lost.

"Akor! Akor! Help me—oh sweet Lady, help me—"

I had her in my arms all in a moment, comforting her with mind and voice and holding her tight to me. "Lanen my heart, I am here, I am here," I repeated. Senseless, I know, she knew perfectly well that I was there, but it seemed to be the right thing to say. She held on to my arms with all her strength and I did not hear her breathe for the longest time, when suddenly between one breath and another she shook me off and stood up. She began to pace the room, her arms crossed before her, her bare feet shaking the floor as she stamped her anger on the boards. She was breathing as though she had run a race.

"Akor—the Healer said—I can't—"

She stopped pacing and stared at me, holding her arms tight round her chest, shaking. "Akor, I'm pregnant. And the Healer said—the Healer said it's killing me. That's what's been wrong with me, why I can't hold down food, why I've been so tired and swollen and had a headache for so long."

I felt the world's fool, but I could not help it. "Forgive me, dearling, I know not that word. What means 'pregnant'?"

"I am carrying our child," she said quietly.

I was very glad that I was sitting down, else I would have fallen. "What, already?" I said stupidly.

"Yes, already," said Lanen, annoyed. "How long did you think it would take? We've been lovers for nearly four moons!" She cracked a little at that and managed a small smile. "And making good use of the time, as well."

"Dearling, you have taught me much, but of the getting of younglings in this body I know nothing. It takes us years to conceive, and the younglings grow for the best part of two full years before they are born."

"Oh Hells, Varien, I'm sorry. I forgot you really don't know," she said, coming slowly to where I sat. "We can conceive after just one encounter, and we give birth nine moons later."

"Nine moons!" I cried.

"If all goes well. And it isn't." She stood again and wrapped her arms about her. "Varien—the Healer said I was warring within myself, that—that it would be better if I could lose the child. And she said"—Lanen started pacing again, striving to speak past the tightness in her throat—"she said it would be as well, that my body knew what it was doing, that it was"—her throat closed again, but she managed to speak through it, her voice rough—"in case it wasn't—in case it was so ill-made it wouldn't live anyway."

That was it, that was the terrible thing past. I sprang up and caught her as her strength left her at last. She wept for a moment in my arms, allowing me to see her weakness as I held her to me. In Lanen that was an intimacy as deep and vulnerable as physical nakedness.

I lifted her tenderly in my arms and laid her gently on the bed, and she sat up against the pillows. I laid the blankets over her bare legs and sat down beside her.

"Lanen, *kadreshi*, your pain is mine," I said, stroking her hair, surprised at how tight my own throat was, "for this child you carry is mine as well as yours." I gazed deep into her eyes. "Dear one, if the Healer is right, what must we do?"

"No!" she cried. "No, I don't believe her! She tried to get rid of it without telling me, in any case, and couldn't." She sighed and put a hand on her belly. "I'm glad she couldn't. She doesn't know about you. Of course it is difficult for the babe." She laughed, harsh laughter through her anger, and said as quietly as she could, "Name of the Winds, Akor, it's got half a Dragon for a father, of course it's going to have a hard time being born."

"Could it be as simple as that?" I asked, stunned. "But surely if I have the form of a child of the Gedri, I am of the substance of the Gedri as well!"

"Are you so certain?" she replied. "You stopped that sword with your arm the night the barn burned, and you were only cut."

"A cut to the bone, and it still aches," I said.

"Akor, if you were a normal man you would now be one-armed if you were alive at all. I saw that bastard, he was huge. And don't forget what you did to the pell—I find it hard to believe that a man of your build could be so strong."

"What has build to do with it?" I asked, confused. "This form I was gifted with is light but very strong, muscle and bone, and—"

"Just like dragons. I've wondered how in the world such

vast creatures manage to fly at all. It shouldn't be possible, unless you have wildly strong bones, hollow like a bird's, and muscles many times as strong as a man's." She paused, looking at me. "And if you are made still of the same stuff, only in the form of a man—sweet Lady—no wonder the Healer couldn't help you! And poor Jamie's pell!"

She was excited now, her anguish gone, her eyes sparkling in the dim candlelight. I love that spirit in her, that will not surrender to despair.

"Varien, that must be it! You are still in many ways one of the Kantri—your form is changed, but you are made still of the same stuff, and"—she glanced down at her belly, suddenly solemn—"and that is what is wrong. That's the war, it must be. This child is—oh Shia—"

Both her hands covered her mouth, as if she were trying to recall those words. I bespoke her, thanking the Winds and the Lady for truespeech.

"This child is what, Lanen?"

In reply I heard an echo in her mind, her memory of a voice I never thought to hear again—Rishkaan, who died half a year ago, speaking what were nearly his last words when Lanen stood trial before the Kantri.

She would mingle the blood of the Kantri and Gedri! Her children will be monsters, the world will fill with Raksha-fire and none to stand between because of her!

I took her by the shoulders and shook her. It made her angry, but it got her attention. "Stop it, Lanen! You are guessing. You know none of this as fact. All that you know for certain is that you are ill with this pregnancy." I managed a laugh, though it was not much of one. "Name of the Winds, dearling, if I were truly of the substance of my old people you would know dreadful pain when we joined in love, if indeed you survived it at all! Be reasonable. The seed of the Kantri would not quicken one of the Gedri, it could never happen. Rishkaan spoke from his hate, dearling. Do not be foolish. It cannot be."

She closed her eyes for a moment, hearing my words for the truth they were. She relaxed suddenly and sat again on the bed. "You're right, thank you, of course you're right. It just couldn't happen." She looked up at me, her eyes bright in the dim candlelight. "But I *am* having trouble with this child."

"Yes." I grinned. "I think we have come around to where we began. The question before us—before you—is, what is to do about it?"

"The—the Healer said we need to find a Mage," she said. "Fast."

"Then that is what we must do. Where should we find such a person?"

"They live all over, there might even be one here in Kaibar, but the school that trains them is in Verfaren. But that's not the worst of it, Varien," she said quietly. "She said I had to find a Mage very quickly or I'd die of this child. Verfaren is three or four weeks away."

A vague idea had begun to form in my mind. "Lanen, do not fear it. There is always a way."

She stared at me, but I did not dare speak of what I was thinking. Not yet.

"In the meantime, am I correct in thinking that Mages are simply very strong Healers?"

"In general, yes," said Lanen. "That woman was only a Healer of the second rank. Mages are more than twice as powerful. Maikel was a Healer of the third rank and you saw what he could do. Mages would be called fifth rank if they could be called anything, but after the fourth I gather that their gifts differ in kind, not just in ability." She frowned. "I would guess there would be someone around here who can help, Kaibar's a big place and trouble in pregnancy isn't all that uncommon."

"Then let us seek out a Mage, my heart," I said. I had caught some of her hope, and combined with the mad thought that had occurred to me, I dared to think that both the child and Lanen might live yet.

Lanen stood and shrugged on her clothes. "Let's get down to dinner and ask Rella, or the innkeeper. Someone is bound to have some idea where we should look."

The smells rising from the common room as we came out of our room were delicious. Lanen clattered down the stair with more energy than I'd seen from her in weeks, and the small grain of hope that had been planted in my heart sent a tiny green seedling into the light and the air.

The variety of foods that the Gedri have created from simple ingredients has never yet ceased to amaze me. There was a thick vegetable soup and a slab of nutty brown bread with it, then a roasted ham served with some kind of root vegetable I had never seen—when Lanen told me it was called "parsnip" I laughed aloud at the sound of the name—and potatoes that had been magically transformed into a fluffy white mush. They were delicious. I was delighted to see Lanen eating heartily. She had lost so much flesh as we travelled, for the food we had carried was intended only to sustain on a journey and after the first se'ennight or so she could not keep it down. The Healer had done good work, however, and for the moment at least Lanen seemed much better. She was still far too thin, but her cheeks were no longer sunken with constant pain. The seedling grew another tiny leaf.

Rella was pleased at Lanen's recovery as well, and seemed almost surprised to see her. "Are you feeling better, my girl?"

Jamie frowned over at Lanen. "Yes, I heard you had a Healer in, lass." He looked long at her. "About time, too. You're too damn thin and I know fine you haven't kept a full meal down for days." His kind eyes belied the gruff words he spoke. "And you've been such a pest this last se'ennight I'd guess you must have been in a lot more pain than you said. What did the Healer have to say?"

Lanen

For the first time, for just a moment, I knew the joy that I had always felt was the right of one carrying a child. "I'm pregnant, Jamie." I grinned at him. "If I live through this, you're going to be a grandfather."

Bless him, his face lit up like a fire in midwinter, and he

leapt up from his bench to embrace me, laughing. "You horrible child, are you in such a hurry to make me an old man?" he said, delighted. "How wonderful! Ah, Lanen, I'm so pleased for you." Then he realised that both Rella and Varien were still looking fairly grave. "And so," he said soberly, sitting down again. " 'If I live through this,' you say. You needed a Healer, all is not well. Tell me."

I sat down and told him what the healer had said. All of it. "But I'm not finished yet, Jamie. I feel so much better now! My stomach isn't heaving, I don't have that damned headache, and my back hardly aches at all."

"Where are we to find a Mage in this town?" he asked.

"My job," said Rella immediately. "The girl's not going to fall over this instant, and I know a place I can go tomorrow where I can learn all I need."

Jamie started to object but I laid my hand on his arm. "I'm not daft, Jamie, and I have no intention of dying. If we cannot find a Mage here, we must find a way to get swiftly to Verfaren, that's all."

"It's three weeks, best speed, my lass," he said heavily.

"Well? I'm no weakling, Jamie. I can do *anything* for three weeks. Besides, there are Healers along our path, are there not?"

"Yes," said Rella dryly, "but probably not as many as you'll need."

"I have managed this long without one, I'm sure I can last between one Healer and the next."

"It's too damned far," said Jamie sharply. I was surprised and stared at him. He glared back. "You have only just managed to get here, Lanen," he said. "You will not be able to ride nearly so far, especially if you are unwell with this babe. We should think about finding a safe place to stay."

"No," I said. "Hideous as that woman was, she was right in one thing—Verfaren is the best place for me to be with this child."

"Hells' teeth, Lanen. Have you forgotten what else is in Verfaren?" he said, his voice little more than a whisper. It barely carried to me. "Berys the Bastard, Berys Child-killer is there. The one man in the world you need to avoid, and he is squatting like a toad in the one place in the world you need to be."

"Then we must ensure that we bring a Mage to Lanen rather than taking her there," said Varien quietly. "Surely, there is somewhere near enough to Verfaren that Lanen need not enter the city itself."

"Well spoken, lad," said Rella. Varien looked surprised at being called "lad," but seemed to take it in good part. "It's true, there are any number of little villages where we could take shelter and simply send for a Mage. We'll have to get a damn sight closer, but at least we don't have to go into the bastard's very clutches."

"I still don't like it," said Jamie.

Rella turned full to him. "Neither do I, Master, not at all, but we all must dance when demons pipe."

Varien turned to me, his eyebrows lifted. *What in all the wide world does she mean by that?"* he asked plaintively in truespeech.

I laughed. It felt good to laugh, to let go the fear and the gloom even for a moment. "She means that sometimes life pushes you into a corner and you are forced to do something you would not choose to do otherwise," I answered aloud, smiling. "As long as we don't draw attention to ourselves, we should be able to creep in under his nose and creep out again when all is done."

Jamie looked doubtful but Rella nodded. "There's a good chance, in any case, that I'll be able to find a Mage here in Kaibar," she said. "Just you take it easy tonight, my girl!"

I laughed. "You have my word of honour," I said.

"Taken and bound," she replied with a smile. "I'm off tonight, I'll see what I can find out."

"Off where?" asked Jamie gruffly. "We just got here."

"Wherever I wish to go," she said, turning to him and laughing. "There is no more I can do for Lanen tonight. I have not been in a city for nearly three moons now, and though I can trail along back roads and through forest and field with the best, I am a daughter of Sorún at heart. Kaibar is only second-best but it will have to do. And I need not answer to you, Master Jameth," she said lightly. "I found myself a different Healer and I've had my back seen to. I too feel better than I have since before midwinter, and tonight I am going to enjoy myself." She grinned, and there was a mischievous light in her eye that I had never seen before. It suited her. "I will see you all tomorrow. I assume we are staying tomorrow night as well?"

"We have seen no sign of pursuit," said Jamie very quietly, "and both we and the horses will be the better for the rest."

"Fine. I'll see you here tomorrow afternoon. Tell them to keep dinner for me," she said to me, rising and putting on her cloak. "It's the best food I've had in ages and I don't want to miss it."

I grinned at her. "Have fun, Rella," I said. She caught my eye and we laughed, leaving the men to wonder what on earth we were laughing at.

I adore Varien, and Jamie is the father I never had, but they can both be so stupid at times.

And sweet Goddess, but it felt good to laugh, if only for a brief moment.

Salera

When the green was just beginning to rise above the cold earth but the trees were yet bare of leaf, I woke one morning as though to the sound of a voice. It was not His, I could not truly be certain that I had heard anything at all, but it had a sense about it of—of family, of home. I shivered and went out of the shelter where I awaited His coming, out to breathe deep of the morning air and see the sky. I heard nothing in that cold clear morning but the voices of our far cousins the birds, so I rose on wings stiff with too much waiting, revelling in the feel of air, and greeted the dawn with a sprightly wing-dance. With me in the air I soon found, to my surprise, some few of my own kind, like me celebrating the warmth of the morning and the simple pleasure of a bright day. All were of the first kind, the Heart-speakers, those I knew I could trust. We came to land as if by consent in a place I had passed through on my journey to the only home I knew.

It was a high place, up in the hills and safe. Most of it was grassy and as flat as any field, save for the two talons of rock that ran out from the high cliffs and enclosed the larger part of it. There was a small wood at one end, and from it the scent of water drew us to a small pool, where we drank.

That was the beginning. By the end of the day a few more had joined us, and as the time went on it seemed that whatever had drawn me into the air had affected all my kinfolk as well.

We gathered, not knowing why, not asking. A few one day, none the next, more the next. We did not question it, nor ourselves. We could not speak but we showed each other visions, thoughts, of the places we had come from. Some came as couples, some with young, and my heart knew pain when I saw mothers and kitlings together. I could not remember my mother's eyes, but I remembered her passing.

I missed him so. He had taken me in, been mother and father to me, given of love freely and kept my own heart's-fire alive. Where was he?

Lanen

"Fire, water, earth and air, keep us in the Lady's care . . ."

I astounded myself by waking to the old words of the traveller's prayer. Jamie had taught it to me as a child, when I was most desperate to see what lay beyond my small world, and now in the bright morning it danced in my mind like the sun through spring leaves.

That was just as well, for spring still seemed a thousand years distant. I opened my eyes, glanced around the tiny inn room, wondered where in blazes I was and nearly jumped out of bed when I realised there was someone in there with me. I woke poor Varien laughing.

He had the grace not to mind. I apologised for waking him, but he smiled at me and said, "Would you apologise for waking me with laughter? Never, *kadreshi*. And there is sunlight as well. A day to celebrate!"

It was such a relief to waken with a light heart, for the first time in what felt like years! Varien and I delighted in that sunlit waking and, foolish though it may have been, made cheerfully passionate love. It was uncomfortable at first and made my back ache again, but it felt so good to join with him that I ignored the twinges and took my pleasure along with him. Varien, I was pleased to note, was getting really quite good at this lovemaking lark.

I felt vastly better than I had, though with my body in less pain for the moment, the voices were back to bother me. I know I am harping on about them, but imagine hearing always in your ears what seems to be a whispered conversation some distance away, the words of which you can never quite make out, and the noise of which you cannot escape. I resolutely ignored it that morning, however, for I was determined to make a right day of it. The light was lingering much later now, the days moving away from the winter dark, and I was feeling the good of the healing and the food from the day before, and of sleeping in a real bed again.

We drifted down to breakfast some time later and found only lukewarm porridge on offer, which we declined. I had a good sum of silver with me and I was suddenly determined to take advantage of the time and go exploring with Varien. He had never really seen a city, for we had left Corlí in a tearing hurry. I bade Jamie farewell, Varien put his arm about my waist and we stepped out into the morning.

I had only ever seen Kaibar briefly when I passed through it on the riverboat that bore me to Corlí in the autumn. I don't usually care much about clothing, but I had found a cloak there, a beautiful green woolen cloak that I adored. It had been destroyed on the Dragon Isle and at the time I hadn't thought twice about it, but now I was determined to find something of the kind to take along with me. I knew I would never find the same shop again, but I was happy enough to wander the streets until some other single lovely thing caught my fancy. I was feeling more than a little shabby and I needed to do something to celebrate my new condition, hazardous though it was. If nothing else, I would put down my wager on the future by purchasing cloth with which to make myself some larger tunics and let out the waists of my leggings!

I know it was foolish to assume that I would need to do so, to believe that I would be able to carry the child—or even that I would live—but I was so thrilled at feeling so much better than I had, that I dared to hope. Indeed, I was fairly drunk on it, as was Varien, and we set out into the city laughing.

That bright morning with Varien is so vivid! I remember it even now as if it were hours ago instead of decades. We wandered down towards the river, past cobblers and fish-mongers and butchers, every kind of merchant's stall you can imagine, all intent, with the best will in the world, on separating every passing soul from as much of their silver as possible.

The smells were nearly overpowering as we came closer to the water. The streets of Kaibar were none too clean—I was glad I was wearing my thick leather riding boots—and the smell of so many people in one place, combined with horses and leather and fish and cooking, was hard on my poor stomach. We had bought hot meat pies from a baker but neither of us could bear to eat them until we came to the river.

There at least the smells were not so vicious, for a brisk wind blew down the Kai and carried them away south and west. We sat on the riverbank and ate our pies but the wind was too fresh to sit in for long. I took Varien down to the har-bour, glancing into every tented stall, looking at everything but caught by nothing until we passed a leatherworker's shop. No tented stall out of doors for this one, but a small room in the front of his home to display his goods. There were leather scrips, baldrics, gloves for use and for show, sheaths for everything from a sword to a tiny ladies' dagger, archers' armguards and quivers, all the usual things, but on a small table by the door there were stacks and stacks of his stock-in-trade, belts of good thick leather with silver or iron buckles. Some were tooled, some were dyed the most amazing colours, some were fanciful carved pieces that were obviously only made for the look of them. I love the smell of leather, always have, and I must have looked happily at every belt on that table without finding anything I particularly wanted. The maker noticed me looking, however, and smiled. He was a neat little man, with a quick smile in a black-bearded face and merry eyes. He beckoned me over. "I have only this moment finished this one, Lady," he said, holding up a tooled belt. The leather itself was nothing wonderful, a thick serviceable belt, but on it he had carved a pattern of leaves and dyed each one a different shade of green. Against the brown of the leather they were perfect. They almost reminded me of the embroidery of my lost cloak. The buckle was of brass, which he made sure to tell me was his very last of a number obtained in trade from the East Kingdom some years ago.

I laughed. "And when I have gone you will bring the other last buckle out, I suppose," I said. He grinned. "It is not impossible," he replied. "How then would five silver strike you, for such fine tooling and my very nearly last brass buckle?"

I enjoyed haggling with him over the price, and as usual we ended up somewhere between our two extremes, but in the end of the day I didn't really care what I paid and I'm afraid he knew it. Still, when he offered to cut it to my size I could laugh and tell him that I was soon going to require a larger size in belts and I'd keep it as long it was. He wished us joy and I walked out with Varien on my arm and the belt around my waist on the tightest hole, most thoroughly pleased with myself.

I also managed to find a clothiers and bought a good weight of material for a tunic in a deep blue that Varien said suited me. We wandered back through the streets towards the inn and found ourselves in a part of the city where a patch of grass and a small stand of trees grew by the edge of a stream. The trees were all bare branches, of course, and with the brown grass I suppose it was bleak enough, but by the waterside sprouted Lady's-bells, their silvery-white heads nodding among the bright green of their leaves, and here and there pale ground roses were just beginning to open, pink and palest yellow. It cheered me just to sit there in the weak afternoon sun before we went back to the inn.

I know this is not the stuff ballads are made of. I suspect anyone who can be bothered to read so far is wondering why I should write such things, that can interest no one but an old woman remembering her past. The truth is that those days were so full of great and terrible things happening, so full of pain and fear and change and darkness, that sometimes I like to recall the times when Varien and I were just being new-wedded idiots together. There were few enough of them. That day was wonderful, without a single care, and I will never forget it. After so long running from pursuit, we felt safe for the moment, and we resolved without a word being spoken to act that day as if all would be well. The Healer's work, despite her manner, was well done and I felt vastly better than I had. Varien dared to tell me of his joy at the mere possibility of being a father, and for the moment I barely heard the voices that whispered at me. It was the Lady's promise of paradise come to real life as a brief glimpse—or so I felt that day, and so I still believe. If there is a life beyond death, if there is a kindly place where we go to be forever with those souls we love best, it would be hard put to it to rival that one bright day with Varien.

Shikrar

Alas! If we had known we might have fought it, but we did not know. I was too blind, too full of the sight of the land running like water to understand the reason behind it.

And yet, what could we have done? Fire was rising against us and we knew not where to turn. We could not fight it with tooth or talon, we could not burn hotter than the fires of the earth. Perhaps in the end we had no choice.

I bespoke Kédra as soon as I reached my chambers. It was now deep night.

"My son, are you well?" I asked quietly.

"We come, Father," he replied immediately. *"Sherók is enjoying his treat, a flight in the dark to visit grandfather Shikrar. Brave soul, my son!"*

I waited.

"We will be there very shortly, Eldest," said Mirazhe, her mind voice amazingly clear and calm. I took heart from hearing her. *"Sherók and I will await you in Lord Akhor's old chambers by the Great Hall. It seems fitting somehow,"* she said, *"for I would guess that we will see Varien Kantriakhor far sooner than we had thought to."*

"There is nothing more likely, dearest daughter," I replied, and could not resist the ghost of an amused hiss. *"He may be ever so slightly surprised."*

"It will be good for him," said Kédra. *"He has hardly spoken with us since he left. If we are a surprise to him, so much the better, it will serve him right."*

"May all the Gedri be as eager to see us, though I fear they will not be."

"Ah, but we have the Lady Lanen to speak for us," said Kédra.

"She is one voice among thousands, and herself declared that she was of no particular note among her people," I said. *"Do you think that those who must be persuaded will hear her, courageous as she is?"*

"Father, I crave your pardon, but you have forgotten," replied Kédra, undaunted. *"This child of the Gedri, of no particular note, managed to talk the Kantrishakrim, assembled in Council, out of killing her and into accepting her as the mate of our king. Name of the Winds, this is a soul that could rule the world."*

I could not help myself. Faced as I was with change and the end of my life as I had known it, still I laughed at the truth behind my son's words. *"Bless you, Kédra, you dreadful kit!"* I said. *"Solemnity now would undo me. Where are you now?"*

"Mirazhe and Sherók are safe in Akhor's chambers, with a fire lit. I come," he said. He was with me almost as his thought ended.

"Welcome, most welcome, dear my son," I said as he came into the Chamber of Souls. We embraced, and I held him to my heart, my wings wrapped about him, just as I had when he was but a youngling. "Ah, Kédra, my dear," I said, and suddenly I could say no more. My throat tightened and I choked on my words. He had been born in that place, my beloved Yrais had died there, the very walls were hallowed with memories and life, and I knew I would never spend another night there. I remained in my generous son's embrace with bowed head and my heart caught in the depths of my despair, when I felt a terrible thing.

We are creatures of fire. We produce fire when we are pleased, when we are angry, when we are deeply moved, as the Gedri produce the salt water they call tears. Few know it, but we also weep, in the last extremity of soul's darkness.

I felt a tear hiss its way down my faceplate.

Kédra saw and did nothing, just held me. I knew deep in my soul that he was remembering the night Yrais died, for then it was he who had wept. I had held him then, been his strength when my own heart was shattered and dead, and now that strength held me up.

Has ever father had such a son?

Blessed be the Winds, but such times are short. I touched his soulgem with my own, that intimacy that only parents and children share, and was again myself.

"Thank you," I said simply.

"I am thirsty, Father. Let us drink before we begin," he said, embarrassed I think.

It is often difficult even for such a one as Kédra to admit to great strength.

We went the few steps out the door of my chambers and both drank deeply of the stream that ran close by. The simple feel of the water, the taste of it on my tongue that I had not noticed for years, the smell of the slow-approaching spring beneath the earth were suddenly precious beyond words.

The thought "you will never do that again" threatened me, but I turned from it. Time enough to grieve later.

Water. Fire. The island alight—no, there could be no mourning until we were safely gone.

With a heart weighted down with sorrow we turned back into my chamber. I had lit a fire in the main chamber both to hallow our actions and to aid us in our task.

We scraped together great handfuls of *khaadish* from the corner where I slept and began to make several deep bowls, breathing fire to melt and smooth the surface and to ease the shaping of them. When they were complete I sent Kédra out to gather moss while I made flat plates about the size of the bowls, bent them slightly that they might act as coverings, and laid them aside. I used the moss to line the bottom and sides of the bowls.

I could delay no longer. As we stood at the opening of the inner chamber, the wall facing us was covered in *khaadish* with the soulgems of our Ancestors set deep in the soft metal. I bowed to the gathered Ancestors of our people, reached up to the highest and oldest and with a careful talon dug it out of its setting. As I placed it gently in the vessel I felt my sorrow as a physical pain, but I could bear it. I had to.

"Kédra, of your kindness make a covering for the cask that holds the soulgems of the Lost," I said.

Poor things, borne here ages ago when first they were torn from their owners, and now forced to return to the place where it had happened.

Alas for us all.

Lanen

It started again that night, of course. I should have known that even so simple a thing as a day of joy has its price.

When we returned to the inn I was tired and I went up to my room to rest. I found my clean, dry clothes folded neatly on the bed and all but danced a jig. I turned my pack inside out, brushed it clean, then turned it back and put my treasures carefully back in, swearing to myself this time to save one change of underwear and one clean shirt against the next time I was truly filthy. When I straightened it hit me, as before, like a dagger had plunged into my belly. I blessed true-speech and yelled for Varien to bring Rella as I crawled to the bed. They were with me in moments. Rella took one look, started swearing and left. She was back soon with a basin of hot water, some cloths, and the assurance that a different Healer had been sent for.

Varien said nothing aloud. He sat beside me, his back to Rella and her ministrations, his eyes gazing gently into mine. Instead of the whispering voices I now heard only his own glorious voice in my mind. There were no words, exactly, but I could feel the strength and love he was sending me surrounding me like a blanket.

"I went looking for a Mage for you, girl, but we're out of luck," said Rella quietly. "Of the three who live here, two are out of town and the third is a bone-setter." She winked at me over Varien's shoulder. "You wouldn't care to break a leg, would you? We could find out how good he is."

I managed to smile back, for the pain had lessened for the moment. "Thanks, Rella, you're a true friend, but I wouldn't dream of depriving you. Just come up here where I can reach you and I'll help you break your own leg, then you can find out."

A man walked in at that moment, someone I'd never seen before. He was middle-aged, of middle height, and he frowned at me. "And what's troubling you, young woman?" he asked, his voice and bearing the very portrait of self-importance. He walked towards me, pushing back his sleeves and starting to glow blue.

"A strange man just walked into my room and started asking me questions," I snarled. Something about him made me want to bite. "Maybe if he said who the devil he was I'd feel better."

"I am the Healer Kidleth. I was sent for," he replied, not bothered in the slightest.

"What happened to the woman who came yesterday?" I asked, as a distraction and to alert Rella. I bespoke Varien as fast as I could. *"Akor, there's something terribly wrong with him. Can you see it? Am I crazy? I don't want him to touch me!"*

Kidleth muttered something and Varien stepped forward and offered his hand. Kidleth took it for an instant, but no more, for Varien dropped it as fast as he could. I could nearly hear him hiss.

"You serve the Rakshasa!" he growled. He was breathing strangely. *"Remember you can't breathe fire anymore,"* I told him swiftly. I heard his breathing change as he stepped forward, towering over the man and forcing him to move away from me and back towards the door. "How dare you come here reeking of the filth!"

The man tried to hold his ground for a moment. "I am the prime Healer with the House of Gundar in Kaibar, young man, you will not address me that way!"

"I am Varien of the line of Loriakeris," growled Varien fervently, "and I will kill you if you do not leave this place immediately."

I shivered. Varien was become Akor again, and saw the evil in this man's soul as deserving instant death, as would be the case on the Dragon Isle. His voice was the same kind of cold I had once heard from Jamie, when he was speaking with a man he was about to kill.

"Leave this instant, you idiot. Can't you see he means it?" snarled Rella. Her hand was on the hilt of her dagger.

The Healer turned and ran without another word. Rella picked up my boots and threw them to me. "I don't care how much it hurts, girl. Get dressed now. We're leaving. I'll go tell Jamie."

"Why?" I demanded.

"Have you forgotten, or didn't you hear for the pain?" she asked me as she swiftly gathered my belongings and tied up my pack. "House of Gundar! I told you when we were on the Dragon Isle—Marik's got demon callers in nearly every branch of his Merchant House, most of them Healers he's turned bad, and this idiot was one of them. If Marik or Berys seek us, they will know where we are within the hour. We have to go. Get dressed and meet me in the common room as fast as you can."

I gritted my teeth, dressed as quickly as I could and we hurried downstairs, but Rella was there before us. "Jamie's out saddling the horses," she said, smiling, calmly paying the innkeeper and chatting about the weather. We followed her outside. The twilight was fading and true dark setting in.

Jamie met us at the door with the horses, who were fractious at being saddled and turned out of their warm barn at such a peculiar hour. As we mounted, Rella said only, "Follow me."

We did. The pain was just bearable, for the moment, and Rella seemed to know what she was doing. I could see Jamie shrug in the light from the inn and turn his horse to follow hers.

We turned from well-lit streets with many houses to an altogether darker part of the town. Barely one house in three was occupied. Many had broken shutters, doors hung off their hinges, and there seemed to be far too many dogs about. The horses were as nervous as I was, and when Jamie's Blaze snorted and backed from a narrow lane Jamie risked speaking. "You do know where you're going, do you?" he called to Rella.

She answered quietly from just ahead of Jamie. "I know they don't like it. Not far now."

We followed, down a short cobbled lane only just wide enough for the horses to enter single file. There was a high gated wall at the end of the street, with a door in it as wide as the lane itself. The door was closed and the gate was dark.

When we were all stood in a line before the door, Rella whistled a series of peculiar notes. Immediately a light was revealed halfway up the wall and the door opened wide. She rode in ahead of us, still whistling, and we came out into a large grassy courtyard covered by a high roof on long poles. How so much room could lurk behind so narrow a street I could not imagine, but I was new to cities and there was much I did not understand. For example, I had no idea where we were, but Jamie looked around and laughed. It wasn't a pleasant sound.

Jamie

I'd heard of the Silent Service all my life and I'd known more than a few of their members, but I'd never dared to hope I'd see the inside of one of their Strongholds. In fact I'd begun to wonder if they were no more than tales. As I glanced around I realised where and why the stories about them had started.

From cobbled lane to grass—so their members would disappear at the end of that impossible road, or appear silently from nowhere and be able to ride hell for leather from a standing start. And the high roof must be designed to fool the eye from above—anyone looking down from a high tower would see only more roofs. It was ingenious and I longed for a little more light, but instead we were approached by three people wearing hoods, who gestured us down from our horses.

Rella, who had dismounted, said, "Don't worry, Jamie. You're not allowed to see any more than you've seen. All of you, please, you'll need to be hooded for a moment or two."

"And you?" asked Varien, sounding none too pleased.

"I work here," said Rella, laughing. "Come, there's no harm in it. I need to talk to my Master fast and this was the only way to do it. If you don't wear the hoods they'll have to knock you facedown on the ground and sit on you. Hoods are easier."

Lanen laughed. "Pass it over, then. I can't see worth spit in this light anyway so I might as well have an excuse." She placed the hood over her own head without a qualm.

We didn't really have any choice so we all did as Rella asked. "I'll be right back," she said. As she left we heard her calling on someone to bring us food and wine. In moments I had a fresh bread roll in one hand and a glass of wine in the other. Couldn't fault their hospitality, and at least there was plenty of room under the hood to allow us to eat and drink.

Rella

If you think I'm going to give away any secrets, think again.

When I reached the Master of Kaibar we had a swift conversation, most of which any bystander would have found impossible to understand. Many of the lesser agents would also be confused, and I am not about to break silence now. However, if we had been speaking normally the mundane parts of the conversation would have gone something like this.

"I assume, Mistress Relleda, that you have a truly fine reason for bringing three Bricks into this Sanctuary?"

"You assume correctly. The idiot innkeeper at the Three Kings sent for one of Berys's twisted creatures when I wanted a Healer."

"I heard you were after healing. You don't look any worse than usual."

"It's for a client."

"A client!" he snorted. "And now you're going to tell me your client is in the courtyard."

"You guess well."

He sat back and glared at me. "Three Bricks in the Sanctuary, Rella. This had better be good."

I crossed my arms and grinned. "Damn right it's good. You would not believe how the strands of fate are crossed and woven in favour of the lady out there. That girl is the one Berys is after. The daughter of Marik. The one in the demon caller's prophecy who's going to rule all of Kolmar."

"You've found her!" he cried, jubilant.

"Found her? I've been with her for months. And I'm not going to give her up now. Do you realise what she's worth? To her mother, to Marik, to Berys himself?"

"Then you intend to bargain with her?" he asked, sitting back, nearly closing his eyes.

I snorted. "Not likely. You know what Berys is after and so do I. I've no time for demons or the bastards who work with them. I'm on duty for her mother, Maran Vena."

"I've heard of her," said the Master, a tiny, greedy smile crossing his face. "I've heard she has something almost as valuable as her daughter."

"The Farseer is not the issue here."

"Why not?"

"Trust me, it's not for sale or stealing." I grimaced. "I tried once. Bad idea. Is the Healer here?"

"I'll send her out."

"And I'll need Post horses for four all the way to Verfaren, or at least to within a day's travel." I was proud of myself. My voice stayed calm and reasonable through that whole sentence.

He sprang to his feet then, spluttering and swearing. "Hells' teeth and bones, woman! Do you have any idea of the cost? Of the wear on the horses, of the loss of speed to our people for a week! Give me one good reason I should let you and three Bricks use the Post!"

I waited, smiling, for him to stop spluttering, then said calmly, "I need to get the new owner of Hadron's horses safely to the best Healers in the world. Then, when she owes us her life—well, we may never have to pay for one again."

Damn, he could move fast when he wanted to.

The Wind of Change Blows Icy Cold

Lanen

We had stopped for the night, a single day out from Kaibar.

We had left our own horses with the Silent Service in Kaibar the night before. In exchange, we might keep the Post horses we rode when our race was over. The Service did well out of the deal, for of course our mounts were of Hadron's stock. Still, it was worth it for the speed. Jamie wouldn't sell Blaze, so he arranged to collect him next time he passed.

The Healer of the Silent Service had been a very kind woman, who had said little but whose gentle touch made her work all the more effective. I felt a little better, but I was beginning to realise that each time someone worked on me the effect was less, as if my body were telling me that there was only so much to be done. I tried not to think about it, and even succeeded for much of that day.

Travelling by Post is astounding. It was hard at first: no one with sense would ever ride a horse that hard, but you never stay on one horse for long. Jamie and I laughed the first time we changed horses, because two of four new mounts were beasts we had sold only a few years ago. Seems Hadron's horses were highly valued by the Silent Service. Jamie muttered something about doubling the price and Rella laughed. "We must have a talk about that sometime in the next few days," she said, "but not right now. Mount up." At the next change we recognised a big gelding we'd sold at Illara just that autumn past. He remembered us, too, and nuzzled at Jamie. We all felt the better for that.

In any case, once we had crossed the Kai—on a dark vessel that made almost no sound—we began our ride on the Post horses and covered huge amounts of distance that night, stopping only to sleep for a few hours in some inn somewhere. I was all but asleep in the saddle and barely managed to stagger into the room we were sent to before I fell across the nearest bed and asleep. Varien must have had to shift me to get in. When we woke it was daylight, all four of us were in the one room, and Rella was up and dressed and in deep conversation with a man at the door. When she closed it she turned to face us gravely and said, "The word from Marik's Healers has come and gone this last hour. They know it was you needing help in the Three Kings, girl, but they don't know where you've gone. Last seen in Kaibar. The farther we get the better."

"Lady, will they not assume that we seek the more powerful healers in Verfaren?" asked Varien. He had hardly spoken all day. "It must be known that Lanen is unwell."

"I'm counting on the speed we left at to save us," Rella replied, throwing her few belongings back into her pack. "We recognised Marik's Healer, we knew he'd report, and we took off. The last place they are going to look for us is in the South Kingdom, where Marik is."

We stared at Rella, unconvinced. She looked up.

"That's the idea, at any rate. Any of you have a better one?"

"Not really," I said, wincing. The pain was coming back, and the voices were loud that morning, and my back was killing me. "If we're going to Verfaren, let's go. At least there I can get some decent healing before they kill me."

Rella seemed to find that funny.

I didn't. But she didn't know—I didn't tell her, or anyone else, but I had started bleeding again. My lower back never stopped aching now, and the riding was making it worse. I wasn't keeping much food down either. I felt miserable and I was deeply grateful that the furious riding left us very little opportunity to speak to one another.

The most peculiar part about that mad dash was how my mind kept returning to my mother, of all things. I found myself wanting desperately to speak with Jamie about Maran Vena, to hear anything he could tell me about her. In fact what I really wanted was to talk to her, face-to-face—though I would have preferred a good shouting match. I had been angry at her most of my childhood and I thought I had grown past that years ago, but here was that same anger back again, formless yet full-blown in its strength. I was even angry at Hadron for being so cold and heartless to me all those years. How stupid! Hadron was dead these six moons, and I had learned from Jamie in the autumn that he had known from my birth that he was not my father, that I was nothing to him, and that he had kept me at Hadronsstead only in memory of Maran—the only woman he had ever loved. Still, the heart does not always make allowances for others, especially in such circumstances.

The worst part of that time, however, arose from my own soul with no reference to any other. I am deeply ashamed to admit it, but in the secret depths of my heart I was furious with the child that grew within me. I know it sounds unnatural and I would deny it if I could, but it happened. The simple truth is that I had been told that it could not survive its own birth and I was angry at it for taking me with it. Despite that day in Kaibar when Varien and I had played at becoming parents, I knew that my life was more than likely to end suddenly and badly, when I had only just begun to live. I was very glad that our speed did not allow us to speak much to one another, and I closed my thoughts to Varien as best I could.

We rode through the day nearly without stopping, pushing the horses and ourselves, changing about every twenty or twenty-five miles. The poor beasts would be useless for several days after, but they were all young and fit and it wouldn't really hurt them. And we had travelled well over a hundred miles in a day, with six changes of mount. It was astounding.

At this rate we would be in Verfaren in another day.

I can hear what you are thinking, those of you who have borne children. How could you do that? Didn't it hurt like fury? Yes, it did. Didn't the riding make the pain worse? Yes, of course. But what would you? I was being forced to ride like the very wind towards the one place in all of Kolmar that I should have been avoiding, for the sake of saving my life. The demons were piping loud and clear and I was dancing like there was no tomorrow, for that was indeed like to be the case.

We stopped just to the north of Elimar, the capital of the South Kingdom. Rella again selected the inn. It was expensive, but it was clean and the food was good enough. She disappeared soon after we arrived, only to return in time for the evening meal. "I've arranged for a really fine Healer to come along to see you, my girl," she said, very pleased with herself. "But not until after we've eaten, so get down to it."

I was intensely relieved to hear that a Healer was coming, but I couldn't eat a thing. I had gone to change my cloth when we arrived and found that I had to change all my underthings. Even I knew that there was far too much blood. The possibility that I might die from this was beginning to become very real. I had been trying to blank out the pain but it was now affecting my every movement, and I was starting to feel light-headed from the loss of blood. I started to thank Rella for her kindness when Jamie interrupted me. He had been brooding and growly ever since we'd left Kaibar and he wouldn't tell me what was bothering him. From the storm on his brow I suspected we were all about to find out.

"That's enough!" he said sharply, keeping his voice as quiet as he could with that much anger behind it. I knew it was coming but I still jumped. "Why, Mistress Rella?"

"Why what?" she asked, tearing a chunk off the loaf on the table. "Damn, I'm hungry. Pass the butter, will you, Lanen?"

"Why all of it?" said Jamie, staring at Rella. "Finding Healers, arranging Post horses—I can't believe it's all part of your work."

Rella looked at him, a bit confused. She wasn't the only one. "Why question a gift from the Lady?" she said calmly. "You know I'm on duty."

Jamie sliced the air with one hand. "Ridiculous!" he snarled. "No one could pay the Service enough to get us all on Post horses, not even Maran."

"What!"

The exclamation was out of my mouth before I could stop it. Too late now to call it back and just listen. Ah, well. I tried to ignore the heads that had turned in my direction—I suppose it was a loud shout, at that—and spoke more quietly. "What do you mean, not even Maran? What does my mother have to do with anything?" I asked. I was much taken aback for, as I have said, Maran had been on my mind all the day long.

Rella was frowning and shaking her head at Jamie, but he faced me and said harshly, "Rella's working for her. She's been in Maran's pay since she joined the Harvest ship with you in the autumn. Since you first met her. Didn't you know?"

"What? No! I thought—Rella, you said the Silent Service wanted Marik, you never—I mean, you said you knew Maran—oh hell," I snarled. "Hells' bells and bloody damnation, Jamie," I said, feeling stupid and angry and betrayed. "I've been an idiot again, haven't I?"

"I suspect we all have, my girl," said Jamie, "but I don't intend to continue in ignorance." He rounded on Rella. "Well?"

She had carried on eating, stopping only long enough to say in her normal tones, "I'm not going to say a word until

I've eaten and Lanen has seen a Healer. Then you can ask me anything you want. Right now, leave me be. I'm hungry."

We had no choice. We were all subdued and ate quickly. I never tasted the little food I managed to eat, but I was feeling awful anyway and didn't eat much in case it came back up. Soon enough we all retired to an upstairs room, where we found the four small beds taking up nearly every bit of floor space. There was barely room to squeeze around them to get inside the door.

I crawled into the first bed I could reach. I was feeling worse by the moment, as the agitation of all that riding caught up with me. However, once we were in and the door closed Jamie turned to Rella with a grim frown and a nasty expression on his face, and I had something else to think about.

"Very well, Mistress Rella," he said. "Perhaps you will now deign to tell us what in all the Hells is going on?"

"You make everything such hard work, Jamie," she said, shaking her head. "But you're losing your touch. Talking about such things in a common room! Honestly. You only had to ask."

"Lady Rella," said Varien gently, cutting off whatever Jamie was about to say, "of thy courtesy, surely the time hath come for truth between us?"

She was taken off guard by him. She knew who and what he was, but I think she forgot from time to time just what it meant to have lived for so very long. Now, with those deep green eyes fixed on hers, and that lovely voice speaking so kindly to her—well, "the eyes of a dragon are perilous deep," they say.

"Yes, my Lord Dragon, I suppose it has," she said with a sigh. She turned to me and smiled. "You are so much like her, you know. I've known Maran ever since she came back to Beskin, about a year and a half after you were born. She has been a good friend to me in my comings and goings for all that time, even knowing who I am and what I do. She is the best friend I have in the world, Lanen. When word reached me that she wanted to hire me to watch over you I was already in Illara, but I signed on that damned ship and went to what I thought would be my death because I had said I would look after you for her. My dearest friend's daughter. Yes, Jamie, she has paid me. Is paying me. Is paying the Silent Service. And no, there is no money in the world that could have got me on to that ship or arranged these Post horses for us all."

She threaded her way across the crowded little room to stand foursquare in front of Jamie and slapped him hard across the face.

"You bastard," she said, quietly but with a startling intensity. "How can you have travelled with me for so long and know me so little? Yes, I am a minor Master in the Silent Service and I may choose my own assignments. Yes, I have more leeway in the arrangements than most, and yes, I was going to ask for consideration from you and Lanen the next time the Service needs good horses. That does not mean that I do everything for pay, or that I seek to use or betray you. Any of you. I've cared about Lanen since I met her, despite all the rules about these things, and I know how sick she is even if you don't care to. I have arranged this swift transport and a good Healer's visit for her because I give a damn what happens to her, as Maran's daughter and in her own right." You could cut the fury in her voice with a knife. "And fool that I am, I was starting to give a damn about *you*, Jameth of Arinoc. Get to the Hells and close the gates behind you."

She stumbled across to the door and turned to me. I knew that "I'd rather fry in the deepest hell than cry right now" look, so I didn't say anything. "I'll send the Healer up when he comes, girl. Don't expect me back here tonight." I nodded.

She slammed the door behind her.

Jamie had not said a single word. He stood openmouthed, his brown cheek showing a good strong pink stain where he'd been slapped. Quite right too, in my opinion.

"If you don't go after her, Jamie, I'm going to disown you," I said. He gaped at me. I glanced up to the ceiling and sent a swift prayer to the Lady for patience. "You idiot. She just said she loves you. Are you deaf?"

"What?" he said stupidly. "But she—she hit me, and, and she said—"

"Go. Now. Grovel, apologise, do what you have to, but go after her," I said. "For Shia's sake don't make me get out of this bed to push you, just go!" He left in a daze, drawing the door closed behind him.

I turned to Varien, who was standing there with his jaw dropping, much as Jamie had been. "Lanen? Whence came this—ah, I shall never understand!"

I grinned at him. "Gedri females?"

"Any females!" he replied smiling. "The females of the Kantri are every bit as confusing as you and Mistress Rella." He stroked my hair, growing more solemn. "However, my heart, what more deeply concerns me is why Jameth suddenly turned on a friend. I thought he admired the Lady Rella?"

"He does, my love. That's the problem. You don't know Jamie like I do," I said heavily, sitting back. All the excitement had brought back my headache, and everything below my waist hurt like every demon ever spawned had been punching me. "It was the Post horses—I asked Rella, and it really does cost a fortune to move this fast, and Jamie knows it better than I. I think he is starting to truly like her, but when it looked like she was being so kind he got suspicious. It's the way he thinks," I said apologetically. "Comes of not trusting people—no, it comes of not trusting women," I said. "He's never had much luck with women."

Varien frowned. "Another mystery. I have watched him, your heart's father. He is a man honourable and brave, skilled both in the art of the sword and in the deeper art of making the earth bring forth food. His heart is true, I would swear it. How should such a man not find a mate?"

I was feeling worse every moment we sat there, but I knew the Healer was coming and fought off the pain. "I suspect it's because he stayed in Hadronsstead with me," I said, glad of something to think of. "He's too much for any of the women around there, they expect a plain farmer and he isn't that at all."

Varien smiled into my eyes. "No, he is not," he said. "And you also are not a plain anything." He leaned over and kissed me, his hands warm and comforting on my back, his lips hard and passionate against mine. Lady knows I felt awful and the last thing I was thinking of was passion, but—well, as distractions go it was a fine one.

Especially when he continued in truespeech. That has never ceased to sway me to his will, the combination of simple physical passion and the wonder of that glorious voice echoing in the silence of my heart, that ancient mind blending with mine to make something new. *You are my beloved, my Lanen, the song of my soul made complete at last. When I thought I could never love you more, when I thought that already you possessed all there was in me to give, behold! I learn that you bear our child below your heart, and love beyond reason springs forth, young and wild, overflowing like a stream in the spring thaw and all, all thine, my Lanen, Lanen Kaelar, Kadreshi naVarien—*

Just as well the Healer came in then, I thought, despite the way I was feeling. I wondered briefly if Varien had done it on purpose. When I thought about it I realised that he most certainly had.

The Healer introduced himself as Jon and asked what troubled me as he summoned his power and sent it gently into my aching bones. I felt it this time, felt the cool blue strength of his work and welcomed the end of pain with a sob. Once the worst was past I could relax and let him work, but even after he finished he gazed long into my eyes, frowning. "Lady, you do know that this child is killing you?"

"Yes, I do. Can you do anything about it?" I asked. He sent his power into me once again and looked long and hard. He tried something, Goddess only knows what, but the moment he put forth any real power it was agony. I cried out from the pain and he stopped, apologising.

"Lady, I know not what to do," he said, sending power again to soothe the pain he had caused. He had a good, kind face, and it was full of sorrow. "There is only one Mage I know of who can help you—Magistra Erthik of Verfaren. She is wise and strong, and her greatest skill is in assisting with childbirth." He would have stopped, but his conscience made him go on. "Lady, I cry you mercy, but I must tell you. I have stopped the pain and the bleeding for now, but it will not last, especially if you insist on travelling. You—forgive me, I must prepare you." He was desperately distressed. He was also a very brave man. "You must realise how near to death you are, Lady. I can see your strength, but you must believe me. What I have done will keep you alive for a few days. If you insist on riding as you have this day, it might only keep you until this time tomorrow. You must stop and rest!"

I was sitting up. I felt a bit ill and very weary and fuzzy-headed, but surely he must be wrong. "I don't feel that dreadful, master," I said. "I cannot believe you. Of what should I die? I am strong, I've hardly had a sick day in my life. Why should this be so dangerous to me?"

"I fear it will come in the end to loss of blood, lady," he said. "The rejection must soon be complete. In a normal pregnancy your body would have miscarried long since, but this is not a normal pregnancy. There is a conflict between something in your blood and something in the blood of the child, and it is stopping the natural process that would protect you." He bowed. "I fear that only a Mage can help you now."

Varien stood beside me and his face was like carven stone. "Is there nothing that can be done?" he asked, his voice calm and quiet even then.

"Unless you find a Mage able to treat the very blood in her veins, then no, there is nothing to be done," said the Healer. "That kind of skill and power are rare indeed, if they exist at all, and where you would find them outside of Verfaren I could not say. And Verfaren is a full week's travel from here." He knelt before me, his genuine concern writ large across his face. "Lady, let me send for help from Verfaren. If I keep working on you while the Magistra comes to us, then perhaps—"

"No," I said. I felt dizzy and confused, but I knew in my bones that I could not stay there and just wait.

"We will consider it, master," said Varien. "My lady wife is weary and needs rest."

The Healer rose to his feet and bowed. "Very well. I have done what I can for you but it will not last. Be warned, lady. You must know what will happen. The pain will return and it will increase. The bleeding will get worse. Your back and your head will ache unmercifully."

I nodded. "I expected as much," I said.

He spoke wearily now. "When you start to pass clots, lady, know that your end has come upon you. May the Lady keep you, for I can do no more."

"I thank you," I said. Varien paid him his fee and let him out.

I had held back the tears very well while the Healer was there, I thought, but I was shaking by the time Varien sat beside me on the bed, and when he put his arms around me I began sobbing in earnest.

For a time he simply held me and let me cry out my fear. However, when I had calmed down a bit, he sat back from me a little and took my hands in his.

"Dear one, forgive me," he said quietly, "I know how you feel but I must say this. What if he is right?"

"No!" I cried. "How can you say that? I am not going to die!"

"Everyone who has ever died has said the same," he replied. I was shocked at the calmness in his voice, but when I looked at him I saw the tears streaming down his face.

"Why should we not at least wait here, dearling? The Healer can wait upon you while Rella and Jamie fetch this Magistra Erthik here." He never took his eyes off me for a second. "And here at least you will be able to rest, to take your ease."

"While I wait for death?" I snarled. "No, I will not! If time is going to be my enemy, at least let me spend it getting as close to help as I can. The Post horses are fast, my love, Verfaren is but a day away at the speed they make."

He stood at his full height, I could almost see him draw the mantle of his years about him as protection as he gazed down at me. "Lanen, you are putting your life in danger. You must consider this again."

"Why?" I asked, growing angry. "I will not sit here and wait for death to take me!"

"And I cannot sit by and watch you die!" he shouted. "Lanen, I cannot bear this! How should I live if you were to die? *Kadreshi*, have mercy on me, I beg you." He knelt before me, his face twisted with grief. In that moment all his protection was gone, all his armour of centuries stripped away in the instant, leaving only a desperate man. "Lanen, do not leave me," he said, that glorious voice all broken with weeping. "I could not bear this life alone."

I took his face in my hands. "I am not going to die," I repeated.

"You cannot know that!" he cried, rising swiftly, angrily to his feet. "And yet you would put what time you have left at risk by riding like a madwoman. What if this Mage Erthik at Verfaren cannot help you? What then? Shall I hold you in my arms as you bleed to death?"

"Varien!" I was shocked.

"Well, what would you? You will not take counsel, you rush headlong into danger for no reason, you refuse to listen to a Healer who has offered to do all in his power to aid you. What is left for me to do but curse the child of our making, or wish we had never met?" He could barely contain his rage, he was shaking with it. "I have kept silent, Lanen, for you did not need to concern yourself with it, but it has been terrible for me to know you in such pain for so long." He stood before me and his eyes locked, blazing, on mine. *"Do you forget, Lanen Kaelar, that I hear your every thought? You have not been careful to shield of late. Every jolt, every gasp, every drop of blood and every shooting pain that you have known has shaken me also this last moon."*

His truespeech was like a sword in my mind. That did it.

"Damn you, Varien," I cried. "What, think you I did that on purpose? I haven't bespoken you so that you wouldn't have to hear it or feel it. Maybe it's good that you have, after all, for the danger is of your making!"

His face had been flushed with anger before, but now he went pale. "What do you say?" he breathed.

"Never mind," I murmured. I was ashamed at having said as much as I had, even if I was dying. Especially if I was dying.

"Tell me, Lanen."

"No," I said. "Don't make me. It was—what did you call it? Those hidden thoughts?"

"Terishnakh," he said. "But the *terishnakh* are dismissed while still in the mind, they do not come to the lips. What do you mean that the danger is of my making?"

"Let it go!" I cried.

"What do you mean?" he said, taking me by the shoulders. I shook myself free.

"It's your child, that's what I mean!" I yelled, and I watched each word strike him like a blow. "It's the blood, yours and mine. Rishkaan was right, Akor!" I cried, and my voice was high and thin with rage and with fear. "We have made a monster between us, and it is going to kill me!"

Varien stared at me in horror as I fought to take a deep breath, but I was overcome and with that breath I screamed with all my might, straight from the gut. I had never screamed before. It was terrible and it was very loud. It frightened me and it terrified Akor, but at least it broke through the anger between us. He came to me and wrapped his arms about me and held on for dear life while I sobbed my heart out. His tears mingled with mine.

"I will fight for you, my Lanen," he told me brokenly in truespeech. He could barely speak even with the voice of his mind. *"If Death dares come to claim you I will fight him, tooth and claw, unto the ending of my life. For how should I live without you in the world?"*

"Forgive me, my heart, I never meant what I said. I've never been so scared in my life, I'm so frightened. I am not ready to die," I replied, holding him with all my strength.

We stood in that desperate embrace until, at last, we both

grew weary beyond bearing. We lay down, still clasping one another so very close, until from sheer exhaustion I fell asleep in his arms.

Will

We slowed when we came to the main corridor that we might not draw attention to ourselves. I collected my cloak and my walking stick as usual, nodding to the young student who was working off some minor misdemeanor by tending the dawn-to-noon shift of All Comers. He yelled to Vilkas and Aral to come talk to him about the tandem work, he had heard all about it and there were no patients, but they declined as they strode past.

We were out the front door, our main objective thus far, and suddenly my perceptions shifted. Outside seemed terribly exposed. We were not prepared, we had no money, no food, only the clothes on our backs and the stick in my hand.

I tried to hang back but Vilkas took my arm and pulled me along. He didn't even slow down. I was impressed, for we are of a height but I would make three of him around. We stepped into the courtyard—and there were three horses, saddled and bridled, a clear gift from the Lady. The groom who held them greeted me. "Will! You haven't seen Magister Berys, have you?" he called out. "He sent for these horses an hour gone and he still hasn't come."

I began to hope. One little falsehood and we would be away, well mounted and far faster than feet could bear us. I was about to answer when Vil replied, speaking in a normal tone as we passed them, "Haven't seen him. Sorry."

He strode through the main gate, followed by Aral at his heels and me spluttering behind. Once we were out the gate and down the street I tried to stop and talk to Vil, but he still had his hand wrapped around my arm. He was a lot stronger than I'd have guessed, though I wasn't seriously trying to stop him. "We can talk as we go, Will, I don't want to stop for anyone or anything."

"Then why in Shia's name didn't we just take those

horses?" I asked, angry. "A gift from the Lady, plain as plain, and you just walk past—"

"Too easy, Will!" he growled. "Too damned easy. An hour they'd been waiting. How long has it been since Berys left us, Aral?"

"About that."

"He's clever, Will. He's very, very clever, and unless I miss my guess he has had this or something like it planned for quite some time. Well, I'm not an idiot either. I think it's time we weren't quite so obvious." He called his power to him as we walked, and his corona covered us all three. I thought this would be much like trying to hide by carrying a flaming torch at midnight, but no one seemed to notice us.

I looked at him and spoke very quietly. "Vil, are we invisible? I didn't think that was possible."

"It isn't and we're not," he said, "but when we pass, we are the least noticeable thing in the world. Even a blade of grass holds more interest than we do. It should slow them down if no one has seen us."

I was impressed. He was good.

"We were meant to take those horses, Will. I know it. That would make it so much easier for him—plant something from Erthik or Caillin in a saddlebag, send a demon to track us, a charge of murder"—and for the first time since we had left his chambers, Vilkas faltered in his long stride and the slightest unevenness afflicted his voice, but he looked straight ahead. "Aral—Goddess, did you see her face? Poor Erthik. I cared about her. She believed in us, and I know as if I'd watched her die that she fell fighting Berys himself."

I didn't question him. It could only have been the Archimage. Both of the Magistri had died without a sound a few feet from us, and Erthik was—Erthik had been the most powerful Mage in the College after Berys.

After Berys.

Aral said nothing. I turned to look at her and was taken aback at how pale she was. For all that, though, her face was set in an implacable mask. Aral has always been a creature of deep emotions. She had not known Erthik very well, but I had seen the two of them together on several occasions, and I had seen a true friendship growing there. Erthik had been delighted by their tandem work and had hoped to get them to teach it to others. Now delight, hope, friendship, all, lay dead in a heap outside Vilkas's rooms. I held back the bile that burned the back of my throat.

We walked on like frightened cats, quickly, every nerve quivering, studiously ignoring the fact that we expected a demon attack any moment. As we passed the last house on the outskirts of Verfaren, however, Aral stopped abruptly and spoke. Her voice was calm and even. She held her right hand up, palm outwards. "I do here speak and swear, my soul to the Lady's right hand, that I shall do all in my power as long as I live to defeat Berys of Verfaren, to oppose him and his works at every turn, and to destroy him should I ever have the chance."

"I do so swear, my soul to the Lady," said Vilkas without hesitation.

"That makes three of us," I said, swiftly. "Sworn and witnessed, our souls to the Goddess. Now can we get moving again please?"

We had turned left when we walked out of the East Gate of the College, so we were on the road going north. "Where are we headed, apart from away?" I asked.

"I'm open to suggestion," said Vil, striding at a great pace. He lifted one hand to waist level and pointed a skinny finger straight ahead. "That way?"

Aral had to do twice the work to keep up as her legs were so much shorter, but she seemed accustomed to it. "Known to some as north," she said. "It's a long way to anywhere in this direction, Vil." She gazed over her right shoulder, as if she could see through the little wood we were passing. "Home's that way," she said, longingly.

"Only your home, and it's hundreds of leagues that way. Be reasonable."

"You two don't remember much, do you?" I said, trying to keep my voice as even as Vilkas's. I couldn't stop seeing Erthik's face, her brown hair disarrayed—no, I couldn't think of that. "I live no more than a few days' walk from here." I glanced behind us. "It's even closer if you go cross-country and stay off the roads."

They were both silent for a moment, though we never slackened our pace and Vilkas's corona still surrounded us. It didn't seem to tire him in the least. "You're in it deep enough as it is," said Vil at last. "You don't need to harbour two murderers. And Lady Shia alone knows who or what Berys will send out to find us and fetch us back."

"He'll start by sending some of the Magistri, and if they can't find us he'll hire mercenaries and pay them for our return dead or alive. That's what you do with murderers," growled Aral. "But my guess is that he'll send demons as soon as the uproar is over. Maybe tonight, maybe any minute now. He had those two he threw at us ready prepared, he must have done, or he'd have needed an altar. I'd guess he must have made some sort of amulet. The spell could take effect long after the summoning was completed, so there would be no evidence of who had done it."

"Keep your corona about you," said Vilkas. "If I were Berys I'd send a demon the instant I was able to, lest we have the chance to prepare our defence."

"No, really?" said Aral sarcastically. "You think so? I wondered why I kept glowing bright blue."

"And as for me, I was there and I saw it all," I said. "I'm your best defence, and I have no way to fight off demons on my own. Besides, if you two think I'm leaving you now you're dafter than I thought. No one knows you were with me at Midwinter Fest, do they?"

"No," replied Aral immediately. "I didn't tell anyone. I didn't want you being pestered. Or me. People get peculiar."

Vilkas took longer to consider, but "No," he said finally. "I remember I didn't want my whereabouts known."

"Hah!" said Aral, showing a glimmer of her usual self. "The Deep and Mysterious Great Mage Vilkas! I know why you never told anyone, it's that Palistra. The golden-haired green-eyed enchantress who's got every lad in the school at her feet except you." I'd never heard Aral so disgusted.

"I'd have thought she'd be busy enough with that lot," said Vilkas, genuinely puzzled, and sounding deeply grateful for something trivial to think about. "I never gave her the slightest encouragement."

Aral managed a small laugh, which under the circumstances was impressive. "Ah, but that's the attraction Vil, don't you see?" she said, pleased despite our plight at being privy to something she knew well neither Vilkas nor I would ever truly comprehend. "I've seen you play Last Man Standing, you should understand the rules. It's the same principle. Without your favour on her sleeve she doesn't have the King. The greatest power to come through the College since Berys the Bastard, keeps to himself, polite but distant, probably doesn't have a lover so still fair game."

"Probably?"

"I can't help what other people think. I've never said word to help them," said Aral reasonably. "Didn't you realise that to Palistra's kind of mind you're completely irresistible?"

"Lady preserve me from that kind of mind, then," he said, shivering, adding a personal comment about Palistra that he would not be proud to have remembered, so I have forgotten it.

"Whatever the reason," I said, "no one knows you were with me then, so if fortune favours us no one will assume that you have come with me now. There's not a soul at Verfaren knows where I live save you two. I say we make for Rowanbeck. My cabin isn't fortified but it is well hidden and a long way from the road."

"I went by the main road with you last time. Is that the fastest way to get there?" asked Aral.

I managed to smile. "Not even close. Do you know Wolfenden? It's a little town about ten miles north of here."

"I've been there a few times, but it's been a while," said Vilkas.

"It's at a crossroads—well, it's where the track joins the road, but it's well marked." I thought for a moment. "Best you should know the way in case we're separated. If you follow the track west into the hills and walk for about three days, you'll come to a great huge green field high in the hills. It sits in a circle of rock walls, you can't see it until you're there. You might have a bit of trouble finding the way in, but now you know it's there you'll find it. Once you're inside you'll be hidden from view. There's a little wood at the western end, and if you go through the wood you'll find the path down the far side. Half a day's walk from there is my village of Rowanbeck. You know how to get to the cabin from there, don't you?"

"I remember," said Vilkas. "But this is all pointless. What good will it do to hide in the mountains?"

"It's a useful place to be if no one expects you to be there," I said. "At least you'll have somewhere safe to make your plans."

"Sounds good enough to me," said Aral wearily.

"I suppose we might as well be there as anywhere," said Vilkas with a bitter edge to his voice. "We've got nothing better to do." It took me a moment to remember that all that had happened would have an extra dimension for the two of them, beyond even the shock of seeing a friend murdered. No Healer above the third rank could ever be taken seriously without the official seal of the College on his warrant to practice. Vilkas and Aral's futures had come tumbling about their ears this day, all in a matter of hours.

"It's settled then. But before we take off into the mountains we need to get hold of some food. The Dragon's Head at Wolfenden, at the crossroads: the food's good there, certain sure. That's where we take the road northwest into the hills. We should get there by sunset, and Gair's a good lad, he'll take care of us." The others looked at me strangely. "Gair, the innkeeper. The Dragon's Head. He's a friend of mine. Good lad he is."

"Then you at least should not be seen," said Vilkas.

"What?" I said stupidly. "But Gair is a friend of mine, and—he—I don't understand."

"Will?" said Vilkas, staring at me. I didn't answer. Suddenly everything was terribly confusing.

Vilkas stopped then, drawing me into the shelter of a small copse of trees off the main road. Aral came behind me, her hand on my arm. I didn't mind that at all. Vilkas looked brighter all of a sudden, and he and Aral were talking, but I couldn't really hear what they were saying. Suddenly I had to sit down for a moment and I seemed to hit the ground right hard with my backside.

The next thing I knew I was sitting with my back against a tree and Vilkas was looking at me like I was a stranger—he wasn't catching my eye at all, just staring in my general direction and moving his hands. I felt oddly as if I was asleep, or had been asleep and was only just awakening, as if—

"Vilkas?" I said, but there was something wrong with my voice. It seemed to be coming from a very long way away. "Aral? Is this a dream?"

Then Aral was there, putting her arm about me, telling me to be quiet for a moment. She was that close I could smell her, smell the summer-flower scent of her. Dear Lady, so near! I sighed before I could stop myself. "Are you in pain?" she asked me gently, and I was in such a state I nearly told her everything, that the only pain I had was knowing she did not love me, but blessed be the Lady, Vilkas's healing finally took hold. I felt terribly, terribly drunk for just a moment, then it passed and I scrambled to my feet.

"What in all the Hells—" I began. Vil put a hand on my shoulder.

"Shock," he said, "nothing more sinister. Aral and I have been protecting ourselves with our power, it's almost instinctive, but we never thought of you. I'm sorry," he said solemnly. I glanced up and caught his eye. He really was deeply ashamed of himself for neglecting me, the poor lad.

"Well, I should think so," I said gruffly. Vilkas apologising was a new experience. "You didn't have anything else to think about, after all. But as for the Dragon's Head, I don't know how I'm going to keep Gair from seeing me. We're going to need food and a place to sleep tonight. The inn's about three hours' walk from here and you may believe me that there is nowhere else on this road."

Vilkas got as far as "It might serve, but I have two concerns."

I was ready to hear them, but the demons attacked just then and I never did.

Shikrar

Kédra insisted that I should get some sleep when we had finally sealed all the soulgems in their containers. I had thought I would never sleep again, but I closed my eyes for a mere moment and woke much refreshed later. Kédra was gone, leaving a scrawled "with Mirazhe" in the earth of my chamber. He had built up the fire again before he left.

I carried the sealed globes containing the soulgems out into the clearing before my chambers, that I might fetch them more easily when the time came—and truth be told, that I might not have to see the Chamber of Souls again, stripped of all that had given it meaning, the empty settings gaping in darkness.

When I first emerged I had found to my amazement that it was very nearly light. The morning was cold and crisp, and by the time I had carried out the last of the containers it was surprisingly bright for so early in the year. Almost I resented such a contrast to the darkness in my heart, and yet—and yet, it was good. If we must make a new beginning, this was a good day to do it.

I set out.

The Summer Field, badly misnamed on this morning of late frost, was full of the Kantri, complaining, confused and annoyed. I noticed to my sorrow that we all fit comfortably there, in a single field. I began to wonder if we might have a fate before us that nothing could turn. Perhaps the time of the Kantri in the world was come to its end and I was fated to see it. . . .

I shook myself and remembered the words I had so often

spoken to my soulfriend Akhor in his youth. *Anyone can give up, Akhor. It is as easy as death. But both death and defeat will find us all soon enough. Fight while you can with all your strength, and choose life over death as long as you are able.*

It is simple enough to say such words. It is much harder to act upon them. Still, they served their purpose, for the memory of having said them to Akhor forced me to live up to them.

I was preparing to speak when Kédra landed beside me. "Good morrow, Father," he said cheerfully. "How fare you this morning?"

"Well enough, my son. The sealed casks await those who will carry them. All is prepared."

"Mirazhe and I have been thinking of our new life in Kolmar, that we will share with the Gedri," said Kédra, smiling. "I am looking forward to it, but it occurred to Mirazhe last night that it might be a good idea to bring with us gifts to ease the sudden arrival of so many of us."

"She is wise, your good lady," I said. "That was well thought. What sort of gifts?" I asked. I had much to say to the Kantri, but I was waiting now for Idai. "What could we possible take that the Gedri would—want—" Even as I spoke I realised what he meant. "Kédra!"

He laughed. "Yes, my father. *Hlansif* trees! We can bring seeds, seedlings, even a full-grown tree or two, and see which survives. I suspect we would then be made most welcome."

"I suspect you are right. To save the Gedri that dangerous voyage—" And suddenly I caught myself. There would be no more wild journeys across perilous seas. Had Kédra and Mirazhe not thought of it, there would have been no more *hlansif* trees in all the world. The Gedri camp, the boundary fence, the Summer Field, our Great Hall, would not be left behind. They would be gone—gone—all burned, all buried under rock, or else drowned deep in ocean for all time. Somehow it all became real to me in that moment.

This was the ending of my world.

I closed my eyes. Ah, but my heart was leaden with sorrow!

"Father?" came Kédra's voice. Quiet, worried, a little fearful.

I could not leave him to do all by himself. There would be a time to mourn when all were safe and far, far away.

I forced myself to smile at my dear son. "We will have to plant a grove of our own and tend it, that we may use the leaves in trade." I smiled at him. "It is very well thought, but we must ask if any of the others are willing to carry such things. You and Mirazhe will be full burdened with Sherók, and I carry the soulgems of the Lost."

Just then a dark shape appeared above—Idai, apologising as she arrived.

She backwinged and landed beside me. "Good morrow, my friend," she said, when with no warning it struck.

The high-pitched shriek, that these days was never silent, suddenly increased until it was acutely painful, and as a counterpoint there came the deep drawn-out rumble that shakes both body and mind, and the ground beneath our feet began to sway violently.

Those who had been balancing on tail and back legs, as I had been, fell over. It was the worst earthshake I had ever been through. It is difficult to explain how confusing it was. That dreadful high shriek had been scraping my nerves raw for days, and then the very earth I was standing on moved like a treacherous sideslip in the air. Trees at the edge of the field toppled over with a great tearing and crashing, I was assaulted on all sides by sound and movement and *I kept looking for the ground*. All my instincts told me that the ground does not move, but what I was standing on was moving and so could not be the ground. I was looking for the solid place and it did not exist. It was terrible.

It felt like ages, but Idai, who had managed to get airborne, told me that it did not in truth last very long. For that I was profoundly grateful. Many, including my son and his family, managed to get aloft with Idai and avoid the worst of it, but those of us on the ground had scrapes and bruises to show for our slow reactions. I would have appreciated time to get over it but I was more than ever convinced that we had no more time.

I called out in truespeech, asking if any were injured or in need of assistance. There was no response, but a dreadful thought occurred to me in the silence that followed my asking.

Until that moment I had forgotten about Urishhak and Roccelis. They were old friends, both afflicted by the joint ill, who had lived for the last kell or so together in a large cave on the north side of the island. I had been in the way of visiting them at one time, for I enjoyed their company, but it had been many years. I bespoke them both, calling with all my strength, but there was no answer.

I called out aloud, "Tóklurik, I pray you, attend me here."

He landed before me and bowed. "Eldest? What can I do?"

"Tók, forgive me—you are kin to Roccelis, I believe?"

"Yes, she is my mother's sister, I—name of the Winds!" He crouched to take off, but I restrained him. "Wait! I know you would seek her out, but first tell me—does she keep the Weh?"

"Her last Weh sleep ended scarce ten winters past," he said, distracted. I knew he was calling his aunt, and from the distress in his eyes I knew he was hearing no more than I had.

"Be at peace, Tóklurik," I said quietly. "The Lady Urishhak does not answer either and she is the last of her line. There are none even to be concerned about her."

"I must find out if Roccelis lives," he cried. "She might be injured, helpless—I must go to her!"

"The Kantri are going to have to leave this island in a matter of hours, my friend," I said. "We may be forced to go before you have time to return."

"Then I will fly after you," he said simply.

"Tóklurik—"

"I go now, Eldest," he said. "If you are not here, which way does Kolmar lie?"

I bowed. "Fly east and a little south. You will not miss it!

But Tók, be warned. If our Ancestors are correct it is a good five days' flight. Gain altitude every chance you get, rest on the wind when you can—" I stopped myself, for he was grinning at me.

"I thank you, Hadreshikrar," he said, bowing gaily to me. "I have not forgotten your lessons, and"—he hissed his laughter—"despite the lack of pupils neither have you, for I would swear the words have not changed since you instructed me full a thousand winters gone!"

"There is a small island south of east from here, that you should reach towards the end of the second day," I said, as he crouched to take off. "There is fresh water there, if nothing else. And the rest of us will never be more than a thought away."

"I thank you, Shikrar," he said. "I will speak with you again as soon as I have learned their fate."

"Fly well and join us when you can," I said.

I had known both Urishhak and Roccelis for many years, and never in all that time had I bespoken them and received no answer from either. I understood the need of their kinsman to seek for them, to know for certain, but in my own heart I knew that they were gone. I was very slightly consoled by the thought that at least those two, best of friends, went forth together, and as they never even cried out they must have died very swiftly indeed.

I found it increasingly difficult to think in the face of the high screech that seemed never to end. The air, as well, was now hazy and full of something that made many of us cough. It was time to go, but there was one thing left that must be done.

"Who keeps the Weh?" I called out as loud as I could. The question was echoed round the field, and two names came back to me through Trizhe.

"Eldest, there are two who keep the Weh, Gyrentikh and Nikis."

"Has anyone tried to rouse them?"

"Not that I know of."

"You are kin to Gyrentikh, are you not?"

"Distantly," said Trizhe, and unexpectedly he grinned. "Though I cannot think I would have fought and laughed with a brother any harder."

"Then call him. Do everything in your power to shatter his Weh sleep," I said fervently. "He took to his Weh chambers some moons since, did he not?"

"Nearly three moons past, Eldest."

"He is young, that should be long enough. Go then, swiftly, stand at his ear and shout if you have to, but wake him!"

"I go," he said, though he looked a little dazed as he took to the air.

I cried out again, thankful for strong lungs and the silence of shock that most of us were in. "Who here is soulfriend to Nikis?" I asked.

Dhretan, little Dhretan stepped forward. He was the next youngest of us all, last born before my own grandson and barely come of age at just over five hundred winters. He bowed to me, very correctly. I could not help but smile.

"Eldest Shikrar, I have that honour. I am soulfriend to Nikis," he said.

"May I bespeak you?"

"Of course," he replied.

There is no time for niceties. Understand, Dhretan, I would not break your faith with Nikis, but her life is in danger if we cannot wake her from her Weh sleep. Know you where her Weh chamber is?"

He looked terribly awkward at the question, as well he might. Unlike the Gedri, we grow larger throughout our lives—I am the largest of the Kantri as well as the Eldest. When our bodies feel the need to grow we are taken by the Weh sleep with very little warning, sometimes a day or two, sometimes only hours. We each have separate Weh chambers, far from our own living chambers, where we go to rest alone. Our old scales flake off and burn to ash, and as we sleep the soft new armour hardens slowly over several months, allowing us to grow without hindrance for that time. In the depths of the Weh sleep we cannot be awakened, and any of our kind who stay near the sleeper are affected and will slumber as well. Therefore we must keep the Weh far from others, and as we are so vulnerable we tend to keep the location of our Weh chambers secret from all save perhaps a mate, or a soulfriend. That secret is given to be kept, not revealed.

"Dhretan, if it were not a question of saving her life you know I would not presume. For her sake I beg you, take me to her Weh chamber. The two of us will go and between us try to wake her or—or perhaps we shall attempt the impossible, and try to carry her here."

Dhretan's astonishment showed clearly, but he had no choice.

"I will take you, Eldest," he said.

"I thank you. My soul to the Winds, Dhretan, you serve your friend well in this."

Before we left, I summoned Idai and Kretissh. Idai was eldest after me, and Kretissh after her.

"My friends, there is not a moment to lose," I replied. "I go with Dhretan to waken Nikis, if it may be done, and to bring her here if that is possible. I must leave all else with you. There are five casks fashioned of *khaadish* outside my chambers, and within them are the soulgems of our Ancestors. Find bearers for them, of your kindness—I had meant to carry the soulgems of the Lost myself, but I may have a greater burden. And I pray you, send another dozen of the swiftest to collect *hlansif* trees, or seedlings, or whatever they can find. Kédra has thought it best that we arrive with gifts, and he has the right of it."

"Arrive where, Shikrar?" asked Kretissh, and around him the question was repeated. "Where do we go? Where is there to go?"

"There is no choice, my people," I said. "We must return to Kolmar."

"No!" cried a great voice, and I was not overly surprised to recognise it as Rinshir's. "Are we to beg house-room of the Gedri, Shikrar? The last time we lived there a single

Gedri killed fully half of us for no reason! Are we then to return and let them complete the task?"

"Please, Rinshir," I said as calmly as I could, fighting back the anger that rose at his words. "I know your objections, but it is not as if we have a choice."

"Alas, my father speaks truth, Rinshir," said Kédra. "Not only did our revered Ancestor Keakhor tell us that there was nowhere else to go; I have set out early and returned only when the light failed, sometimes flying for two long days before I turned back, most days of the last two moons." He bowed his head. "My people, there is nothing but barren rock, and little enough of that, for many days in any direction save east. There I found a small green island at the limit of two days' flight. It is barely the size of this field but there is a pool there with sweet water, and room enough to stand. We may at least rest there on our way."

"Shikrar, I still do not—" began Rinshir, but I was done with patience.

"You fool!" I cried, standing in Command. "Our doom shakes the very ground beneath our feet and you waste time on talk. Go then, fly from the fate the Winds place before you, fly south or north or west until your strength fails and the cold sea claims you, but do not hinder those of us who wish to live!"

"My people," I continued, raising my voice to carry, "Kolmar was our home for many long lives of our people before we chose exile on this island. I was born here, we all were, and all the lives of our parents before us were passed in this place, but before that we shared Kolmar with the Gedri for all the mingled lives of both our peoples. This very island we named the place of exile. My people, our exile is done. We are going home."

"Very good, well said. I think they have understood it at last," muttered Idai in my ear, "but unless you get moving no one else is going to raise a wing." I crouched and prepared to go aloft, but Idai stood directly before me for a moment and addressed me silently. "*And precisely how do you intend to waken Nikis? You know that the Weh affects all who go too near the one who sleeps."*

"Idai, that was proven true by one who sat outside a cavern in the sunshine. I suspect there will be enough to think about to keep me wakeful." I replied. *"Still, I would be grateful if you would bespeak me every few minutes, lest the Weh take me unawares."*

"Humph. So you do have some sense after all," she said roughly. Her words in truespeech were far kinder. *"Go carefully, my friend. We are beset with dangers, and of us all we can least bear to lose you."*

"I shall take good care of this old hide." I replied lightly. "Go with the Winds, and get you aloft with as many as will follow you as soon as you can," I said aloud. "Do not wait for me, Idai. Get aloft, fly high, find the air currents if they are there to be found. East and a little south. Kédra knows the way."

I turned to Dhretan. "Let us go," I said, and leapt into the air.

"Eldest, a question," said Dhretan as we flew.

"Nearly youngest, an answer if I have one," I said, trying to keep my tone light. He was very young, after all.

To his credit, his voice was calm. *"What shall we do if we cannot wake Nikis?"*

"If we cannot wake her, littling, then I will bear her hither myself. We will not leave her behind." I said, wondering at my own presumption. Still, it was not the journey from her Weh chamber that concerned me. That, I felt certain, I could do. It had never been done before, but I did not doubt that I could do it.

How we could bear a full-grown lady on borrowed wings for five long days, however, was another question entirely.

Rella

I walked straight down the stairs and out the door. I instinctively avoided making myself obvious, but a lifetime spent in the Service made me notice what kinds of folk were there. Mostly local Merchants of the lesser houses, farmers—oh, and the Healer had stopped for a drink as well—one or two young couples—a minstrel in the corner, playing to no one as usual—a particular type of nod and gesture from a figure in the corner, that was a colleague, I replied with the "all's well." A quiet night, then, with luck.

All this I noticed while I was hurtling through the common room and out the door. I never cease to be amazed at what one person can do in just a few moments.

AYE, RELLA YOU IDIOT, LIKE SLAPPING JAMIE. OH, THAT WAS BRILLIANT.

I hate it when that voice in my head starts talking back. I started pacing up and down the street outside the inn, my anger rising nicely to the boil.

Could have been worse, I told that other voice. *I could have really hit him, like I wanted to. Bastard! What brought all that on, anyway? When have I ever played the mercenary since I met—Hells, even since I met Lanen?*

AND HER WITH THE EYES OF MY SWEET THYRIS, MY BEAUTIFUL LITTLE GIRL, TAKEN FROM ME ALL THOSE YEARS GONE. I KNOW, I WAS LOST. WHEN SHE STARTED BEING KIND TO ME FOR NO REASON, YOU KNOW, I COULDN'T TREAT IT LIKE JUST ANOTHER ASSIGNMENT. MARAN'S DAUGHTER AND ALL—POOR MARAN, I'VE HARDLY SENT WORD ONCE A FORTNIGHT, AND THE CONTRACT SAYS FOUR TIMES A MONTH.

That Farseer's not wasted on her. She'll know what's going on.

AYE, AS FAR AS SIGHT WITH NO SOUND CAN TELL HER. I'M THREE REPORTS DOWN. SEND ONE TONIGHT, THAT WAS ONE OF OURS IN THAT CORNER. STRANGE. WHAT'S HE DOING HERE? STILL, ELIMAR'S A BIG PLACE.

You're avoiding the issue. Jamie. What are we going to do about Jamie?

WHAT IS THERE TO DO? ASIDE FROM WANTING TO KICK HIM I CAN'T HELP GETTING FOND OF THE MAN, HE'S A DAMN GOOD FIGHTER. I'VE WATCHED HIM TEACHING VARIEN, HE'S PATIENT AND CLEVER, HE'S A GOOD MAN—.

The fact that he's our age and well made and moves like a dancer doesn't hurt, and he treats us—treated us—like a

*normal person, and when the light is right he's quite comely
enough to be getting on with—*

AND WE'VE GOT A CROOKED BACK THAT IS GETTING MORE PAINFUL
EVERY YEAR. HELLS, HE THINKS WE'RE PAID DEMON FODDER, RELLEDA MY
GIRL. HE WOULDN'T GIVE US A SECOND GLANCE IF WE WERE THE MOST
BEAUTIFUL WOMAN EVER BORN. BESIDES, HE'S GOT A FLAME IN HIS HEART
YET FOR MARAN, DESPITE EVERYTHING SHE HAS DONE TO HIM. I HEARD IT
IN HIS VOICE THAT NIGHT.

Aye, and she has one for him. Remember?

HARD TO FORGET.

I suspect I'd have come up with something sensible just
then, only somebody tapped me on the shoulder.

I drew a dagger and whirled, all in a motion, but he wasn't
near enough to hit. There stood Jamie, standing well out of
my reach, with the light from a distant doorway just about
enough to let me see the laughter in his eyes. Not mocking,
just amused.

"Just making sure you're not losing your touch," he said
carelessly.

"If you'd been any closer, you idiot—" I snarled, sheath-
ing the dagger.

"If I'd been any closer I would be an idiot." He stood with
his hands behind his back. "In fact I'd be a bleeding idiot,"
he said with half a smile. It was an old scrapper's joke and
not that funny, but I found the other half of the smile for him.
Damn his eyes. I wanted to stay angry, so I stood and faced
him there in the street. "What was it you wanted, Master?" I
asked, planting my fists on my hips. I'm afraid the anger in
my voice might not have been entirely convincing, but it's
hard to fool another of your own profession.

"To apologise," he said, and he bowed to me right there in
the street. I was starting to feel flattered until I realised.

"Fine," I said, angry again. "You can go back to Lanen
and tell her you've made peace with me. Just let me alone."

Jamie smiled then—not a wry grin or a mocking grimace,
just a plain smile. Goddess, he had a good smile. "Oh, no.
Not yet. You may not know it, Mistress, but for the most part
I'm a stranger to the ways of women."

"No, really?"

"Not that I haven't shared a bed with a few," he said happily. "I have, and heartily enjoyed it too."

"I'll bet."

"And I never had any complaints from the other half of the exercise, so you can stop sneering." He began to walk slowly towards me, like a smug salt-and-pepper cat, and I swear my heart started thumping so loud I expected him to hear it. *Rella you ass, you're over forty, stop this foolishness,* I growled at myself, but I didn't appear to be listening.

He stopped just a handsbreadth outside my reach with a dagger. Standard practice for personal conversations between fighters. "But I've not spent much time with anyone since Maran and I were on our travels," he said. I'd never noticed how pleasant his voice was, just that trace of a northern accent. Focus, Rella, keep calm—

"Until now. We've been together two full moons now. I've come to admire your skills and your courage, and the Lady knows you're sharper than I am, but you know, I had never seen even a glimpse of your heart before tonight." His brown velvet eyes were locked on mine. "It's a damn good one, Rella," he said, "but I may have the match for it."

And he stepped inside my guard.

Several thousand thoughts clamoured for attention and the trained part of me was yelling *Threat!* and trying to get me to draw a weapon, but sometimes you just have to ignore your brain and your training and listen to an older wisdom.

I can't remember who started kissing whom, but after a very short while it ceased to matter.

xii

Of True Names and the Web of Fate

Salera

I knew great pleasure in those days. I had never thought there were so many like to me. Waking each morning was great joy, flying at dawn with brothers and sisters I had never known. It was food for my hungry heart and balm to my lonely mind, and for a brief time I did not think of Him. However, one day near noontide one of the two-legs walked through the gap on the side of sunrise. It was scrawny and it made a loud noise when it saw us and then it ran away, the smell of its fear strong on the air behind it. Its fear confused me. What were we, to be afraid of?

The others did not share my confusion. They seemed content enough that it had left, even pleased. I knew frustration again such as I had not felt for many years. I wanted to know what my kinsfolk were thinking, why they were pleased to see the two-legged one run away in fear.

I had no words but I wanted desperately to talk to them.

I remembered again the voice of the one I loved most in the world. It was deep and pleasing, and it shaped sound. He was not much of a singer, but he made pleasant noises and I missed his voice. However, there were two shaped sounds he had made the same way over and over, until I understood.

I suppose it is not true, then, to say I had no words at all in those days. I knew two sound shapes and I kept the memory of them close in my heart, trying to make the sounds myself when I was alone. The short one was the harder, for though I did not realise it, the sounds were made for a different mouth than mine. The other was the sound He used when he was talking to me, and I knew it was the sound that bound me to him.

Sah-rair-ah. He shaped it so, and I had practiced it again and again through the years, until I could nearly make the sound the same way. It made me think of him.

It wasn't quite right, but it was as close as I could come at the time.

Berys

I was disappointed that they didn't take the horses, but it didn't matter. Erthik and Caillin were found dead, none had seen or heard a struggle, therefore they must have been killed by those they knew.

Aral and Vilkas were outlawed by early evening. To have killed not just two people, not just two of the Magistri, but Erthik, their great proponent and mentor! It was monstrous.

Obviously.

It was Rikard, oddly enough, who made most trouble at the Assembly. He suggested that it was not clear exactly how they had died and perhaps we should consider a spirit summoning. He was shouted down by the others, who of course consider that procedure demonic. I did not bother to join in the debate, for unlike the others I knew that there were only a few hours after death in which such a summoning would work, and that the time was long past. I would have been happy to attempt to summon that which would not come.

Once the Assembly was over and Vilkas and Aral charged with murder, I retired sorrowfully to my chambers and begged to be left alone with my grief. I closed the door behind the departing Magister, locked it and cast a spell of silence on my room.

Only then could I laugh. Ah, what a splendid day it has been! It is no use sending Maikel after him now, for Vilkas's powers are intact. And because Vilkas is too strong and too used to dealing with the Rikti for one of them to concern him, I have sent a score. It did not take long or cost overmuch in the way of lansip, and it will be worth it to me to know that he is dead at last. The end of their price is the delivery of his head. I have a special box all prepared.

And to cap this delightful day, I have the final drop of good news I have needed. The Healers from Kaibar have sent word and a scrap of cloth by Rikti messenger—the cloth she left behind in the inn where she was staying.

Poor thing, she must have been bleeding badly, for it soaked into the cloth and stained it.

Blood from the one sought. This is what I have needed so desperately. Lanen is mine, and behold, there is my weapon ready to hand. I will set Maikel onto her this very night. Soon I will have in my hands that which I have sought for so long. I shall have to tell Marik his daughter will be here soon.

However, the deepest hours of night approach. I have renewed the players' paint on my face and hands and thrown the residue into the fire. No more. This night I will complete the work I have planned for so many years and set in motion nearly two moons ago. I will need to rest after this summoning, but on the third day Berys will be dead at last. Malior, Master of the Sixth Hell, will then rise triumphant with the fate of the world in his hands, and woe to those who would hinder me.

Will

There was no warning. One moment we were sitting discussing what to do, the next Vilkas had disappeared under a frantic crowd of demons, biting, tearing, fighting another to get at him.

Aral impressed me mightily. I was yelling blue murder and, I am ashamed to admit it, trying to get away. She, who had been covered by the faintest of light auras, instantly shone in the dim shadows under the trees like a blue star come to rest. She swiftly drew a pouch on a long string out from under her shirt and extracted what looked like a ruby the size of her hand, then she did the most extraordinary thing: she seemed to focus her power through the jewel, at least that's where the light went, a shaft of bright purple light straight through to Vilkas—

Who with a grunt emerged from under most of the demons. He had made a shield around himself of the power Aral sent him, but he could not keep them all off. A raking talon got through here, a bite there, and in a very short time Vilkas was looking much the worse for wear. He was doubled over, I guessed to protect a wounded side, and his face was bleeding badly.

I could not take my eyes from him, though I was not capable of assisting him. I am a gardener. I know nothing of demons and to fight them I had only my staff. Useless.

Aral, never stopping the flow of power she sent to Vilkas, drew her belt knife and held it out to me. "Will, help," she said. "Hard to talk. Take this."

I took it, stupidly staring at the blade.

"Cut me," she said, holding out her left hand, but with all her concentration on the jewel clutched in her right hand and the strength flowing through it to Vilkas. He struck out with the power she sent him, but it took a great deal of time and effort for him to deal with even one of the creatures, and there were so many, so many . . .

"Will!"

"What? I don't understand," I said, "why should I—"

"Hold the blade for me then!" she cried. "I need blood!"

Without thinking I sliced the palm of my own hand. The blade was very sharp, I hardly felt it. "Here," I said, holding out my hand to her.

It was her turn to stand amazed, but only for a second. Vilkas called out, "Aral, quickly, I can't last much longer."

The strain in his voice shocked me, he who never had to exert himself. From Vilkas that was a scream for help.

I was starting forward, but Aral grabbed my wrist and put my hand on the jewel, so that my blood flowed freely over the glowing surface.

What I had thought was a bright flow of the Healer's power gleamed now like the sun at noontide. I felt the most astounding sensation. Caught up in the fight, I felt just for that moment what it must be like to be a Healer. My strength was used as I could never have used it: every impulse to help Vilkas, every drop of friendship I bore him, and (I guessed) all the deep love I bore for Aral joined with her own power and whatever was in the jewel.

Now where the light touched the creatures, they hissed and screamed. Aral began to step forward, and of course I went with her, my hand on the jewel.

That was not a bright thing to do.

The creatures could not take their prey so they decided to attack the next best thing; since Aral was the source of their pain and deadly to them, the next best thing was me. I dared not remove my hand from Aral's, so I used my staff in my left hand—very badly—to try to beat the things out of the air. They had physical form, I could knock a few of them back for a little while, but there were so many of them. In moments my arms and my back were covered with the things, biting, slashing—I began to fear for my life and I had to let go of Aral's hand to use my staff.

They turned again to Vilkas when the bright stream of Aral's strength was cut off, but he was ready for them this time. With a word and a gesture he made a great globe of power that surrounded them and kept them captive. Aral moved to my left side, placed my cut right palm again over the gem she bore, and reached out to touch the creatures with her left hand. I tried to restrain her, but she reached right through that globe and touched the nearest.

To my everlasting astonishment it screamed and vanished. Just like that.

It took a very short time thus to dispel the rest of them.

When they saw what was happening they tried even harder to escape Vilkas's power, but it might have been iron for all they could affect it. Each time Aral's touch burned them, broke them, sent them back to the lowest of the Hells.

I counted fourteen despatched thus when the last of them had gone, and Aral said later there had been another half-dozen destroyed while I was fighting one-handed. I began to feel a burning in the bites and slashes that covered me, but I was most concerned for Vilkas. The moment he released the prison his power had made, he fell to his knees.

He was in a terrible state. I hurried towards him, idiot that I am, but Aral was there before me. Her hands were empty again, save for the kindly blue glow of the healing power. She sent it to Vilkas, wrapped him gently in it, drawing out the poison, knitting torn flesh. I watched it happen. If you have never seen a high-ranked Healer at work on deep wounds—well, it is astounding. It is to believe again in the sacred nature of healing. To watch the demon-tainted blood turn from black to red, to see the open mouth of a cut close seemingly of itself, and watch even the red seam of that wound fade and mend—there was no question in my mind that this was the highest gift of the Lady, of the Mother of us All.

In a very few minutes Vilkas stood, unsteady on his feet but whole. He put his long arms about Aral, gently and awkwardly, holding her tight against his chest. "Thank you," he said simply.

I knew what she was thinking, I could almost hear her. I knew she would have given worlds for Vilkas to stay like that forever, close in her arms, but she knew too well the nature of that embrace and she wanted his love as well. For all the depth of the bond between them, for all that they had just now saved one another's lives, she knew the embrace was friendship and gratitude and nothing more. Even I could tell as much from afar. I swear I could almost hear her.

Or perhaps it was the beginnings of delirium, for I was badly wounded myself and the poison of demon wounds works swiftly. Vilkas, seeing me waver, left Aral instantly and sent healing to me himself. *Drat you, Vilkas,* I remember thinking as I leaned against a tree for support for the second time in an hour, *if you can't love her, for Shia's sake, you could at least have let her heal me so I could hold her too.*

Healing leaves Healer and patient both weary. We staggered back to the road. There was no longer any concern about Gair recognising me. None of us cared. We were desperate for a place to stop and to rest, and we had three hours at least of walking still to do. We took it slow, and Vil and Aral took it in turns to keep their power called about them and ready. The shadows of afternoon began to lengthen and the clear air grew cooler. Aral stumbled. "Damnation, I'm tired," she muttered. "Goddess, somebody start talking so I can think about something apart from sleep and demons while I'm walking."

She turned to Vilkas. He shrugged. "Nothing to say."

"You're so helpful, Vilkas." She turned to me. "You've usually got some kind of tale to tell, Will. Who is Gair, then, how do you know him?"

"Do you care?" I asked, managing to smile.

"No, but if you don't talk to me I'm going to fall over and we need to get to Wolfenden."

"True enough. But Gair's no subject, trust me. Even older than I am and never been five miles from his doorstep. I do indeed have a story, and a true one, that you two should hear, as we're going to that inn." Vilkas glanced at me with one dark brow raised. Aral was delighted. "But there's a price," I said seriously. "To be paid before I tell my tale."

"Name it. Unto half my kingdom," said Aral, grinning. "Of course, my kingdom at the moment consists of the clothes I stand up in and they wouldn't fit you, so I'm fairly safe."

"That's what you think," I said. I couldn't help grinning back at her. "Do I get to choose which half?"

"Will!" she exclaimed, batting at my arm. "And here I thought you were a gentleman." She laughed. "Though it might be worth it to see you in skirts!"

"You're not wearing skirts, idiot," said Vilkas dryly.

"Trust you to miss the point," she said, with a loud sigh. "But come, Will, your price?"

"The answer to a question."

"Ask."

I turned to Vilkas. "Why?"

"Why what?" he said, striding along unperturbed. "And I do not recall volunteering to pay your price, Aral."

"Oh, Vil, it won't kill you. I need a story badly."

"Very well," he said with a sigh. "Why what, Will?"

"Why did you not use your power back there?" I asked. "Berys obviously fears your strength, Aral tells me every few moments what a great mage you are—"

"Liar," came Aral's voice. We both ignored her.

"I've seen you doing things half-asleep that most of the Magistri couldn't do the best day they lived. Why did Aral have to do all the work when those demons attacked? You could barely defend yourself."

"Ah," he said. "You noticed."

"It was hard to miss, Vil. A bloody great horde of demons land on you like a flock of starlings on a seed store and Aral does all the work!" I said. I gazed steadily at him in the late-afternoon light.

"What is it, Vilkas? Why could you not disperse those demons?"

He turned away from my gaze. "You tell him, Aral," he said. "I need to stretch my legs. You both walk so damned slow." He changed his gait, and between one step and another he was walking twice as fast as he had been before, his hands behind his back, his face set in a scowl. I watched him distance himself from us with a certain surprise.

"Don't worry, Will. It makes him furious that there's something he can't do," said Aral softly. "In every other task we've ever tried his power is astounding, but he can't disperse even the least of the Rikti. Lady help us if we ever have to face the Rakshasa. More to the point, Lady help me."

"What happens when he tries?" I asked. I was amazed. I had thought Vil could do anything.

"I—um. I don't know," she said, worried. "He's never been able to do as much as try since I've known him. He just won't. When I asked him about it he didn't answer and he didn't speak to me again for a week. When I finally saw him again he tried to tell me, but he wasn't using words very well and what he did say didn't make sense."

"Vilkas not using words well?" I snorted. "That's not possible. When did this happen?"

"Not long after we'd met. About a year and a half ago, I'd say."

"Then he's had enough of a rest and it's time someone asked again," I said decisively, and took off after Vilkas. It took a bit of effort but I caught him up. Most of his height is in his legs, the man walks as fast as most folk run.

"You can't run away from it, you know," I said firmly.

"I was taking the opportunity to walk at my normal speed rather than the snail's pace you two keep. I am not running from anything."

"Liar," I said loudly. That stopped him in his tracks, but it stopped me as well. The look on his face was the blank wall I'd fought so long to break through. It meant I must have hurt him very badly indeed.

"Vilkas, I'm sorry," I said. "You know I don't mean it. But if you can't even speak about your failure with the Rakshi you will never overcome it. It won't go away for being ignored, you know. And you have made a powerful enemy whose chief weapons are demons. You have to think about this."

He closed his eyes briefly, and when he opened them again the wall was gone. I let out the breath I hadn't known I was holding. Being a friend to Vilkas was never easy.

"Once," he said as Aral caught up with us. "I'll tell you this once." He glanced from Aral to me. "Come, let us be moving," he said. "There's a long way to go yet and I would gladly maim for a beer."

We returned to a pace that Aral could keep up with while Vilkas collected his thoughts. The day was fading slowly from the sky, but there was enough yet of twilight for us all to see each other.

"It happened many years ago," he began. Aral tried to say something, but he stopped her. "Later. Just listen. I was barely ten winters old but I was already working with the Healer in my town, learning what I could. I knew even then that I was damned good and a lot stronger than he was, and I was very sure of myself. Then an old woman came in demon-touched and asked us to help rid her of the taint." He stood up straighter as he walked, as if he were having to literally face up to the memory. "Sandrish thought I could use practice on demons, so he showed me what to do and let me loose. I sent my power into the poor soul, and since the very idea of demons has always sickened me I poured my heart and soul into the healing. I put everything I had into it, hard and fast."

Aral gasped and I heard her whispering "Goddess, no. Oh, Vil, no." Vilkas ignored her. "The woman started screaming, so I tried even harder. She stopped screaming almost instantly." His teeth came together with a click. Neither Aral nor I dared say a word. We hardly dared breathe. Vilkas's tale was like a blow with a club.

"Sandrish did what he could but she was stone dead. I had—ha! I, the great healer, the wise child who was so very strong!" He spat the words out. "I boiled the blood in her veins, Aral, and when I heard her screaming I seared her heart."

We said nothing, we just waited until Vilkas was breathing more normally. Until we were all breathing more normally. To my astonishment, Vilkas spoke again. "I used to have dreams after that—well, you'd expect it, wouldn't you, but the dreams had nothing to do with my killing that poor woman. There was one in particular that I kept having." His voice paused. "I keep having.

"I am standing on the top of a mountain—I know this sounds stupid, but it was a dream—I have fought my way to the top of this mountain and I can touch the sky. *Really* touch the sky. I just reach out a finger and I can feel the blue-ness of it, and the soft clouds. Then I am the ruler of the world. The whole world is at my feet." He shivered. "After that, though, the dream can go two different ways. In one I became some kind of sky god, like the stories you hear of the tribes in the Far South who worship the sun—I am all-powerful and beneficent and everything is wonderful, I use my power to its fullest extent and I make the world a glori-ous place."

After we had walked in silence a little way, Aral said the obvious, because someone had to. "And when it goes the other way?"

Vilkas spoke in the flat tone I had come to dread, for I was learning more of him in this one day than nearly two years had taught me. When he could not trust his emotions to stay in check he wrapped them in iron bands, hid them away in deep impenetrable caverns of darkness and spoke as if he were discussing the weather.

"When it goes the other way I am the Death of the World." He said the words as if they were a title. "It always happens the same way. I am fighting one of the Rakshasa, one of the Lords of the Hells, and it stabs me in the heart but I don't die. I instantly turn into a demon a thousand times worse than the one that has stabbed me. I kill it with a flick of my power, for by then I have power that has grown as vast as the world, and then I—then I kill every living thing, and to end it all I reach out and crush the sun in my hand."

He stopped for a moment, to control his voice again. Dear Lady, I thought, what does he do with all that passion? I had never seen a man run so desperately from himself.

"And I laugh. Every time. While I'm killing demons and people and breaking mountains, when I'm putting out the sun—I'm laughing the whole time," he said, striding for-ward again, and despite his best efforts his voice was thick with disgust.

I kept pace with him and demanded my answer. Without stopping to think, without any consideration for the depth of his feelings, I demanded an answer of him, "Why, Vilkas?"

"Why what?" he snarled.

"It's important. Why are you laughing?"

His voice shocked me when he answered, for he spat out the words with a deep self-loathing.

"Because it feels good. No, it feels bloody damned *fantastic*. There is no difference between being the sky god and being the Death of the World, Will. *No difference!* In the dream, the feelings are the same no matter which I choose: ultimate release and fulfillment, and self-indulgence, and—fate."

I dropped back to join Aral, who was in truth no more than a step behind. However, Vilkas had not yet ceased to astound me. Having had his say, having damned himself forever in his own eyes as being at once too weak, too strong and irredeemably evil, he made a stunning effort to seem reasonably normal. We all knew he was only bearing up by virtue of his indomitable will, and neither Aral nor I would have pricked that particular soap bubble just then for worlds.

"There," he said pleasantly, "will that do you for your price?"

"Vilkas, I—"

"I'll take that as a yes. At least we're not thinking about how tired we are anymore." He snorted, then sighed. "Hells' teeth, this day is long as years! How far are we now from that inn of yours?"

"A little over another hour, I'm afraid," I said. The sun was long since down and the light had leached slowly from the sky as he spoke, leaving darkness to settle cold on all our shoulders. Exhausted as we were, at least the walking kept us warm. The Súlkith Hills away west stood outlined sharply again the last fading glow of twilight. The stars were beginning to make themselves known, even some of the shy ones, for the moon was very young and the night cloudless. The trees on either side of the road were reduced to dark shadows on the starfields, and away off to our left as we walked north, the hills grew very slowly closer and higher. The sight of them lifted my heart. I had forgotten how much I missed my home.

"Then, in Shia's name tell us your story," said Vilkas.

"And it had better be a damned fine one. I'm getting bloody cold."

I smiled to myself in the darkness. "Well, it's not as bad as stories go, and none the worse for being true." I took a deep breath. "Salera saw I first in fire—sorrow sealed her, lone child and lost. . . ."

I had only just finished the tale of my life with Salera when we all saw a light ahead. There was nothing else for miles in any direction, it had to be the little village of Wolfenden and the Dragon's Head. I stood up straighter and ran my fingers through my hair, wishing I'd brought more silver with me. I hoped the bloodstains on my cloak weren't as obvious as the ones on Vilkas's tunic.

The smell of hot food wafted through the cold night air and gave us all heart. "It's as good as it smells, I swear," I said cheerfully.

"I don't care if it's braised liver of cat, I'm having some," said Aral. To my surprise she took my hand as we walked in the darkness and held it, briefly. "I hope you find Salera again, now you've left Verfaren," she said softly.

"I do too," I replied. Her hand in mine felt so right, so good—and then it was gone. I kept my foolish thoughts to myself and the three of us hurried into the warm, well-lit common room of the Dragon's Head.

Shikrar

Dhretan led me as swiftly as he could fly up the east coast of our island. We had passed Akhor's old Weh chambers and were beginning to approach the southern cliffs and the Grandfather when he began descending. It was difficult to keep behind him, and to be honest it was difficult to fly that low, but the poor soul was working so hard.

"There," he told me in truespeech, pointing with his snout. *"That cavern there, with the tiny clearing before it."*

"Lead on, Dhretan, but be warned, I am going to shout," I replied.

I began in truespeech.

"NIKIS! NIKIS, AWAKEN!" I cried, as loud as I could. I kept shouting her name, and when we had come to land and Dhretan showed me the entrance to her Weh chamber I hurried inside and began shouting aloud.

"Nikis, it is Hadreshikrar who speaks! You must waken, your life is at stake!" No response. "Nikis, our home is dying, we must leave this place." As if to echo my words, there was a deep rumble and a brief earthshake even as we stood there.

There was no response from Nikis.

"Go close and call her by her true name," I said to Dhretan. "I will go out. Shout it at her and fear not, I will be too far away to hear."

I walked into the forest to find the stream I had smelled, and drank while Dhretan was yelling. I tried very hard not to hear what he was saying.

"Eldest, she does not waken!" he cried. *"She has not so much as twitched."*

"Touch her hide gently," I said as I returned to the clearing. *"See how tough it is, that we may have some idea of how much longer she will sleep."*

I heard him cry out aloud before he bespoke me. *"Alas! It is barely hardened at all. Her scales bend, lord!"*

As if in sympathy with his dismay, another deep rumble rolled through and the earth shook, a little longer this time. My heart was beating fast and every muscle cried out to be gone from this place, but having come this far I could not leave her there.

I sped into the cavern and noticed this time that my wings, folded tight, still brushed the sides of the entrance to her chamber. We would not be able to work together to lift her out.

Dhretan must have noticed as well, for as I ran to Nikis he asked, "How are we to do this, lord?"

I got my first good look at Nikis—strange how you notice such detail when time is of desperate importance. She was a lovely young creature, her delicate new scales the colour of dark iron, her soulgem like a deep yellow topaz. She was only a few kells older than Dhretan, which was a blessing, but she was still larger than I could carry easily or for long. "Help me turn her over," I said. "Swiftly, swiftly!"

Together we managed to get Nikis on her back. "Fold her wings in carefully," I said, "take care that they lie to the side and not under her. Now let me get hold of—"

I was interrupted by a loud explosion. Too close! It was swiftly followed by another earthshake, which began as the slightest of movements and grew worse. And worse.

I could barely keep my feet, but I managed to grasp Nikis's shoulders under her wing-joints and cried out to Dhretan. "We must get out now, we are too close to the fire-fields! Look to her wings!"

I dragged Nikis backwards, scrambling as swiftly as I could, desperate to be out of there. I fell onto her twice, thrown off my feet by the movement of the ground. It was terrible and hideously slow; I knew her hide was being scored and her wings bruised and battered, but as long as I got her out of that cavern I did not care.

When I finally reached open air I could pull much faster, putting my back into it, and she was out in moments.

However, moments were all we had. The earth had stopped moving but the smell struck me as soon as I had emerged. When Dhretan followed Nikis out he too smelled it. "Eldest, what is that on the air?" he asked. "And the sound—it roars, Lord Shikrar!"

"It is fire, youngling," I said, trying desperately to remain calm. "Help me turn her on to her chest that I may lift her." As we struggled with the dead weight I added, "And whether it is earth or forest that burns, we have very little time before it reaches us." I shuddered, for the stench was growing thicker by the instant, and Dhretan seemed to be moving at a snail's pace. "Her back legs are tangled—quickly, Dhretan! We have no more time."

"But the smell," he said as together we rolled Nikis back onto her chest. "That is not wood."

"No. It is rock. Now get aloft, I am going to have to lift her." What I would give for a cliff top to leap from, I thought longingly. It was hard enough to lift myself from the flat ground, and Nikis must weigh a third of my own weight. I sent a swift prayer to the Winds and wrapped my forearms about her chest. I could only just reach so far. However, I managed to interlock my talons in front of her.

A crash from far too close, the acrid smell of molten stone far too near, a gleam of yellow-red moving through the wood.

"The fire is upon us! Fly!" I cried. Inspired by terror I crouched, gave the greatest leap of my life with my back legs and flapped as hard and as fast as I could.

To my everlasting astonishment, I felt myself lifting from the ground. *"Get underneath the instant you can, Dhretan, take some of this weight for me."* I gasped out in truespeech, fighting for altitude. *"Quickly, quickly!"*

Dhretan maneuvered underneath Nikis as soon as I had lifted the two of us clear of the trees. He managed to take some of her weight, allowing me to fly a little more steadily. I glanced back to see where the molten stone was, and where it had come from.

We were barely two wingspans above the ground and still flapping madly when the fire-rock covered the clearing behind us, hissing violently and sending up a cloud of steam when it took the pond I had drunk from moments before. "Faster, Dhretan, 'ware the downdrafts!" I cried. For twelve hundred years I had taught every one of the Kantri how to fly: better than anyone I knew what would happen if we were too close to the ground, so desperately unstable, and were hit by the downdraft ahead of the swiftly approaching thermal created by the molten rock.

We managed to fight our way to a decent height and establish a kind of rhythm. Never before had I so blessed my wingspan, but that was all there was to be thankful for. I glanced behind me just for an instant, and in that glance I saw where the molten rock had come from.

The southern cliffs stood sentinel no longer. There was a stream of fire pouring over the edge at the lowest point, and the stream widened even as I watched—a red-gold firefall. A great pall of smoke was rising from the forests as they burned. It was like seeing the death wound of one I loved.

"*My people, we have no more time. Fly! The southern cliffs are breached!*" I cried, broadcasting truespeech to all who could hear. "*The fire comes! Trizhe, what news?*"

"*Good news, Teacher Shikrar,*" replied an unexpected voice, and with a deep sigh of relief I realised it was Gyrentikh. "*My cousin has wakened me. It is as well he has the gentle voice of a rockfall, for I slept sound.*"

"*Welcome, Gyrentikh, praise the Winds you are with us. Idai?*" I called.

"*Peace, Shikrar, I am wide awake, I thank you,*" came Idai's wry comment. "*I am aloft with nearly all of our folk. I can see the island—and I can see you. Name of the— Kretissh, swiftly, with me!*" she called out.

"*I would not have asked, Iderrisai,*" I said softly to her alone as she rode down the wind to where Dhretan and I struggled, "*but I will be glad of your help.*"

"*And should I have left you thus?*" she asked. "*Move, Dhretan, you have saved this old idiot, more honour to your courage, but Nikis is too great a burden for you. Join the others.*"

"*As you wish, Lady. Brace, Lord Shikrar, I am diving,*" said Dhretan.

"*My thanks for the warning,*" I replied with a grunt as he left and the full weight of Nikis hung from my locked forearms. Name of the Winds, but she was heavy!

"*We have caught the thermal that rises from the eastern cliffs, Shikrar,*" said Idai, coming up under me and taking much of Nikis's weight on her back. "*I thought you would be glad to hear it.*"

"*If I had the breath I would laugh, Iderrisai,*" I replied. "*Are we all here?*"

"*Tóklurik has not yet bespoken me, but it is a long flight to the northwest where Roccelis lived—Shikrar, between us two, have you any hope for them?*"

"*None, Idai, and I do not believe Tóklurik does either, but the heart must follow its own path. Roccelis was kin to him.*

Perhaps he only hopes to recover their soulgems. Soulgems! I take it—"

"Enough, Hadreshikrar!" Idai said acerbically. *"I appreciate your concern, but the rest of us really are quite capable of looking after ourselves. Yes, the soulgems of the Ancestors and of the Lost are safe. Even Kédra's daft idea of bringing hlansif trees is being attempted."* Her mind voice softened. *"A few small artefacts, some seeds, and a small stone brought from the Summer Field: those will be all we have to show for five ceats in the Place of Exile."*

I managed to hiss my amusement. *"Those and the lives of every soul of the Kantri now living!"*

"Well, if you put it that way," she said. The air of quiet amusement in her voice was a great relief to me. I looked back and down. It was hard to see past Idai's wings, but I could just glimpse the island where I was born. It was half covered in a pall of dark smoke, and in the northern half, even in bright sun, I could see patches of vivid red that must be vast firefountains to be seen from so far away.

Idai glanced up at me. *"Shikrar, my friend, have done,"* she said sadly. *"We know it is gone. There is no need to watch the last of the destruction. Remember it as it has been, not as it is. The deep truth of any living thing is in its life, not its death."*

She was right, of course. I closed my eyes and turned away, concentrating on carrying Nikis, on gaining altitude, on heading east and a little south.

But I kept looking back, as long as I could see even the clouds that covered it.

Lanen

I woke the next morning feeling reasonably well. Varien had moved only far enough apart to let me sleep, but the other beds were empty yet. I was just worried enough to get to breakfast early but Rella and Jamie were there first, drinking chélan and laughing quietly.

When Varien joined us, he drew me aside, and for a

change there was joy in his eyes. "Lanen, it is a wonder," he said earnestly. "There is hope for you, and for the babe."

"What?" I said. He hesitated. "Look, it's too early in the morning to confuse me and it's no challenge at this time of day," I said sharply. "What are you talking about?"

"I have dreamt of our younglings, Lanen," he said.

I laughed despite myself. "One at a time, please!"

He smiled. "That is what I thought, and truly it is difficult to tell ages in dreams. They might have been years apart. But I saw us, all four of us, standing in a high place on a glorious summer's day." He cupped my face in his hands. "I cannot tell you what a comfort this is."

I took his hands away as kindly as I could, but it was hard. "I'm glad you are comforted, my dear, but dreams tell us only what we wish to hear. And just so you know, please don't do that." He looked startled. "Holding my face in your hands," I said angrily. "It might feel good to you but it makes me feel like either a child who's being yelled at or a horse that's being sold. I was waiting for you to look at my teeth."

He just looked at me.

"I mean it," I said angrily.

"Very well," he replied, gazing deeper into my eyes than I wanted him to. "And to your anger and your fear, *kadreshi*, I say that I hear you. However, you must know that I recognise true visions when they come, even if I do not require the Weh sleep any longer. This was the echo of a Weh dream I had not sixty winters past, Lanen."

I was astounded. "Truly, Akor?" I asked him.

He kissed me. "Truly, *kadreshi*. Therefore, let us hope once more, no matter the cost!"

I smiled at him, for I knew what we both were thinking. We might not have another night to spend together, but at least we had spent the last one in each other's arms.

"Drink up your chélan, my heart," I said. "We need to go."

The Post horses were waiting, spoiling for a run, bless them, and we gave it to them. The speed was balm to me even as the ride shook me out of my comfort and back into pain. I could not tell how far we managed to go in the morning but even Rella seemed astounded. We did not stop to eat, for I knew—we all knew—that every moment I lived now was borrowed. As the morning wore on the aches and the sharp pains grew worse, but I kept quiet as long as I could. It wasn't too bad at first.

Between us we had a flask of wine, which helped, and at every change we managed a swift draught of chélan for warmth. We only ever stopped long enough to change horses and answer calls of nature, but once when the lads were off round a corner I called to Rella. She rode over to join me.

"So—I gather you and Jamie have made your peace," I said, trying to keep a straight face.

"You could say that," replied Rella, one corner of her mouth curling into a smile.

"I could say a damn sight more but it can wait," I replied, laughing. "And what was that about a concession the next time the Service wants horses?"

She laughed back. "I'm amazed you heard that!" She looked at me then, a little surprised. "I really am surprised, you know, but you heard me fine. I'd have thought that Post horses for three days for four people would be worth a few of Hadron's horses next time we're in need."

"Not a few, Rella. Two."

"Two! But that's nothing to the cost of—"

I interrupted her before she could dig herself in too far. "Yes, two. A stallion and a brood mare. Will that satisfy you?"

She stared back at me openmouthed for an instant, then laughed. "You've done it again, you wretched girl! I ask for bread and you gift me with a feast."

A twinge hit me just then and I must have grimaced, for she moved her mount closer. I held up my hand. "Just get me to Verfaren alive and in one piece and you can have your breeding pair this very autumn."

"Agreed," she said, holding out her hand. I clasped it and held on for a moment. "Rella—I'm so glad that—I mean— be good to him, will you? He deserves it."

"Do you think so?" she asked dryly, letting go my hand as the men reappeared.

"Yes," I said simply.

She looked across at me, her expression softening. "So do I," she said, and we were away again.

We rode well into the night, for we were still travelling faster than Rella had dared to hope we could. The stars were out in a dark night of a young moon and we were passing a range of high hills to the west, away off on our right, when it hit. A deep, sharp pain that time, and so unexpected that I cried out in agony.

They all tried to rein in but I kicked my horse. "Come on!" I yelled. They didn't have much choice. We all knew my only hope was to get to the Mages. How we were going to get a Healer to come to me in the middle of the night without Berys finding out about it wasn't clear, but to be honest I was leaving that to the others.

I wished then I had asked Varien more about what he had dreamt. I tried to see it in my mind, a picture of health and a glowing future, but there weren't enough details. True-speech is a wonderful thing.

"Varien?" I called.

He didn't answer, or if he did I didn't hear him. I tried again. *"Varien, can you hear me?"*

I opened my mind, listening, but I wasn't prepared at all.

Hundreds of voices, shouting, frightened—no, terrified.

"Varien!" I cried out. He turned. I tried to bespeak him, but again he couldn't hear me. I gestured to his saddlebag and then to his head. He nodded, drew forth his coronet and put it on.

He wasn't prepared either.

Varien

I was overwhelmed by the noise. I could not even hear Lanen through the chaos, though I tried to bespeak her. She frowned over at me as we journeyed, but I could not make out her voice. I called, therefore, to the one voice I had known longest, and like the worst fool the world has ever spawned, I called him by his true name. I would give worlds, I would give years of my life, to have that name back.

"Shikrar! Hadretikantishikrar! Soulfriend, namefast friend, hear me in all this madness and answer I beseech thee!"

"Akhorishaan! Blessed be the Winds, I could not reach you. We are aloft, Akhor, all of us."

"What? Why?"

"See, my brother. Alas for us all! See in my thoughts the fate of our home."

He opened his mind to me and I could not help it, I cried out aloud, a wordless cry from the heart. In truespeech I could manage no more than, *"Name of the Winds. I cannot believe it. When, Shikrar?"*

"Not yet two days past. We have found the Sea of the High Air, blessed be the Winds, but the most of our journey lies still long before us."

I had only flown that high sea twice in my life. It was a current of air that ran strong and sure from west to east at certain times of the year, but it was hard to find and rested near the very limit of our capacity: the air was thin and cold so high up. *"At least you may ride upon its broad back for a little time. Are you all—Shikrar, you are weary already. What burden do you bear?"*

He sighed. *"It is Nikis, daughter of Kirokthar who was taken by the Winds two hundred years since. She keeps the Weh sleep"*—I could hear his mind's laughter—*"though how she can sleep through being carried half by me and half by Idai I have no idea!"*

"Kretissh is next after Idai in size, is he—"

"He and Idai take it in turn to bear what they can of her weight on their backs. However, I cannot think how I might loose her from my grasp without disaster, at least until we find the green island Kédra spoke of. We should find it soon."

"How long, Shikrar?" I asked grimly, for the pain of us-

ing truespeech was assaulting me. *"How long will it take you to get here once you have rested, for I assume it is to Kolmar that you fly?"*

"There is nowhere else, my friend," he said resignedly. *"We look to land on the island this night, and two or three days after should see the Kolmari coast, but that is only if we meet with no other checks. The winds are with us much of the way, but the Storms lie between and they are always treacherous."*

I was about to reply when Lanen cried out again. I shivered. She sounded much worse. I tried to bespeak her but to my deep dismay there was no response. *"Shikrar, forgive me,"* I called to him, *"Lanen is in pain, I must go to her. I will speak with you again soon, my friend."*

I moved as close as I could get to Lanen as she drew her steed to a halt: Luckily Jamie was on the other side of her, for when she fell off her horse she fell away from me.

Marik

I was listening. I couldn't help but listen. They had violated my mind, torn it open against my will, and I could hear every word the two of them spoke as long as I was awake. I knew it was them, the two who had made me mad, sent me into that darkness that lurked still beneath the thin layer of sanity just waiting for me to fall.

I heard it all. Everything the one called Shikrar said, no matter who he said it to. I heard all their debates, knew everything—well, nearly everything they said. Sometimes the other whispers were too loud, sometimes I was asleep and remembered things as in a dream, sometimes it was like speaking to someone in a large crowd; I would hear about every other word. I could make sense of some of it, though.

I wrote it all down, even that long unpronounceable name, shaking as I realised that they were coming. All of them, all the dragons, were coming to Kolmar.

Berys would be pleased. Maybe he could kill them. I knew that was what he was planning.

I hoped he was planning fast.
I couldn't stop shaking.

Jamie

"Rella!" I cried as I caught Lanen, barely. Rella returned at a canter; in the darkness she hadn't noticed right away that we'd stopped. Well, that Lanen had stopped.

I managed to hold on to Lanen until Varien got off his horse and took her weight from my arms. "Jameth," he said, his calm voice shaking only a little, "we must get her somewhere warm and safe, and find a Healer."

"Warm sounds good," came a quiet voice. Lanen had recovered, enough to speak at least. "And sooner sounds better," she added.

"We're almost at Verfaren," said Rella sharply. "We can make it—"

"No," I said, at exactly the same time as Varien. "She is too cold, lady," added Varien. "I fear for her. Should we make a fire here?"

"No," said Rella. "There's an inn somewhere near here—Wolfenden can't be far, and the inn there is good enough."

"How far away are the Mages?" asked Varien urgently as he helped Lanen back onto her horse for the moment. Damn, he was strong. He lifted the long weight of her up in the air with no trouble at all.

"A good hour," replied Rella. "But one of us can make the run to Verfaren once we get there if we can find a fresh mount. It's a good ten miles beyond Wolfenden."

"I'll go," I said, vowing that I would run on my own legs if I had to. Seeing Lanen like this was breaking my heart. My lovely girl, daughter of my heart if not my body, so weak and ill. I was on the way to cursing Varien for fathering a child on her when I realised she wouldn't take that very kindly. Still, it was hard to keep my mouth shut. I held her steady while Varien mounted his own horse, then he reached out and drew Lanen into his arms. He held her there, her head against his shoulder, and we set off again.

We rode slowly, Lanen lying motionless in her husband's arms. I hardly knew her in this dreadful condition, and despite my entire lack of faith in any god ever made I begged whatever powers might be watching to get us to this inn quickly, and her to a Healer who would be able to do more than relieve her pain for a day.

To my intense relief I smelled smoke after a very short while, and when we rounded the next bend in the road I smelled food as well and saw light ahead. As we drew nearer we saw clearly the open doorway and the glow of a fire shining through it on to the road. We were at the inn door a quarter of an hour after Lanen fainted.

Maybe there is something to these wretched gods after all.

Berys

I sent the Rikti hours, ago and they have not returned. I have badly miscalculated Vilkas's power. Damnation! Twenty of the Rikti I sent after him and not one survived to report to me!

Swearing will not help. I have two separate tasks before me this night. I shall begin with the simpler, sealing the fate of the fool Maikel. Then the last stroke of the knife, the last drop of blood, the last word of the spell, and I shall know how to control the Demonlord.

And when I have learned what that control is—ahh, I have worked these long years to bend the world to my will, these long months to learn how to summon and control the strongest demon master who ever lived. It will not be simple, for he is not strictly a demon, though if he accepts my offer to live again he will be bound under the terms we agree. When he knows I have Marik of Gundar's blood and bone in my power, he will be tempted. When he finds that I plan for him to dispense with the few remaining Kantri he will not be able to resist.

After I have recovered from the second of my tasks—it will take a few days—there lacks only the final summoning and sacrifice to set all in motion. Then he will rise again and serve me; the Demonlord, who sold his name and his soul for ultimate power, will be my servant, bound to come and go at my will!

It is good. He will accomplish for me the death of the Kantri. Ah, somehow I must arrange to see at least one of them die.

What would be the point, otherwise?

My robes await me in the anteroom to my hidden chamber. I have drawn my blood into a sealed vessel and healed the wound. I have the scrap of cloth from Kaibar, and the last of my lan fruit in my scrip. Its worth is a thousand times the value of the dead and dried leaves, this living piece of the island of my foes. It is precisely the sacrifice I require.

Oh—and I must find a student along the way. Or a Magister. I need a heart from a living body to sacrifice to the Lord of Hell for the control spell—but there are so many hearts walking around that it's not really worth planning in advance. I shall simply take what I can find.

Now for it.

A plain lantern to light my way this night, Durstan at my side. I passed no one on the way to my summoning chambers. I may have to go to All Comers and see who is available, but I have a minor task to accomplish before I require whoever it may be.

Once inside I renewed the spell that renders this room unnoticeable, for though I was still in need of a heart there was too much at stake to risk interruption.

While speaking the appropriate prayers and binding spells, I lit the seven candles placed on the boundary ring, each at the point sacred to one of the seven Lords, and with a word I charged the fire under the main brazier on the altar. In moments the coals began to glow red. I lit the incense from the candles and breathed deep. The familiar scent was like coming home.

Durstan, robed now and prepared to assist, helped me on with my robes and handed me my knife. I called my power about me and began the familiar words of the invocation, pierced my fingertip and offered seven drops of blood. They hissed on the coals. I had spoken the invocation so often I felt that I hardly needed to concentrate, but I knew that feeling so well I laughed at it. Ever the Rakshasa attempted to trap the unwary. I concentrated as usual, avoiding the stutter in the fourth line that would have changed the meaning and left me open to instant attack.

In any case, this was a slightly different summoning. I had planted a demon in Maikel while he slept, drugged, at my mercy. It bore in its claws two ends of a demon line, one out and one back, the other ends of which were in these very chambers. The spell on Maikel was subtle and had cost me dear, in time and blood and lansip, but it was worth it. Once I set the spell in motion Maikel, out wandering the world even now, would follow whoever I told the demon to follow, thinking that he had his own reasons for doing so, and when the prey had come to rest he would stop and build an altar. The instant it was built the demon would burst forth, plant the demon lines in the earth and disappear. I could then travel to wherever it was, take my prisoner and travel back in the blink of an eye. Maikel will most probably live long enough to watch me appear. I will enjoy that.

Above the altar, in the red air, a shadowy impression of the demon within Maikel took shape. "Sso, prey, you dare ssummon your death! Despair as you die, for I am—"

"I am Malior, Master of the Sixth Hell. You have taken my blood, little Rikti. Serve me or die," I said, tightening the binding charm.

"Ssspeak, masster," it spat, tearing at the charm like a rope around its neck.

"I have your quarry," I said. "Taste the blood on this cloth. Send your host to seek her and build an altar where she stops, but it must not be before three days' time."

I was proud of that detail. I had calculated that the summoning that would follow this minor one would leave me drained for two days, giving me one day to prepare for Lanen's arrival. The instant she was safely in my hands I would complete the summoning of the Demonlord, but it would be folly to attempt it until I had her safe. I knew she had Farspeech—Marik had warned me—so she would have to be silenced as swiftly as possible once I had her.

The creature objected and threatened, of course, but it had no choice. "Ass you command, masster," it hissed finally.

"When the altar is built, plant both of the Swiftlines you carry. When that is accomplished you will return to me and inform me that all is done. You will then be free to go."

"Ssoon, ssoon, masster," it begged.

"Three full days from this moment at the earliest. You submit?"

It cursed and hissed and struggled to escape, but I could hold such a creature captive in my sleep. "I ssubmit. Three daysss at the earliest, and when the prey iss at resst."

"Yes. Go now. You will return and tell me when all is done."

"Yesss," it hissed as its form dispersed into nothingness.

I threw lansip on to the altar to sweeten the air. The simpler of the two done, but I had known it would be easy. The smoke from the lansip leaves was pleasant enough.

Now for the second of my tasks. I renewed the incense and began to prepare myself for the ordeal ahead, but the truth was that I knew most of what I needed already.

There was a certain simplicity to it, overall. I had pondered long on the problem: How should anyone be burnt to powder by the Kantri and laugh all the while? Either he was completely insane—and I refuse to believe that one who could destroy True Dragons at will was mad—or he must have found a way to do in life what has only ever been heard of in legend. It was that thought that had led me to realise that the Demonlord had performed the spell of the Distant Heart.

There are many children's tales of such thing, the mythical wizard who removes his heart and hides it away, making himself invulnerable. The heart is always removed to a great distance, hidden and guarded: in the stories it is some variation on the theme of "inside an egg inside a duck inside a box hidden in the trunk of a hollow tree," guarded by fabulous beasts or simply by obscurity.

But I know where it is. Fabulous beasts and all.

For thousands of years the true death of the Demonlord was within the grasp of those who hated him most, and they never knew it.

The heart of the Demonlord was hidden on a green island in the west, inside a series of caves too small to admit any of the creatures who lived there. The final stroke of irony is that, vulnerable and without a body to use, his heart continued the destruction of the beasts he so longed to destroy. In their exile they thought they were so safe, so wise and strong, and all the while his heart beat in the mountains and poisoned the air, the water, the very land they lived upon. They are fewer now than they have ever been, barely enough to breed.

I must be sure to tell them before they die.

The Wind of Shaping Like Fire Burns

Will

We sat as close to the fire as we could get. The inn was all but empty. I'd have preferred it to be full, that we might not be so obvious, but to be honest I was too tired to care, and I was the most wakeful of us three.

Vilkas and Aral slumped down on to the bench nearest the fire while I went to find Gair, but I noticed as I left that Aral still had her power about her. They were talking quietly.

Gair emerged carrying a steaming pie, and for two coppers I'd have taken it out of his hands, but he saw my face and pulled it out of my grasp.

"Ho, Will, it's that way is it? Well, there's another in the kitchen with your name to it, just let me serve these good folk and I'll be with you."

"We need food fast, Gair, these two are famished. Can I fetch beer and bread for now?"

"A moment, Will, I'll be right with you," he said, placing the pie before the only other people in the place, an older couple. I just stood and waited. Gair was like that.

I couldn't help taking note of the two he was serving, a sharp-featured man with dark hair sprinkled with grey, and a woman with a crooked back. They both looked done in, but while the man was slicing the pie into quarters the woman said, "I'll need something stronger than wine. What else have you got?"

"Is she in that much pain, then?" asked Gair kindly. "The poor lass! I've some Kygur, or there's a bottle of Kairhum wine."

"Stronger than wine, I said," the woman said sharply.

"No, mistress, you see—it's boiled down, like, and the water's drawn off and leaves the alcohol behind. It's strong, right enough."

The man barked a harsh laugh. "Kairhum is it. That stuff'll take the shine off old leather, Rella, and Lanen's not used to spirits. Trust me, it'll help her until we can fetch a Healer from Verfaren."

"Bring it then, quickly," said the woman.

Gair turned to me. "Will, I—"

"Go. I'll get our beer, you help these folk."

I brought a brimming jug and three leather tankards to the table Vil and Aral had dragged over to the fire. "Did you hear any of that?" I asked quietly. I glanced at the older couple. They were eating quickly, but more than half of the pie sat untouched in its dish.

"Not a thing," said Aral. She drank off a full tankard of Gair's best brown ale and sighed deeply. "Blessed Shia, that tastes wonderful. Where's the food? I'm starving."

"Coming. Gair's fetching strong spirits for those folk— seems there's more of their party and one of them's in a bad way." I lowered my voice. "They're heading for Verfaren to fetch a Healer."

To my astonishment, Vilkas rose instantly without saying a word and moved towards the corner where the others sat. Aral and I, of course, followed after. As always. I'll say this for the lad, he'd have made a fine player.

Vil stood before them and bowed. "Your pardon, my lord,

my lady," he said. "My friend could not help but hear your conversation. You seek a Healer?"

The man just frowned at him, but the woman stared straight into his eyes. "Yes. We need the best Verfaren has and we need them quick. What has it to do with you?"

Vilkas drew himself to his full height. He was in a dreadful state, dishevelled and weary as he was, but there was a light in his eyes that would not be ignored. I think the day had been too long for him, too full of death and battle, too close to the dark places in his soul. He was at the same time exhausted and in that strange place beyond exhaustion where we are stronger than we ever imagine. Certainly, he risked a damn sight more than he should have.

"Everything, lady," he said. "At Verfaren today, one of the people I loved best in the world was killed by the head of the College because she dared stand up for me and mine. I would keep even a chance-met soul out of the clutches of that demon master lest the same fate befall them. I am a Healer, in the service of the Lady Shia, the *mother* of us all. It is my duty to serve those in pain. How can I help?"

"Hells' teeth, you puppy," muttered the woman, staring around her to be certain we were the only souls about. "How dare you say such things about the Archimage?"

"Because they are true," said Vilkas loudly. He was burning bright now, not with his corona but with a bone-deep anger that had at last found an outlet. "I am no fool, mistress," he said, his brilliant eyes alight with his fury. "I know all too well the powers ranged behind Berys the Bastard, but from this moment I refuse to support his lies. He is a demon master and a murderer and I will do all in my power as long as I live to bring about his downfall."

"And if I were to tell you that I am an assassin, and in his service?" said the woman harshly.

Vilkas wrapped a shield of power about her instantly and she was held motionless. The man beside her hardly moved, but he was watching carefully. "Aral," said Vilkas.

Aral moved forward and joined her corona to his, muttering,

"Great, thanks Vil, now we're both in it." She gazed closely at the woman through her corona. "It could be, Vil. She has killed before—but I'd swear she has not the slightest touch of Raksha-trace."

Vil released her and bowed. "If you are truly what you claim, I can only beg that you will drop your allegiance, else I will be forced to fight you and it would not be an equal contest. I am trained to healing, lady, and your death would weigh on my soul, but I cannot have you following me."

The woman smiled. It was a good smile. "Then be glad I'm not in his pay. My soul to the Lady, lad, it's good to see such courage, even if it is misplaced. I've hated Berys for years—but you should be more careful who you declare yourself to. Be glad there's no one else in here. How do you know about Berys?"

"I am his Enemy," said Vilkas simply. Cold, burning simplicity, like a new-forged blade plunged into the heart of ice. He might as well have shouted it. I shivered and felt Aral take my hand for simple comfort. I am afraid I found myself thinking that if the Death of the World were ever to speak, that would be its voice.

The woman stared at him, trying to take his measure. The man, however, stood and held out his hand. "Then you are welcome here, lad, but if you're going to call yourself Berys's Enemy you're going to have to stand in line. What's your name?"

Vil hesitated. The woman looked up at him. "Don't bother thinking up a false one," she said dryly. "I'm Rella, he's Jamie. Our real names. Who are you?"

"Vilkas," he said, taking the man's offered hand. "My soul to the Lady, I swear to you I am the strongest Healer you will find in or out of Verfaren who isn't demon-touched. How can I help?"

Well, that was enough of that.

"Your pardon, gentles," I said, coming up and putting a mug of beer in Vilkas's hand. "Drink," I told him, then turned to the couple. "His name is indeed Vilkas, he is what he claims, and before he can help anybody he needs food and a chair. Will you join us at the fire?"

They glanced at one another and the woman shrugged. The man, Jamie, got up and closed the door and latched it. Gair, who was just coming in with our food, put it down on the table and began to protest, but Jamie said, "If it means you lose custom I'll pay you for it. We need privacy."

Gair looked to me. "Up to you," I said with a shrug.

"Five silver will get you privacy and a closed door," said Gair decisively. Despite the atmosphere, I restrained a grin with great difficulty. He'd be lucky to make that much in a week.

Obviously, Jamie knew as much, from his laugh. "Make it two, master, and I'll find it easier to believe!" he said.

"Don't bloody haggle," snarled Rella. She stood and Gair took a step back. There was that in her eyes that made me nervous as well. She drew out three silver coins. "There's for our beds, a closed door and food. Now where's that bottle of spirits?"

"Just coming, mistress," he said, taking the money and bowing his way out.

Aral and Vilkas were already eating like starveling waifs. Healing is a wearying business, I'm told, and they had walked ten miles on top of all that had beset them. Their youth was in their favour at least. Hard to believe that so much had happened in so few hours.

I should never think such things. Mother Shia seems to take it as a challenge.

A great cry came from somewhere beyond the kitchen. Before it had ceased we were all four on our way.

Varien

Lanen gripped my hands with all her strength while the pain swept through her. The moment the spasm relaxed I helped her to lie back against the wall. She could not lie flat, but at least this way she could relax a little. She closed her eyes as I covered her with a light blanket.

I tried to bespeak her but met only silence. It terrified me.

"Dearling, can you hear me?" I asked gently, and added in truespeech, *"Oh, kadreshi, sleep not on the winds, not yet, I cannot bear it."*

"Of course I can hear you," she said. She tried to keep her voice light, but it was taught with her pain. "I may be falling apart at the seams generally, but for the moment there's nothing wrong with my ears."

"Lanen, look at me." She opened her eyes wearily, and the agony behind them struck me like a blow.

"I'll admit the view is a fine one, Varien love, but I need to rest. Just let me close my eyes for a moment—"

She cried out then, in surprise as much as pain as another spasm seized her. "Akor! Oh Hells, it's worse!" She gave a great shudder. "Oh Hells," she said, and her voice sounded terribly distant. "Akor, help me—dear Shia it hurts—"

I happened to glance down from her face and saw a rapidly spreading bloodstain on the blanket. They tell me I shouted to bring down the roof tiles. I have no memory of it. All that remains to me of that moment is the memory of the bone-deep fear that I was going to lose Lanen, and the sickening knowledge that I could do absolutely nothing to help her.

Will

I had never heard anyone yell like that. There were no words in it, but it was a command sure as life. Vilkas, already blazing blue and ahead of all, turned to Jamie and said "Where?"

Jamie pushed ahead of him and opened one of the many doors. Everyone else hurried in so I kept out of the way, but I caught a quick glimpse of the folk inside, for the bedroom was well lit and had a roaring fire in its own grate. There was a woman sat up in the bed, held in the arms of a silver-haired man, sitting in the middle of a spreading stain. I could smell the blood from the doorway.

Gair came rushing up. I sent him away again to fetch boiling water and soap and a fresh set of sheets, and told him to prepare food and drink for healers and healed after the work was done.

I only hoped the sheets wouldn't be needed to wrap a corpse in. The lady was so very white, and there was so very much blood.

Salera

It was a night of the young moon when I sensed him. I woke from my rest. All around lay my new companions, curled neatly around one another to share warmth and the comfort of another heartbeat. I had slept alone this night, and now though dawn was yet hours distant, I woke as to a voice calling me.

It was his voice, or the echo of it. In the deep heart of me I knew he was near and my heart rejoiced to think he drew nigh, for the longing I had to see him again was stronger than ever. I was drawn east, walking away from the late-setting moon. I sought for any trace of him, drank in the wind: but his scent was not there. Still he drew me east—perhaps I would catch his scent higher up.

I climbed up one of the rock spurs that encircled much of the plain. It led soon to a ledge on the outer wall of the high rocks that might have been made for such a purpose. I leapt off and caught the air while my kinfolk lay sleeping. There was just enough lift to assist me, so I spiralled up and glided across the high meadow I had just left. It was a deep feeling, still and sacred, to be aloft when all the world was unaware. I saw distant lights to the north and much nearer lights south, and knew that he might be in either place, but still I was drawn eastward.

Not far in straight flight I noticed another light below and smelled smoke. I began to spiral down. Do not think I was using reason in any sense, for reason was not part of me then. Not yet. No, I followed some deeper instinct. How does a wolf find its mate in the deep forest, or a hawk its other half in the broad sky? There is a something that draws loved ones together that has no name and cannot be explained by reason.

I finally knew he was there as I came lower. Did I smell his trace on the air, catch the scent of his passing or of his footsteps grown cold on the frosty road? No.

But I knew he was there all the same.

Jamie

It was an evil sight that met our eyes. Lanen was bleeding badly and Varien looked completely terrified. The lad Vilkas hurried in and with a curious gentleness sent his power to aid her.

"She lives yet," said Varien, "though I know not for how long." I think hearing that dead flat voice from him was the only thing that could make me take my eyes off Lanen. He stood beside the bed and held her close, as though daring death to come for her. I had never seen a living man so pale.

"My lord," said the Healer, Vilkas, never turning his face from Lanen, "make room, I pray you, I must come closer to the lady." Varien, with great difficulty, laid Lanen flat on the bed.

"I thank you, my lord. Be assured, she sleeps now, I have released her from the pain—"

Varien reached out and grasped the front of the Healer's robe and lifted him off the ground, all in one swift motion. Varien's eyes were blazing and his voice, far from flat now, echoed in the room. "I have heard these Gedri phrases for death before. If thou hast let her die, false healer, behold thine own death before thee!"

No one else moved but the lady Healer spoke softly. "Master, my friend speaks not of death but of the Healer's sleep. It is as if your lady had fainted, she does not feel pain. She is not dead, nor will be if you will let her healer get back to his work."

"Forgive me," said Varien, putting the healer gently back on the ground. "I cannot hear her, I feared—Jameth, help me—"

I came and took him by the shoulders. Just for that mo-

ment he didn't resist. "Can we be of any assistance?" I asked
the lady Healer.

"Take him back to the fire and feed him, if he'll eat."

"I will not leave her," said Varien, shaking off my light
grasp. He looked to the Healers. "I will not interfere, my
word to the Winds and the Lady, but I will not leave her."

"Let him stay," said Vilkas, deep in his healing trance.
"The rest of you, out."

The little lass looked me in the eye then, and her brown
eyes were kind and reassuring in her honest face. "She will
live, master, if it is within human ability to save her. Vilkas
was not boasting, though I know it's hard to believe chance
met as we are. He really is one of the strongest Healers
alive." She stopped for a moment and smiled. "But if we're
not down in half an hour, send up food and wine, and a jug
of water. Even Vil needs food." She laid her hand on my arm
and gently but firmly pushed me towards the door. "Now go,
and take Will and your lady wife with you. We need quiet." I
was helping Varien to the door when she called out, "Oh—
what is her name?"

"Lanen," said Varien from the corner. All credit to him,
his voice was steady. "Her name is Lanen Kaelar."

The little healer turned back to Lanen without looking to
see if we had gone. She moved her hands and spoke a short
prayer, and her Healer's blue corona grew brighter as she
moved towards my heart's daughter.

I glanced over at the bed as I led Rella and the big fair-
haired stranger, Will, out of the room. Berys's Enemy over
there was completely absorbed in his work, and to my relief
he was surrounded by what looked like a small blue sun.
Maybe he really was that good.

Lanen slept.

Aral

That night was the first time I ever saw Vilkas working
at—well, I thought at the time it was his full capacity. Cer-

tainly he was drawing on power that I had only suspected he had. I don't know if it was the relief of having finally told someone about his dreams, or that he was too tired to hold back, or if it was just that he was so glad to have a simple problem of healing to work with rather than having to hold off demons, but he threw himself heart and soul into helping Lanen.

It wasn't swift or simple to aid her. The obvious problem was that her body was rejecting the babes. I said out loud, "She's healthy otherwise."

"Yes, but—Aral, take a look at her blood," said Vil, in the faraway voice he gets when he's concentrating. "Not the stuff in her veins, just look at the blood around the problem."

I did as he asked, then I looked again. "What in all the Hells is that?" I said aghast. "That dark stuff, it's like there's a battle going on within her blood—sweet Shia, Vil, what is she carrying?"

"They are too young to see easily, but they look normal," he said. "And she has no taint of the Raksha about her, none at all." He looked up. "I've got her stable and asleep, but I'm working flat out just to keep her there." He turned to the silver-haired man, who now stood silent, watching every move with his great green eyes. "You—what is your name?"

"I am called Varien," he answered, far more politely than Vilkas deserved and with immense dignity. "And you are called?"

Varien

"I am Vilkas, and my colleague here is Aral of Berún," said the young man. "You are the father, are you?"

"Yes. Lanen is my wife and bears our child."

"Children," snapped Vilkas from the bedside. I was too astounded to reply.

He finally looked up at me. "Come here a moment, Varien, if you will. The difficulty your lady is having is not one I have seen before, and I must examine you to understand it and heal her. Do you permit?"

"Yes," I said. "But you should know, the last time a Healer tried to assist me he could not."

"I can believe that," said the young man as he sent the blue strength of his power to surround me. "I can't see a thing—a moment, I pray you." The glow about him brightened, and suddenly he gasped and straightened, staring into my eyes. Lanen had often said that my eyes were yet the eyes of Akhor of old. Perhaps it was that which made him step back.

"By our Lady," he swore. "Woman never bore you, nor man never fathered you. Of what kind are you? And what is that which should sit there but does not?" he asked, touching my forehead.

"That is my secret," I said quietly.

"Don't be a fool!" said Vilkas, angry in the instant despite his wonder. "Your wife is dying because there is a violent battle raging in her body over the children she bears. Your children. If I am to keep her alive I must know what it is that she fights." His eyes were hard.

"I see," I said. "Very well. I suppose the time of concealment is past, at least with you. Know, Healer Vilkas, that this knowledge is life and death to more than Lanen." I glared at him. "Know also that death will be thine at my hand if this knowledge goes beyond this room."

In full view of both of the Healers I drew forth my circlet and put it on. They both gasped at the sight of the golden thing, for gold is very rare among the Gedri. Blessed be the Winds, the moment the soulgem touched my forehead I felt my old self sweep through me, and since I was not using truespeech my head did not ache. I did, however, feel all my years come back and settle quietly on my shoulders, and I grew impatient with this unfledged youngling.

"Behold, Mage Vilkas," I said. "This is what I lack, this is what I bore through all my years that now is no longer a part of me."

Before I could stop him he reached out and touched my soulgem. I heard his flesh sizzle, heard him cry out, and in a breath I was Akhor again, at what Lanen calls my stuffy best.

"You young idiot! What did you hope to learn from that? How could you forget that another's soulgem is sacred and never to be touched this side of death? Now stand you bold before me and show respect for your elders. If you want to know something, *ask*, but keep your claws to yourself unless you want to feel mine."

A thousand and thirteen winters are not so easily shed, alas.

He healed himself with a thought, swiftly and efficiently, and stood foursquare before me as I had so severely demanded. Already I regretted my words. His jaw hung open just slightly. I could not help smiling to myself. Add the head held just so and the wings thus, and he would have been standing in pure Amazement.

"Hells take it, I never meant to say that," I sighed.

Vilkas took a great gulp of air, as though he had only just remembered to breathe, and managed to gasp out, "Claws?"

I sighed. "Yes, Vilkas. Claws. And fangs the length of your arm, the proud four, though the rest were smaller. And horns, and wings, and scales, and breath of fire."

"Sweet Goddess, how can it be? But you are, aren't you?" He drew the blazing blue about him and stared at me with all his might. "Dear Lady Shia," he whispered, "you're a dragon." He staggered backwards a step before he caught himself. "But how?"

"The story is long in the telling and now is not the time," I replied. "I am no longer one of the Greater Kindred of the Kantrishakrim," I said, a little sadly. "But so I was, Mage Vilkas. And so in my heart I shall always be. Before I became human I was one of the Kantri: the True Dragons, Lanen used to call us. My name was Akhor and I was the Lord of my people."

Vilkas was mastering himself and even thought to bow. "I—I thank you, Lord. It—that makes sense, it would explain—please, I must see your blood, and I cannot see past your skin. Can you spare a few drops?"

I drew the belt knife I carried and pierced my fingertip. "How much do you require?" I asked.

The Healer made a glowing blue cup of his hands. "Just a few drops will do. Into my palms—yes, that's fine, thank you."

He raised his hands before his eyes, and what he saw there returned him to himself and to the healing before him. "Look Aral, it's the same," he said excitedly. "This is it, the dark fluid, it's his blood. Her body's fighting it."

I bowed my head. This was what I had feared from the beginning. "If my blood is yet the blood of the Kantri, it is no wonder that her body cannot bear it," I said as sorrow took me. "Of your kindness, save her life. The younglings cannot live, half Gedri and half Kantri. Poor creatures." I closed my eyes. "May the Winds bear them up and guard their souls," I muttered, beginning the dedication of the dying. "May the souls of the Ancestors—"

To my astonishment, Vilkas slapped my face. "Stop that," he commanded. "I need your help. No one is going to die if I can help it. Speak to her. Call her."

I was so surprised I did as he asked.

Lanen

I heard Varien's voice calling me, but he must have been several fields away, I could barely hear him. I stood up in the stirrups and shouted back but he didn't seem to answer. I couldn't see him either.

I looked around me. I had been having the strangest dream, all about being sick and riding a lot of strange horses forever in a far country. I was delighted to have wakened to find myself strong and whole. Still, that far country had been lovely, what I had seen of it. I was tired of Hadronsstead, I wanted a change. I nudged Shadow into a gentle trot and went looking for Varien.

Suddenly, out of the stead came a tall dark-haired man. It

seemed perfectly normal to see him, and it wasn't until he turned a sour face to me and grunted, "What are you doing here? Be off with you," that I realised with a shock who it was.

Hadron.

I half-jumped, half-fell off of Shadow and backed away. My dear mare Shadow. She had died in the fire. Hadron had been dead since last Autumn.

I ran with all the strength of terror towards the far fields, crying, "Varien! Varien! Where are you?"

Varien

I called to her aloud but she did not so much as twitch a finger. There was no help for it. I called to her in truespeech. *"Lanen! Lanen! Come, you must waken."*

"Varien! Varien! Where are you?" she called, her mind-voice weak and confused.

"Here, dearling." I said gently. *"Come, I am here. Waken and come to me. You do but dream."*

"Akor, damn it, get me out of here!" she cried. Her thought was oddly distant, as though we spoke through water. She was far away, so very far away, and death so near.

"Lanen Kaelar, Kadreshi na Varien, I call upon thee." I said with all the strength of my thought, sending all the depth of my love to her with all my strength, using her true name, sending love like water in a cold clear stream to one dying of thirst. *"Come to me, beloved, my own Lanen."* I said, reaching out to her in the regions of the mind. *"Come, littling. Thine hour of death is not yet come. Leave thy dream and waken to healing."*

"Akor?" she said, much nearer and stronger. *"Akor, I can't see you."*

I laughed. *"Forsooth, dearling, it is no great wonder. Your eyes are closed! They are comely thus, it is true, but I love them better open."*

I felt her hands take hold of mine an instant before her eyes opened. "Good point," she said. Her voice frightened me, it was so very weak. "Makes it easier to see, you're right."

I leaned over to kiss her. "It is good to have you back."

"Varien, I had the strangest dream," she began quietly, but I interrupted her.

"I will hear it later, dear one. Behold, these folk are healers to tend thee. This is Vilkas, a great mage, and this lady is his companion the healer Aral."

"Work faster, will you, great mage?" she said with a strained smile. "It still hurts like all the Hells."

"I am holding the pain at bay even as we speak, Lady," said Vilkas. "When all is done it will be gone, but not yet. You must understand what is happening and what you and I must do about it."

"We? You're the Healer," she said weakly.

"I am, yes, but—I have never tried the kind of healing your body requires," he said. "You know that at the moment your body will not consent to keep these children any longer."

"Child. Yes, I know. But it will not consent to leave." She frowned and turned to me. "I only wish it would not take me with it."

"You are not going to die!" cried Vilkas angrily, to my surprise. "There has been enough death. I have lost one I cared deeply for this day. By the Lady, these children will live if you will it, Lanen." He turned to me. "She knows what you are, does she?"

"She knows full well," I said, smiling down at my dear one.

"So I do," she replied. Her voice was stronger now. "You're an awkward so-and-so, but you're my husband so I have to put up with you."

"Lady, this is no time to jest," said the Healer solemnly. "You know that this man was once a dragon?"

"Of course, you idiot," she replied. "He just told you I knew. What of it?"

"It is the dragon in his blood that is causing the problem with your pregnancy," he replied, ignoring Lanen's insult. "I have stopped the bleeding and begun to repair the structures in you that are causing you pain, but unless you help me with the underlying cause the healing will not last."

"Very well, O great mage. What can I do?" asked Lanen.

Vilkas stood, thinking. "I do not know exactly how to say this. You must—it is a matter of acceptance—"

The lady Aral spoke then, and her voice was soft and gentle. "Lanen, it has a great deal to do with the way you think of things. Vilkas can do wonders, but you have to accept the strangeness of these children in your mind and in your heart, or your body will never let them live."

"I have tried," she cried, "but it is killing me! I don't want to die!"

Aral came close now and said, "Lanen, look at me." She grinned. "No, not like that. I'm a girl too, remember? Now really look at me."

Lanen relaxed a little.

"Forget your fear and anger for a moment and listen to me. It's important. Have you and your husband ever worried about the children?"

"Of course, I have been ill from this for nearly a moon now."

"No. I mean, knowing what he once was, have you feared what your union might produce?" The little Healer took a deep breath, swore briefly and said, "Monsters, Lanen. That's the word. Have you been afraid that you were carrying monsters?"

Lanen wept, all in an instant.

"Oh, Goddess," she said, her voice breaking. "Yes! The words, they haunt me, Rishkan's words—oh Varien, help me! He said our children would be—would be—"

"What did this Rishkan say to her?" Aral asked me, "and why did it make such a deep impression?"

"He had a dark vision of world's ending," I said. "He tried to kill her, and only my friend Shikrar prevented it. Rishkaan said—"

"He said I would mingle the blood of the Kantri and the Gedri, that I would bear monsters, that the world would fill with Raksha-fire and there would be no one to stop it because of me," said Lanen, her tears falling unnoticed. "Is it true? Oh Goddess, no, is it true? Are they monsters?"

"Don't be stupid, woman. They are perfectly human creatures, if that can be said of babes so tiny," said Vilkas sharply. "But the mingling of the blood is not happening, and it must happen. If they are to live, the two must blend and become something new, something that will sustain both them and you."

"What in all the world can *I* do about it?" Lanen asked.

Aral spoke again. "It's all in your mind, Lanen—well, at least that's where it starts. This is all very new and we don't really have words for it, but I think—I think you have to let these babes be what they are, both dragon and human, no matter what you think of it, and—Vil, is this right?"

"Yes," he replied. All this while he had been sending a steady stream of power into Lanen, giving her his strength. "But there is more. For this change to happen, Lady," he said, gazing into her eyes, "you must love them. As they are, what they are, who and what they will become—you must love them and be willing to be changed by them, shaped by them, as they have been shaped by you and your husband."

"First is the Wind of Change, Second is Shaping, my Lanen," I said, with a shiver. "Although it costs me nothing to speak thus, for it is thou who art being shaped." I grasped her hand tight, making her look at me. "Kadreshi—"

"No, Akor," she said, and her voice had some of its usual strength. "They're right. Lady—I can't remember—"

"I'm called Aral," the little Healer said.

"Aral. What do I do?"

She smiled. "First, we ask the one who's the focus of the healing. Vil?"

He looked up, his face carefully neutral. "We will work together, Mistress Lanen. You must welcome the dragon—"

"Kantri, please," she said. "They call themselves the Kantri."

He managed a small smile. "You must welcome the blood of the Kantri into your body, and I will work to change your own blood that it might support both Kantri and human at once." He gazed at her. "You must understand, Lady. This is the only way you will be able to survive, but it will change you forever. You will not be able to go back to the way you were."

My valiant lady laughed, despite her pain and fear. From her true heart, in despite of all that beset her, she laughed. "Akor, you see, all is well. This is my turn!" She grinned at me. "Mind you, I have the easy part. I have these kind folk to keep the pain at bay, and I'm not going to be growing wings or losing anything I had before."

"Are you certain, my heart?" I asked.

"Certain sure, Varien," she said. "Very well, O great mage Vilkas. When shall we begin?"

"When you are ready, lady," he said.

"Then let it be done now," she replied.

He stood up, not touching Lanen at all. "Aral, I need you," he said. I was surprised at the flare in the girl's corona at those words, but she said nothing as she drew nigh to Lanen. They stood one on either side of the bed and raised their hands—well, Aral raised and Vilkas lowered—so that their palms were a finger's breadth apart. They stood thus with their eyes closed, allowing their coronas to combine. Together they were far brighter than they had been separately.

Aral, however, opened her eyes and regarded her companion. "Vilkas," she said gently, "this is too great a work to approach half-made. Behold, you are safe. There are none here that you need to fear, all is well, all is healing and the work of the Lady. We cannot do this with the tiny portion of strength you have restricted yourself to. We are going to need your true gift, my friend. The time has come, as you knew it would."

Aral

I have no idea why I said that, but as the words passed my lips I knew they were true. Lady, it scares me when that kind of thing happens.

"I am not prepared, Aral," he answered me, but it was an excuse and we both knew it.

"You do not need to be prepared. All the power you could ever need is within you, at your command, as it has ever been. Call upon it and loose it gently, Vil. All will be well. Gently, slowly, under control. The power that is in you, release it to serve the Lady Shia and the Lady Lanen who lies before us in her need, blessing and blessed," I intoned.

I suppose I should have expected it, but how was I to know?

When next I looked down Lanen was floating above the bed at waist level. Vilkas's waist level. Her eyes were open and aware, but only aware of Vilkas. I don't think he meant to do it; my guess has always been that it was just that his back was aching and he needed to see closer, so he brought her closer, but it was certainly a first.

I looked at Lanen, so near to my eyes, and was almost blinded by the blue Healer's fire from Vilkas. It was astounding. She was all but transparent—I could see every bone, every organ in her body, her very blood as it was flowing through her veins.

I stood amazed as Vilkas poured strength into her, as he watched the blood circulating, as he looked deep into the structure of blood itself and understood.

Then he spoke. Blessed Shia, that voice. I freely admit that Vil's voice is one of the best parts of him, but when he spoke from the heart of that healing sun he sounded wise and strong and—older. A lot older. Several hundred *years* older.

"Lanen Kaelar, it is time," he said.

"Whenever you're ready," she replied, and managed to add, "Name of the Winds, Akor, he sounds like the Kantri!"

Vilkas raised his hands high and summoned all that blaze of power into a ball the size of his hand. It glowed blue-white and was soon too bright to look at. With a gentle gesture he pushed that blue-white sun into her body, where it spread in an instant to fill her from top to toe. For a moment she floated there, pulsing with that power that beat with her heart's rhythm. Then I saw Vilkas—this is so hard to describe—as if he held back the last note of a song, or the last drop of water that will make the jug overflow. It glimmered in the palm of his hand.

Then suddenly I felt the pulsation begin to falter. Lanen cried out. Vilkas shouted over her cries. "Bear with it, it changes, all is well, all is well—Lanen, know the truth of it, Kantri and Gedri become one, like your beloved but deeper, allow it, in the blood, in the bone—yes, that's it—Lanen, *now*!"

And he threw the last bright drop straight at her heart.

She screamed just once, a scream that shook her whole body, and then she lay still.

Vilkas lowered her then, oh, so gently on to the bed, where she lay still, so still—then I saw the bloodstained cotton gown rise a little. Fall. Rise again. Blessed be Shia, she was breathing.

I was shaking so that I could hardly stand. Vilkas had to take us both down, to release my poor little nimbus back to me, and—with what reluctance!—to let go the glory he had so briefly owned.

With the last of my strength I looked at Lanen with the fading remains of my Healer's sight. All the battle that had raged in her blood was gone. She looked now like any completely exhausted, perfectly healthy pregnant woman.

"Vilkas. Vil, my heart, my dear one," I said, too tired to be careful, "You did it. Wonder and glory! You found your deep power and used it, Vil! You did it. She's fine."

"Thank the Goddess for that. Mother of us All, but I'm weary," said Vilkas, and collapsed in a heap on the floor.

Will

I heard the scream and ran to the room. I arrived just in time to see Vilkas collapse and Aral sink to her knees.

"Aral, what happened?" I demanded.

"All's well, don' worry," she murmured. "Need food, sleep—help Vil—"

I would have gone to Vilkas, but the silver-haired man was there already. He lifted Vilkas into his arms as though he weighed no more than a child. "Let the keeper of this inn bring food and drink to the finest room he has, that these two who have laboured so mightily may be cared for," he said, with the manner of a king.

Everyone else was right behind me, including Gair, so Vil and Aral were taken to the nearest bedroom and made comfortable. I knew just enough about Healers to wake them and force a little watered wine down their throats. Vilkas woke long enough to say, "Need sleep more than food, Will, bu' leave it here." He was asleep again almost before he finished speaking. We left them with food, drink and a good fire and closed the door.

When I went back to the common room Jamie was the only one there.

"I've seen Lanen," he said, relieved, and for the first time I saw that he had a good face. It had been sharpened by his fear before, but his brow was clear now and his manner very nearly gracious. "Rella and Varien are making her comfortable—changing sheets and bathing her and so on." He passed me over my drink.

"We owe you everything," he said, "you and your friends. No gold could ever repay you for what you have done."

"Gold, eh?" I said, grinning. "Well, you're right, of course, such service is beyond any amount of gold, but you could certainly try to make it up to us. You could just start piling gold on the table, we'd tell you when it was enough."

He laughed with me, a laugh full of deep relief. "Alas that I have no gold with me on this journey!" he said. "I fear we will be forced to offer silver. Will that serve?"

"I should think so," I replied, not really thinking about it. "For now, food and a place to sleep are a good start."

He smiled and said, "Aye, that of course, but we can discuss true payment in the morning. I have been riding since dawn—though to be honest, you look worse than I do."

I yawned and felt my jaw creak. "Ah, well, I am that

weary, but as the other two are sound asleep I thought I would—well, master Jamie, truth is that one of us must be awake and wary and there's only me left to do it."

Jamie looked long at me. "Will, I think you're a good man," he said finally. "You know nothing of me, I know, and have no call to trust me, but I tell you true, we are keeping watch as well. Rella and I have the first shift, and believe me, we're good at it. Get some sleep. I give you my word I will watch over you and yours, and wake you should danger threaten." He held out his hand.

Well, you have to trust people at some point, don't you?

"Willem of Rowanbeck," I said, shaking his hand.

"Jameth of Arinoc."

"Well, Jameth of Arinoc, I am going to believe every word you say," I declared, "partly because I saw the way you looked at that poor girl in there and partly because I have had hell's own day and I could sleep through the end of the world," I said, standing up. "Wake me if anything untoward happens."

"I will that. Sleep well, Willem."

I rose, staggering, and stumbled to the room Gair had pointed out to me. I fell on the bed and I swear I was asleep before my head touched the pillow.

Shikrar

We lay huddled together on a hilly green rock in the ocean. There were a few trees and there was fresh water, but there was little else. Barely room for us all to lie down, but that did not matter—the whole island was a mass of upraised wings, as those who were less tired kept the rain off those who slept. Beneath the shelter of friendly wings were heads resting on furled wings resting on nearby backs resting against other backs.

Idai and I lay curled around one another. It was very intimate, or it would have been if we were in a dry cave. As it was, we were simply huddled together against the cold, with

Idai's wings over our heads to keep off the lashing rain, talking.

"Shikrar, my friend, I do not believe that we can bear Nikis so far again," said Idai wearily. "And by all accounts, the second leg of the journey is the harder."

I tried to move my aching forelegs. Even thinking about it hurt. "I fear you may be right," I replied. "I have not been this stiff and sore for many a long kell. Even with the assistance of you and Kretissh I nearly dropped her twice. But what choice have we?"

Idai looked at me. "We could leave her here, Shikrar," she said. "For a short time only, while we find somewhere to live in Kolmar, while we make our peace with the Gedri." She snorted. "While the wretch gets over the Weh sleep."

"It is hardly her fault, Idai," I began, but she was laughing.

"I know, Shikrar, but you do realise that she will be re-membered among us forever as being the only soul to sleep through our return to Kolmar! Nikis the Weary, perhaps, or the Unlucky." With a groan Idai fluttered her aching wings, shaking off the water. "Though in my present mood I would be inclined to call her Nikis the Lazy."

I snorted at that. "The thought had crossed my mind as well. Especially last night, when so many of us could rest on the High Air and you and I had to keep working!"

"It might be a good idea for more of us than Nikis alone to wait here, Shikrar," she said quietly. "I have been thinking. Perhaps one or two should go first, to meet with the lords of the Gedri and speak with them." She hissed her amusement. "We are, after all, going to be something of a surprise."

Idai has always been able to make me laugh. "Ah, Iderri-sai, I thank you," I said. "It was well said, and I agree with you. It seems quite reasonable to send one ahead first. I will go."

"Either you or I, or possibly Kretissh," she replied. "Do not forget, Eldest, you are our lord while Akhor—while Varien is away."

"That was never decided, Idai," I said gently. I knew she

still felt pain speaking of Akhor, whom she had always loved. "Our King is chosen by acclamation, after all. Varien offered to give up the kingship, but still he is our King until the Kantri in lawful Council decide otherwise."

She snorted. "It was decided by everyone except you. And you are the Keeper of Souls, and—"

"Kédra is perfectly capable of performing the Kin-Summoning," I said, "and when I go to sleep on the Winds, you will be Eldest in your turn. What is a leader for, if not to lead?" I stretched my forelegs again, wincing at the cramp. "Besides, I cannot think of another way to avoid carrying Nikis for three more days."

"Ah, Shikrar, now I believe you!" she laughed. Trizhe, lying nearest us, raised a mild complaint about the noise.

Idai lowered her voice. "Besides, Teacher-Shikrar, I spoke easily just now of making our peace with the Gedri, but that may not be a swift or a simple thing. There are those among us"—she glanced at me sideways—"who despise the Gedri and will always do so, no matter what you may say or do."

I acknowledged her point, for until the year just past I was among those who felt that way. However, like the others I had merely been repeating the words and thoughts of my elders. When I finally met one of the Gedri—the Lady Lanen, now so dear to me—I was forced to reconsider the foolish opinions I had held for so very, very long. I was proud of myself for being able to admit to my own ignorance and to change, though with all that Lanen had done for me and mine I would have been the world's worst fool not to have done so. Still, Idai was undoubtedly right.

"What then should we do?" I asked mildly. "We cannot force the Gedri from their lands. Would those who refuse to share the land with them consent to take to the high mountains, or the deep forests? Surely in all that great land there are places where the Gedri do not live?"

"Surely," echoed Idai. "It is a very large place, and we are few." She sighed. "We are very few, Shikrar. Think you we will have any kind of a future in that place?" She dropped her voice to the merest whisper. "Or any kind of future at all?"

I turned to her, surprised. "You are unusually bleak-hearted, my friend. Of course there will be a life for us. The Kantri and the Gedri have lived in peace for many long years. We forget, we children of a latter day, that it is the exile and the separation that are unusual. We are going home, Idai," I said quietly. "Kolmar is home to us, heart and soul and bone and blood, and the Gedri are our cousins. What other race can speak and reason, aside from our life-enemies the Rakshasa? Do not fear this change, Idai. All will be well. I know it."

She sighed and let her head drop heavily onto my flank. "Your words to the Winds, Hadreshikrar, may they prove true. And I am soaked through. Shift over and lift up those stiff old wings, O wise one, it's your turn to keep the rain off."

Varien

Lanen slept now, a deep sleep granted by the Healers to help her recover her strength. Rella and I had cleaned her and changed her garment, and I held her in my arms while Rella helped the innkeeper bring in a new mattress and clean sheets and bedding. I laid Lanen gently down and Rella drew the quilts softly over her.

"I'm off to keep watch, Varien," said Rella when I tried to thank her. "Jamie and I will keep wakeful. You get some sleep."

"Lady Rella—"

She smiled. "I know, son, but save it for morning. You're shattered."

I put my hands about her waist, lifted her up and kissed her soundly. "Dear youngling," I said as I put her down. She was sputtering a bit, but it was good for her. "In the span of my life you were born yesterday, and Lanen this morning. I thank you for your kindness—daughter."

She laughed at that. "Wretched bloody dragon! Right enough, I do forget sometimes."

"Watch well. I will take the duty tomorrow night."

"Done. Goodnight then, grandfather!"

I closed the door behind her. I still wore my circlet, still felt like my old self, and as long as I was not using true-speech it brought me no pain. I began to wonder if it might not be wise to have it remade to be smaller and lighter, that I might wear it always. Shikrar had fashioned it in a stolen hour when first I was made human, that my people might know me. It was deeply kind of him, and I thought of him every time I wore it, but our talons are made for fighting and rending, not for such fine work as this. It could be half the size and still hold my soulgem securely.

As I sat there, my gaze on Lanen, my thoughts wide-scattered in my weariness, a great stillness arose in my soul. I welcomed it and let it sink deep, let it soothe the ragged edges of pain, let my wandering thoughts return and fall like leaves gently down inside it.

I rose and opened the shutters at the window to let in the night, breathing deeply of the cool air and taking pleasure in the starlight and the sharp scent of pine. In the darkness and the silence I was more alone than I had ever yet been as a Gedri. Lanen, in her healing sleep so close by, merely made the loneliness stronger. In sleep our loved ones are utterly beyond us, separate, locked in their own thoughts and un-touchable. The Kantri call sleep *invorishaan*, the little death, and so it is; a kind of preparation for us all, to make true death easier when it comes.

Death had nearly come for Lanen.

I rejoiced that she was healed, but my heart was almost as heavy as if she had not been. The anger that had taken me in Elimar had astounded me with its vehemence. I had not known it was there. My anger was not truly aimed at Lanen; it was a mask for the fear that chilled me. The dread of los-ing her I loved most in all the world went bone-deep. I had watched Shikrar mourn his beloved for eight hundred years, and I knew in my soul that I was every bit as devoted as he.

I had been furious at Lanen for defying the Healer, for putting safety aside in pursuit of true healing—but I knew that I would have done the same. Who would have the courage to sit and wait for death, relying on help that might not come, knowing that death would soon find you in any case if you did nothing? I did not have that kind of courage, but I had asked it of Lanen.

I also admitted to myself, in the soft silence of the moonlight, that I was beset by fears for the future. What manner of strange creatures did Lanen bear now? What was to become of them, and of her? Her blood was now mingled truly with the blood of the Kantri. I shuddered as Rishkaan's words echoed in my heart. With a great effort of will I rejected them and clung to the truth of my own Weh dream, a bright vision of standing with Lanen and our children in the beauty of a new day. I let out a sigh and a prayer to the Winds that I might be proven right.

In this strange sadness I lifted the heavy circlet from my head that I might gaze upon it. My soulgem. How far beyond understanding, to be able to hold it in my hand while still I lived! In the normal way of things our soulgems are severed from us only after we die. Once the fire within is unleashed at death, it consumes the body; the soulgem remains as the sole physical remnant of our existence. It is our link with our past, with our loved ones, it is—

Akhor, my heart said to me starkly. *It is your soulgem. It is no longer part of you. That means only one thing. You are dead, Akhor. You are dead, and all your life before is dead with you.*

The knowledge beat upon my brow, beat in my heart against the cadence of life. *No! No! I live!* I cried silently, gripping my soulgem with all my strength, feeling the facets dig into my flesh, sharp against my palm. *I live!*

Yes, I live. And Akhor is dead.

I knew in that moment that both were true, and the knowledge was agony. I would rather have been struck through the heart by the sword of an enemy, for surely it would not have hurt as badly.

Was I to lose *all* that I had been? Was I become human to be no more than human? A young man's body with a thousand years of life and memory trapped within, with the knowledge of half a lifetime full of things that none would ever care about. I knew where the best fish shoaled off the coast of an island that was dead or dying. I knew how to catch the early thermals, where they lingered latest on a winter's night, a hundred tricks of flying that Shikrar had taught me and a hundred more I had learned myself. I knew the joy of dancing on the wind at midsummer, of singing with all my people in a great chorus to shake the heavens with a voice that I no longer possessed. To fly with all my strength up to the High Air on a summer's day, to find that broad wave and ride it, to dive swift as a falling stone and sweep back up into clear air at the very last moment, the fierce and soaring joy of it—never again with my own wings.

Never again at all, Akhor. Varien. Changed One.

So much that I knew, so much I had known and lived through, all useless now, all vain, all lost to me forever. The knowledge pounded against my breast like waves crashing on a rocky shore. I had been the Lord of the Kantrishakrim, the King of my people, ever restless, ever searching, desiring only their good in all that I did. In a moment I had cast it all away, when I bound myself to the woman who had caught my heart. It was a great shame to me to admit that I felt such a profound regret but I could deny it no longer. I loved her still, I always would, deeply and truly, but I was forced to admit to the silence of that deep night that my love for her would ever be touched by what I had lost. She had not changed me into a human, that was the work of the Winds and the Lady and we might never know the reason for it—but if I had never met her, I would be the Lord of the Kantri still.

The young moon sent gentle rays to bathe my hands and to bring a passing gleam to my soulgem, so bright in life—I twisted it this way and that, trying desperately to catch the moonlight again, to bring even a single moment more of life from the depths of it, severed from me for all time—ah, my heart!

I knelt in the pale rays of the moon with my soulgem cradled in my hands and wept. For the first and last time, alone in the soft moonlight, I mourned in my deepest heart the passing of Khordeshkhistriakhor, he whom I had been for more than a thousand years. All before and behind me was darkness and I was terribly alone.

It is often thus. When sorrow takes us, when after bearing overwhelming burdens we feel that the last weariness is come upon our souls and we would leave this life, it is because the Winds are preparing us for the next step. There must always be death before there can be new life. The soul understands no other way. Without darkness there would be no dawn; without winter, spring would never come.

This is a truth, but it does not make the winter less cold or the agony of death any easier to bear.

Still, perhaps I would not have been lost so deep in despair had I known that outside the window, even as I wept, stood my future.

Berys

My second task was to my first as darkness is to shadow.

I assumed my robes of state, for this time I called no Rikti. Only one of the Lords of the Seven Hells would serve my purpose. As a Master of the Sixth Hell I could command Rakshasa of the first through the fifth circles, and could negotiate with any of the great demons up to and including the Lord of the Sixth Hell. The only human who had ever dealt with the Lord of the Seventh Hell was the Demonlord, and it cost him his name, his memory and his life, in that order.

The task I had set myself in this second summoning was to learn how to get rid of the Demonlord once I had summoned him, in case he proved troublesome. I had learned much over the years I had worked on this final problem, but it was clear that I would have to summon the Lord of the

Fifth Hell to learn what I needed to know. That Lord is the greatest demon that I have certain power over.

And still they try to tempt me, the fools. The Rakshi whisper words of power even as I prepare: so great a mage as I am has no need of precautions, my power is such that with it alone I will prevail over the degraded race of the demons, protection is for the weak—hah! Pitiful, pitiful. The screaming of spiders! I am no fool to give in to such obvious flattery. Before I complete the summoning I must know how to overpower him. I must be able to dispel him if I tire of him, or when I require him no longer.

Good, they have stopped. Annoying things. My robes of state, tied at the waist with knots that protect me, to bind the demons I summon to keep within their allotted places. Incense, thin and light that my mind would not become fogged as I concentrated.

I checked the scribed circles and the sigils at the seven points—all were undamaged. I lit fresh candles at the seven points, drew back my sleeves, lifted my arms in greeting and began the Invocation.

"I, Malior, Master of the Sixth Hell, do here make sacrifice of water and blood"—I broke open the sealed jug and poured the dark, dank liquid on to the glowing coals—"of lansip and living flesh, to summon to me the Lord of the Fifth Hell."

I threw two handfuls of lansip leaves on the coals, then swiftly before I could think about it I drew out my knife, sharp as a razor and smeared with a salve to kill pain, and cut a strip of flesh from my arm. Even as I threw it on the coals I sealed the cut with my power to stop the bleeding. The pain was intense, but it helped me focus. The incense was fogging my mind despite my precautions.

Not the incense, fool, the Rakshasa. Don't stop!

"I bind thee by knife and by blood, by lordship earned and sacrifices offered and taken," I said. There before me in the coals a face began to form. "O Lord of the Fifth Hell, I summon thee"—and here I spoke his name. It was a spell in and of itself. I dragged the long syllables out of my memory, forced them past my lips. As ever, the end of the name was the hardest. I could feel the pressure of the Raksha on my mouth, on my lungs, trying to get me to speak too fast or stumble over my words, or best of all to fall silent—but I was not a Master by chance. Such things are commonplace when dealing with demons. If I were not able to resist and repel such attacks I would have died long since. I finished the name and stood back, for on the instant I completed it there was a creature sitting in the coals.

It was sitting because there was not room enough for it to stand in the small room. I had seen this Raksha before and knew it to be full eight feet tall. However, sitting comfortably on the glowing coals, in a semblance of a normal human body, it was surprisingly restrained. "What is it now, Gedri?" it asked. It sounded bored.

I knew better than to even appear to relax. "Thou art bound, thou art sealed to my service until I release thee."

"Yes, yes, I know," it said coolly. "What do you want?"

I had never seen this behaviour. It was disorienting. I almost stumbled over the chant I kept repeating in my mind to keep it out of my thoughts.

At that slightest suggestion that I might falter it screamed so loud my ears rang, and it leapt at me, transformed in the act into a ravening monster, horned and fanged with eyes of flame, reaching for my face with talons the length of my arm, like every demon of a child's nightmare.

I never stopped my internal chant, never loosed my hold on the spelled bonds that held it. Its lunge ended at the scribed circle as though at a brick wall. "Pathetic," I said, my voice calm and controlled. "Spare me your theatrics. I require information from you. Tell me what I need to know and I will release you."

"We have watched you, you know," it said mildly, retaining its new appearance but resuming its seat in the coals. "You entertain us."

"You are bound, creature."

"I know what you want. The way to rid yourself of the Demonlord."

"Yes," I said. The internal chant took less and less thought to continue.

"What have you to offer to me for so great a power as that knowledge would give you?"

"The price is paid already, creature. Blood and water, flesh and lansip. That is the price."

"Ah, but this is knowledge deeper than a simple summoning. You must know that." It grinned, showing several mouths in unlikely places. "You seek to change the balance of the world, little human. That is not purchased with a little strip of flesh, however tasty. I must have more."

"What more, monster? Tread carefully, foolish one. If you demand more than the knowledge is worth you will be bound to my service for a year and a day."

"You can barely hold me as it is, prey," it hissed, in a voice thick with contempt. "Sooner or later you will falter, or forget, or stumble on your words, and I will dine well with a sweet sauce of triumph."

"Stop wasting my time," I said, drawing the binding spell tighter. "What more do you demand? I would know how to rid myself of the Demonlord once I have summoned him. It is not so great a knowledge."

"It is worth much to you."

I sneered at it. "It is life and freedom to you, demon. Whose is the greater need?"

It shifted to the form of a great serpent and hissed at me, its coils writhing among the flames. "A price worthy the name, then. Lan fruit, little human! A lan fruit, whole, or you may summon the Nameless One and die at his hands for all we care."

I did not laugh aloud, for that can be deadly, but in the privacy of my thoughts, behind the chant that kept it at bay, I laughed heartily at the demon. My sources had been right, it was not blood or flesh that would buy this but something far more rare. A lan fruit. Something no human could be expected to have. Until the autumn just past there had not been a lan fruit in Kolmar for nearly three hundred years.

"Then speak up, slowly and clearly, and tell me what I wish, for here is a lan fruit, its skin unbroken, whole and perfect."

The demon's whole body shivered with its greed. I held the fruit just beyond its grasp.

"Behold, O starving one," I said, waving the precious thing back and forth through the air that the creature might smell it. I leaned forward, keeping both myself and the lan fruit out of its reach, and whispered intensely, "Paradise."

It roared and the whispers began again, though they were now only one word, repeated a thousand thousand times.

give give give give give give give

"First the information," I cried, for the voices were growing louder. "Tell me now or I eat it before your eyes."

"NO!" the thing screamed, slavering, its eyes never off the ripe gold of the lan fruit. "I will speak, I will tell you, then if you eat it I will be free to rip open your belly and take it for myself."

"Tell me what I want to know and it is yours," I said.

It sat back then, in its nearly human form again, and looked deeply pleased with itself. "There is only one way to be rid of so powerful a demon master," it declared, "for before he died he ensured that if he lived again he would live forever. Still, for the great spell of the Distant Heart to work there must always be a way to destroy the wizard who casts it. The Demonlord declared that he could only be destroyed by a creature that, when cut, bleeds both Kantri and Gedri blood."

"No such thing exists!" I cried. "It is impossible. You lie, demon! I know the strictures of that spell, the destruction must be physically possible."

The demon shrugged. "The spell of the Distant Heart worked, so it must be possible. However, that is not my business. I have told you what you desired to know. It is truth, there is no other way to be rid of him," the demon said smugly. "Now, prey, give give give lan fruit."

I threw it at him in disgust. "Take it and get thee gone,

wretched slave, be damned for all the good you have been to me," I said, but I was distracted by the news and forgot for a split second to banish it immediately.

It instantly took the chance and struck out at me, hoping to keep me off-balance long enough to free itself. In moments it had worked itself loose from half of the bindings I had laid on it, but I was racing through the exorcism and had completed it by the time it had shaken off the binding charm. I put the seal on the dismissal and banished it even as it reached for me.

I was left, shaking, alone, in the red glow from the brazier with the certain knowledge that if I called up the Demonlord I would be stuck with him.

The third task lies before me still; the final summoning of the Demonlord, the embodying of that powerful soul and the binding of it to my service. Once I have Lanen in my hands I will speak the end of the spell and set it in motion. It will work, I know it. But after the Kantri were dead? I would still have the Demonlord on my hands, striving always to free itself. Could I—

I laughed aloud. What thoughts were these, what foolishness had I been considering? Of course I could contain the Demonlord! What matter that I could not banish him? Binding spells could be reinforced easily enough. Long enough at least to find that heart of his and see whether my arts could not create such a creature as his condition demanded, or whether the physical heart he had once owned could be destroyed by simpler means. It would be a challenge, indeed.

And if all should fail? If the dragons win, if I summon the Demonlord and cannot banish him, if I cannot find Lanen, if one of a thousand things goes wrong—well, what then? I have lived now almost eighty years, and the lansip elixir has given me back fifty of them, for in the mirror and in myself I am now no more than thirty years of age.

If I am successful, I shall rule all of Kolmar until I grow tired of life and stop taking lansip. If I lose, I die. It is all one to me. Do you imagine I give the slightest damn about what happens to the world when I am gone? Not I. All is the great game. Evil is the same as good, you know, it is simply the other side of the scale. Dark and light, good and evil, life and death—it makes no difference. Only weak fools fear one or the other. I fear nothing. Not death, not demons, neither success nor failure. I am untouchable for I have no fear, and fear is the only reason that anyone ever does anything. Fear of being alone, fear of death, fear of pain. These are nothing. There is only the game, only the moving of the pieces on the great living board. And only the one without fear can win.

That is why I have spent years planning and working and waiting, like a great spider sitting quiet at the heart of my web until the prey is well caught. To see a soul helpless, begging for mercy—ah, that is true power in this world! Life and death, being or not being—and the knowledge that I do not care one way or the other is the best sauce.

I am not insane, you know. I do not recklessly kill. There is a far deeper, more exquisite pleasure in prolonged pain. To keep them on the edge, leave just enough hope for them to cling to until I am ready, then knock away the last support and let them die in despair. Ah, now, that is worth the doing, deep in the blood and the bone. Delight far beyond mortal ken, that knowledge, to watch a soul crumble in on itself. It takes me to the pinnacle of joy. For that I would cheerfully light fire to the world, could I only have the power to know the world was aware and screaming as I lit the kindling.

I was born into the wrong race. I have read what few of the Demonlord's writings still remain, and he said the same thing of himself.

I would make a better demon than any of the Rakshasa I have ever met.

The Telling of Tales

Lanen

I woke to find myself alone and free of pain at last. I sat up, feeling cold, and realised the shutters were open. The moon was nearly set, but there was still enough light to make out a dark shape in a heap beside the low window, covered in a silver waterfall that caught the last gleams of moonlight.

I rose quietly and went to stand beside him. He had fallen asleep with his left arm on the window sill, his cheek resting on his arm and the circlet bearing his soulgem cradled in his right. Like all sleepers he looked vulnerable, but when I knelt beside him to look into his face I caught my breath. He looked—oh blessed Lady, he looked so terribly sad.

The expression on his face pierced my heart. I was not certain whence his sadness came, but the circlet in his hand spoke of the Kantri. Had he been speaking with his distant kindred? Or had sorrow turned to regret so soon? I had watched Varien working with all his strength to accept his weakness as a human. I knew, in my deep and secret heart, that had I been one of those glorious creatures, I could not have borne to give up my form for anyone, no matter how dear to me.

It was not as if either of us had been given a choice; it had just happened. We knew that somehow our very gods were behind his transformation, but that did not make it any easier for either of us to bear. No matter how great his love for me—and I did not doubt it—I knew that he mourned what he had lost. How could he not? When he had truly realised, that day in the Méar Hills, that he would never fly again, the sorrow on his face had torn at my heart and I had felt a desperate guilt deep in my soul. Jamie was right. I had gone across the sea to change the world and I had done it. If the price had been demanded of me I could have borne it, but it was the Lord of the Kantri who had died.

We were come to a crossroads now, Varien and I. Now that I was safe from the threat of imminent death there was much we had to say to one another, for the words we had spoken in our fear and anger had a kind of truth behind them and would have to be faced. We had accepted the will of the gods and of fate swiftly enough when Akor was transformed, but it was as if the dream was finally done and the clear light of morning shone harsh and merciless upon us at last. We had to accept the reality of what had happened, and it was neither simple nor without cost on either side.

I didn't mean to call to him in truespeech, but I needed to reach out to him and it seemed only natural. I didn't know if he could hear me, or if I wanted him to hear me, and I didn't use words. I didn't have any. What could I possibly say? There was only one thing left to cling to in all the shifting ground that we stood upon, and it filled my mind and rang in my heart—the song we had made together. When we had flown in thought the Flight of the Devoted, while still he was one of the Kantri, we had made a song together that blended our souls, that was our love made real. That, at least, was true. Our souls, no matter what the shape of the bodies that held them, were the match of one another. When words failed me for the love I bore him, for the desperate sorrow I knew was in him, still that song echoed in me. I knelt beside him. I did not touch him, but I opened my mind to him and sang that melody softly and with all my heart, letting it take its force from my love and my understanding of his pain, sending it to him through the intimate link of truespeech that we shared.

That was when I began to realise that the song had changed, was changing. It had grown deeper and more complex, it spoke now of sorrow, of pain, in places where before had been only joy and wonder. It was—I know not how to describe it. I closed my eyes, listening even as I sang, as the voice in my mind took me places I did not expect. The melody was the same, but now it had a greater richness to it. It was deeper and more varied and somehow more real. It took unto itself all that had been happening to us, touching Varien's sorrow and mine, weaving it into the very melody—

I looked at him then, smiling, knowing that he was awake. I could never do that with music, but the Kantri were the greatest musicians who ever lived. His eyes gleamed in the darkness, for the only light we had was starlight from the window. I guessed the gleam came from eyes bright with tears as we both rose to our feet, singing together softly now in truespeech, and he held his hands out to me, palm up. I placed my palms to cover his, lightly, shaking, as the voices of our minds blended, drifted apart, blended again, and fell away into silence at the same moment.

Together.

When the last note faded I stood unmoving, my eyes closed. I knew now that the sorrow that was come over Varien was deep in the bone and not to be kissed away like lovers' hurts or soothed with soft words of devotion. I could not have moved if I had wanted to. I needed to know if his love was greater than his pain, if his sorrow was now become regret deep as the sea and old as time—

"Lanen. Lanen. My heart, my life, how can you think it?" he asked, his fingers closing gently around my hands.

"Come, Lanen Kaelar, look at me," he said. "Look at me," he repeated aloud. I opened my eyes. It was very, very dark.

"I can't see you," I replied, my voice catching. Damn.

"You are using the wrong part of you to look," he replied. Dear Lady, his voice was wonderful. *"Look at me with your heart, my Lanen. Truespeech is only a part of the full Language of Truth, use it in its wider sense. See, my darling."*

"I can't do it, Varien, you know that," I said, impatient. *"I've tried this before and—Lady keep us!"*

I cannot describe to you how I saw what I did, for many kinds of sight were involved. It was most like a painting but that falls far short of the grandeur. Imagine a great swirl of red and gold over the heart against a background of pulsing green the colour of Akor's soulgem and the shape of Varien's body but much larger—then see the red and gold, ever moving, extend to cover the whole physical body, see a shadow in some parts, no longer denied, that adds depth and fullness. Then add in a melody, high and far, but always present—the song that rings ever in both our hearts. And then lift it all from the imagination, give it shape and weight and make it real, and you will have some faint idea.

I was astounded. "What was *that*?" I asked. "Varien, I saw—"

"You saw for a moment as the Kantri see, my dearling," he said, and in the darkness the joy in his voice was plain. "Do you believe me now? That is the truth of my love for you, my Lanen. It colours everything I do, even unto mourning my severance from my people." He caught hold of me then and held me close, his arms so tight I heard my ribs creak.

"Lanen, my dearest Lanen," he murmured as he held me. "Well I know that I wear this body as the kind gift of the Winds and the Lady, and that in my old self I have died—but Lanen, hear me, hear my words and believe them. I do not love you only for a season, or only as long as it is easy to do so. Sorrow is not regret, *kadreshi*," he said, and I began to cry. "I do not regret what has happened. Like any creature,

Kantri or Gedri, sorrow takes me sometimes, but it is not an evil. Sorrow is part of life, as death is part of life and comes as surely. Believe me, my heart. We both made the choices we made of our own free will." He released me just enough to look in my eyes. "It is true that if you had not come to the island I would not have changed, I would not have died. But Lanen—Lanen—if I had not chosen to act as I did, I would not have changed no matter what you had said or done. What has happened was the fault of both of us, or of neither."

I was weeping so hard now I could barely speak, and my mind had little to do with the words that came out. They flew straight from my soul. "Varien, forgive me, forgive me! I would have paid any price to be with you but I never wanted the payment to be yours. Forgive me—"

He made me look into his eyes. "Lanen Kaelar, Lanen my wife, I forgive you. Will you now forgive me for the pain our love has cost you, and for the change our babes have forced upon you?"

"I forgive you from my heart." I reached out to stroke his cheek. "We are both changed now, my love. It is well."

I saw again the gleam of tears in his eyes. "I love you," he said, simply. "And Lanen, I do not regret."

I had needed desperately to hear those words. When he spoke them I clung to him and wept like a child. When the tempest of weeping had passed, though, I recovered myself a little and stood back. "I have desperately needed your forgiveness," I said. "But Varien—I know these feelings will return. They run too deep to be dealt with all at once. By the love I bear you, do not fear to speak to me of them." I drew myself to my full height. "I would always rather have to do with spiky truth than with comfortable lies. Always."

I held out my right hand to him and he smiled and took it in his. "I give you my word, Lanen Kaelar," he said, the beauty of that deep warm voice threatening to break down my hard-won self-control. "Always the spiky truth."

We gazed long at one another in that quiet darkness, our hands softly clasped. It was a vow as great as our marriage vow and we both knew it. Finally he stepped forward to seal it, with a kiss so strong and sweet I thought my heart would break. We held each other close for a long moment of utter silence. I remember my thoughts as though I stood there this moment—I would gladly die in this truth, with him.

I should have known it was too good to last.

We stood unmoving, drowned in that silent place of joy and pain mingled, until we heard someone shouting "Demons!" down the corridor.

Ah, well.

Salera

I stood at the edge of the dark winter wood in the deep night. The moon had set and dawn was yet distant, but I could smell him now. The longing that had drawn me there was grown large within my breast. I knew he was inside the large pile of cut stone that stood before me, but there was—ah, there was another smell that disturbed me greatly even as it sent a shiver through my wings. Faint, familiar yet never known before, wild and strong, so far beyond me I hardly dared even to breathe it in.

At first it kept me away, so deep went that scent into my soul, but I could not stay away. *He* was there. I walked around the piled stone until I found the place where his smell was strongest. Strangely, it was the sound that stopped me. I had forgotten, but when I heard it again the memory rushed over me.

I had forgotten the sounds he made when he slept. I knew the rhythm of his breathing as I knew my own heartbeat. Fear fell away as I moved close to the small patch of wood in the stone. I remembered that there had been such things in the place we had shared. Those had swung open. Perhaps there were the same?

I reached up and pulled.

Will

Well, I had been dreaming about the demons that had attacked us, and I wake slowly from deep sleep, so it makes sense I'd have thought what I did. For I woke with a start at a strange noise.

There is was again, the sound that had wakened me.

Something was outside my window, pulling at the shutters trying to get in.

"Demons!" I shouted, hoping to goodness someone would hear me, scrambling out of my bed towards the door. I threw it open and shouted. "Vil, Aral, quick, it's demons, in here—"

Vilkas appeared, rumpled and weary but already ablaze, followed immediately by Aral. "Where? What? What's happened?" he rumbled.

Jamie and Rella came round the corner with a glass-sided lantern. "Where?" demanded Jamie, though I could see fear on his face.

"There's one at my window!" I said.

Rella snorted and the others relaxed. "It's being very restrained, don't you think? They don't usually both to knock."

I was a bit more awake by then, and a small measure of courage had returned. The noise had stopped as well.

I went sheepishly back into my room, followed first by Aral, then by Vil, then by Jamie and Rella who were muttering and laughing quietly to themselves. I lit the candle by my bed from the lantern—well, light gives courage, doesn't it?—then went to the window, lifted the latch and threw open the shutters.

I was promptly knocked onto my backside by the armoured head of a large friendly dragon the colour of new copper with eyes the blue of the sky in spring, or of a little healing flower—

"Salera!" I cried, delight warring with amazement as I drank in the sight of her.

To my everlasting astonishment, she looked me in the eye and said, very softly, "Sssahhrrairra."

Then she licked me.

Maikel

I had been wandering ever since I escaped unnoticed from the College. The magnitude of my realisation, the knowledge that I was right and Berys had bewitched me for months, hit me like a physical blow and for a time I drifted vaguely away from Verfaren, mostly north and east, sleeping as little as I could for dread of the dreams that sleeping brought, and eating only enough to keep myself alive, for food had no savour. In a curiously detached way I began to fear for my own life.

That changed one evening, between one breath and another. I know not how long it had been since I had left Verfaren, but when I woke to myself again it was sudden, and as potent as cold water in the face. There seemed no reason for it—one moment I had been staring into the fire in an inn somewhere, the next I was ordering food and enjoying its taste, my mind vigorous and my own again.

I was most conscious that my vague fears for Marik's daughter Lanen had grown until I could deny them no longer. I must find her before Berys or Marik did, warn her, help her if I could. I prayed to the Lady that my strength would serve me so long, for even the act of prayer brought a sick feeling to my gut. I prayed the harder therefore, pleading my case to Mother Shia, for I had only my healing ability to provide me a living and I sought only to assist the young woman who had been so unjustly pursued by my old master.

After beseeching the Lady's aid, I turned my face south with utter certainty. It was as if her presence beat upon me from a distance, like the sun. I blessed the Lady in my deepest heart for her assistance and started walking. My gut was painful and distended, but I could not spare the time to heal it. I sought the lady Lanen now with all my strength. It was all there was in me to do.

I was caught so deep in the spell that I did not even question my too-easy knowledge of where in all the wide world Marik's daughter might be.

Will

I scrambled to my feet, never taking my eyes off Salera. She was too big to come inside anymore, I thought sadly, until she folded her wings up small and sort of flowed over the sill into the room. So much came back to me—her way of moving, the feeling of being near her, and the fact that sharing a room with her was very like having a horse in the house, simply from the point of view of the available space. I didn't care. I had already thrown my arms about her neck when I realised that the others were still there.

Salera didn't seem to mind overmuch. In fact, she seemed curious. I glanced up to see the other four staring. I laughed, and Aral at least relaxed and laughed with me. "Will, she's glorious," she said, moving forward. "Would she let me touch her, do you think?"

I grinned. "Littling, this is Aral. She's a friend. Aral, this is Salera."

Aral held out her hand awkwardly, as to an unknown dog. Salera ignored it, of course, but she gazed at Aral for a long minute and then took a deep sniff of her. I'd seen her do that before, when she first met my sister Lyra. It was her way of learning a new person.

Aral said quietly, her voice heavy with wonder, "Salera, you are so beautiful. Will told us about you, but he never said how lovely you were."

Salera gently touched the tip of her long snout to Aral's nose, like a formal handshake; then she pulled away just a little. Aral reached out slowly—I was pleased, that was just the way to behave—and touched the copper-hued faceplate that was so close.

"It's warm! I mean, she's warm," said Aral, amazed. Salera seemed as interested in Aral as Aral was in her, so I left them to it and went over to the others. It wasn't far to go—Salera was managing to take up most of the room.

"You never mentioned that you had a pet dragon," said Jamie quietly. There was a quaver in his voice, but I couldn't tell if he was scared or amused. "I'd no idea the creatures were ever so friendly with people."

I laughed. "She's no one's pet, master, and I haven't seen her in many years." I turned back, it was hard to take my eyes from her. "Far too long, eh lass?" I said.

She made some kind of sound, as she used to. I always wondered back then if she was trying to speak. She'd spoken her name to me right enough, or something awfully close to it. I still didn't know what to make of that.

Vilkas stood stock-still by the door, watching everything that happened but keeping well out of it. It wasn't like him, but I got a better look at him when I went to light more candles. Shia, he looked exhausted. He nodded at me, murmured, "Some demon," and finally released the corona he'd summoned to him. When it was gone he looked like a man who was asleep standing up.

Rella, on the other hand, had moved into the room to have a closer look. After a minute she lifted one corner of her mouth. "At least she's a more manageable size than the other ones." She stepped forward and bowed to Salera. "I bring you greetings from your cousins Shikrar and Kédra of the Kantrishakrim," she said, grinning. "They think about you all the time, you know."

"They do indeed," said a new voice. I looked up to see the silver-haired man in the doorway. Couldn't recall his name. He was fully dressed, as if he had been watching with Rella and Jamie, and he wore—

It was a night for surprises and no mistake. He was wearing a heavy band around his head that was made all of gold. I'd never seen so much in one place before. And I've not yet mentioned the emerald set in the middle of it, the size of Aral's fist! I tried to think if there were any princes of any of the Kingdoms who matched his description.

His lady, as tall as he was, stood behind him looking like a different person than the poor pale creature I'd seen earlier. Vilkas had certainly done her the world of good.

Neither of them could take their eyes off Salera. Mind you, I could understand that. They both approached her with wonder in their eyes, but the man was entranced, bewitched. He walked right up to her—and by my hope of heaven I swear she was as enthralled as he was.

She ignored me, Aral, everyone, to come up close to him. She looked him all over and took her deep breath, then another, then another. He stood before her and closed his eyes. I began to wonder if he was right in the head.

Varien

"Little sister, little cousin, I welcome thee, I greet thee in the name of the Kantrishakrim. Wilt thou not bespeak me, little one, dear one, so dearly met at last?"

I was overwhelmed. The Tale of the Demonlord I knew was history, but it happened nearly five times my life span in the past. That is very nearly legend—but here was legend stood before me, made in the true image of my own people but a tiny fraction of the size.

The sight of her pierced my heart. Sherók, whom Lanen helped bring into the world, was the first of the Kantri to be born in five kells, five hundred years. My people were dying, and here was one who looked for all the world like a youngling. I kept waiting for her to speak, I could not stop myself, as long as I wore my circlet I tried to bespeak her, but to no avail. If she had appeared even in some small measure different from the Kantri—but she was not. No matter how long separated our two peoples had been, she was our image made small, undeniably of our blood and our Kindred. Her eyes gleamed brightly, I could tell she was intelligent—but she did not, could not answer me.

Then my eye was drawn to a detail. There was a raised lump in the centre of her forehead, almost exactly like the structure in a Kantri youngling that protects the soulgem before it is fully formed. However, in the Kantri it is a scale that loosens over time. On this beautiful creature it was still part of her faceplate.

I spoke aloud. "Do you permit, littling?" I asked, reaching towards her face. She took my scent and approved—those gestures at least were the same. I reached out to touch the raised surface on her faceplate, longing to encounter a thought, wondering if a touch would make the difference.

It did not. I felt nothing beyond the smooth warmth of her

armour. "Alas, little sister," I said, my hand lingering on her cheek ridge, "if you speak, I cannot hear you."

Will

"What do you mean, if she speaks? Of course she does!" I said. "Didn't you hear her?"

"Goodman, I did not. I am Varien rash-Gedri. What are you called?"

"Willem of Rowanbeck," I said. "Salera is—well, I raised her. We're friends," I said, then I started laughing because Salera was making that very obvious. The room was cold and she must have remembered that I felt the cold that much more, for she settled down by wrapping herself around me and resting her head on my shoulder. I leaned against her, forgetting all the troubles that beset Vilkas and Aral and me, forgetting everything except that my Salera had found me again.

Then Varien smiled, a smile like sunrise, deep and powerful and brave through sorrow. "There is a word, Master Willem, for such a depth of friendship. Soulfriends." He gazed at the two of us as though his life depended on us. "Soulfriends," he repeated softly.

Then his lady came up beside him and wrapped her arm about his waist. "Yes, love. And they haven't seen each other in years, and most of the rest of us are asleep on our feet." She put her palm on his cheek, turned his face towards hers and kissed him. "You can adore her again tomorrow," she said, grinning. "Right now I'm claiming a wife's rights. Goodnight, everyone!"

Vilkas was already gone, claimed by exhaustion. When the new-wedded pair—for what else could they be?—had left, everyone went back to wherever they had been, calling quiet but cheerful goodnights.

I hardly paid them any heed. That tall lass had been right—"adore" was the right word. I sat and talked to Salera until the sky began to lighten, and I found I had to touch her somehow—just my hand on a wing, or admiring her size and strength. She was half again the size she'd been when last I saw her. I couldn't help it, I kept telling her how beautiful she was. I don't know that she understood, but she dropped her jaw and hissed at me—that's a kind of dragon laugh, I remembered when she did it—and kept wandering around me, always touching. She was as bad as I was, after so long apart we almost needed to be reminded that the other was real.

"Ah, my girl," I said finally, when the sky outside the window began to brighten in earnest. "I'll need a *little* sleep at least. Are you weary then, however far you've travelled?" She just gazed at me. "Ah, you look fresh as spring itself, lass," I said, grinning. "Will you mind if I get some sleep?" I laughed at myself. "Truth to tell, I hate to close my eyes in case you're gone when I wake."

I don't know if anything I said meant anything to her, but when she saw me lie down she more or less wrapped herself about the bed, with me on it, and rested her head on my chest, gazing at me. I kept my eyes open as long as I could.

Soulfriends. I liked the sound of that.

Lanen

It was a blessing and a wonder to wake to life and health and sunlight. I lay for a moment just revelling in the feeling of not being in pain any longer. The voices had receded to the merest whisper for the moment, though they had not gone away. I was almost beginning to be used to them, though I still wondered what they were.

Then I really woke up.

"Varien! Varien, we've found them!"

A bleary voice issued from the other side of the back I was looking at. "Found whom, my dearling?" The back uncurled, turned over and became a groggy semblance of a man. I had to smile—what a difference from the first day of our wedded lives! He looked more than a little dishevelled now, rather than being a vision of perfection. His face was acquiring lines of character, his skin was no longer nearly so soft for our travels had kept us out in all weathers, and his travails of late had put dark circles under those glorious green eyes. I put my arms about him and kissed him. He had been stunning before, a perfection to astonish, awe-inspiring. Now that he was touched by life he was irresistible, for the awe was still there but now so were the wrinkles.

I had certainly found the way to waken him, for he kissed me back with a will and—well, we were but lately wed, and I had been so ill . . .

"And a good morrow to you, Lanen Maransdatter," he said sometime later, when we were recovering our breath. "I am as ever your willing pupil. Fool that I am, my thoughts began to chasten you for waking me when first I heard your voice. Blessed be the Winds that I learn swiftly! However," he said, sitting up. "I am left in suspense. Whom have we found?"

"The Lesser Kindred, of course," I replied, not moving. Even his back was lovely. *Oh, Lanen, you're deep in, aren't you?* I thought to myself, and sat up. "The little dragon, Salera. She's amazing, isn't she?"

"Alas, my love, I bespoke her but she did not respond," he said.

"And did you expect her to?" I asked indignantly. "She's so young. And I'd swear she understands Willem, at least a little." I grinned at my husband. "If they've known one another so long, we are not the first!"

He laughed as I had hoped he would. "It is hardly the same, though, dearling." He stared at nothing for a moment, thinking. "They are soulfriends, it cannot be doubted, but—it seems more like to a father and daughter than aught else."

"I'll believe you. How wonderful, when she just curled about him! Come on," I cried, bounding out of bed, "let's go see if she's still here."

Varien rose and caught me to him, holding me far too tight, as usual. "Lanen, my Lanen, it is good to have you back," he said.

"Believe me, I'm glad to be here," I said. I kissed him as

hard as I could and then leaned back in his arms. "I love you with all my heart and soul, my Varien, but I'm absolutely starving. Food and dragons, in that order."

We were in the common room in five minutes. That's when we realised that it was nearly midday. And that we were not the last to emerge.

Rella

Jamie and I had kept the watch together, before and after the little dragon appeared. True, we were best suited to the task, but it was also one of the best ways to find a little peace and time to talk. Such things are far simpler when you are young; there are no complications and no lurking comparisons, and the wounds to be healed are generally not so deep. I will not bore you with all our talk. We were honest to the point of pain with each other and with ourselves. The eventual result was an unarmed truce, which for two old fighters is not a bad start.

When dawn came I was all for waking that lazy dragon Varien and letting him stand watch for a change, but Jamie tapped me on the shoulder and pointed at the shutters. I opened them and found that the sun had come up, quietly, behind a screen of light grey cloud.

"Hola, mistress, a good morrow to you!" said a loud voice from outside and away to my left. "You rise with the sun! A moment and I will have the fire—oh."

I turned and enjoyed the scene. It was the innkeeper, come to light the fire and to prepare breakfast, and he had found two of his guests already present and quite a decent fire in the grate already.

"We've kept it in, I thank you," said Jamie, very kindly I thought. "But breakfast sounds wonderful. I'd cheerfully maim for a pot of chélan." The innkeeper laughed and disappeared through a door. He emerged moments later to put two pots on the main fire to boil, one water, one a smaller vessel that he kept stirring. "I hate to intrude, but the kitchen fire is taking a while to get going. Soon have chélan and porridge for you. Did you sleep well?"

We looked at each other and laughed. "Not yet," I said. "But after I've eaten I'm going to go and give it a damn good try."

You grow used to such strangeness when your life is lived as it comes instead of according to a plan. Neither Jamie nor I had trouble falling instantly asleep after we'd broken our fast and knew that the innkeeper would raise an alarm if need be.

When we finally wakened again the early cloud had dispersed and the sun was bright and high. We both felt rested but wondered why none had sent to waken us. We washed quickly in cold water and entered the common room together—

—to applause. Lanen and Varien sat next to the two healers. Varien, I noticed, was wearing his circlet openly now. Will sat a little apart from the rest with the most amazing expression on his face.

"Well done, Jamie," called Lanen, laughing. "For once in your life you're later up than I am. I'm proud of you!"

"Be silent, wench, and pass me some of that chélan," he growled. She laughed again and brought mugs for Jamie and me. We sat with Will at the other table.

The innkeeper was serving a midday meal, and after we'd all eaten we drew two tables together and—well, wondered what to do next.

I turned to Lanen. "My girl, you're looking fine for a change. How do you feel?"

"Like spring after winter," she said. "Mage Vilkas, I—"

"Please, just Vilkas," that young man said. He seemed pleasant enough, if only he'd smile now and again.

"Vilkas, I owe you my life," said Lanen simply. "How can I possibly repay you? What fee can you charge for such a gift?"

"None," he said. "For you were not the only one whose life was changed last night." And my wish was granted, for he smiled then, a broad glorious smile that lit up his face and showed the joy that danced behind his eyes. "In fact it seems that few of us escaped unscathed by the whirlwind of the powers that were abroad last night. Will here is away with that dragon of his, no matter where his body might be."

"Where is she then, Master Willem?" asked Jamie over Will's protests.

"She's gone out to hunt, but she'll be back," he said. Turning to Varien, he added, "That reminds me. Why is she so fascinated by you, and how in the world do you know so much about dragons?" He turned to me next. "And you! What were those names you said, and what did you mean, they sent her greeting? I—"

Varien interrupted him. "Master Willem—"

"Just Will, if you please," he said.

"Will, the full truth is a very long story that must wait another time, but Rella, Lanen and I were on the Harvest ship that returned from the Dragon Isle last year. We have all spent time with the Greater Kindred—with the True Dragons that live there, and several we know by name. One in particular, Shikrar, has spent much of his life seeking to contact the Lesser Kindred."

"The Lesser Kindred are Salera's people?"

"Yes."

"Why do they want to contact them?"

Varien smiled. "I saw the love you share with her last night, like father to daughter. The Lesser Kindred were brought into being by one known only as the Demonlord. He sent an army of demons to rive their soulgems from them. The ones who were attacked were changed in other ways as well." Varien paused a moment. "Our history says that they became as beasts, but it is wrong. Salera is not a beast, not in that sense. She is of—of the same kindred as the True Dragons. So were all the Kantri who were changed by the Demonlord. They were made smaller in stature and bereft of their soulgems, but kindred none the less."

"What's a soulgem?" asked Aral. Interesting as all this

was, she seemed particularly fascinated by my circlet. "And if you'll forgive me, what is that stone you wear?"

Varien

I looked long into her eyes before I answered her. There was something I trusted there, so I told her the truth.

"The answer to both of your questions is the same. A soulgem is the only physical remnant of the Kantri, the True Dragons, after they die." She gasped, her eyes wide, and put her hand to her chest. "This stone I wear is a soulgem, lady," I said slowly, not releasing her from my gaze, "though I think you knew that before."

"Not until this moment. Oh, Shia, it makes so much sense!" She drew forth a pouch from under her tunic, opened it, and gently took from it a soulgem red as ruby. It might have been Shikrar's.

I could not stop my body, though it was not acting on my command. The instant I saw it I sprang to my feet and grasped her by the throat. "Where did you steal this from? Where did you get it?"

"Varien, stop it! Stop it! **Akor, let her go you idiot!"** cried Lanen in my mind. I only gradually became aware that everyone was shouting. I released the Healer with great difficulty.

"Think, man! None have disappeared from the Place of Exile, have they?" demanded Lanen. "What, do you think this Healer has killed one of the Kantri from all this distance and brought the soulgem back to taunt you with?" *"Put yourself through the Discipline of Calm, Akor, or something like it,"* she added in truespeech. *"This woman helped heal me, she's not demon-touched. You're overreacting."* I heard her mindvoice smile ever so slightly. *"Bloody Dragons, they're all the same."*

I tore my eyes away from the soulgem and with an effort managed to bow and say, "Your pardon, Mistress Aral. Forgive me, I pray you. I am ashamed. This is ill repayment for your healing. I crave your pardon. Lady, Mage Vilkas. La-nen is right, I reacted without thought. Please understand, it is how you would feel if I revealed that I carried a human skull about with me as a trophy."

"There's no need to kill me for it. I didn't know," said Aral, massaging her throat. She called up her Healer's power and let it spread around her neck. After a moment she breathed a sigh of relief. "That's it fixed. Damn." She glow-ered at Varien. "You could have killed me. You don't know your own strength. That hurt like all the Hells."

Lanen

"Aral, I beg your pardon. I'm sorry my husband reacted so violently. Can I do anything to help?"

"No, I'm fine now," she said. "Damn good thing I'm a Healer." She turned to Varien. "It's not like I have this set as an ornament. I wear it next my heart. It is very precious to me."

"He was a Dragon, Aral," I said quickly, before Varien could respond. It seemed pointless to me to keep Will in the dark at this stage. "I know he told you last night, but it can take a while to sink in. For the purposes of argument he is still one of the Kantrishakrim, and you've just shown him that you wear the mortal remains of one of his kinfolk round your neck."

"Oh," said Aral. She was embarrassed. "I didn't realise—sorry, Varien," she murmured.

"The Kantri can talk to their Ancestors, did you know that?" I added, as lightly as I could. She didn't know, poor soul, and she had the grace to look appalled as I explained. "They use the soulgems to contact them. In his eyes, you have kept this particular Ancestor prisoner for—well, they left five thousand years ago. Prisoner for about that long. Do you wonder now that he's angry?"

Aral said something extremely rude that was, on the face of it, physically impossible. I was impressed. I'd been col-lecting oaths for a while now and it was a new one to me. I made a mental note of it. "I'm truly sorry, Varien," she said. "I never meant—I didn't know, how could I?"

"How do you come to have such a thing?" I asked.

"That's what I wanted to know," said Will. "She used it yesterday—sweet Shia, was it only yesterday?—to fight off demons. It was amazing."

I put my hand out to restrain Varien, but to my surprise he nodded. "We are the life-enemies of the Rakshasa. Did the Ancestor grant you assistance?"

Aral nodded. "It—it always reacts violently when there are demons around, and if I channel my healing power through it I can disperse them with a touch." She frowned down at the gem gleaming in her hand. "I had cut myself once, by chance, and my blood touched it—then the power was amazing."

"Astounding," said Varien. "Perhaps the life in the fresh blood quickens the memory of the Ancestor." He sat down again, obviously relieved. *"If the Ancestor assists her, it means that he or she approves of the holder,"* said Varien to me privately. *"Though I have never heard of one so willing before, or one who worked with the Gedri. I must ask Shikrar who this could be!"*

"Whence came you by so precious a thing?" he asked Aral again.

"My mother carried it," she said, "and her mother, and hers, back to my great-great-grandmother. She—well, it's a long story, but they say she found it in the deepest chamber of a cavern in the mountains when she was in need of aid, and that aid came to her soon thereafter. She carried it always afterwards, in memory and in a kind of gratitude. When she knew she was dying, she passed it to her daughter, and so on until it came to me." Aral was staring into the gem's depths. "I am the first Healer in the family. It was pure chance that I learned it was proof against demons."

She looked up. "You are certain this is a soulgem?"

"Absolutely certain," said Varien. "There can be no doubt—though if you must have proof I can supply it," he said. Taking off his circlet, he touched the gem in Aral's hand with his own for just a moment. They both began to glow gently from within, unmistakably the same in kind.

Varien replaced his circlet. The glow in the red gem faded swiftly to darkness.

"I hate to disturb you," said Vilkas, his voice unexpectedly harsh, his smile gone forever it seemed. "It is gratifying to know that the power that has been assisting us is glad to do so, but that does not alter the fact that we have wasted a good deal of time this morning. We are bound westward this day and we should be leaving," he said, glaring at Aral and Will. "We do not wish to stay too long in one place lest Berys should find us."

"Polite as ever, Vil," sighed Aral. "We both needed sleep and you know it, but you're right. We only left Verfaren yesterday and we were attacked by a score of Rikti before the day was out. Who knows what he might do given time to think about it?"

"Which raises a question," said Rella, looking at me. "Where precisely are *we* bound, now that you are well? If Berys is coming out into the open with his powers, it would be madness to try to get to the library at Verfaren now."

I laughed. "Thanks to Will we do not need it! Unless in your time there you learned more about Salera's people than you knew before?"

"No," he replied. "No, I read all the books the library had to offer and none of them said any more than the common knowledge. They certainly didn't say where they had come from," he said, gazing at Varien. "So they are truly kin to the great dragons away west?"

"They are," said Varien. "I was hoping that in all this time—we try to speak to them every year, as I tried last night, but they cannot hear us nor we them."

Will bristled. "She hears as well as you or I."

"I spoke of the Language of Truth. Lanen tells me it is called Farspeech among you." He sighed. "The mark of a sentient people is that they can speak and reason. I have little doubt of Salera's ability to reason, to some extent, but she cannot speak."

"But she can! She said her name to me the moment she arrived!" cried Will.

Well, that stopped everyone cold just long enough for the room to be suddenly full of dragon.

Salera

I watched as He slept and my heart was light with the joy of it. The touch of him, the smell, the sound of his voice, the sound even of his night noises, eased my fear and calmed my soul.

I had much to think of as I lay near him. The other two-legs I had seen were so different, especially the silver and green one. That one haunted me, for his touch was like cold water on my face, like flying out of a cloud into birght sunlight.

Like dawn.

When He woke I nuzzled him to reassure him, then I went out to hunt. It was a good place for hunting, the small creatures did not know my scent and I could catch them easily.

However, as the sun rose overhead I found myself restless again. I had thought that finding Him would settle my heart but it did not. I could not stay in that place, where there were so many of his kind and none of mine. Perhaps all would be well if we returned to our old home, and on the way he could meet my people.

The thoughts were not so clear as that, you understand. All I felt at the time was that I had to return to the high place with Him. But the result was the same.

I entered in the open door of the place he sat eating, surrounded by the other two-legs.

I wrapped the very tip of my tail around his leg.

Will

I had to laugh. "So you want to go as well, do you? That you and Vilkas should join forces against me! It's not fair you know, kitling," I said, reaching out to stroke her neck.

She tugged ever so lightly at me. I knew how it would go if I didn't move. "Very well! I must pay my shot and get my cloak, then we'll be on our way." She knew the tone of voice and let me loose as soon as I stood up. I shooed her out the door—she knew what I meant and left—and I turned to the others.

"I don't know where you're bound, friends, but I'm going home. I've just been told." I grinned. "She's a good persuader."

Vilkas and Aral stood as well, and Gair came over. No idiot, my friend Gair. He knew the signs and he'd seen Salera leave. I expect the sight of her had kept him distant, true enough—Gair is not made to deal with wonders, or even with beasts other than horses and dogs—but once she was gone he made sure he was in amongst us.

"Was all to your liking?" he asked briskly, not letting anyone answer. "Good, good, I'm glad."

Rella was not best pleased. "We've paid, master," she said.

"Not for a ruined mattress and sheets," he replied promptly. "And Will, I can't let you have this on account I'm afraid. I'll need silver."

Damn. I'd forgotten I had not a single copper piece with me. Just as well that Lanen took over.

"Of course you will, master innkeeper," she said. "That is my concern, for it was I who ruined your goods. Now come, let us not disturb the others . . ." She drew him away, her arm around his shoulder.

"You wouldn't believe that girl had never done a thing outside farm work until the autumn," said Jamie, with a kind of awed pride on his face. "She's amazing. You mind out," he said, turning to Varien. "She'll have you wrapped around her little finger if you're not wary."

"Alas, Master Jameth, I am already lost," said Varien, gazing after Lanen.

It takes all kinds, I suppose, I remember thinking. You must remember I didn't know her then, and she wasn't that much to look at. Certainly it was good of her to pay for our bed and board, but I was going to have a word with Vilkas. How did he expect to live on the nothing we had brought with us? The woman had been near death, he could have charged her a few silver coins at least for his pains!

Salera called from outdoors, a kind of half-roar. I hurried to collect my cloak from the room I'd slept in. Lady knows I had nothing else to carry.

When I returned everyone was outside. Jamie and Rella had gone to saddle the horses, and it turned out that Lanen had paid for our room and board, arranged food for the journey for both parties and had purchased blankets for Vil and Aral and me, which she had rolled and made ready to tie on behind various saddles so we wouldn't need to carry them. I was embarrassed and offended and grateful all together—and if you don't know what I mean then you've never been poor—but when I tried to thank her she shook her head and said, "Oh, no, Master Willem, take no offense I pray you. These are in the nature of a bribe, pure and simple. The four of us beg your leave to accompany you and Salera wherever you may be bound, and in earnest of our good faith we offer food, and blankets that are soon going to smell very strongly of horse."

I stared at her. Jamie was right, this one was cut from a different cloth. I blinked.

"Well, Master Willem? Will you allow me and mine to travel with you for a time?" she asked politely, but her eyes were twinkling. There was a smile deep down in there somewhere.

I couldn't help it, I grinned. "Caught you, Mistress La-nen! What would you do if I said no?"

She burst out laughing. "Follow you anyway!"

"Of course you would." With that expression on her face she looked half her age, a happy girl with a passing resemblance to my little sister. "Come then and welcome," I said, and my last doubts about these strange folk fell away. "My place is small, but it's a roof and four walls and I'm sure we'll manage somehow. I live about four days' easy walk up in those hills. Let us be off, before this wretched child knocks me off my feet again," I said, for now that we were outside Salera was stood beside me, nudging me with her head. "You're not very subtle, are you?" I said, patting her neck and murmuring happily to her. "I'm so pleased to see you, littling."

When the horses came up they had to be convinced about Salera. Her kind were uncommon enough that they had never encountered one, and there was a certain amount of snorting and backing and a kick or two, but Jamie knew what he was doing. Salera, too, did what she could to calm them, standing still to be seen and smelled.

"A moment, Will, of your kindness," said Varien, when the horses were calmer. He had kept quiet ever since I'd said that about Salera saying her name, but it was obviously something he wanted to get clear before we got moving. He came up right close to Salera, staring for all he was worth. She stared back at him. "You said she spoke to you?"

"She said her name," I said, proud of her. "Clear as day."

It was a most peculiar setting: a bright copper dragon with eyes as blue as the spring sky above, sitting with furled wings on the road outside a wayside inn listening intently to a man who looked unsettlingly like her, though I couldn't tell you how exactly.

Varien came around to stand before her, with Lanen right behind him. He bowed, then tapped himself on the chest, clearly indicating himself. "Varien," he said, and then he pronounced it a little differently. "Varian. I am Varian." He held out his hand, indicating her.

She started trembling. I'd never seen her do that. Everyone else came near, sensing that something important was happening.

Varien tried again. "Varian. Varian," he said slowly, tapping his chest. Then he pointed at me. "Will. Will."

She made that sound then, the one I had always assumed was just noise.

Hooirrr.

I stood there stunned. *Will you idiot, she's been talking all these years, you just never understood, idiot, idiot!* If you didn't have lips, and if your tongue wasn't made to form an "l" behind your teeth, Hooirrr was as close to Will as you could hope to get.

Salera had got up on all fours. Her wings were rustling in her agitation and her tail was twitching like a furious cat's, but her eyes were locked on the figure before her.

"Again," said Lanen softly, her own eyes shining. "One more time, love."

Varien pointed to himself once more, slowly, and I noticed he was trembling as well. "Varian. I am Varian." To me. "Will." To her, and waited.

"Ssarrairrah," she said, triumphantly. "Sssarraaairrah!" she cried again, and rising on her back legs she flapped her wings and sent a quick breath of fire into the air. When she came back down she butted her nose against me so hard I nearly fell over and said "Hooirrr." Then she touched her nose against his chest and said—well, the first sound was a hiss between closed teeth that was only faintly like an "f," but the rest came out very like "Hffarrriann."

Varien fell to his knees; Lanen, behind him, had her hands on his shoulders, and they both were staring openmouthed and wide-eyed.

Varien

"Speech and reason, speech and reason," my thoughts kept repeating. *"Lanen, that's it, the mark of a true people, speech and reason. She understands what a name is, knows her own, has—Name of the Winds, she has spoken mine. Lanen, Lanen, she is—they are—"*

"They are their own people, aren't they?" Lanen replied. For once she was the calmer of the two of us. Her hands on my shoulders were all that kept me upright. *"Ready to burst into full life."* Her mindvoice faltered as she added, *"They are become a new race, Varien. They are no longer the mindless beasts the Kantri believed them to be. The Lady knows I rejoice for this glorious child and her people, but alas for the Lost!"*

"Lanen?"

"I am such a fool, my love. I had wondered in my deep heart if—"

"If the Lesser Kindred could be reunited with their soul-gems to restore the Lost. I know, my dearest, and if you are a fool I have been one for hundreds of years, for I had thought it too. But if they are all as she is, they are a breath away from full sentience."

"I know it. We must think of some other way to bring peace to the Lost."

This whole exchange of thoughts took mere moments, and it did not in the least make less of the wonder of that recognition. Salera understood. She was aware.

I stood and bowed to Salera, as Shikrar always bowed to a youngling when first it used truespeech. "I welcome thee, Salera, my cousin."

She bowed back, but I could see her shaking with the effort of containing herself. I scrambled to my feet, laughing, for I knew what was coming as though my own muscles were shaking so. She took the others by surprise as she leapt into the sky, sending Fire aloft to hallow the time. I would have joined her if I could.

"Why did you say Var*ian*?" asked Lanen quietly, not even glancing at me. Her eyes never left the little one.

"Fewer sounds to learn all at once," I replied. Salera filled my vision as well. "We all learn thus when we are young."

Will stared for some moments, slack-jawed. "I'll be damned," he said, watching Salera as she danced in the air.

Aral sighed loudly and started walking. "Very likely," she said, shoving him as she passed. "And unless we get moving and get off the high road we are all going to be damned to-gether. Berys is still around, you know."

"A point to Aral," he said, starting off after her.

We all set off towards the lowering sun, into the Súlkith Hills, following the faint path west and up.

* * *

Marik

Berys finally replied to my message by sending Durstan to bring me to him.

"It's about damned time, Berys, what in the Hells have you been doing?" I growled when I was shown into his rooms.

"A few necessary things," he said, not bothering to rise. He was stretched out on his bed in what looked like a nightshirt.

"Like neglecting me, for example," I snarled. "You were in such a tearing hurry to heal me so I could be of use to you. Do you have the slightest interest in what I have learned from the dragons? Or would you rather laze about like a bored merchant's wife?"

"If you were not so useful, Marik, I would have your throat cut for that," said Berys offhandedly. The worst of it was that, despite his tone of voice, he meant it and I knew it. He would happily kill me if it suited him and I never forgot it.

"But I am useful. I am suddenly the most useful man you know, Berys, and you will soon believe me on that score." I sat beside the table and poured myself a cup of wine. "What have you been so busy doing?"

"Ensuring my victory," he purred. "Maikel pursues Lanen even now. In three days' time—no, just over two days' time, now, when I am recovered from my labours, or as long as it takes him to find her—he will build an altar and conveniently die when the demon emerges to plant the Swiftlines."

"What in the hells are Swiftlines?" I asked. "You never told me about this. I thought you said you couldn't find Lanen!"

"Swiftlines are—well, some call them demonlines. They are instant transportation. I don't even have to know where the other ends are, for there are two, one each way. I can step through, capture her and be back before anyone notices. As for Lanen—remember the report from our healer in Kaibar?" I nodded. "It was accompanied by a sample of her blood which I have made good use of."

I snorted. "Ever find out what that dragon was that the Rikti said was protecting her?"

Berys, for all that he looked exhausted, managed to sneer. "The Rikti was mistaken. She passed through Kaibar and there was no sight nor sound or smell of a dragon. Or perhaps the Rikti was right and it has left her. In either case I do not fear the wrath of the Kantri here in Kolmar. My folk would have heard if one had been seen, and they cannot make themselves invisible!"

I laughed, low, almost to myself. "Well, Berys, I wish you good fortune. That girl finds protectors in the strangest places. Didn't our man in Kaibar say the humpbacked woman was with her again?"

"Yes, Rella seems to have joined her," said Berys casually, "along with two men he didn't have the names of and I don't recognise. It makes no difference. They will not be able to prevent me."

"They may not have to," I said grimly. "That is what I've come to tell you. The Kantri are coming, Berys. Here. Now, as we speak. We've got about—well, what a coincidence. About two days or so."

It was worth the bald statement to see Berys's face. He seldom allows anything as minor as surprise to affect him, but there, this news would change a few of his plans.

And the Walls of the World Came
Scattering Down

Varien

It was the strangest of journeys. We set off from the inn at Wolfenden in the early afternoon, and the rest of the day was bright and warm. We walked together, the seven humans and Salera at Will's side, exchanging stories. I learned how Will and Salera had met, and Lanen and I told them a short version of our own meeting. It made the time pass easily. We camped in the shelter of a small wood that night and woke early in the morning to the most extraordinary day.

Overnight, winter seemed to have given up the battle and early spring had leapt up all around us. The small flowers, the ground roses, that were fighting to bloom in Kaibar were here full-blown. I would have expected the year to regress as we walked higher into the hills but it did not. Will assured me that as we went higher, towards the high field that was the pass through these hills, the shoulder of the sharp pinnacles of rock ahead would be cold enough for my taste. Indeed, I could see snow lingering on some of the peaks, but at least in their lower reaches it seemed that the Súlkith Hills were disposed to be kindly. Lanen showed me as we walked the brilliant red and yellow blooms on their short stalks, and in a warm and quiet dell blessed by sunlight, the fragrant queen's chamber, a many-blossomed purple spike of a flower, scented the air.

Strange, is it not, that it should be the flowers that I remember? In the midst of my sorrow for my lost kindred, in the depths of my acceptance and my grief and in the joy of the new and deeper peace Lanen and I had made, it is the strong colours of spring in the mountains that most affected me.

Lanen walked beside me, unusually silent. The feelings between us were not simple nor could they ever be again, but in turning to face the darkness we had overcome the worst of it. She knew at last, truly knew in her soul, that she was not to blame for the change the Winds had thrown upon me—and so, at last, did I. And now she was changed as well, of her own free will, to a strange hybrid creature—nearly as strange as I—there was much to take into both of our hearts and consider, of gifts and bereavement, of death and life and the mingling of souls.

I remember the flowers.

Shikrar

I had my wings tucked close in, the surface as small as I could make it. The winds of the eternal Storms that blow between Kolmar and our island were ever potent and threatening. The flying was difficult to say the least.

I had left Idai only a day past. We had found that most of the Kantri were willing to rest for a little time before undertaking the second and more dangerous half of the journey, especially as the rain had stopped and the sun shone, and even that little green rock felt safer than the unknown perils of Kolmar for many of us.

I declared that I would go on ahead to learn what I could of the effects of the Storm winds and to meet with Lanen and Varien, that we might discuss how best to prepare the Gedri for the return of the Kantri. Idai frowned at me and told me that her thoughts would be open to me day and night. It was an extraordinary offer, to be open and listening for days on end. She has always had much of generosity about her, the Lady Idai.

However, at that particular moment I would have exchanged all the generosity in the world for a body beside me in the air. Two can read the currents better than one and I felt very alone, high above the wind-whipped seas. Every muscle was aching from carrying Nikis the Weary—I had heard her so referred to by others now, the poor soul—but thus far they all served me still.

I had left at dawn and encountered the Storms only an hour from the Isle of Rest. It had been a long day of effort, followed by an endless night of work, striving to keep high enough that when the air dropped suddenly away it did not bring me too near the water. I was weary beyond belief, which would explain why I was so foolish as to relax my vigilance when the headwind dropped for a moment. I let out my breath and allowed my wings to lock, just for a moment's rest—

—when a wall of air rose up like a wall of stone before me. I was thrown on to my back, and though I managed to turn over and glide up and out of the drop, my right wing was throbbing in the main joint. It had not broken, thank the Winds, but the pain ran deep. I had no choice, days from land in any direction, I had to use it.

I was most fortunate. I found that the wall of air I had hit was the trailing edge of the Storms. I forced myself higher, every beat of my wings sending out a jolt of pain.

I was glad then that Idai was not there, for I could not restrain myself. With no other soul near me to pity or assist, I cried out with every downbeat. It made it a little easier to bear, but I began genuinely to wonder if, injured, I could go so far alone.

There is no choice, Teacher-Shikrar, I told myself. *You*

have taken this task to yourself on behalf of the Kantri and you are hours from land in any direction. Wind and life or sea and a slow cold death, Shikrar!

That choice was simple enough. I drew in a great breath and roared out my pain to the Winds as I forced myself higher. *Kolmar lies ahead, Kolmar and Akhor and a new life. It is well.* I stopped talking to myself long enough to adjust my angle of rise. *Besides,* I told myself, *if you think Nikis faces years of laughter at her expense, imagine what would come your way should you fail in this flight. Name of the Winds! You would give every soul you ever lectured about flying the chance to taunt you for the rest of your days.*

It seemed to take years to reach the High Air, but it was my only chance. Every time I had to lower my wing I cried out. Eventually I fell silent, for the air was growing thin, but the pain did not lessen.

I knew that my life depended on gaining altitude. I would have given ten years of my future for a rising thermal, but the cold sea ran below me unfeeling, uncaring, cold watery death awaiting me.

We can swim, of course. In the summer we enjoy the water, and in truth it was known that flying very close to the surface took less effort—but I dared not risk it, for it is impossible to take to the air from the water's clutches. If once I touched the sea, I was dead.

The thought sent me higher yet. I may be the Eldest of the Kantri, but in the normal way of things I had still before me a good two more kells of life, and I had a strong desire to see my grandson fly.

When at last I found the broad river on high, when at the end of my strength I caught the edge of that strong wave and could ride it with locked wings, I learned what I needed to know. It led me swiftly and easily over the top of the Storms and that terrible wall of air. I bespoke Idai and told her, that she might guide the others through more gently than I had managed.

Ahead in a clearing sky the winds dropped and the wave in the High Air disappeared, but as I glided down I found another current leading eastwards that was strong enough to bear me. I rode it, wings locked, giving thanks, breathing again. My injured wing throbbed but I was better able to bear it when I could glide and did not have to stroke the air.

The absence of pain seems a simple thing until you possess it no longer.

Once I started allowing myself to glide, however, I found it desperately hard to think. I held on to the little that I knew—according to the Ancestors, I had just over a day's flying yet to accomplish. I was weary to the bone, but I knew I would have to seek height again as soon as I had rested. Just a little rest, just a little, now that the pain was gone—

"Shikrar? Hadreshikrar, it is Idai who speaks. How fare you, my friend?"

I woke with a start to Idai's voice. I was flying through a cloud and was terribly disoriented, but from the pressure I feared that I was far lower than I should be. In the few moments it took me to rouse, the air had grown a great deal rougher. Strange, I thought, this feels like the turbulence you get when water meets—

I came out of the cloud and hit first a powerful updraft that carried me safely up and over the cliff that rose high above the water's edge, and then encountered the downdraft on the other side which threw me unceremoniously to the ground.

Not the welcome I was expecting, I thought briefly as the darkness took me.

Maikel

I found them halfway up the mountain. They were a long way ahead of me, down a valley and up another hillside from where I stood, and there were more of them than I expected. I saw one that I assumed was Varien, for his silver hair was hard to miss in sunlight, but I knew Lanen the instant I saw her even from that far away.

At last, at last, that stopped me where I stood.

How in the Lady's name could I possibly be certain of that distant moving speck being Lanen?

I looked again. I could not tell how many people there were—more than four. There were at least three horses, but there might have been four or five. There was a strange creature with them at first, though it left as the sun was going down. It moved very fast. It might have been a light chestnut horse, I couldn't really tell. But I knew Lanen was there, and which of the tiny dots she was.

That was not possible.

I tried to think what might make me feel so certain. I felt pity for the girl, certainly, but there was no bond between us. I had asked for Lady Shia's aid but this did not feel like divine guidance. My gut wrenched at the thought of the goddess and I could not think clearly.

I drew food from my pack, for it was growing dark and I would have to stop. From what I could see the others were setting up their camp; I saw fire spring forth, friendly and welcoming on that far hillside. The longing grew in me to go there, to speak to Lanen again, to warn her, to be with good people again—to warm my hands and my heart at that fire.

At the very thought I was doubled over with cramp. I could not stand or walk long enough to gather wood for my own fire. The cold food helped, but my gut was dreadfully painful. Enough, I thought, I must do something about this. After I had eaten and rested a while, I sent a prayer to the Lady and summoned my healer's power to me.

There is a kind of half-trance that accompanies healing. I was so weak that my own corona made me dizzy, but I fought the feeling and called in my power. Only the faintest nimbus answered me. I drew on it, weak as I was, to help heal the pain in my belly, but the slightest effort swiftly exhausted me. The pain was as bad or worse after I had finished.

I sat propped against a stone with thin blankets wrapped about me to keep out the night, but the cold and the pain were sharpening my mind.

Finally.

The very things that beset me were making me realise that all was wrong. All. Everything I had done since I left Verfaren made no sense. I had meant to go east and north, and I had done that, but at a snail's pace and towards no destination. I hadn't eaten for days—foolishness. And the sudden urge, no, the *need* to find Lanen and warn her—how in the name of the Mother had I had even the slightest idea of where to go?

I shivered, not with cold. For I had found her, in all the great world I had found her in a matter of days. That was sickeningly not right. What was guiding me? What was pushing me, and why?

I shivered again as a pain cramped across my gut. Oh dear Goddess, sweet Lady Shia—*ahhh*!

Oh Hells' teeth. The pain hit me worse every time I prayed, or even thought sincerely of Shia—a spasm clenched me even as I realised.

I drew in my power again, ignoring the weakness that demanded I stop at the appearance of the merest nimbus. I am a Healer of the third rank, I can heal broken bones in minutes, knit torn flesh, relieve fevers—I had saved Lanen's life when she was very near to death indeed.

It was a struggle, but finally at least a useful portion of my corona surrounded me. I gathered my courage as I had gathered my power and looked with the healing sight into my own body.

I spewed forth my meagre meal and kept heaving long after there was nothing more to come. No one should have to see that in themselves. Oh Mother, oh kind and blessed Lady of the ground below and the water around and the moon in her gentleness above, keep me man alive long enough to fight back.

Wrapped around my gut, with claws in my spine and a spiked tail flicking back and forth, was a demon. I had not called it, I had not allowed it into my soul much less my body, it had been put there against my will. By Berys, of course.

I had heard of such things, but I had never believed that it could—it never happens to you, does it? It was a Sending. A major demonwork that cost the summoner dear one way or another, but not nearly as much as it cost the chosen host.

There was no way to be rid of the thing. It was the cause and the force behind the compulsion that had made no sense. I didn't know why Berys wanted me to track Lanen, to be near her when she stopped, but I "knew" it was something I had to do. No, I corrected myself. It was something that Berys, through the demon, wanted me to do.

The only way to be rid of a Sending is to kill it where it sits, but the victim cannot do it for himself, for the demon will sense the threat and stop the muscles from completing it. If I could not find anyone to kill it for me, I would simply have to wait for it to become active and kill me when it emerged. A Sending is death one way or another. For me, it would have to be the worse of the two.

It was a terrible moment, that realisation, alone in the cold on that barren hillside, without even the comfort of a fire. But I resolved the very next instant, with every fibre of my being, with all the strength of my soul, that I would fight its every move and deny it to the limit of my strength. That might not last very long, but every delay was a gain, a victory over that which would destroy me in the end no matter what I tried to do. At the least I would go down fighting.

I had just made that decision when a wave of unbearable pain swept through me and I fell senseless to the ground.

I dreamt of fire and darkness.

Salera

When the sky darkened I left them. Every moment with Him was a joy, but I was called also to be with my brothers and sisters. I ran for a little time when I left them until I found a good jumping-off place, and then I flew high in the dying light until I crossed the sharp teeth of stone and came again to the high field where we had gathered.

I knew joy at seeing them again, so many of us in one place. More had come even in the last few days. I had never dreamed there were so many of us. I remember looking to see if any of the Hollow Ones had come, but I saw none. I greeted those I had flown with, those I knew best of these my newfound kinfolk.

We did not know why we were there. It was joy to be together, but we did not wonder at the "why." I tried to shape sound at some of them. I spoke the sound that was me, and the impossible sound that was Him, and tried again the noise of the Silver One who wore the wrong body. I think some tried to speak after me, but we were not used to such things and it was so hard then.

I looked up at the moon, older now and moving towards the full, and smiled at the smiling face that gazed down at me. They would come, the next day they would come, and all would be well. I drank, and slept, and missed Him even while I dreamed in the midst of my own people.

Will

Salera left us at twilight on the second day, but I watched her hurrying upwards and guessed we'd meet her at the pass. We had made good time—the shelter of the high field was no more than a long morning's walk from here. It would be a good place to stop, and from there it was an easy day's journey to Rowanbeck.

Jamie, Rella and I were in the lead, mounted when the road was not too steep, leading the horses when it was. The two of them divided their time between bouts of scouting ahead and around, and bouts of old-fashioned chattering. They had both done a great deal with their lives and I was happy enough simply to listen much of the time.

I hadn't forgotten the two in my care. Aral quite happily spent the journey walking with me, walking with Vilkas, and pestering Varien and Lanen. Their story amazed her and she spoke to them about it as long as they could bear. Lanen eventually had enough and sent her away, kindly but firmly. Aral didn't seem to mind.

The one I worried about was Vilkas. He had kept to himself even more than usual, and even Aral had trouble getting through to him at first. Aral had told me what had happened, that Vil had managed to tap into some of the great store of power that he hid even from himself. It seemed to me a cause for rejoicing, but Vilkas seemed to spend an awful long time thinking about it.

By the time we lit a fire that night I found myself shivering, deep inside. I was pleased to be going home but there was more to it than that. I couldn't tell if it was fear or anticipation or just plain cold, but as the night went on every part of me took up the shaking. I felt like a bee sounds in a clover field. It wasn't anything you could see, but it kept me awake most of the night. I wasn't the only one.

Vilkas

I walked along in silence for most of the journey. I was aware of a growing wrongness in the air and almost mentioned it, but I have learned over the years to conceal my feelings. I could have been mistaken. It might simply have been the altitude. Besides, I was in the midst of trying to understand so much all at once that I might only have been sensing my own roiling emotions. Aral spent a little time with me, enough to realise that I was restraining myself. She occasionally dropped back to walk with me in companionable silence, for which I was grateful, and once she muttered something along the lines of "You're doing well, Vil. I know it's hard, but best to wait until we can stop for a while." It did not make things any easier, but it was gratifying that she was aware of my self-control.

In fact she had no idea how controlled I really was. It had been simple enough for her to tell me to let loose my power that night, but I was the one who had actually done it. The thought still made me shake inside.

I had dared to harness the sky god, or forced the Death of the World to do something useful if you looked at it that way. I had undone the work of a decade to meet Lanen's desperate need, and not only had both the world and I survived, it had worked.

I was still in a kind of shock. It was not possible to do

what I had done. I had changed that woman's blood to some unheard-of mixture of human and dragon and she was still alive. That wasn't possible. I felt that I was walking simultaneously in two worlds, the one that surrounded me at the moment, and the other in which reason had its way and she lost the children or died or both. Those were the only possible outcomes of her condition. At best I might have helped her to live, but the babes would die and life would go on.

That hadn't happened. I had let loose more of my power that night than I had dared to use for many years and the woman lived and would bear her children. What they might become I could not imagine, but *that* they would live was my responsibility.

Deep within me, where I could just bear to listen to it now, arose the thought that I might just be able to accept my power and use it, all of it—

All of it

—and choose the way of the sky god after all. Lanen was a good person. With just a portion of that power I had kept her and her children alive and healthy.

What is the point of being the Death of the World in any case?

There's never anyone around to see you succeed.

By the time we camped the second night I had come to my own peace with what had happened, but I appeared to be in the minority. Will volunteered to take the first watch and we let him; anyone could see he had no chance of sleeping. Lanen and Varien weren't far behind. Only Rella and Jamie seemed to sleep well that night. I wondered if anyone's conscience could be that clear.

Aral had come and sat beside me when the fire was starting to die down. "Vil, I know you feel it," she said softly. "What in all the Hells is going on?"

"If I knew that I'd do my damnedest to do something about it so I could get some rest," I replied. "I've been trying to ignore the lot of you for hours now. You are a dear friend, Aral, but please, I haven't recovered yet from that healing session." It was a polite lie, but still it was better than simply asking her to go away. She raised an eyebrow at me, expressed dubious sympathy and left.

I lay down and closed my eyes, trying to ignore the atmosphere. Ever try to sleep through a night filled with a wildly raging wind? It was much the same thing.

Lanen

Dawn couldn't come too soon. I had managed a few hours' sleep at the tail end of the night, but I woke feeling more weary than when I went to sleep and Varien wasn't much better. The misty grey morning didn't help any of us—we all woke slightly damp and a lot colder than we had been. Will had kept the fire going all night, which was a blessing. I wondered how he managed—he said he hadn't had a wink of sleep but he seemed more alert than the rest of us.

Oh—except for the old campaigners. Rella woke with her usual stiff back, which Jamie was learning to loosen; he said his side was paining him, but I caught his eye. "You're just out for any sympathy going," I said, laughing at him over my second mug of chélan.

"You know me too well," he said, stretching. "Next time I'm leaving you behind."

I would have kept on teasing him but to my astonishment Idai's voice interrupted me. *"Varien? Lanen? May I bespeak you?"*

"Of course, Idai," replied Varien, who had taken to wearing his circlet at all times. *"What is the trouble I hear in your thoughts?"*

"Have you heard from Hadreshikrar?" she asked, and now even I could hear the concern in her mind-voice. *"I bespoke him just now and I heard him begin to respond, but after that came only silence."*

"I have heard nothing, Lady," said Varien. I was staring at him, completely confused, but he took my hand and muttered aloud, "Not now, I will tell you in a moment." *"I take it you fear for him,"* he added in truespeech.

"He should have been there by now, Akhor," said Idai. I managed to keep back a yelp, but not very well. Fortunately, Idai heard nothing but Varien's voice reassuring her. *"We will find him if we can, Lady,"* he said. *"Shikrar has not called to us either—perhaps he rests after his journey?"*

"That might be, Akhor, but I like it not that I cannot hear him. I pray you, take the time to find him, and rouse him if you can."

"We will do what we can," said Varien. He winced, and I realised that his head must be throbbing now with the pain of truespeech. It seemed worse for him at the moment than it was for me, and I found it hard enough.

"We thank you, Lady, for letting us know your concern. Let us all seek him and who finds him first tell the others," I said, and released the link as she agreed.

Varien took off the circlet and rubbed his temples, grimacing.

I just stared at him. Eventually he looked up at me. "What do you—ah," he said.

"Ah, indeed," I said, not knowing whether to be amused or annoyed or delighted. "How long have you known that Shikrar was on his way here?"

I gathered from the subdued spluttering noises that Rella had overheard.

"I have only known that for—ah—Lanen, in my fear for your safety I have neglected to tell you—a great deal has been happening among the Kantri of late," he ended lamely, looking for all the world like a small child who has forgotten to carry out its mother's errand. "Lanen—perhaps you should sit down." He smiled then, almost a mischievous grin. "It is a truth and it is most definitely spiky. In fact, it is also horned, tailed and taloned, and it is not he, it is they."

"They?" I asked weakly. "They who?"

Not to be outdone, Rella moved up to join us and added swiftly, "They who what?"

"They who will arrive here in Kolmar in a short time, although I know not precisely when. If Idai is correct, Shikrar should be here already."

"Who are *they*?" I all but shouted.

"The Kantri," he said, almost as if he did not believe it himself. "The Kantrishakrim, my people of old. They are coming here. The Dragon Isle, as you call it, is overrun with fire and ash and would have killed them all if they had stayed. There is nowhere else for them to go. They are coming here. The Kantri are coming to Kolmar."

I would have bet that six people could not stand silent that long for anything, and I would have lost.

Rella

When I could breathe again I laughed, long and loud. One of the Healers sent what I suspect was a treatment for shock to all of us, but I kept laughing.

"Either tell us what's so funny or stop cackling like an old hen," said Jamie dryly.

"Berys—it's Berys," I gasped out. "Oh, Lady, I'd give a year's wages to see his face when he finds out!" The others waited. "Don't you see?" I said, "He's got all his hopes pinned on his demons, that's the one thing he has that almost no one can challenge, and now—hahaha!—oh, now the creatures who can get rid of the damned things with a *breath* are coming here and there's nothing he can do about it! Oh, it's wonderful!"

Well, that seemed to cheer everyone up. I kept laughing on and off for an hour or so, while we got moving. Trust Varien to forget to mention it to anyone!

Seems my friend Shikrar was going to be the first to arrive. I had spent more time with his son Kédra than with him, but I respected Shikrar. He was a fair soul. The only problem was that he was a fair soul in an absolutely huge body. He was half again the size of his son. He had been fine on the Dragon Isle, but I was having a hard time imagining him in Kolmar. He seemed to be made to a different scale entirely. Still, see him in Kolmar I would, if they could find him. According to Lanen and Varien there was no sign yet.

The cloudy morning brought in a sunny day, like the old

songs say. I was glad of it as well, my bones aren't as young as they used to be and the cold was getting into them. Still, I walked rather than rode all morning as we went higher and higher. It was getting colder, and the air a bit thinner too, when Will pointed up ahead and said, "At last! That's the entrance to the high field."

"Not a minute too soon, I'm starved," said Lanen cheerfully. "But where, Will? I don't see any entrance, just more rocks."

He grinned at her. "That's the beauty of it. Unless you know it's here you'd never find it—follow me." He mounted one of the horses and went on a little ahead, and before our eyes he seemed to disappear into the rocks. I thought it would be easier to see the entrance as we came closer, but until we were right on top of it you'd have sworn there was nothing there but stubborn rock. We went in, one by one, leading the horses between us—it was a narrow entrance—and found ourselves in a great round green field surrounded by high rock. At the end farthest from the entrance and a bit to the left there was a small wood, but it was half hidden by one of the two spurs of black rock that curved down from the high walls into the green grass. They almost looked like great ramps, dwindling swiftly to nothing from the great height of their origins in the cliffs and mingling with the ground.

All this I saw in the first moment—it's the Service training, you get used to looking for the lay of the land and a quick way out. I saw no exit at first glance, and then I stopped looking.

The whole place was brimful of Saleras.

Maikel

When I wakened I was already walking, down the valley, up the far hill, following. I did not remember rising or taking food, and I did not have my pack with me. Alone, then, without aid, without even the most basic necessities, I began the war.

At first it was not so hard. A little delay here, a forced rest there where I did not need one, anything that would slow it down and keep it from its goal. It wanted me to walk quickly so I concentrated on walking slowly. I learned then that if I thought of my fight in the abstract I would lose it—"walking slowly" could speed up without my noticing it until I was at the speed the demon wanted. So I took each step, each single step, and slowed it down. I forced myself to concentrate on every single step.

Sweet Shia, it was hard. Still, from the way the demon fought back I must have been accomplishing something, so I bent all my will to it.

I had worked hard to become the best Healer I could be, taking my natural talent to its utmost limit through study and perseverance. It had been difficult but I had learned a great deal about bending my own will to a task until it was completed. That training stood me in good stead now, when every step took concentration and dedication. The demon fought, of course, but I used one of the techniques we were taught to overcome its first struggles. If the Healer is wounded he cannot work as well, so we learn first to heal ourselves. If there is no time for that, there is still a way to distance yourself from your own pain. I used that distance now to protect myself, though I knew that I would pay for it later.

I nearly laughed. The habit of life is so strong! For me there would be very little "later."

I discovered then the truth of the old saying that he who has nothing to lose is most to be feared, for he fears nothing. To prove the point I stood still, ignoring the desperate demands of the demon, concentrating on simply gazing about me on the new-blown spring, hearing the song of the small birds, breathing in the clear air filled with the spices of life and living. I stood on that sunlit hillside and wept, but not from the pain.

The sheer beauty of life was all around me, and I stole a moment in the midst of the struggle with death to rejoice in the wonder and glory of the world that surrounded me before I was forced to leave it.

Varien

The Lesser Kindred stood assembled all before us. The high field was full of them, of every imaginable hue from old iron to Salera's bright copper. We were all struck dumb with wonder.

Salera stood forth to greet us, Will first—a nudge of her nose and a happy "Hooirrr," then she came to me, bowed and said "Hffffarrriann." There was no mistaking it. She knew my name. She was so near to speaking it hurt. I could not help myself, I reached out to her again with truespeech.

"Come, littling. You are so close, Salera! I am Varian, you know what names are and you can learn—oh, my sweet cousin, hear me, make that last step, so small after all you have done!"

There was no response. Lanen took me by the shoulder. "Come, my dear, we have walked long this morning and the sun is nearly overhead. There is food and drink."

"You do not understand," I said, trembling. "This is not the way of these creatures. I was told they lived lonely lives, in ones and twos, scattered. . . ."

She looked at me with a crooked grin on her face. "I *do* understand. I live here, remember? But I also understand that you didn't have any breakfast, and if you don't get some food inside you soon, you are going to fall over. That wouldn't be setting a very good example, would it?"

I looked at her. Her eyes were shining bright as mine, she knew, she truly did know how astounding a thing this was. She also knew the limitations of a human form better than I. When she put a thick slice of bread and cheese into my hand I ate ravenously, washing it down with water from the little stream in the wood. Lanen had carried that water, followed all the way there and back by curious creatures who closely watched her every move. It was strange to do so everyday a thing as breaking bread in such a place, but it was right as well.

When we had finished our rapid meal it was the height of the day. I had been calling out to Shikrar regularly through the morning, as often as the painful use of truespeech allowed, and had no reply. My fears for him were growing, and I decided to make one final attempt before—before whatever the Winds had planned took place. I put my whole heart and soul into the summons.

"Shikrar! Hadreshikrar, my friend, where art thou? I fear for thee, soulfriend, thou hast been silent too long. Speak to me, rouse thyself from sleep or injury, speak to me!"

To my intense relief I heard his voice, fainter than usual but very much alive.

"I hear thee, my friend! Blessed be the Winds, I am here! I stand on Kolmar—albeit rather shakily, if truth be told. I have injured my wing. I can yet fly, but it is painful."

"Shikrar! Blessed be the Winds indeed. Where are you?"

"A moment, my friend, let me look. Ah. I am on a high grassy cliff at the sea's edge. I know not whether I am north or south of the Gedri lands, but all the land is untouched about me. Where are you?"

"In the southern half of Kolmar, below a great river that divides the land in two," I said. *"If you can bear it, take to the air and you will see that river if you are anywhere near. South of it and away west there are high hills that lie between two great cities. I am in those hills, on a high green field—there cannot be another like it. And oh, Shikrar, it passes belief—the Lesser Kindred are here!"*

"What do you say?!" he roared, his mindvoice sparkling with wonder.

I laughed. *"You heard me right, my friend, the Lesser Kindred. We have found them—or they have found us. Shikrar, they are so close to sentience!"*

"Have you tried to bespeak them?" he asked excitedly.

"I have, my friend. They are silent yet, but they are nearly able to speak aloud. One, Salera, has learned to say my name. They are so near, Shikrar! Come, find us, my friend," I

pleaded. Now that I heard his voice and knew him near it was almost physical pain to be separated longer. And I knew my Shikrar. *"Perhaps you will be able to teach them."*

He laughed. Blessed be his name, he laughed with delight. *"Akhor, to see the Lesser Kindred I would crawl on four broken legs. What signifies a slight injury to a wing? I will find you if I have to smell you out!"*

"The Winds attend your flight," I said, astonishment and joy dulling the swift, sharp pain of truespeech. *"Come soon, my brother."*

"I come, my soulfriend. I come."

He would find us from the air, and he would come. It was well. I turned to Lanen. "Did you—"

"I heard, my dear." She took my hand. "Let us go among them, Varien. I have the strangest feeling. Come."

The great crowd of the Lesser Kindred opened before us and closed behind as we were carefully observed. All of us moved among them, submitting to curious sniffs and strange noises. I tried with all my will to understand what they might be saying, but to no avail. And finally, in the centre of that great field, we met with Salera once more. She stood before us and would not let us pass, moving swiftly to stand before us, stretching her wings out to stop us from passing by.

"What is it, my lass?" asked Will. He reached out to touch her, but she would not let him. Instead she turned to me. "Hffffarriann," she said. "Sssaahhrrrairrrah."

And she moved her head on her long neck, reached out and touched my soulgem with her nose. "Sssaahhrrrairrrah."

I shivered. I felt with every mote of my being that something astounding was at hand. The world seemed to shrink, and for that time all of existence consisted of Lanen, Salera and me. Lanen was shaking as I was, a swift internal shiver that brought a blush to her cheeks and fire to her eyes.

I tried to bespeak Salera again, almost out of habit—it is the way my people communicate—but Lanen stopped me after the first word. "No, Varien. That is too far ahead. Start further back." She indicated the raised lump on Salera's faceplate. "Start here."

I reached out to touch Salera's face. She stood bravely still as my skin touched her armour. A swift jangling ran up my arm and I withdrew my hand instantly. "There is something there, you have the right of it—but I do not understand, I touched her faceplate before and there was nothing—" I began.

"You weren't wearing your soulgem then," Lanen reminded me quietly. "Could it be as simple as that?"

"As what? The touch of my hand on her face affects us both, but—"

"No. Not with your hand," she said. Her voice was strange and filled with awe, almost as if she spoke for another in that strange close-focused world that held only the three of us. "So simple. If this works—"

"Lanen?" I asked.

"Your soulgem," she said, placing her hand delicately on Salera's neck. "Varien, touch that raised part of her face with your soulgem, while you are wearing it."

"That is a gesture between parent and child only, Lanen," I said.

"Yes, I know," she said calmly. She sounded so certain.

I was trembling so that I could barely stand but I did as she said. I leaned over in the intimate contact that is normally restricted to mothers and younglings, and touched with my soulgem the place where hers should be. Again, the contact all but set off sparks, but—

There was nothing. I sighed and dropped my head against hers in sorrow, my soulgem still against the place where hers was not. *So near, so near, my beautiful cousin*, I thought sadly. *Alas, I had such hopes of this meeting! Perhaps in another year, or another ten, or—*

And then Lanen, who was touching Salera, put her hand on my shoulder to comfort me.

A raging fire swept through me in the instant, all-encompassing but not destructive. It roared through my mind, dizzying, spinning, as thoughts and words and ideas—as if they were looked at and recognised and returned. I was dizzy on the instant, so I focused as I always had—through

my soulgem, which still touched Salera. The fire gathered itself from all the corners of my mind and sprang like flame
from breath to kindling, through my soulgem to her. In moments I felt the swift heat returning to me and had to stand
away from her.

It was too late. The hard covering of the raised lump was
burning, and Salera was crying out in pain. Will, Vilkas and
Aral were suddenly with us—though they might have been
standing near the whole time for all I knew. Will put his
arms about Salera, not knowing what else to do in the face of
that dreadful burning armour.

Vilkas was suddenly blazing even in the midday sun. Aral
stood beside him not nearly as bright until she drew forth
from the pouch about her neck the soulgem of that lost
Kantri. The instant it touched her skin she cried out and took
Vilkas's hand. Together they reached out to heal, to save
Salera from the burning, to quench the fire around—

Around her soulgem.

The burning stopped once the new soulgem was free of its
prison. The Healers sealed the raw skin around it and took
away her pain. I was astounded that they could think of such
a thing. I was also astounded that their healing worked on
the Kantri, but I did not think of that until long afterwards.

We all gazed in awe, in disbelief at the gleaming gem,
bright blue in the sun like Salera's eyes, as she turned from
us to look directly at Will. He was standing behind, he had
only heard her cries, and could do nothing but stand by her
and hold her against the pain of the fire, as he had done from
the first.

He gasped, amazed, when he saw the brilliant blue in the
centre of her copper face. She turned to face him, sat up on
her back legs, looked into his eyes, and said softly, "Ffa-
therrr."

"Salera," he replied, his voice breaking over her name.
Without more words she rested her great head on his shoulder and he put his arms about her neck.

I could have beheld them thus for hours, but I was not allowed. Something nudged my arm.

I turned to find a creature much smaller than Salera gazing up at me. He was grey as steel, with a fine healthy sheen to his scales. He nudged my arm again.

I turned to where Lanen stood gazing in rapt astonishment at Will and Salera. "Your pardon, dearling," I said smiling. "I think our task is not quite over."

She looked around and down at the importunate youngling, then around the high field, full to overflowing with the Lesser Kindred, then back at me and grinned. "Thank the Lady we ate, Varien. I've a feeling it's going to be a long day!"

The hours swept by in a confused swirl of minds and fire. Now that I knew something of what was coming, I was better able to allow the questing soul to see my thoughts and take what it needed of language and some basic learning. In the hours that followed I became reasonably adept at it. We also found that if Lanen was touching us both before I let my soulgem rest on the littling's faceplate, it was less of a shock for all of us.

Lanen and the others forced me to stop at intervals to rest, to eat, but I could no more sleep than I could deny my aid to any of these who asked it of me. It struck me in those brief moments of rest that this must be some jest of the Winds. I was very much aware of the fact that I was giving to these wondrous, gleaming new creatures that which I no longer possessed myself.

Did I envy them? Deeply.

Was I jealous of them? Completely and absolutely.

Did I ever consider not assisting them? Not for a single instant. My jealousy and my envy were genuine and I could not ignore them, and I did not, but they were overwhelmed entirely, as a candle by the dawn, by the vast joy that lifted my heart each time a new soulgem was revealed. Ruby, sapphire, opal, topaz yellow, emerald green like my own, as various as the colours and temperaments of the creatures who now bore them.

The only other thing I remember happened not long after the sun had gone down. We were resting for a few stolen moments and the moon was high now and bright, when of a sudden the new-made ones took to the air with breaths of flame and danced aloft in the moonlight, singing their delight, their joy and wonder with voices never used before.

That moment is graven in my heart forever. Come death, come life, come sorrow deep as time or joy to move mountains, still the vision of that bright young race aloft for the first time, rejoicing in air with the brilliant moonlight flashing from their soulgems like so many flying stars—the piercing beauty of that moment is mine forever.

And then another importunate head touched me on the shoulder and we all were needed again. At times I felt every one of my thousand years, like an ancient tree giving life by its death—at times I was renewed, body and spirit, by the gratitude and the honour done me by the new-found souls.

I did not notice time or light, cold or weariness. I only know that by the time the last soul found its freedom and had bowed its thanks to me, before turning rejoicing to its kindred, true dawn was upon us. I looked up, seeing for the first time since—"Name of the Winds, Lanen, has it been so long?"

"Since what?" she asked wearily.

"Salera was brought to herself just past midday—"

"Yesterday," sighed Lanen, and she smiled at me. "You have been like a man possessed, my heart. And quite right." She looked out, as I did, in wonder at the first day of the new lives of the Lesser Kindred. "While one soul ached in silent darkness, we could not stop," she whispered.

I stood and stretched, stiffness catching me in a hundred places as I sought to stand upright. Lanen laughed, a clear laugh straight from the heart, and I joined her. There was no other way to release the soul-deep wonder, the sheer glory of it all. We laughed and kissed and hugged and laughed again, until the very stones rang with it.

And behold, there was yet more to tell Shikrar.

Maikel

By nightfall I had reached only the outer ring of stone. The demon within me was certain that Lanen was just beyond and it pushed me to scrabble around the stones, looking for a way in. It was dark, which favoured me. I was caught up in the fight and I was prevailing, for the moment, when the Sending used the single worst weapon it possessed.

Despair.

It showed me images of hideous death. My death. I saw in that dark place a rain of fire over the beauty that had so blessed me earlier, a vision of all I loved or had ever loved come to nothing, and finally of my own body rotting on a hillside, untended, uncared for, food for worms and ravens.

That was the battle. There, alone among the cold stones, outside anything that might be happening in the circle of life beyond, I fought with all the lonely strength of my spirit to overcome despair, whose talons are sharper than swords and whose breath of fire is straight from the deepest hell. If ever I began to overcome it would torment me afresh with dark visions of death and ending. Almost I gave in, almost I stopped fighting, but I was learning that the fight itself fuelled a will in me that strove still.

Then a sound distracted me and I looked up. There, over the rim of sharp stones, dragons flew. They were dancing a-wing in the moonlight, and there was that about them that sparkled, that reflected the light in scattering joy. The demon chose that moment to strike at me with pain but I did not even notice, for the joy of those creatures was made my joy, their song of thanksgiving the echo of my life, and in that moment pain had no more dominion over me.

However, I had forgotten in that transcendent moment that pain can cause a purely physical reaction. I lost consciousness, but the last things I saw were the dragons, wheeling, soaring on the wind in pure delight, and my heart flew with them as my mind fell away.

When I woke again to pain I was moving. It had got me through the gap in the stones unnoticed, and was now creeping around the southern rim of the field. It should have been impossible to go so far unmarked, for the field was filled with creatures of all kinds—horses, humans, and more of the little dragons than I had imagined existed. There must have been more than two hundred of them, but all their attention was focussed on something happening in the centre of the plain.

I tried to cry out but I had no voice. It was like an evil dream, in which time slows so that you run at a crawl, and you cry out for help with all your might but only the merest squeak comes out of your mouth. If I could speak I might be able to call for help, someone to kill the beast for me.

But I could not speak, and there were none to aid me.

The demon was in a hurry now, so I spent my strength on keeping my steps as small as that nightmare pace. I was still fighting for every step, but it was nearer its goal and I had to work ever harder to stop its advance. I could feel the sweat drenching my clothing as I used every muscle to deny it. By the time it—we—reached the stony outcrop I had been striving against it for almost ten hours without ceasing and I was weary to the bone. We were then two-thirds of the way across the field. It seemed to be heading for a darkness on the far side that I guessed was a wood.

After that I lost ground to the force of will and the pain, for my weariness lay upon me like a great weight. I no longer counted victory in steps, but in breaths. That breath I did not move forward. That breath I resisted, but it moved a little. That breath I rested and it took half a step, but this breath I have stopped it again.

The night moved like years, until suddenly it stabbed me again with agony and I could bear it no longer. I released my hold on it long enough to take a deep breath and rest, just for a moment. In that time I covered half the remaining distance. I managed to look up as we entered the wood and blessed the Lady, for the sky was growing light and that endless night was all but over.

I decided to choose my final battle and let it walk unhindered towards the hidden place it sought, but while it was moving I began to draw in my power. It felt what I was doing and tried to stop me, but my will now was iron and pain meant nothing, for my death was upon me and I knew it. I called to me every scrap of will and training and innate power I had ever possessed, commended my soul to the Lady, and unleashed it at the thing I carried.

I heard it scream as the power of the Lady Shia struck it like a lance. I sent wave after wave of power at it, drowning it in the blessed light of the Goddess. If I had been stronger, or if I had known more of the nature of demons, perhaps I might have been able to kill it, but it had reached its destination. I was no longer needed.

I was grateful for the swiftness with which it severed the great cord in my back, for the pain was stopped like the snuffing of a candle. I felt nothing as it clawed its way out, and I kept the clear light of the Lady around me until the last second. The last sight I saw in life was the first rays of true dawn striking the great peaks round about and gleaming off the scales of the beautiful dragons, and I blessed the Lady with my final thought as I took beauty down with me into darkness and death.

Shikrar

I had rested some hours after I spoke with Varien, but as the first hint of false dawn lightened the sky I leapt into the updraft that had kept me from crashing into the cliff. My wing ached but it bore me yet, and the updraft carried me swiftly to a decent altitude. I had to fly a long way north to find what I sought, but I knew it at once when I found it— the river was unmistakable, the only feature so large that it could be seen from so far away. The hills were away to the west of where I flew, but not too far.

"Varien, my friend, how fare you?" I called, as dawn rose bright behind me. *"I am near, I believe. I have found the great river, and the sharp hills lie before me."*

He did not answer me, so I tried bespeaking Lanen. *"Lady Lanen, is Varien—?"*

"I am here, Shikrar," he replied at last. His voice sounded extraordinary. *"You are as welcome as a summer's day in midwinter, my friend."*

"Varien, what news? What news now of the Lesser Kindred?"

"Come find us, my brother," he said. *"Oh, Shikrar! It is the unknown and the Word of the Winds both together. I have no words. You must see."*

He sounded weary but very happy. I glided towards the sharp peaks ahead, wondering what there was for them to show me.

Berys

Where is it? The damned thing should have come to me by now. It should have been here hours since! Dawn is here already, the best time is past, if it comes not swiftly I shall be forced to—

Ah. Good.

"Masster, all iss done. The prey awaitss you, the Swift-lines are planted in the heart of the host and both are open to you."

"You are late," I growled. "You should have been here hours ago."

"The hossst wasss ill chossen, Masster," it hissed happily, knowing I had not specified a time limit. "Healersss can work againsst uss. He wasss a sstrong Healer and killed himself before I could force him to build the altar. I wass forced to built it mysself, and that wass not in the price we agreed."

"You speak truth, little demon," I said, throwing an extra handful of lansip onto the flames. It inhaled the smoke greedily, its reward sufficient. "All now is achieved. Our pact iss concluded, all iss done, live in pain and die alone," it intoned, spitting at me as it vanished. I ignored its petty complaints.

All was prepared now for the summoning of the Nameless One, the Demonlord, for I would undertake it the instant Lanen was in my power. There was much to do, and it must be done swiftly, but all was in readiness for my return.

I took with me every set trap I had to hand. Such things were very useful—all the work had already been done, I had only to break the thin clay discs the spells were encased in to summon up the demons in question. If I encountered difficulties I had anywhere from one to a legion of the Rikti at my command, and in extremity I could call up a Raksha from the Third Hell. That should take care of most things. It would even slow the Kantri down long enough for me to appear, take the girl and get out.

The most useful set trap against the Kantri, of course, would be a Ring of Seven Circles, but there had been no time. The making of such a thing took far longer than the two days' notice I'd had from Marik. Bastard. He should have told me before.

Still, I was prepared. My robes of black and silver, woven about with spells of protection, would serve as armour—not for long, but for long enough.

I stood in my summoning chamber among lighted candles with Durstan at my side. "Be ready to silence her the instant we appear," I told him.

"I am prepared," he rumbled. "Success, Master."

"Always," I replied, and stepped into the circle that marked the outgoing Swiftline.

It took no time that could be measured. Between one breath and another I travelled to the far end and stepped out into a small wood. I looked quickly about me. I could not see Lanen, indeed I was hard-pressed to find any humans. There on the field before me were hundreds of the little dragons that commonly haunt the woods. I broke a disc and a single Rikti appeared. "Find the living humans in this crowd and come and tell me where they are," I commanded.

I had not known I would need to deal with these creatures, and I did not know what their response would be. I watched its flight from my hidden place in the wood and saw that it was pursued by several of them. Then, to my satisfaction, I heard a voice cry out, " 'Ware demon!" That voice was human enough, and I could tell where it came from, so the thing's death by the paltry flame these little creatures could command was no great loss.

There were the humans, out in the open and looking terribly confused. How delightful. Ah, and there was my prey.

I was feeling extravagant. I drew out nearly every disc save the one that summoned the Raksha and broke them. The air was suddenly black with Rikti awaiting my command. I pointed. "Leave alive that human, the tall female with the long hair. Kill the rest," I shouted, to be heard above the yells and hisses of the creatures in the field.

They massed and attacked, and I strode forth to claim my prey.

Varien

Into the midst of our celebrations the first of the demons came alone and died swiftly. If it had not been for Will's shout we might have had no notice at all. As it was, we were at least a little wary when a great cloud of them appeared and came straight for us.

My first instinct was to rise up and flame them, but when in the next instant I remembered, instead I called out in truespeech to the brother of my heart.

"Shikrar! Haste, my friend, the Rikti attack!"

His voice rose in a song of battle. *"Behold, they are their own undoing and it is good. I know now where you are for I can smell the evil from here. I come, Akhor!"*

In the meantime, for I knew not how far away Shikrar might be, I drew my sword as my only defence, for tooth and claw and breath of fire were denied me—but they were not denied the Lesser Kindred. I had not known for certain that they would react in the same way as the Kantri; our hatred of the Rakshasa must be deep in the bone. The Lesser Kindred rose in flame and struck with claws and teeth.

Lanen, beside me, had drawn her blade as well. Vilkas stood in the centre of his blazing corona, no whit diminished for all that he had laboured all night to aid the Lesser Kindred, but the fear on his face was plain. Aral, beside him, also had drawn her power about her, but her corona was barely visible in the early-morning light. She only just had the time to draw forth the soulgem of the Ancestor before the things attacked.

I could not see Jamie and Rella, and Will was off somewhere in the midst of the newfound ones. I saw him fighting his way back to be with Vilkas and Aral in the brief moment before I was set upon by three of the demons. Out of the corner of my eye I saw Lanen swinging her sword with a will.

My own sword was not to their liking, for their bodies are physical and they can be hurt, but I was too slow. I cried out as my back and my face were raked by two separate Rikti, but to my astonishment both the attackers screamed and the other that threatened drew away from me. I could only see the one that had struck at my face; I watched in amazement as the claws that had drawn my blood burst into flame as it screamed and fled. Other of the Rikti came nigh me to attack but ever they veered away before they could strike. It was as if they could smell—

Of course. My blood. Whatever else had changed about me, it seemed that was still the same. An idea struck me that normally I would not even consider, but in the heat of battle I acted upon it immediately, for there was nothing to lose. I swiftly wiped away the blood that was running down my cheek with my hand, and spread it upon the blade of my sword.

Lanen, only a few feet away, was hard-pressed—I saw blood on her arm and on her face. The sight roused me to fury and I started to fight my way to her. The first I struck with my bloody sword screamed and vanished—it had worked! With a fierce joy I slew the Rikti that kept me from my dearling.

Will

I was caught far from the others, for I had been walking with Salera. She had more words now, though there was still much to learn, and we had been trying to speak with one another when the demons attacked. I had not even my staff with me. I tried to run back for it, but there were too many dragons in the way, for many of them took to the air to fight. There were too many demons as well, and when one fastened on the arm I'd raised to protect my face I thought sure I was doomed, when a strong arm plucked the creature from me and tore it apart. I stared. Salera stood beside me, her new soulgem blazing. She sent flame after the next one and managed to scorch the one behind it as well. She had to push me down to get at one that was attacking from behind, and I realised that I was only in the way. It wasn't very heroic, I admit, but then I'm no hero. I stayed down, curled up at her feet, while my valiant Salera kept all harm from me.

Vilkas

I could not do it. I had thought that once I had released it I could claim all of my power, but I could not. The old deep injunction that kept me from fighting the Rikti still held. I cursed and fought to tap into that power, throwing all my will behind it, but I met only the same blank wall. When the Rikti attacked in force I could only put up a shield to surround myself—though my fury at my own failure made it strong. I would have extended it to Aral, but she shouted "No!" and I had to obey. As was now becoming her custom, she held the jewel—the soulgem—in her hand and sent her power through it. She kept the creatures away from both of us for a time and managed to kill a few, but there were just too many. The best we could manage was protection for ourselves until we saw, not far away, Jamie and Rella. I have never seen such combined ability with a blade—they appeared to be surrounded by ten swords—but even they were tiring and injured. Rella's clothing was torn and blood showed through some of the tears. Jamie's cheek was opened to the bone. They, like we, could do little beyond delaying the inevitable.

I turned to Aral. "Can we protect them as well?" I

shouted, pointing, for the noise of the battle was growing. She nodded. We strode over to them, Aral dispelling as many of the demons as she could as we went, but it was like trying to empty the sea with a cup.

We did not reach them an instant too soon. Just before my shield could defend Rella one of the creatures landed on her back and bit her neck. She cried out just once and fell. Aral destroyed the demon and in the next instant my shield protected the four of us, but Rella was badly injured.

"Vil, can you do two things at once?" asked Aral. I was shocked to hear the deadly weariness in her voice. "I'm about exhausted and she's in a bad way. I have stopped the bleeding but I haven't the strength to heal her."

Blessed be the Lady, I thought. At last, something I can *do*.

Keeping the shield raised all the while, I looked over at Rella, who measured her length on the grass. Aral was right, she was badly injured. Healing, simple healing, safe, blessed by the Lady—and the depth of my strength came to me, the fullness of it, as it had that night in Wolfenden. It was like cold water in my face, I roused and shook myself. I raised Rella with a thought to lie on the air before me. The demon had severed the great cord of her spine. It was a delicate task and required deep concentration to reconnect, and I had to maintain the shield to protect the four of us.

Do not think me boastful. I was useless against the Rikti; all I could do was keep a simple shield around myself and perhaps a few others. But healing—healing ran through me like warming fire. Even in the madness of the battle it was not hard for me. Rella was unconscious, for a blessing. I remembered first to cleanse the wound of Raksha-trace, cleaned the severed ends and reconnected them, forced the re-growth of the cord, of the muscles around it, of the skin above. When I finished and looked up there was but a thin red line on the back of her neck.

I was concerned at first by the expression on Jamie's face. He was astounded, plainly, but he seemed frightened as well, a disconcerting emotion for such an old campaigner.

"It isn't possible, surely—no one can heal such a wound so quickly, it's unbelievable."

Aral saved him. She put her hand on his arm for just a moment.

"Told you he was good," she said with a grin, and turned back to the battle.

Berys

I gave the Rikti a little while to wear them down, to keep their minds on the little individual battles that surrounded them. It worked well enough.

I prepared the second Swiftline and strode towards the pair in the centre. Lanen and the silver-haired man. Halfway there I stopped and broke the final disc, and a Raksha of the Third Hell stood before me. I interrupted the inevitable posturing.

"Behold, I provide you with a selection of prey, but you will take him first." I pointed. "The one with the silver hair. Kill him," I said, "then you may have the rest of them."

It flew on bat wings to obey me. I followed it.

Varien

The Rikti had learned that my sword was death, so that Lanen and I had a moment's rest. As I was renewing the blood on my sword, Lanen turned to me with tears of frustration in her eyes. "Damn it, Varien, I can't help you," she said. "I'm too slow with a sword and I can't hurt them otherwise. I hate being helpless."

I took her hand with my free one. "I know. Would it help to imagine for one last time that I am Akhor of old, defending you with tooth and claw against the Rikti?"

In the midst of the battle, she laughed. "It would indeed. I thank you, Akor," she said.

Then a movement away to the side caught our attention and held it. I committed my soul to the Winds and bespoke

Lanen. *"I fear our doom is come upon us. Find safety where you may, dearling. I will distract the creature. Go. Now."*

It was a Raksha, and it was flying straight toward us.

Berys

My plan was working beautifully. The silver-haired one wasted his time preparing to meet a Raksha with a sword and sending Lanen away to find cover. She had seen the other group of humans not far away and was making for them when I cast a simple Sleep charm upon her. It should have worked instantly, but something in her resisted long enough to discover who had sent the charm. When she saw me her eyes widened and she tried to cry out, but Silence is swiftly cast even from a distance, and it is very effective. However, Marik had warned me that she had Farspeech, so I called to two of the Rikti and had them bear her back with me as I ran to the Swiftlines. Speed would make all the difference.

I had not planned on having to deal with one of the Kantri so late in the battle.

Shikrar

I flew as fast as my wings would bear me. The strain in my injured wing threatened to give way, though, and I could not allow that. I was forced to fly more slowly than I would have wanted lest I fall from the sky altogether. I bespoke Varien to tell him that I was near but he did not answer. There again, I thought grimly, he would not reply from the midst of battle.

By the time I was near enough to hear what was happening I was frantic with the Raksha-smell and the silence from my soulfriend. I approached from above, sacrificing surprise that I might know what I faced. It was an evil sight—what looked like a legion of Rikti, and there to one side a Raksha, fighting—

Fighting Varien.

I could see blood on his face, and I heard Lanen crying out his name in my mind.

I came roaring and flaming from the sky, straight towards the Raksha. Varien dove out of the way as I came near. The Raksha turned to face me and raked my armour as I closed with it, but it only had that once chance. I was in a fury, and the Eldest and largest of our race. It was dead with one bite and I destroyed the body with cleansing flame the next instant.

Varien was gone.

Varien

I looked for Lanen the instant I heard Shikrar calling me, though I could not answer while my sword still defended my head. The Raksha was distracted—I am told that they can smell us as we can them—and it only fought with half its strength, for it knew that one of the Kantrishakrim was near and it began to fear for its life. From the corner of my eye I could see Lanen moving towards the others, towards the protection of the healers, when suddenly she fell. I was struggling to get away from the Raksha to help her when two of the Rikti caught her up and dragged her at a terrible speed across the field and away towards the wood at the far end.

She called out to me in truespeech. *"Varien! I am bespelled, I cannot fight back—help me! Shikrar, to me!"*

"I come, Lanen! **Shikrar, swiftly, she is taken!***"* I cried. I saw Shikrar diving at the Raksha. It turned its attention away from me, and like an arrow released from the bow I sped towards Lanen.

If the field had been empty I might have reached her, but ever the Rikti attacked me as I ran and I was forced to fight them off. *"Shikrar, help her!"* I screamed in the agony of my frustration, as my blood-soaked sword dispelled the last of the Rikti about me. Shikrar's vast shape ran past me then, scattering the Rikti as he went, and I followed after faster than I had thought I could run.

I felt as though I were running through deep water. Every muscle, every beat of my heart threw me towards Lanen, but I felt a great darkness gather round about me with each step as I watched her carried away from me on demon wings.

All my strength, all my love, all that I was or ever had been I poured into my desperate need to be by her side, but to no avail.

The Rikti reached the wood. At its edge stood a man, young and strong, who stank of the Rakshasa as though he were one himself. *"Shikrar, the Gedri, he is the source, destroy him for me I beg you!"* I cried in truespeech, and spared the fraction of an instant to rejoice when cleansing flame surrounded that abomination.

It did not touch him.

The demon-master laughed and gestured to his tame Rikti, who dropped Lanen into his arms.

"NO!" The scream ripped from my throat, agony. ***"Stop him Shikrar!"***

Too slow.

Too late.

I wake still at nights to the memory of those last moments. I see Lanen catching sight of me, struggling to get away from Berys, stretching out her arms to me, crying my name desperately in truespeech as bespelled silence holds her.

"Varien! Varien! AKOR!"

I threw down my sword and flung myself across the last few feet that separated us, but the bastard who held her captive took one step backwards and disappeared.

With her.

"NO!" I cried, falling to my knees, scrabbling insanely in the earth where he had stood. *"LANEN! LANEN!"* I screamed in truespeech and aloud.

Silence.

Shikrar went wild then, I think. Like me he followed instinct, but he dug stone like earth, as if Lanen had disappeared down a hole. When finally he realised that he could not follow her, he turned his incandescent anger on the remaining Rikti.

The Lesser Kindred had fought well, but they had not the flame nor the strength of a Lord of the Kantri in his wrath. I had never seen any of our people in a killing frenzy before. The Lesser Kindred drew back in awe as he roared and flamed until all the Rikti were dead, then he rent the bodies of the dead when there were no more to kill.

I bespoke him finally, from that small part of me that still lived. *"Shikrar, it is done. They are dead. Burn them."*

Great gouts of flame roared over the mangled bodies, burning the ground clean down to the rock. The cleansing flame seemed to rouse him out of his madness, for he shook his head and gazed about him, his glance finally coming to rest on me.

"Varien—Varien, I could not save her," said Shikrar brokenly. His voice in my mind was appalled. *"I tried with all my strength, I could not—Akhor—they were too far ahead."* He bowed, shaking, and said aloud, "Akhor, Akhor, I cannot hear her."

I tried to answer him, but my voice was trapped in my throat and would not obey me. *"Shikrar my brother,"* I groaned in truespeech, *"I cannot hear her either."* I tried once more, calling into silent darkness, as I feared I would call for the rest of my days.

"Lanen! Lanen! Hear me, answer me—Lanen!"

There was no answer, and there was no more strength in me. I knelt there on the grass in that bright spring morning and stared helplessly, stupidly, at the place where she had disappeared.

I could not weep. My soul was lost in a desolation far beyond tears—but my heart kept up its litany long after my mind had fallen into darkness.

Lanen—Lanen—Lanen—

The Nameless One

Berys

Once I had her safely in my chambers in Verfaren I cast yet another bespelled sleep upon her. She fought it, but I was too strong for her. I sent Durstan to put her in a demon-guarded chamber and hurried to begin the great summoning.

I did not wait for Durstan to return with my sacrifice for there was much to be done first. I moved surely but swiftly, rejoicing all the while—Marik of Gundar's blood and bone were in my power at last!

I drew forth and lit the incense I had made a year since from a list of ingredients obtained from ancient sources. Mixed in with the rest was a rare and precious scrap of parchment the Demonlord himself had touched. It had taken me half a lifetime to find and a small fortune to purchase.

I threw more coals on to the fire, renewed the candles, sealed the seven sigils at the points each with their pre-scribed element. The circles were carven into the stone floor but I swept them again, ensuring that each was clear and complete. I opened a small chest against one side of the room and drew out the robes I had made for this work. Woven into the fabric of the cloth were the sealing symbols of spells of protection, binding, containment, control and mastery. I threw off my battle-stained garments and assumed the deep red robes. As I wrapped the cord around my waist I repeated each of the spells, sealing each with a touch to the symbol, that my very robes might act as protection and reinforcement of the spells I needed. I finished tying the cord with the binding spell.

Where in all the Hells was Durstan with my sacrifice?

I threw a handful of the priceless incense on to the coals. It instantly sent billows of pungent smoke into the air, a heavy cloud that seeped into the brain and made limbs heavy and speech slow—or would have if I had not taken the precautions I had. The symbol for protection glowed bright in the murky chamber.

Ah, the door at last! I had told Durstan to send in the sacrifice—I could not see who it was for the smoke, but it was alive and that was all I required. Durstan had not subdued it, however, so I had to cast Sleep upon it before I could drag it on the altar. The smoke was so thick I could barely see the shape as it lay not two feet from my eyes. Still, I could find its chest fast enough.

It was time. I called up my power and began the chant I had spent so long learning. Every word was a spell, weaving a full tapestry of spells to call and to bind.

From the moment I started I sensed a presence. There in the mist, somewhere in the cloud created by the incense that carried the single point of essence of the Demonlord, there was a mind watching mine. It was more intelligent than any demon and it was without fear that I could see.

I was delighted. At last, a kindred spirit.

I proceeded with the summoning, invoking the strictures that would keep it under my control.

"I'm not a demon, you know," said a quiet voice from the mist.

I continued with the spell.

"You're trying to bind me like a demon. It won't work.

I'm human, just like you. Well, no, not like you. I'm much brighter than you are." It giggled. "I know when to leave the dead alone."

There was a brief pause in the spell. "Forgotten it already? You are pathetic," it said, ending on a hiss. I felt a presence now, much nearer, above the altar.

The summoning was working. The words grew harder to say, sticking in my throat, but I bent all my will to speaking them aloud despite the pressure not to. My will prevailed.

It had stopped its inane comments when the binding took hold, but it did not writhe as the Rakshasa did. I had wondered if it would—but no, it was not embodied yet, I could inflict no pain. That would come in time.

I gathered my thoughts and ran quickly over the end of the spell.

"You'll never manage it, you know," it said loudly, confusing me. I had to begin again, going over the syllables, and again it interrupted. "It's too hard. You'll never do it. Give up now and I promise I won't hurt you."

I sent what was left of my Healer's aura to encompass the presence. Corrupt as my corona was with Raksha-trace, still there was enough in it of the Lady to injure the creature. The presence, to my satisfaction, screamed loudly. I went over the spell once more, this time without interruption.

I took up my sacrificial knife and ripped open the garment the sacrifice wore. As I pronounced the final words of invocation it stirred, and when I plunged the razor-sharp blade into the chest of the victim it screamed. I had done this often enough that I hardly needed to look as I cut out the heart, but I usually enjoyed the look of horror on their faces when I held their still-beating hearts before their eyes. I glanced down just for a moment.

It was almost my undoing. My eyes met those of Durstan. Somehow I had mistaken him for whoever he had tried to supply, and of course, I had put the sacrifice to sleep instantly.

It is as well I never cared much for Durstan. I was annoyed that I would have to train up a new servant, but it was a small inconvenience. I showed him his heart and found that I felt my usual pleasure. That was all right, then.

I threw the beating heart on the coals. "Arise now, Demonlord, thou who didst surrender thy name in the service of darkness these long aeons since. Arise as my servant, that together we may destroy the Kantrishakrim once and for all, and have the whole of Kolmar for our own."

The voice became only a little louder. "You have not provided me with a body. How then shall I arise, you fool?"

"A body is prepared for you, ancient one. Look to the west, see there an island in its death throes."

"I see it," the voice answered. It sounded curious.

I explained the arrangement. The Demonlord laughed, long and loud.

"That is not enough!" he said. "Oh, you are such a clever fool! No, little demon caller, that is not enough. I must have you."

"I am not part of the bargain," I replied.

"Ah, but you are," he said. "Without a piece of your own body I am not bound. I told you, I am not a demon. I require a sacrifice from you, yourself. The heart of this man is good, it nourishes me, but it is not yours."

"I will make a sacrifice of blood," I began, but he interrupted me.

"No, not blood," he said, "that is too simple. No, I need something of you that you cannot replace." It stopped for a moment to ponder. "Your left hand, I think."

"You ask too much!" I cried, but I knew what its response would be.

"Those laws of what is too much or not enough only apply to demons. I told you, I'm not a demon." He smiled. "So, what happens now, little demon-spit? Do I eat you where you stand, or will you do as I bid?"

I was trapped, but those of my profession must ever consider the possibility that such things can happen. It was not that much to lose, after all.

"Once accepted and given, you are bound to me. Blood and bone binds deep, Demonlord. Once accepted and given, the sacrifice binds you to me."

"True. I'm waiting."

"On pain of perpetual servitude, do you accept this sacrifice of my left hand?"

"Damn," he said calmly. "I was hoping you'd cut it off first so I could refuse. Yes, I accept the sacrifice."

I did not stop to think or wonder if I dared. I took the bloody knife and brought it down with all my strength upon my wrist. I took the instant of shock to seal the wound with my Healer's corona and dispel the pain, for I had to keep my wits about me a little longer.

It was peculiar, though, lifting up my own hand and tossing it on to the coals. It hissed and was taken.

"Bound to me, Demonlord, bound and mastered!" I cried.

"It is well, Malior," he answered from the heart of the coals. The voice was much stronger now. "I go now to the island to take up that which arises, and I will come unto thee in the body thou hast prepared for me. It is fitting. I will aid thee in thanks for the sacrifice, and then—ah, then, we shall see, little demon-spit. At the least I will take joy in the death of the Kantri, and thy death thereafter."

"Arise, then, and come to me as swift as the wind will bear thee," I cried.

"I come, O Master," it said, its voice light and mocking.

And it was gone.

The spell was complete. I had done it.

I closed off the invocation, sealed the brazier and doused the coals, blew out the candles.

It was done. I was in a daze, for the shock was taking me, but I took the precaution of looking again at my hand—at the stump where my hand had been. As I suspected, it was hazy with infection. I would have to have it seen to.

Out of habit I called for Durstan to help me with my robes, but he lay on the altar most decidedly dead. I just managed to rouse balefire to consume him—it was a kind of swift and useful sacrifice I kept always ready by me. It allowed me to summon the Rikti at will, for they always received the leftovers of my sacrifices. This much fresh flesh would supply me with another small army of Rikti should I require one.

I dressed with difficulty in my usual robes, left the chambers and closed the door behind me. I staggered to All Comers with a tale of a demon attack. The Raksha infection was purged, my stump was examined and sealed carefully with a skin flap. I was carried back to my chambers to rest, amid general dismay.

I spent the journey to my chambers in quiet delight. My lost hand bothered me hardly at all. Now that I had in my grasp all I required for victory, the only question that remained was deciding which of the College servants I should choose as Durstan's replacement.

Jamie

I had watched it all. I saw Berys under the trees, laughing, fifty years younger than he should be. I had tried to get to him while the demons were massed against us; thank the Lady, Vilkas and Aral restrained me. I'd have been killed instantly. It brought me up short, reminded me I was thinking with my heart not my head. Stupid.

But when he took Lanen, when he disappeared with her, I went cold from head to foot, felt my heart contract to an old and unwelcome ice. I fought it for the moment. There was too much to do first.

I waited until the last demon was dead, until Vilkas dropped his shield against the demons and healed the gash in my cheek. I thanked him for his kindness to me and to Rella, carried her gently to the fire we had been tending through the night and roused her from her healing sleep.

"Rella," I called softly. "Rella lass, coom nah, waken oop," I said, slipping for an instant into the thick accent of my youth. " 'Tis broad daylight, Rella. Come, lass, waken to me."

She stirred and opened an eye. "I'm weary, Jamie," she

said sleepily, "go 'way—oh Hells." And between one breath
and another she was awake and very aware of her last memory. "Oh Goddess, am I—but—how?" She lifted her hand to
her face, then stood shakily with my help. "It can't be. How
can I move, how can I stand? I felt that thing cut me down
like a spider off its web, I dropped and couldn't feel a thing.
How—?"

"Vilkas," I said. "Never seen the like." I took her hand.
"You're right, lass. You were done for. I saw the cut. The lad
has a blind spot about demons, but by all the Hells, he's the
stuff of legend when it comes to healing."

"Amazing," she said, stunned.

Well, I'd best get it said and over so we could get on with
things.

I took her by the shoulders and made her look me in the
eye. "I must tell you, my girl. When I saw what had happened, before Vilkas said he could help, I had already drawn
my sword. I was going to send you on ahead."

That was merc's cant, in such circumstances, for the mer-
ciful blow you give a comrade who will otherwise die a slow
and painful death.

Rella drew me to her and kissed me soundly. "Thank the
Goddess, you're neither fool nor coward," she said, her eyes
locked with mine. "It's a long death, that one. I wouldn't
wish it on anyone." She touched my cheek. "I'd have been
grateful."

She released me and looked around. "What's happened to
Varien? In fact, what's happened to—Lanen—" Her face
changed and she looked appalled. "Oh Jamie, no, she
isn't—"

"No, she's not dead, at least not yet," I said. "Berys came,
I saw him, and he summoned a big bastard of a demon to
take her. He's got her, Rella." I gazed into her eyes, into love
so late found and so precarious still. "Berys stole her from
under my nose. And I must go after as long as I have
strength to try to get her back. I'm leaving, now you're
awake."

"Just make sure you can keep up with me, old man," she said, smiling, her voice light, as if this was just another stage in our journey. If I hadn't seen the bright track down her cheek gleam in the sunlight, I'd never have known she wept. "But Jamie—I know it goes against your every instinct, but you *must* wait. There is too much we do not know."

"I have waited long enough!" I cried. "She could be dying!"

"And where would you run to, to find her?" Rella demanded. "And what would you do if she is protected by demons? Think, Master Jameth," she said. "We cannot rush after her like green recruits. We must plan this campaign. If he wanted her dead, why bother to take her away?"

"How should I stand here a moment longer when she is in his power?" I cried, even though I knew in my heart that Rella was right.

"Because you know you will be of no use to her dead. Come. We need to think, find out who is with us and how best to use our strength. How fares that young Healer—" she said, glancing around the field. There was certainly plenty to see. "Bright Lady! Jamie, you idiot, you didn't tell me there was a *dragon* come to call!"

I followed her slowly as she hurried to talk to it. Truth be told, I was a bit afraid. This creature's presence, its friendship with Varien—well, there, I'd been inclined to believe him of late in any case.

Varien. There he knelt in the grass, still in shock. He loved her, aye, true enough, I thought, gazing at his back. But I had the prior claim by more than twenty years.

I shivered as I felt it again, a cold wave sweeping over me, but this time I welcomed it. My heart was swept clean for that instant as I made my vow, as I declared my only purpose. I had always known, I suppose, but the time was now come.

I would go and speak with the great Dragon. Perhaps it would help us find Lanen.

And if it would not, no matter. For my only purpose in life now was to find Berys the Bastard, Berys Child-killer, come day come dark, come pain or death or all the Hells, and make him give me back my shining daughter.

On my soul I swore it.

Shikrar

The other Gedri came to me and to Varien then, a little tentative at first because of my presence, but it seemed I was not completely unexpected.

They had seen what had happened.

Two of the Gedri came first and tried to lift him from his knees but he would not move. I spoke to them. "Forgive me, littlings. You are young, even in the span of your people, are you not?"

The man bowed. The woman answered, "Yes, we are, but we're Healers. He needs help."

I lowered my head that I might be nearer to her level and spoke more gently. "Lady, he is beyond help at this moment. I have known him all his life. I pray you, leave us. When he comes more to himself we will seek you out. It will not be long. What are you called?"

"Her name's Aral, Shikrar, and he is Vilkas. They're only trying to help," said a familiar voice. I found a solemn joy in that dark moment when I realised who stood before me, bedraggled and bloodstained.

"I greet thee gladly, Lady Rella," I said, bowing. "I believe that they act for the best as they see it, but please, come away with me all and we will speak of it further."

They followed me to a good distance, where Varien would not hear my words. "It eases my heart to see a familiar face, Lady, although I did not expect to see yours," I said to Rella as we walked.

She smiled. "Ah, there I have the advantage of you, for I knew you were coming. Now, why did you stop these two from helping Varien?"

"His wounds are not of the body, Lady, as you know well. He needs time." I lowered my voice to the merest whisper. "You do not hear him as I do. He calls to her even as we stand here, speaking on her name over and over." Aral the Healer put her hands over her mouth. "I know his pain, for I lost my mate after so short a time together—"

"And I lost my child when she was barely ten years old," said Rella sharply. "Death comes untimely to all who live, Shikrar, not only to the Kantri."

I bowed. "True, Lady. I did not mean to imply that my pain was worse than another's. But Akhor waited a thousand years for the deep love of his heart to blossom, and it has been in flower so short a time. Please, in this let me serve my friend."

Rella stood with bowed head for a moment, then looking up she reached out suddenly to touch my faceplate. "Help him if you can, Shikrar. He needs you. But time is of the essence. If he takes too long to rouse, I will help him myself." She turned and strode rapidly away.

I had the time, as I walked back to rejoin Varien, finally to look at the creatures that looked so familiar but kept their distance. I knew Varien was with the Lesser Kindred, but I had not realised they would be so beautiful or so in awe of me as they seemed, or that they—

Soulgems. They had soulgems.

"*Akhor!*" I cried, reaching out in my surprise, without thinking, to my oldest companion.

I heard his mindvoice, indeed, but it was no answer. Soft, barely to be heard, the refrain of a distant, dying song.

"*Lanen—Lanen—Lanen—*"

Idai

I waited with the others on the Isle of Rest. I had heard no word from Shikrar, so I expected that it would be some days yet before the way could be ready for us to arrive in Kolmar.

Kretissh and I had spoken long together, and we both recognised that without the strength of Shikrar it would not be possible to carry Nikis any further. Even if all the rest of us left for Kolmar, one or more would have to remain behind to look after her until she woke from the Weh sleep. I found myself stupidly growing angry with her. In an effort to think of something else, I remembered Tóklurik and wondered how he fared. In fact I began to worry about him. Why had he not bespoken us before?

Unless he is already in Kolmar laughing at us, I thought to myself as I called to him.

"Tóklurik? Tóklurik, answer me I pray you, it is Idai who would speak with you."

I heard a faint response. It worried me more than silence would have. *"Tók, it is Idai. Where are you? Are you in need of aid?"* I asked, my heart sinking even as the question left my thoughts, for how could we aid him wherever he might be?

"Idai, Idai, blessed be the Winds," he answered, a little stronger. *"It is good to hear your voice, Idai, here at the end of life."*

"Tóklurik, what has happened? Where are you? Are you injured?" I asked, standing up and flexing my wings even as I spoke. I was eldest after Shikrar, surely I could assist Tók if he needed help.

"Idai, I hear you. Stay where you are," said Tóklurik weakly. *"I am beyond aid but the sound of your voice cheers me. Of your kindness stay with me, Lady."*

"I am here, Tók," I said, sorrow sweeping over me full-blown upon the instant. For Tók's sake I did not let it show in my truespeech. *"As long as you want me. Where are you?"*

"In our old home, in the Place of Exile." His thoughts faltered for a moment, then recovered. *"We would not choose to be exiled here now, Idai. Every inch is black with the earth's blood made stone. The air—the air is tainted. The fumes that were afflicting us before are worse now, and I cannot get away from the foul air. And the ground shakes continually, stronger and stronger."*

"What happened?" I asked gently.

"I found my aunt Roccelis and her friend Urishhak," he said, *"as I vowed to do. Their soulgems lay on the floor of their old chamber but there was no way of knowing how they*

died. I can only guess, for the air in the cave was appalling, but I retrieved them. I had their soulgems clutched safe in my talons and was rising on a thermal ready to follow you when the mountainside beneath me spewed forth liquid rock. It caught me, wing and body. I fell gravely wounded and I have lain here, burned and bound into the rock in and out of wakefulness, since then. Has it been more than two days since you left?"

"A little more, *Tók*," I replied. *"It does not matter."*

"It does not," he said. *"The end comes soon—Name of the Winds, Idai, the ground wakes!"*

Suddenly, his mind voice was sharper and clearer. So was his pain.

"The ground groans deep, Idai—Winds keep us, the mountains! The mountains are falling!"

"Tók, what are you—"

"The Grandfather! Idai, the fire comes—I am dead, remember me—Idai, beware, the Grandfather rises!"

And then there was only silence.

Rella

I was afraid that Varien would waste hours in grief. He was absolutely unreachable, but I gave him no more than the half of an hour before I approached Shikrar again.

"Has there been any change?" I asked quietly.

Shikrar bowed his huge head down to my level and it was all I could do not to shrink back. Goddess, but I'd forgotten just how big he was. "He no longer calls her name, Lady, but he will not let me speak with him." He looked at me, and even if his face couldn't show anything, those eyes were expressive enough to convey what he was thinking. "I confess I am at a loss as to what I should do to aid him," he said.

Right.

"I've got a few thoughts on that score," I said, and stumped over to where Varien knelt. He had not moved since Lanen had disappeared.

"You're going to have the most awful cramps in your legs, you know," I said as lightly as I could.

"Leave me," he said distantly.

"No, I don't think so," I said, moving to stand before him. "No, Varien, I'm going to stand here and talk at you until you break yourself out of this."

"Begone," he said.

"No," I replied, and slapped him, lightly, on the face.

"How dare you?" he growled. Well, that was better than nothing.

"I dare because I think she's still alive, Varien, and we're not going to do anything to help her by kneeling here in the grass."

He finally looked at me, then, and saw that depth of resolve in my eyes which echoed his own thoughts. I extended a hand to help him up and he took it. Even for so young a man—well, you know what I mean—it was difficult for him to stand up after so long.

To my amazement, the moment he got his balance he leaned down and kissed me, a quick brush of the lips. I couldn't help but notice that he smelled amazing.

"What was that for?" I asked gruffly.

"For rousing me. It is time." He looked around, and seemed to see his oldest friend for the first time. He walked over to Shikrar and embraced him awkwardly, putting his arms as far about that great neck as they would go. "My heart's friend, I have not thanked you for my life. You saved me from that Raksha, for I was demon fodder in another moment."

"It is always my pleasure to rend the Rakshasa, Akhor, you know that," said Shikrar, trying to keep his voice light. "On the contrary, I thank you for the chance. Alas, would that I had been faster!" he cried out suddenly, turning his head away. "Akhor, soulfriend, I ran as fast as I could but she was too far away—"

"Enough, my friend. You did all in your power. Name of the Winds, Berys had a legion of the Rikti at his command and the battle was not going well. We all owe you our lives."

"True enough," I said. "I'll thank you later, Shikrar, but for now the only questions before us are, where has he taken Lanen and how are we going to get her back?"

Varien winced from the pain of my words, but he followed me back to where the rest of us sat around a small fire.

Vilkas

I had healed all who needed it as soon as that huge dragon had destroyed the demons. Some of the Lesser Kindred were injured as well, but when I went to heal them my power would not touch them. It was not until Aral joined her power with mine that we could clean out the poisons and knit their torn flesh.

Only when all was done did Aral and I allow ourselves to rest. I was astounded that we had kept useful so long, for we had been putting forth our power all the night long, before the demons arrived, sealing the soulgems of the new race. Jamie and Rella had built a small fire in the shelter of the little wood and we joined them beside it, drinking from the stream nearby, eating whatever we could find in our packs.

A thousand thoughts were chasing each other through my mind. I wanted to thank Aral and to tell her that I would not have survived without her, I wanted to take the time to rejoice with Will, that he finally could speak with the astounding creature who now called him Father; and I wanted desperately to speak with the True Dragon who had saved us, and with the amazing dragons whose emergence into full sentient life I had witnessed and aided.

I could not imagine that any other event in my life, no matter how long I lived, could ever come close to the incredible joy of that time, of standing by and watching the light of reason take root behind the eyes and glow in the soulgems of the Lesser Kindred.

However, the unavoidable truth is that healing is exhausting for the Healer, and I had been working from roughly noon on the day before, with few breaks and no real rest. I asked Will to waken us when things started moving, and could only hope that Lord Varien would understand that we shared his sorrow but could keep our eyes open no longer. Aral slept already and I lay down beside her in the long grass. I remember putting my head on my arm but no more.

Will

I sat tending the fire in a kind of daze. I was as sad as I could be that the Lady Lanen was taken and I'd gladly help to save her if I thought I'd be of any use, but I have no defence against demons. While everyone was trying to come to their senses I came to the only possible decision I could. I would go with Vilkas and Aral wherever they fared, for my fate was twined about theirs.

A bump on the shoulder reminded me that my fate was linked with another as well.

"Hhow ffare hyou, Ffather?" asked that wonderful voice, and suddenly Salera was curled about me. I shivered with relief and relaxed as her warmth wrapped me round about.

"Thanks to you, littling, I am not only alive but very well," I said, reaching out to stroke her cheek ridge. "You saved my life, Salera. I thank you, my kit."

"A liffe ssaved also hyou ffor me, hwen kitling trruly I wass," she said solemnly, gazing at me.

"You remember that?" I said, astounded.

"I remember, Hooirr," she said. She dropped her jaw and hissed. "Hyour nname iss so hard to ssay!"

I smiled at her. "Then you can stick to Father."

"It iss good. Ffather, of hyourr kindness, come with me to the Great One. I long to sspeak hwith him."

I laughed quietly. "You don't need me, lass. You're all grown up and glorious and come into your own. I'm sure he will be delighted with you."

"Yess, I know," she said, her eyes gazing sharp and intelligent into mine. "But I hwould have him know you."

I glanced at Vilkas and Aral, drowned deep in sleep. They didn't need me for the moment. I added another few sticks to the fire and prepared to step forth with my strange and wondrous child. We didn't have far to go, though, for everyone was coming towards us.

Shikrar

She walked towards me as I was following Rella and Varien towards the fire. She moved carefully, almost fearfully, and at every other moment she would touch a tail or a wing-tip to the Gedri who walked with her for reassurance. He was a kind-looking—man, that was their word, man, with hair like old *khaadish*. I wondered how such a friendship could have been formed in so short a time.

When she came up to me she bowed, very skillfully. I returned the courtesy. "Welcome, little sister," I said, when she did not speak. "I rejoice that I may be with you on this first day of your flowering. It is a great wonder and a great blessing for the world."

"Hwat iss 'blessing'?" she asked.

"A very great good," I answered. I could not take my eyes from her. "You speak very well, littling. It is amazing. How have you learned so much so swiftly?"

"Ffrom the Ssilver King," she said. "He who wearss the wrong sshape but iss drragon nonetheless." She gazed up at me. "Hwere iss the Lady taken?"

I shook myself. She understood! It would take me a little time to realise that even if they looked like younglings, even if their speech was yet new to them, these creatures were aware and intelligent and to be treated as such.

I was a little ashamed of myself.

"We do not know, littling. Forgive me, I would call you by name. I am Shikrar, Eldest of the Kantrishakrim and Keeper of Souls," I said, bowing again.

"I am Ssallerra," she said, managing the 'l' reasonably well for so new a speaker. It is a hard sound for us to make. And then she astounded me again, for she nudged the man who stood now a little behind her to come forward. "Tthis iss my ffatherr."

He bowed and laughed. "I am called Willem of Rowan-beck, Master Shikrar," he said. "I never dreamt I'd ever meet one of your people. I'm honoured to know you. I am no more Salera's real father than you are, of course, but I raised her from a kit and I love her like a daughter."

"It is well, Willem of Rowanbeck," I said, hissing my amusement. "You have been singularly blessed. She is a wonder."

"I know it," he replied, full of delight as he gazed at her.

I enjoyed that moment of joy even as it passed. Varien called us to join them all at the fire.

Varien

Finally we were all met under the shelter of the trees. The bright morning had clouded over and it was grown cold. Vilkas and Aral, roused from the sleep of utter exhaustion, sat nearest the fire drinking chélan.

Many of the Lesser Kindred had left the plain, and those who remained had congregated at the far end of the field. I learned later that Salera had asked them to leave us in peace for the moment. It was well thought, for I had seen how they watched Shikrar's every movement. There would be time after our council for a wider meeting of our races. We had other things to consider now.

We shared out the cold food from our packs as we talked, for none of us had eaten much since the night before.

"You're not going alone, you know," said Rella to me as she passed around her store of oatcakes. "You'd have to kill Jamie to stop him."

"I would as soon cut off my right arm," I said. Jamie caught my glance and nodded. I saw then the coldness that had taken him. It saddened me, but I recognised it. Indeed, at that moment I welcomed it.

"That means you get me too," said Rella, raising an eyebrow. "Just so you know."

I bowed. "Three," I said.

"Alas, Varien. After so many years of life I had hoped you

would be able to count by now," said a voice from high above. Shikrar settled on one side of the fire and brought his head down to a level with mine. "Four, at the very least. Or perhaps I count for more than one, if only by virtue of sheer bulk?"

"Four, then, Shikrar. Forgive me, my friend. There is no levity in me."

"I know it," said Shikrar gently. "But for all that, keep hope, Akhor. If he wanted her dead he could have killed her here. Keep hope, my friend."

I sent him a swift thanks in truespeech, grimacing at the twinge even so small a usage brought.

"The real question is, where do we start to seek her?" I said.

"Find Berys," said Jamie, his voice like ice. "Verfaren, surely."

"Not necessarily," said Vilkas. "Though that would be the first place to look." He spat. "Those damned demonlines can go anywhere in an instant."

"Demonlines?" asked Jamie. Cold, cold his voice, even the one word.

"Hard to set up, costly to the maker, but once they're in place you can go from one spot to another in the blink of an eye. Then they're gone. Once through only."

"Hells, Vil, how did you know that?" said Will, startled.

"I can't fight the things with my power, Will," said Vilkas grimly. "I've made damned sure I know all there is to know about them in case I can fight them any other way."

"Even if we know not where Berys may be, we must begin somewhere," I said. "If he is not there at Verfaren, perhaps we can find those who will know where he is gone."

"Only if he doesn't know we're looking," said Rella. She glanced at Shikrar. "Forgive me, Shikrar, but you might just be a little obvious."

He snorted. "True enough, lady, but I am only the first. Soon there must be some kind of reckoning, for the Kantri are coming to Kolmar."

"When?" she asked.

"A moment," he said. I heard him bespeak Idai and knew he had left his truespeech broadscattered that I might do so.

Idai

Shikrar bespoke me at last, his voice subdued and weary. *"I am safely arrived, Idai,"* he said, *"though I have ill news. There has been a great battle here. A* rakshadakh *called Berys sent an army of Rikti on to Varien and Lanen. She is stolen away."*

"And Akhor?" I asked, hardly daring to breathe. He had no armour to protect him, no flame, no talons to rend or fangs to bite, what if he . . .

"Varien is well, save that his heart is riven in twain for fear of Lanen's fate," he said. I breathed again.

"Alas, Shikrar, would that I had better news to lighten your heart. I have—alas, Tóklurik bespoke me as he was dying," I said. My heart was heavy with that loss, and now Lanen gone as well. *"It is an evil day."*

"It is, my friend. Let us then do what we may to mend it. How fare the Kantri?"

"Rested and restless." I replied. *"Is the way prepared for us?"*

"I think now that it cannot be, Idai," he said. *"There is none to ask and none to grant permission. However, there is a great demon master arisen in this land. All happens for a purpose, Idai, though the Winds might not make all clear at once. The Gedri have no defences against the Rakshasa."* I felt the tiny smile in his mindvoice as he added, *"I suspect if we simply follow our own instincts and rid the land of the Rakshi, we will be as welcome here as we could desire."*

My heart lifted. My soul to the Winds, I had never dreamt of such a thing, but to arrive in all our power when the Gedri were in need—ah, yes, it would be the best introduction we could hope for.

"Come, then, Idai. Bring the Kantri home," said Shikrar. He told me again to keep high, and how to avoid the wall of

air that was the edge of the Storms. *"A moment, my friend,"* he said.

Shikrar

"I need your counsel," I said, turning to the other Gedri. "Where should we meet with the Kantri?" I hissed a little in faint amusement. "Where is there room for all of us to meet at once?"

"There's a plain just north of Wolfenden," said Will at once. "How many of you are there?"

"A hundred and eighty-nine," said Varien quietly.

"Then there should be enough space," said Will. "It'll be a good place to meet, there's little enough traffic comes down that road this time of year."

He told me how to find it and I bespoke Idai once more.

"Very well, my friend," she said, when I had instructed her. *"We will meet there in about three days' time."*

A thought crossed my mind. *"What of Nikis, Idai?"*

A dry little laugh escaped her. *"Kretissh has said he will stay with Nikis for now, until we think of an easier way to carry her or until she wakes. All is well, Teacher-Shikrar. We come."*

"Come then swiftly, my friend," I said. *"We will meet in the plain in three days. Fly well and strong!"*

Varien

It was done, then. The Kantri would arrive soon. But I had no intention of meeting my people on that plain.

Jamie turned to me as if he read my thoughts. "There is no need for us all to be there," he said. "I will not go. I am for Verfaren as fast as I can make those horses run. How much longer must we wait?"

"But a moment more, Jameth," I said. "I am as anxious to be gone as you are." I turned to Will and the young healers. "You have not spoken, Will, Vilkas, Aral. What will you do now?"

Aral opened her mouth and, looking at Vilkas, thought better of it. He spoke.

"I go with you, if you go to seek out Berys. The Lady Lanen will need us all, I think. And in any case I have a vow to fulfil." He glanced at Jamie and at me, half smiling. "Between the three of us, we may give Berys something to think about."

"Vil, you can't count any better than Varien," said Aral. She looked up. "Lord Shikrar, I hope you will forgive us for not accompanying you, but if we are to reclaim our lives we must seek out this bastard. Not what I'd choose to do, but there it is."

Shikrar nodded, but he was troubled. "I understand your desire for speed, my friends, but on behalf of my people I beg you to spare a brief hour to greet the Kantri." He gazed at each of us and I found that I was ashamed. "We have lost that only home that we have ever known, and we have flown to the limit of our strength to come here." He gazed full at me, then, and I heard the rebuke in his voice. *"You at least must be here to greet them, my friend,"* he told me in truespeech. *"For all that has changed, you are yet the Lord of the Kantri."*

I bowed. "You speak truth, Hadreshikrar. I at least must meet with you all. La—" My throat closed as grief threatened to overwhelm me, but I took a long breath and spoke again. "Lanen would wish it so, I know it," I said.

It was Rella, ever practical, who then said dryly, "That field is right close to the road, and at this stage a small delay won't hurt. Surely we can all meet together and form a plan of action, rather than rushing into Verfaren waving our swords?" She turned to Jamie. "I don't know about you, but I'd rather have all the help I can muster."

"The Kantri are life-enemies of the Rakshasa," added Shikrar quietly, and I saw the smallest touch of the Attitude of Amusement in his stance. "If you are to face down a demon-master, what better weapon could you hope for than several hundred souls who delight in destroying demons?"

Vilkas and Aral nodded, and we all turned to Jamie.

"No," he said quietly, in the dispassionate voice that fell

cold as ice on the ear. "I see the sense of your words, but I will not wait even so short a time." He turned to Rella. "We should get back to Wolfenden in a few days. When we come to the road, you go with the rest and talk to the dragons. I'll go ahead on my own to Verfaren and learn what I can about Berys. Meet me at the gates to the College of Mages at noon the day after we split up."

"Are you sure, Jamie?" asked Rella quietly, her face and voice carefully neutral.

"Sure as life," he said. I shivered.

She turned back to Shikrar. "Very well then, Shikrar. All but Jamie will meet with the Kantri. Perhaps together we can find a way to defeat Berys and get Lanen back."

"We do not yet speak for all, Lady Rella," I said, turning to the two who had not spoken. "Will? Salera?"

Salera

I was proud of myself, for I could understand all that was said. It was harder to form words than to understand them, but I was certain that would improve in time.

The strangest part of that time was how swiftly we of the Lesser Kindred took to our newfound senses. We had been but a breath away in any case, so perhaps it was not so strange after all, but when Aral asked what Will and I were doing I did not have to stop and think.

"Hhow sshould I not seek to aid the Lady of my people?" I asked. "Sshe it wass who brought uss reason, sshe and the Ssilver King. It iss a great debt. I sshall go with you."

Will laid his hand on my neck. "Then off we go all. We can plan the subtleties on the way, but I for one cannot wait longer."

We all stood and began to gather up our packs.

Rella

Only one thing more happened to delay us. We were preparing to leave when a great shout came up from deep in the trees. Aral had gone to fill her water skin when she caught sight of something lying in the wood.

It was the body of poor Maikel, Marik's healer, near an altar surrounded by demon symbols. Vilkas said it was the base of the demon line and performed a swift ceremony to dispel the darkness. "There is no way to tell where it goes, but Berys was in Verfaren when we left. There's a good chance he has returned there," he said grimly. "As long as he didn't have another one ready, we may have a chance."

Vilkas seemed to think that Maikel had paid the price of service to the demons, but I saw the expression on that poor dead face, above the ravaged body, and I knew in my soul that Vilkas was wrong. Maikel's face was at peace, almost there was a glimpse of joy about him. He had died fighting, for my money, and I sent a swift prayer for the soul of a solitary warrior winging to the Lady. We buried him beneath the trees and built a cairn over his grave.

The sun was setting as we left the high field and set off down the mountain.

Lanen

I woke after what seemed like many long hours. I tried to speak, to cry out aloud, to call to Varien in truespeech. I could not make a sound.

I had been plagued by evil dreams, but to be truthful the waking was little better. I woke to find myself lying on a hard bed in a cell deep underground, or so I guessed from the cold and the damp. There was a lamp at one side, a heavy wooden door that was locked from the outside—of course— and a tiny grate with a tinier fire in it. I rose and threw on more coals. There seemed to be plenty.

I knew Berys had caught me, I remembered that much of the battle. At least, I had assumed that the man with the hideous face was Berys. I also seemed to remember seeing Shikrar arrive just as I was taken. I could only hope it was so. I remembered Akor and the efficient contempt with which he had killed demons. Perhaps Varien and the others lived after all.

There came then a rattle at the door. I looked around wildly for anything to use as a weapon. I had started towards the lamp when the door opened.

It was Berys, if that's who he was. He had the body of a lad only a little older than me, but he moved more like an old man. It was deeply unsettling.

He smiled at me and that was more unsettling yet. He waved his hand in a curious pattern and suddenly I found I could speak.

"Who in all the Hells are you?" I demanded. "And where am I?"

"My name is Berys, and you are mine," he said smugly. "Marik of Gundar's blood and bone. Are you comfortable?"

"It's cold as midwinter down here. A blanket or a cloak would be useful."

"I will arrange for a cloak to be brought to you," he said. He lifted his left hand to make some gesture and I realised with a shock that "hand" was the wrong word. There was only a stump.

"Oh, don't concern yourself," he said lightly. "It is nothing compared to what is going to happen to you."

"I see. And now you will mock me and threaten. So brave. Why haven't you killed me yet?" I said, snarling. Thank the Lady, I really was for that moment too angry to be afraid.

"Oh, no. You are not for death. Not yet," he said. "I have preparations to make. Even I must take a little time to properly welcome a major demon."

"May the Kantri find you and fry you where you stand!" I cried.

"Oh, I don't think that very likely," he said calmly. "I know they are coming, you see."

I was shocked at that.

"Oh, yes. They will be here any day now, I suspect," he said. "But the Demonlord will be here any moment, under my command. And this time he will be able to complete the work he began so long ago." Berys leaned forward and I got a good look at his face. It was young and fair in seeming, which made it worse. My stomach churned. I had the feeling that if you cut him he would bleed maggots.

"And I will have you to offer in fulfillment of prophecy, Marik's daughter. Your soul to demons, your body to rule Kolmar just long enough to wed with me. And then, ah, well"—he smiled a terrible slow smile. "Then I will amuse myself with you. There is so much pain that can be inflicted without causing death. You will be a challenge."

I leapt for his throat and just for a second I had him. I squeezed with all the might of my fury, but in a moment he summoned his power and threw me off.

"You will live so much longer in agony for that," he snarled, opening the door and hurrying out.

"Not if I get hold of you first," I shouted at the closing door.

But then I was alone, with a fate much darker than death before me.

"*Varien, Varien,*" I cried in truespeech, knowing I could not be heard. The darkness of my future pressed me close, but I clung to the love I knew was in the world and seeking me. "Come soon, my heart," I cried aloud, in truespeech, deep in my soul, knowing none could hear me on any level.

I had little real hope that my loved ones would find me, but even the sound of their names was comfort in so dark a time and place.

I listened then, for the sound of a bird or a beast or even a guard outside the door.

There was nothing.

I was alone.

Shikrar

I was better than her word. It was but midmorning of nd day after Lanen was taken that I heard her voice.

ere coming down from the high hills to the cross-

re we would go our separate ways.

"*Shikrar, I see the coast!*" she cried in my mind. "*All green and glowing. It is glorious, Shikrar!*"

"*It is home, Idai,*" I answered. "*Come, follow my voice, I would speak with you.*"

I was learning much of the Gedri on our travels. Varien was different, I knew him from of old, and the fact that he had banished despair and replaced it with a grim determination did not surprise me. That Jamie, who was Lanen's father, had done so as well impressed me deeply. I had come to appreciate the differences between them—Vilkas, Aral, Will the Golden. It is certain that large-souled creatures come in many forms.

Rella was my most constant companion after Varien. She asked after Kédra and his family, and demanded the whole history of our leaving the Dragon Isle. It eased my heart to speak with her. She reminded me in some ways of Idai.

The littling, Salera, was a constant delight in the midst of all our sorrows. Her speech improved by the hour it seemed. She was intelligent and gentle, knowing always who required speech and who needed silence as we walked. The very sight of her brought joy, for she was lovely in body as in spirit. I began to think very seriously that another name would need to be found for the Lesser Kindred. That had described beasts, not a free people. I must consider it.

It was Will who saw them first. We were come out of the hills and the others had pointed out what they named an "inn" in the distance, when he shouted and pointed upwards. The rest of us looked where he pointed, but there was no need. We would have heard them in a moment in any case. My heart gave a great leap as hope returned.

For the Kantri had arrived, the whole of our people rejoicing after loss and long travail, to a sunlit morning brightening a good green land, and they were singing. T   nd was hauntingly familiar to me as I rose to join th   I did not know it at first. I realised, though, as I   throat to add my voice, that it was in two parts.   the theme of our old home, the Place of Exi more, and the second—the second was a new song, of hope and peace and sun on the grass.

It was a song of homecoming. Our long exile over, the sunlight flashing on wings and striking sparks from soulgems, the Kantri were come home.

In the deep ocean west of Kolmar there was once a large island, green and lush. Many ages ago a small box with a beating heart inside it was brought to the island by a demon and hidden deep in a great mountain.

The mountain looked, at first glance, a little like a vast dragon. The demon had a strange sense of humour, or the one who controlled the demon did, for the island was soon the home of the great dragons of legend.

Over the years the essence of the heart seeped out into the earth, the water, the air of the island. It poisoned all it touched, but not enough to kill. No, the poison was only enough to make worse the natural ailments that afflicted them—joint ill, early aging. A low birth rate.

Finally, there came one who sought the heart from afar. His searching shook the island to its foundations, for the heart did not wish to be found. The dragons fled, to escape the fire and the molten rock that sprang up to cover the island. There was only one who saw the ending, and by that time he was no longer capable of thought or speech.

The end came when he who owned the heart decided that he wanted it back. It was deeply buried under old and new stone and he had to reach down into the vitals of the island to retrieve it. The rocks burst asunder with a roar to shake the heavens at this final insult, and the mountains fell crashing into the sea.

But before death took Tóklurik of the Kantrishakrim, he saw a wonder. Rock and ash and fire began to cling together. Made from the substance of the dying island—from raw molten stone, from the yellow dust that filled the air and Tóklurik's lungs, from the poisonous gas that burned ~~h~~ his armour and choked him, from the fire that flowed over him and killed him at the last, there grew from out the death throes of the Place of Exile a vast shape, black and grey and red and sickly yellow. It rose into the air on hideous, impossible wings and circled the black smouldering rock that was the last remnant of the Dragon Isle.

Until at last, with a cry that sang joyfully of death, the great black dragon turned and flew swiftly to the east, towards the lands of men.

Acknowledgments

As ever, first and last, I must thank my gift-from-the-gods Editor, Claire Eddy of Tor Books. I consider it a great honour to work with a woman who is so completely brilliant at her job that she has turned it into an art form in its own right. Thank you, my friend, for patience and encouragement and for your own fine work.

To Margaret Lynn Harshbarger, I owe the fact that this book has some semblance of a reasonable plot. Oh, and the Kantri owe their lives to her as well, for she reminded me that, as realistic as it might be for earthquake and eruption and all to take place at once, the pressure wave which would have tossed them about like sparrows in a force-ten gale would in fact be composed of poisonous gas and I wouldn't end up with bruised and shaken Kantri, I would end up with very dead Kantri. It is vitally important to have friends who realise such things. For your solid friendship, your forbearance and your ace plotting skills and artistic instincts—hey, shouldn't your name be on the front of this book too?

With grateful appreciation for her patience, I owe a large

vote of thanks to Derval Diamond, stable manager at Dragonhold Stables, who very kindly took the time to answer my questions about the behaviour of horses and how (for example) they react to burning barns. Only when one speaks with an expert does one learn the true depths of one's ignorance. It was lovely to meet you, Derval, and you were a great help.

I owe my heartfelt thanks also to that talented and gracious lady Anne McCaffrey, for her kindness and patience in answering my endless questions about horses and, latterly, the whole writing biz. I'm so glad we've met, and I can't thank you enough for your friendship and your solid support through all the varied craziness, Anne. Thanks a million. You're an absolute star.

My thanks are also due to:

Stephen Hickman, for providing so wondrous a portrait of Salera to grace the cover.

Dr. Penny Smith, glider pilot and occasional Mistress of the Revels (or, if you insist, Senior Production Editor) at Monthly Notices of the Royal Astronomical Society, who has very kindly and on several occasions told me about large things that glide through the air and how they do it. Any idiotic mistakes concerning the flight of dragons are my fault entirely, however, and have nothing to do with the information young Penster has provided.

Catherine MacDonald, brilliant baritone in our Sweet Adelines quartet, who is a midwife in real life—largely, I suspect, to support her singing habit. Catherine has been my advisor on matters of midwifery, for which I am very grateful, but again, any dreadful howlers that may have arisen in that area are all my very own.

Christopher, for regular assistance in seeing things logically from Berys's point of view, for talking me out of hydroplaning dragons, and for helping to keep me as sane as I ever get anyway.

Deborah Turner Harris, ever and always, for helping me out with plot problems, always knowing what questions to ask, and for being for so many years a terrific writer and a true friend of my heart.

And finally, though not in any sense last, I here thank my partner, the amazing Dr. Steven Beard, for patience high above and far beyond the call of duty, and for always being amenable to providing a cheery word, a sandwich and a cup of tea when I was not of this world, or a really awful pun when drastic measures were required.

I couldn't have done it without you, gang.

—Elizabeth

TOR

Award-winning authors
Compelling stories

Please join us at the website
below for more information
about this author and other great
Tor selections, and to sign up for
our monthly newsletter!